A DEVASTATING OPPONENT

Deveraux leaned casually against a broad tree trunk, his arms folded, the smile which Rorie always found so infuriating playing around his mouth.

"I had thought to partake of the cooling waters, myself. Were I to defer to your wishes, Miss Shelbourne, how shall you recompense me for my disappointment?"

"Another proposition, Captain?" she spat caustically.

"Perhaps."

"And what shall you bargain with this time?"

"Why, my silence, of course," replied Cameron matter-of-factly. "You seem to have a talent for being caught in rather compromising situations. It might lead one to almost think they were planned."

Advancing to the water's edge, he slipped off his shirt to display a hard, muscular chest which tapered down to a slim waist.

"Shall we proceed?"

The Homeward Heart

kathy Kelter

LEISURE BOOKS ❧ NEW YORK CITY

A LEISURE BOOK

Published by

Dorchester Publishing Co., Inc.
6 East 39th Street
New York, NY 10016

Printed in the United States of America

Prologue

South England, October, 1749

The old gypsy matriarch looked up at the man who stepped into the light of her campfire. Though his features were carefully hidden beneath a hooded cape and he tendered no name, Magda knew his identity. In truth, she had been expecting him. The cards had foretold it. And even if they hadn't, she would have known his kind by the demanding arrogance in his stance.

It amused her how the nobility shunned her people by day, only to seek out their women by night—the young girls for sexual favors, the older ones to prophesy the future. Usually, Magda silently spat upon their hypocritical souls while gleefully taking their coins. But not tonight.

Motioning for the man to seat himself on the opposite log, the gypsy woman continued to stir the black kettle as though time was of little consequence. The man snorted derisively and fumbled in his cloak for a gold coin, certain that she was stalling for her fee. But Magda shook her head.

"I take no fee to foretell a man's doom," she said.

The low, flat monotone of her voice lent such an air of foreboding to her statement that the man recoiled as though he had been slapped. And, for a moment, he remained silent and motionless.

"Explain yourself, old hag! Dare you to tell me I have no future?" he demanded shrilly, rousing from his shock, his nasal voice rising with emotion.

"Nay, everyone has a future, if only for a few minutes," answered Magda matter-of-factly. "Some are rewarding, others are to be feared. Whichever the case, 'tis of one's own design," she warned him.

The man shifted uncomfortably. "And what of mine? What say ye then?"

The old crone cackled. When the potion began to boil, she took five leaves from a pouch and threw them into the pot. And as she watched the particles float into position to show the tally of his deeds, she suddenly felt a bone-chilling coldness traverse her body. This was far more than she had been prepared to see.

The pale moon hung heavy in the sky, momentarily obscured by wispy clouds. In the distance, shouting could be heard as men wildly danced around a fire, raising flaming pitchforks high in the air to ward off demons and witches. With a certain irony, Magda noted that this was All Hallows' E'en, the night when every kind of evil spirit roamed the earth . . . and one sat before her now.

"What is it, old woman! What do you see!" the man shouted, grabbing her arm.

6

The hood of his cloak fell back, and Magda looked deep into his eyes. She saw that the leaves and the vision had not mislead her, and she shrank from the cruelty she saw in those dark, hawklike features.

"I see much blood on your hands—blood ye shall never wash free—blood to which ye must soon answer," she replied tensely. "And I see another who yearns ta place the cloak of death about yer shoulders."

Roger Thornton, duke of Lyndeforde, abruptly stood to pace the clearing, acute agitation apparent in every step and in every nervous stroke of his chin. Even in the dim firelight, Magda could see that he had visibly paled.

"Who!" he screamed, suddenly yanking the gypsy to her feet and shaking her like a rag doll. "Who seeks my death!"

"Nay, 'tis not death I see, though there are many who wish yer return ta the devil. But one shall deal ye the fate ye deserve as the days end the May," Magda whispered raggedly, struggling to break his hold. "The name . . . ye will know only then."

"You old crone, 'tis ye who shall see the devil," Thornton hissed. And his fingers closed tighter and tighter around her neck with cold deliberation. Magda's eyes grew huge before rolling back into her head. When her body went limp, the duke released his hands to let her slump to the ground.

Pulling the hood over his head, he left in the darkness from whence he had come.

1

Charleston, South Carolina, January, 1750

Stripped to the waist in the unseasonable afternoon heat, Captain Cameron Deveraux supervised the unloading of one of his company's ships just docked from the West Indies. He worked alongside his men hefting hogsheads of sugar, rum, and molasses, heavy bolts of cloth, and large crates of dyewoods and coffee. Oblivious to his surroundings, he rarely stopped, and then it was only long enough to issue further orders.

Ladies, young and old, strolled along the colorful quay. Beneath twirling parasols, they covertly cast admiring glances at the vigorous, bronzed, black-haired captain as muscles rippled across his strong back and broad shoulders to cord in powerful arms. Though a large man, Deveraux had the sleek movements of a cat—quick, agile and purposeful, with a sense of restrained energy and strength. By all appearances, he was a man who wasted little time. Were it not for his six-foot-four-inch stature, the clear blue of his eyes and the sharp angularity of his aristocratic features, one might have mistaken him for a savage.

Signaling for his men to continue the unloading of the ship, Deveraux shrugged into a loose-fitting shirt and made his way back to the office to study the manifest. It had been a profitable haul, and he was well pleased. Just two more such trips and he would have the coin to expand into the China trade. His mind full of plans, he was dismayed to find that his manservant was impatiently awaiting his presence with obvious unpleasant news to impart.

"What is it, Rawlings?" he demanded brusquely, taking his seat behind the worn desk. "I've much work to finish before the day's end."

In answer, Rawlings threw a tattered London paper on the captain's desk, his finger drawing Cameron's attention to a spot heavily outlined in faded ink. Deveraux's eyes narrowed, and his lips drew together in a harsh line as he read the "Proclamation for the Writ of Enclosure."

"What's it mean, Cap'n?" asked Rawlings anxiously.

"It means that His Grace, Roger Thornton, duke of Lyndeforde, has petitioned the government for full control over the lands of Drumfielde Village," replied Cameron tightly. "That bloody bastard!" he cursed, wadding the paper into a tight ball and angrily throwing it against the far wall.

"Ken he do this—rob the villagers of their rights to the open fields?"

Cameron rose to his full height and went to stand before the window, his gaze going far out to a sea as tumultuous as his emotions at that moment.

"The man is within his rights," he acknowledged in a steely voice. "Centuries of wanton use of the open lands have so depleted the soil that British productivity has suffered a serious decline. Parliament has sought to correct the problem by permitting landed gentry, who promise to improve crop yields and overworked soil, to enclose and adjoin all surrounding free lands to their estates. And it has not been without success."

"It ain't right, Cap'n!"

"Few things in this life are, Rawlings," Cameron responded with a bitter edge to his tone.

"But the villagers depend on the free use of them open fields to graze their livestock and to plant crops!" exclaimed the valet, his anger rising to a feverish pitch. " 'Tis always been their birthright."

Deveraux turned to regard his servant. "Aye, and 'twill now most likely be their ruination as well as that of Drumfielde," he observed quietly. Though inwardly Cameron raged at the injustice of the law, he had to admit to the necessity for it. But he couldn't help feeling that there was a more equitable way of implementing the program so that all could benefit.

"Beggin' yer pardon, Cap'n, but ye knows as well as me that Roger Thornton ain't intendin' ta improve no crop yields."

"Yes," agreed Deveraux tersely. "Knowing His Grace the way we do, I'll wager that there is more to this story than we yet know." Cameron suddenly turned a more discerning eye upon Rawlings. He knew his servant well enough to recognize the signs. The nervous gestures and averted eyes usually meant the wiry little man was holding something back. "Rawlings, what aren't you telling me? Come! Out with it, man."

"There—ah—there was a sailor in town inquirin' 'bout Reed Delacroix," confessed Rawlings haltingly, wondering how his captain would react.

But Deveraux merely raised a questioning brow. When he spoke, his voice was controlled and coolly detached. "So, they still seek Reed Delacroix. Is the sailor in port yet?"

"No. He shipped out fer the Indies this morning. He didna find nothin' nither. More 'n likely jest askin' as matter of course in ev'ry port."

"If I've learned anything, Rawlings, nothing is just a matter of course," responded Deveraux, kneading the knotted muscle at the base of his neck. "I think it is time now to lay the past to rest."

"What d'ya be meanin' ta do, sir?"

"Tell Ian to collect the crew and to have the ship ready to sail by the end of next month. We'll be charting a course for England."

Rawlings's leathery face lit up, the glint of battle in his faded eyes and a hint of challenge in his bowlegged stance. He had waited a long time for this day when, at last, some wrongs would be righted. The cap'n was no longer the brash youth. This time the odds would be in his favor. But just as quickly, the valet lost his swagger as another thought intruded.

"Your grandfather, sir, he will have much to say on the matter," Rawlings bleakly reminded his employer.

Deveraux frowned. That was an understatement. The dapper and fiery Claude Deveraux would be most disturbed by his grandson's decision to return to England. And Cameron was not looking forward to the explosion certain to follow the disclosure.

Aloud he said, "Be that as it may, the past demands satisfaction, and I will not delay any longer—not even for Grandfather's sake. The crafty old fox has succeeded in postponing my revenge for too many years. 'Tis time now that he realize I have a date with destiny which will not go ignored."

In the distance a muffled clap of thunder sounded, and Rawlings echoed the captain's own thoughts when he observed softly, "There be a storm brewing this night, and I dinna mean jest the weather."

2

Drumfielde Village, England, April, 1750

It was spring in Drumfielde Village. Leaving
behind the lean, hard months of winter, the
town sprang to life. All around, there was a
flurry of activity as every able-bodied male
rushed to finish the cutting and planting in the
forest before the early thaw, for none could risk
the ox-drawn carts, heavily laden with timber,
churning up sun-warmed soil already in culti-
vation.

Soaring gracefully in the sunlit sky, thrushes
serenaded the village with their cheerful songs.
A wild array of purple cotton thistles, pinks,
White Johns and jonquils carpeted the meadows,
providing a feast for the eye. And the air held a
freshness that intoxicated the senses and infected
even the most work-hardened individual with a
delightful giddiness. Indeed, spring brought a
necessary respite for the soul, a rebirth of the
spirit—and new hope for the future.

In a glade at the edge of the woods, Rorie Shelbourne yawned and stretched languorously on the bank of a meandering creek, beneath the dropping branches of a willow tree. There was a momentary recess from the frenzied hum of the saw and the jolting vibrations of felled trees while the workers enjoyed their noon repast. And it was during this time of the day that Rorie would sneak away to her favorite retreat by the stream to vicariously relive the adventures in Squire Balfour's books.

With a sigh of longing, Rorie turned the last page of her latest escapade. At nineteen, her thirst for knowledge of the world beyond the narrow existence of her little village was a driving force within her; she felt certain that the sheer intensity of it would eventually consume her. Propped on her side, she idly plucked at the cool grass beneath her fingers, staring moodily off into space. Men weren't encumbered by impractical clothes, shackled by ridiculous conventions or confined to a dull, thankless existence, she fumed. They were as free as they chose to be to make their mark upon the world, to seek fame, fortune and adventure wherever they would.

"Ah, if only I were a man," she lamented for the thousandeth time.

"I thank the stars tha' yer not," came a masculine voice from behind her.

Rorie started at the nearness of the unexpected intruder. Heart pounding, breathless with fear, her first instinct was to gather her skirts and run. She was fleet of foot, but she knew she wouldn't get far, hindered by the damnable petticoats. Silently she cursed a society which demanded that its females be trussed like a pig ready for roasting. Then her fury at this intrusion into her Eden rose to the fore. Jumping to her feet, her fists clenched, Rorie whirled around to face the interloper who had dared to trespass upon her daydreams. She hated fear—it made one weak and unable to think clearly—and she desperately fought the rising emotion. One thing she did know for certain: she would fight any man who dared lay a hand on her.

Chuckling, the dark figure began to emerge from the shadows. Just as Rorie was about to dart past him, an arm went around her waist, and a hand clamped over her shoulder. Rorie's eyes widened in surprise, and she knew a moment of paralyzing terror as she realized that a second party had come up behind her. Her whole body shuddered as she was immediately transported back to the memory of another time—a hellish nightmare she had sought to banish for six years.

With her mind caught between the past and the present, Rorie fought blindly, kicking, screaming and clawing with all her might against the restraints of her captor. She was conscious of nothing but the terror which drove her. Judging from the low-pitched groans, she could only deduce the success of her defense. She was just about to break free when a familiar voice penetrated her muddled senses.

"Easy, Rorie! God's blood, 'tis just me and Wiley!"

As recognition dawned, Rorie's body went limp and she started to sob in relief. But as reality took a firm hold on her, her temper flared anew, and she rounded on her brother in a flash of fury.

"Terence Shelbourne, what do you mean by

coming up behind me and frightening me out of a year's growth! Are these the manners you're learning from the likes of your new friend?" she spat.

Terence held up a hand to stem his sister's fiery tirade. "Hold on, Rorie," he broke in sharply, massaging a tender shin. "Wiley and I were on our way back to work in the forest when Aunt Molly asked me to find you and send you home. Something about some unfinished chores. And we weren't intending to sneak up on you, either," he snapped irritably. "But your nose was buried so deep in a book, we thought to teach you a lesson. Another of the squire's acquisitions?" he inquired with a disapproving lift of his brow. "Sneaking off to the Grange and talking Mary Balfour into giving you the run of her father's library is courting trouble, sister dear."

"And just who else is to read them?" Rorie retorted defensively. "Mary says the squire only bought the books for the status their ownership brings and understands them little. Books are so dear, 'tis a sin to own them and never read them."

"You had best have a care, Rorie. You know how the squire feels about a learned female. If he found out that a village lass was not ony raiding his library, but instructing his daughter as well—"

"Bah!" Rorie scoffed. "Mary and I are most discreet and time our visits to his absences. God's teeth, the squire can't see his feet for his belly. How do you expect him to see what is not in front of his nose?"

Terence shrugged, knowing it was useless to

argue with his headstrong sister. He bent to pick up the leather-bound book. "What is it this time, *Gulliver's Travels*, or *Robinson Crusoe*?"

Rorie's face turned crimson, whether from embarrassment or latent fury, she wasn't sure. She lunged to retrieve the cherished book, as though it were a window to her very soul. Terence was quicker, though, and held it high above his head. He gave a hoot of laughter as he slowly read aloud, "*A General History of the Robberies and Murders of the Most Notorious Pyrates.*"

"It needs be some story fer a lass the likes of ye ta wish ta be a man," quipped Wiley Pate.

Rorie remembered Terence's friend then, and she turned to see him rake a discerning and appreciative eye over her. Refusing to show her uneasiness, she cocked her head and gave Wiley a long, considering look in return.

Although he was of average height, stocky and firm, and attractive enough with his short, brown hair brushed forward from the crown in the style of the country menfolk, she didn't trust the sleepy look in his hooded eyes. And she distinctly disliked the smug curl of his lips, as though he were enjoying a private joke. Around the village she knew him to be something of a Lothario, and that, in itself, served to make Rorie all the more wary of him. Lovers rather than laborers, the Wiley Pates of the world would always seek the easier path, she concluded with lofty disdain. Already, at the age of twenty, he was showing every sign of following in his dissolute father's footsteps, and his name, she thought, was most befitting. Decidedly, Rorie shared her aunt and uncle's dim view of this friendship. With a shrug of her shoulders and a toss of her blond hair, she dismissed Wiley and turned back to address her brother's bantering.

Her bold defiance both startled and delighted Wiley. This girl would not play the coquette, he surmised, and the sleepy look in his eyes was instantly replaced by yet another look, easily defined by any lusty male. Once again, he took the measure of her assets. The swelling of soft flesh above the snugly fitting bodice testified to full, rounded breasts in need of caressing, the long, thick mass of golden hair begged for a stroking hand, and the full, pink mouth invited kissing. Altogether they bespoke of a passionate nature yet unawakened. Although slightly taller than most girls he knew, he gauged her to fit very nicely beneath his bulk. Yes, the promise of glorious womanhood lay upon her brow, and he figured to be the one to make this little flower bloom.

"I hardly think," Terence was saying airily, "that a book of pirates' exploits is what Father had in mind for broadening the boundaries of your mind."

"And I hardly think," Rorie shot back, "that frequenting taverns and tumbling milkmaidens in the hay is what Father had in mind for broadening the boundaries of *your* mind!"

Wiley chuckled. "She has ye there, mate."

Terence flushed to the roots of his curly, red hair and glared at his friend.

"Let up, Rorie," her brother warned firmly, in a tone that would brook no further argument. "Take yourself home. Aunt Molly is waiting." And with that, he angrily threw the book to her.

Rorie bit back the stinging retort on her lips,

for she saw that her innocent taunt had struck closer to home than she had intended. Terence had quit his apprenticeship with the apothecary over his failure to cure their parents of a fever last year, and he carried a deep grief and a heavy guilt with him. Shortly thereafter, Wiley Pate had come along to assuage his hurt with other, less illustrious pursuits. At eighteen, he needed more than the company of musty medical journals, Terence argued heatedly each time Rorie had tried to persuade him to return to his studies. Finally Rorie took her aunt and uncle's advice and stepped aside to let him make his own way. Since then, she had painstakingly avoided the subject—until now—and she cursed her waspish tongue.

Seeing that there was nothing to be gained by further argument, Rorie swallowed her pride and departed with all the dignity that she could muster. In spite of the firm set of her chin and her proud carriage, she felt like a chastised child. Digging her fingernails into the palms of her hands, she angrily muttered epithets under her breath as she heard Wiley's laughter—and felt his gaze—follow her down the path.

A short while later, Rorie sheepishly entered the neat little thatched cottage of the Fenton farm. She braced herself for the tongue lashing she knew to be due her.

"Rorie Shelbourne!" her aunt greeted severely. "Ev'ry time I turn around yer nowheres ta be found. If 'tis another book wha' stands betwixt ye an' yer chores, I'm bound ta take the stick ta ye."

Molly Fenton was usually a good-natured woman, tiny and plump, who barely reached her niece's shoulders, but the tone of her voice and the spirited flash in her gray-blue eyes told Rorie she would not get around her aunt so easily this time.

"I tol' yer mother, God rest her soul, 'twas unseemly fer yer papa ta be learnin' ye beyond yer station, even if he was the village schoolmaster," she continued to lecture, wagging the wooden spoon in her hand for emphasis. "It jest makes ye yearn fer more 'n ye ken have. No matter how much ye knows, ye ain't gonna be more 'n a village lass. Why, yer head is so full of silly notions of adventure and such, there ain't no room for ye ta be thinkin' on a husband—even if ye could find a man hereabouts wha' ain't already felt the lash of yer tongue. Ye mark my words well, miss, 'tis only trouble yer bound fer—"

"Aunt Molly, please accept my humblest apology for the shameful neglect of my duties. You are right to chastise me, and I accept your rebuke," interrupted Rorie glibly. "Now if you'll excuse me, I shall be about my chores without further delay."

Molly Fenton was speechless as Rorie then bent to give her a quick peck on the cheek before disappearing into the dairy room off the kitchen.

"I—I'm not finished," the older woman sputtered. But already knowing the futility of further argument with her niece, she threw up her hands in defeat. Rorie did this to her every time, confusing and sidetracking her with such grand language that Molly didn't know if she was being blessed or cursed.

" 'Pon my soul, child, ye hath the tongue of a devil an' the beauty of an angel. What's ta become of ye?" she muttered to herself with a shake of her head.

Rorie had just finished separating the cream a few hours later, when she heard her uncle's voice in the kitchen. She knew something was amiss, for nothing of small importance would interrupt the felling of trees at a time when they were in a losing race with Mother Nature.

"What is it, Uncle Will?" asked Rorie, emerging from the dairy, her curiosity getting the better of her. "What has happened?"

Will Fenton, a large, burly man with graying red hair, just waved her off. " 'Tain't nothin' ta concern ye, lass. Go back ta yer chores," he answered brusquely, hurrying out the door.

Rorie looked questioningly at her aunt. The worried frown on those small, round features only deepened her resolve to know the truth of the matter.

Well acquainted with her niece's stubborn determination, Molly sighed in resignation. "There's ta be some announcement from the duke in the square within the hour. As though the village hasn't known trouble enough."

"What announcement?"

"No one knows, but I'll warrant 'tis nothin' good. An' where do ye think yer off to, miss?" Molly demanded as Rorie whipped off her apron and pinned up her hair beneath a white linen cap.

"My father may have died from fever, but 'twas the duke's last announcement closing the village school that robbed him of the will to live. And mother—Aunt Molly, I have to go. I would know if that scoundrel has the courage to show his face this time," Rorie shouted over her shoulder, throwing on a shawl and running out the door.

Molly nodded in understanding. She knew it was useless to stop the girl when she put her mind to something. Besides, perhaps it was time for a day of reckoning.

3

"Here ye, here ye, by order of the Parliament under His Majesty King George II, the common-fields of Drumfielde shall henceforth be enjoined to the estate of His Grace Roger Thornton, duke of Lyndeforde from this the twelfth day of April in the year seventeen hundred and fifty under the Act of Enclosure—"

Her emerald green eyes wide with shock, Rorie echoed the murmurs of stunned disbelief that swept through the crowd to drown out the last of the herald's words. Never would she forget the incredulity, the uncertainty, and the anger which kaleidoscoped across the dazed faces of her kinsmen as each quickly compre-hended that his way of life, his most ancient birthright, was to be no more. A shrill, wailing scream of unspoken betrayal suddenly rended the air, sending a chill up the most stalwart spine and galvanizing paralyzed minds into action.

Other shouts of protest soon erupted, and a rock whizzed overhead to mark the herald.

Suddenly, rage over the years of injustice and hopelessness these proud people had been forced to endure was unleashed with a vengeance, as men, women, and children began to pelt the hapless messenger with pebbles and stones.

Rorie gasped when blood streamed from the man's head, and he crumpled to the ground in a lifeless heap. Though she could well understand their fury, she was dumbfounded that people she had known for most of her life—good, kind, gentle people—could be capable of such violence. Anxiously searching the crowd for her brother, she could see her uncle standing atop a wagon, struggling to control the situation. Rorie could feel the tension in the air as Will Fenton's steady voice fought to carry over angry tones. At first, no one appeared to be listening, but then Rorie heaved a sigh of heartfelt relief as several people began to drop their stones.

As the crowd started to disperse, inflammatory epithets issued from behind, to once again incite the masses. Rorie whirled around to locate the source. Was the man mad? In attacking the duke's emissary, the townspeople had already crossed over that line with consequences that boded ill. Although they felt as though they had nothing more to lose, they still had their lives, and if they didn't stop soon, those would be called to account, too.

Rorie had barely finished her thought when the guards who had accompanied the herald, began to charge the townspeople with sabers and bayonets. Rorie stood rooted to the spot, unable to believe what was happening. When the village miller fell dead at her feet, his sightless eyes staring up at her, seemingly begging her for aid, she drew back in horror. Yanking her skirts from the clutch of the dead man's bloody hand, Rorie ran dazedly through the desperate and bewildered crowd.

"Terence! Uncle Will!" she screamed until her voice was hoarse, but in all the confusion, her cries might just as well have been silent.

As the crowd was pushed back, Rorie found herself hemmed in from all sides, unable to move. Again, urged on by that disembodied voice, the mass surged, and she fought with all her strength to keep from falling and being trampled underfoot. Billowing black clouds suddenly filled the air with acrid smoke that burned her eyes; Rorie realized that the dry thatched roofs of some cottages had been set aflame.

She felt the press of the crowd lessening then, as people began to scatter in every direction, seeking cover from flying sparks and charging guards. Everything became a blur to her as she was shoved and jostled in the panic, while she blindly groped her way to the edge of the square. It was happening so fast, she was having difficulty accepting the reality of it all. Her cap and shawl had been lost long ago; her dress was torn and stained, and her waist-length hair was breaking loose from its mooring of pins to fan about her like a golden cape. But she was aware of nothing save the need to find her family and escape from the nightmare. Where were her uncle and brother!

Nearby, two men observed the scene in angry and helpless frustration. As the duke's guards regrouped to attack again, one cursed and started forward.

"Easy, Rawlings," cautioned Captain Cameron Deveraux, clamping a restraining hand over his manservant's bridle. "We can do little in the face of those guards except to warn the duke that the villagers now have an ally. Our work requires secrecy if we're to succeed, and 'tis unfortunate that a few must be sacrificed to save the whole."

"Aye, I be hearin' ye, Cap'n, but I don't like it."

While Rawlings continued to vent his anger in colorful expletives, Deveraux's attention was drawn to a small child toddling out of the square, crying for his mother. Cameron's eye traveled to a rearing horse, that had just lost its rider. Realizing the path the horse would take in its fright, Deveraux forgot his own edict. The child and the terrified horse were on a collision course. Letting out a loud yell, he spurred his mount to action. Stunned into silence, Rawlings could only look on in disbelief as the captain flew toward the square at a fast gallop.

At the same moment, Rorie emerged from the crowd. Upon seeing the little Johnson boy, she was hurrying over to console him when a singular warning cry penetrated her senses above the din of hysteria. Looking up, she saw the wild, riderless horse, its nostrils flaring in terror, charging directly toward the toddler. The blood drained from her face, and she opened her mouth to scream but no sound came out. Without further thought, Rorie ran to the child. In a few seconds he would be under the horse's hooves.

In a desperate effort, she lunged for the boy, throwing him as far afield as she could, taking

```
09   843.01.01.10  03/21/88 15.14 6440
B.DALTON BOOKSELLER     PLEASANTON, CA

*  9570063                        2.50
*  8007314                        4.50
*  8004897                        3.95
*  8007691                        3.95
*                   SUBTOTAL     14.90
*                   SALES TAX     1.04
*                   TOTAL        15.94
*                   CHECK        15.94
*

-----------------THANK YOU-----------------
```

his place in the path of destruction. The last thing she saw was the white of the horse's rolling eyes as the gelding bore down on her. She had just thrown her arms across her face when a force grabbed her around the waist and seemingly catapulted her off her feet, high above the ground, before slamming her body against a hard but tractable surface.

The wind was nearly knocked from her body, and it took a few minutes for her to realize that someone had pulled her from the horse's path with a split second to spare. A muscled arm now held her securely against a rock-hard chest atop a huge stallion.

"Are you hurt?" demanded a voice when they had reined to a stop.

Startled by the nearness of the deep-timbred tone, Rorie could manage only a shake of her head. Twisting around to see who had saved her, she let out a cry of surprise as she was suddenly handed unceremoniously to the ground, out of harm's way, without a further word. By the time she had staggered to her feet, the rider was in the distance, a black cape billowing in the wind behind broad shoulders.

Still shaking from her narrow escape and uncertain of her emotions, Rorie became angry at the rudeness of her benefactor, then grateful for her life. Now, having recovered somewhat, she was curious. Why had the man run off without giving her the chance to thank him? Unless he was trying to protect his identity. And to what purpose? Though she hadn't the chance to see his face, she had no doubt that he was a stranger to these parts, for she could recall no one of that large size and breadth in the village. But she had little time to dwell on the matter, as her uncle and brother hurried anxiously to her side.

"Rorie, I thought—When Uncle Will and I saw that horse charging—" Shakened to the core, the lanky youth merely shook his head, unable to finish.

"Are ye together, lass?" Will Fenton broke in more tersely, his eyes searching her for any sign of injury.

Rorie nodded. "Just a little bruised," she said, managing a wan smile. "Are you and Terence—"

"We're fine—two among the lucky few," he assured her tensely. His coarse, weathered features hardened then, as he turned to survey the smoldering remains of the village.

"And the child—is he safe?" asked Rorie.

"Aye, thanks to you," said Terence. "But, Rorie, his father didn't fare as well. Tom took a sword through the midsection," her brother added quietly.

"Oh, no," cried Rorie. Tears welled up in her eyes and spilled down her cheeks. The Johnsons were decent, hard working people, just a year older than herself, and she had known them since childhood. Now Sally was a widow with a young son to raise in the worst of times. Rorie was heartsick, for it had all been so needless.

The smell of gunpowder and smoking thatch still clung to the air; people aimlessly wandered the field of battle, helping the wounded and seeking an explanation to this madness. All totaled, Rorie counted ten dead, four of them children who had been trampled in the panic, and twice that number of injuries. Not a sound penetrated the eerie, unnatural silence, however. The mourning would come later, she knew, when the shock wore off. In actuality, the revolt had occurred in less than half an hour, but it would last a lifetime in their minds.

"Uncle Will, I think this was not by chance—" began Rorie angrily.

"Hush, lass! We'll talk later. 'Tain't safe here. Now off with ye ta fetch yer Aunt Molly and her liniments whilst Terence and me lend a hand here."

As night fell, an uneasiness settled upon the shattered village, but not even the darkness could blot out the horror of the day. Worn down by shock, sorrow, and hours of ministrations, Rorie, Terence and their aunt and uncle collapsed wearily onto the benches around the trestle table at the Fenton farm. Their bodies were slumped in resignation, their features etched in exhaustion.

"Uncle Will, I think the revolt was neatly plotted," said Rorie, breaking the heavy silence. "Someone in the crowd was deliberately stirring the people to riot. And judging by the strange behavior of the man who saved me this afternoon, I would venture to say 'twas him. Do you think him to be a spy for the duke?"

"Nothing is fer certain—except this carnage," Will Fenton added bitterly. "Though I owe that man a debt, I hold no one above suspicion after this day."

"Bah, Rorie, must you always question everything!" exploded Terence, giving way to his pent up emotions. "The villagers have lost their birthright. The duke waits until the fields are planted with the spring seed before announcing the enclosure and then, as always, the bastard doesn't even have the decency to show his face. Soon, people we have known all our lives will be forced either to tenant farm or to seek their livelihood in the mines in Cornwall. Either way, they become nothing more than slaves. And you don't consider the matter worthy of revolt without prodding? God's teeth, give our kinsmen their due!"

"I'm doing just that," retorted Rorie. "Someone cleverly manipulated that crowd to violence because, thankfully, the majority of the villagers do not share your trait for impulsive action before rational thought. We're no longer talking about a birthright here, brother, now 'tis a matter of an attack on the duke's emissary."

"Hold yer tongues! Enough battle has been waged this day, and I'll not stand for it under me own roof!" thundered their uncle. "Much as I fear the thought, I'll warrant that Rorie speaks the truth in this matter."

"But why? What's ta be gained by forcing a revolt where unrest was certain ta be present?" queried Molly Fenton, pale and drawn. Anxiety and concern had replaced the usual twinkle in her eyes.

Will stood up to cross the room, his stocky frame throwing a great shadow against the whitewashed wall in the dim firelight. As he reached for his pipe on the mantel and slowly began to fill it, his bushy red brows were drawn together in puzzlement.

"I kenna tell ye who is ta blame or what was ta be gained by bringin' the villagers to this end," he responded at length. "There ain't nothin' more ta take from them. But I'll wager there be more ta this than meets the eye. If only the duke's herald had not been stoned . . . Rest assured, His Grace'll not be turnin' another cheek ta this. I ain't got an answer now, but by the heavens, I'll find one." Will slammed his great, beefy fist on the table in determination. "I'll not let Lord Chardwellende's hard work go for naught because his nephew and heir fancies a larger estate."

"Now, Will Fenton, don't ye be exchangin' yer temper fer good sense," admonished his wife worriedly. "Lord Chardwellende, God rest his soul, has been dead neigh on ten years—"

"Aye, an' we all know who's ta blame fer tha'," Will interceded tightly. "Ain't nothin' been the same since then."

"Hush, husband, keep yer tongue in yer mouth! Lord Chardwellende's nephew is the duke now, good or bad, an' he's got spies everywhere. He ain't got a kind eye fer ye as 'tis. Ye've weaned away his tenants to help them set up their own communal farm on a piece of our land to escape estate taxes, and ye counseled the village ta set up its own barter outside of the Market Fair so's no one has ta pay the duke's high prices an' be forced ta sell his wares too low ta him. There weren't nothin' he could do to ye then, because we be freeholdin' an' Lord Chardwellende give us this land 'til our death to do as we please. But iffen ye give the scoundrel further cause—"

"Aunt Molly is right," said Rorie. "Let me talk to Mary. Mayhaps she can convince her father to approach the duke on Drumfielde's behalf. After all, he is the local magistrate."

"Squire Balfour!" exclaimed Terence with a derisive snort. "The fat lout lends a hand to no one who doesn't feather his nest, including his own daughter. Her only value to him lays in raising the importance of his bloodline through some illustrious marriage."

Molly sighed regretfully. " 'Tis truth, Rorie. The poor lass has always been under her father's thumb, and even more so since Mistress Balfour has become an invalid."

"Be that as it may, we must find help in some quarter, and we can ill afford to leave the smallest stone unturned," Rorie said firmly.

Will nodded his head in agreement. "Aye. We got ta take our miracles where we ken find them an' make 'em where we can't."

4

Armed with an old riding skirt that Mary had once given her as an excuse to call on her friend, Rorie picked her way down the rutted lane to Balfour Grange, ever conscious of the palpable silence. There was no humming of the saws or quaking of felled trees today, just an unnerving quiet. Not even the cheerful songs of the thrushes had been able to penetrate the pall which now hung over Drumfielde Village like a heavy mantle, and so it seemed they no longer tried.

Ever since Roger Thornton had proclaimed himself the new duke of Lyndeforde and lord of Drumfielde on that long ago day, it seemed that uncertainty had become a part of their daily lives, thought Rorie sadly. Though he had never resided at his estate and was never seen, he had made his presence felt just the same. If the blackguard wasn't raising taxes or closing the school, he was finding some other insidious way of stripping them of their pride and dignity.

As Rorie passed by the south fields, her anger mounted until she thought she would choke on her rage. The bailiff and his men were setting about brambles and hawthorne bushes to enclose the fields, fields that by right of the most ancient law in England, belonged to the village.

"The Devil take you!" Rorie cursed under her breath through clenched teeth. "And if I must pledge my soul, I'll see this injustice undone," she vowed.

Remembering her mission, Rorie drew new strength from her anger, and she arrived at the stately Balfour Grange full of steely determination. As usual, refusing to bow to convention and present herself at the servants' entrance, Rorie boldly stepped up to the massive oak door and knocked loudly. A woman dressed in gray linen with a white muslin round-eared cap fixed securely atop her head opened the door. Although the housekeeper had always had a special fondness for Rorie, the distress on her face was evident as she viewed the girl on her doorstep.

"Oh, Rorie, things do not go well here," the housekeeper cried in alarm. "Ye shouldna come today. The cockfight was postponed, and the squire be at home—"

"You misunderstand, Mrs. Simmons," interrupted Rorie. "There's no need to stand guard for me now. I'm not here to raid Squire Balfour's library. I'm here to—to return Miss Mary's riding skirt, which she bade me embroider," fibbed Rorie smoothly, holding up the skirt for inspection. "Mary is expecting me."

The housekeeper took the garment and examined it skeptically, knowing that Rorie Shelbourne was not above a few high jinks to get

34

her way. But the skirt was undeniably one of Miss Mary's—one that she hadn't seen in a very long time. Shifting uncertainly and casting anxious glances over her shoulder, Mrs. Simmons finally motioned for Rorie to step into the large, marble entryway.

Glancing into the empty library, Rorie had to smile as she recalled her first visit to Balfour Grange two years ago. She had accompanied her mother when Sirena came to display her lace to the mistress. Rorie had been left waiting in the kitchen. But having known only crude huts and cottages, Rorie had been agog at the overstated opulence of the Grange and quite soon conveniently forgot her place when the cook's back was turned.

It was in the library that Mary had come upon her, reverently running her hands across the spines of the leather-bound manuscripts. Rorie had counted three dozen in all and was struck speechless by the squire's prodigious wealth, for books, printed and bound by hand, were very dear, indeed. Though their paths had rarely crossed, Rorie recognized Mary at once, and she cringed in expectation of a stinging reprimand, for a village lass simply did not roam through a gentryman's home at will. Her legs had nearly buckled under her from surprise and relief when Mary, instead, smiled shyly and asked if she liked to read.

The two girls were opposites in every way, not to mention their social differences. Where Rorie radiated the confidence and exuberance of young womanhood, Mary was small and underdeveloped for her age, her eyes reflecting only resignation of her father's will. Yet they had been instinctively drawn to one another. When the visit ended with Mary offering to lend Rorie books, the seeds of an enduring friendship had been sown.

Mary had been true to her word, opening her father's library to Rorie during the squire's frequent absences. In exchange, Rorie had taught Mary to read with greater proficiency and comprehension, opening her mind to knowledge outside of the village limits. For Rorie, exploring books was an adventure, but for Mary, it was an awakening of her social consciousness.

Great shouts of anger suddenly filtering out from a room down the hallway, which Rorie knew to be the drawing room, pulled her mind back to the present. Etiquette demanded that she remain in the entryway until she could be announced, but as the squire's booming voice continued to issue forth, punctuated by sounds of hysterical weeping, Rorie bowed to her curiosity and quietly followed Mrs. Simmons down to the room.

As Mrs. Simmons stood helplessly in the doorway, unable to break into the highly charged diatribe to make her announcement, it was Mary who first saw Rorie standing behind the housekeeper.

"Oh, Rorie, thank God you've come," she cried, cutting her father off in midsentence. Pale, hollow-eyed, her face tear-stained, it was obvious that Mary had spent long hours crying.

Squire Balfour whirled around in amazement at the interruption and gave Mrs. Simmons a withering glare.

"I thought I gave ye instructions that we weren't to be disturbed, Mrs. Simmons."

"Ye—yes sir," the housekeeper stammered, "but Miss Rorie said tha' Miss Mary be expectin' her."

"Nonsense!" boomed the squire angrily.

To his mind the Shelbourne girl was too forward for her station. Her keen intelligence and educated background, which he knew to surpass his own, was irritating to him. She was clever with words and, on more than one occasion, he had come out the fool in verbal exchanges with her so that he avoided the girl whenever possible. Now here she was intruding into a matter of a most sensitive and private nature.

"I'm afraid ye'll have to take yer leave, missy. 'Tis a matter of extreme personal importance of which we speak. Take up yer business with the housekeeper—in the kitchen," the squire commanded imperiously.

Before Rorie could open her mouth to respond, Mary astounded them both with an emphatic "no!"

"Please don't leave," she cried, looking at Rorie in supplication, her wide gray eyes looming too large in her delicate white features. "I have no one else to turn to. I need your help."

"This is preposterous," blustered the squire. "A squire's daughter asking a peasant for aid, and against her own father no less!"

Rorie looked uncertainly from father to daughter, wondering what she had blundered into. Already she had overstepped her bounds. But though she bemoaned the girl's timidity and meekness, Rorie admired Mary for her genuine concern for others and her lack of silly pretenses, which separated her from the other empty-headed females of her class. Having allowed her father to orchestrate her every thought and action in a desperate effort to win his affection, she seemed younger than her twenty-two years. Once, when she had shyly confided her desire to enter a convent, Rorie had encouraged her to do so, for she could think of no more fitting place for a girl of Mary's sensitivity.

Taking Mary's trembling hands in hers, she asked, "How can I help?"

Tears of gratitude welled up in Mary's eyes. She bowed her head as though in shame and sobbed brokenly, "Father has betrothed me to—the duke—of Lyndeforde!"

The shock Rorie felt was evident as her expressive, green eyes flew open to survey the squire as though he were some repulsive creature.

"You would give your own daughter to the scoundrel who chokes the very life from this village! Did you hear nothing of the enclosure!" she cried, heedless of her position.

Squire Balfour's florid complexion became even more flushed as he quite unexpectantly found himself on the defensive, and he had the decency to look momentarily contrite.

"Well, ah, yes, events of the past day were unsettling, I must admit, and ye ruffians should be grateful for the leniency I've shown thus far as magistrate. But 'tis neither here nor there," he added with an impatient wave of the arm. "The fact remains that marriages of convenience are arranged every day, and I must look to the practical side. A female's duty is to the betterment of her lineage. 'Tis what every young woman is raised to—or should be," he added pointedly, glaring at Rorie. "Anything else is of small concern."

The squire hadn't believed his good fortune when the duke's emissary had approached him about the betrothal, and he wasn't about to let the opportunity slip through his fingers—enclosure or no. The man was a duke, and that was all that mattered, reputation aside. He would at last see his daughter married. Happily or not was of little consequence to him, for it would settle the silly notion she had of entering a convent. She would be a duchess, and his grandson would be heir to extensive holdings. The next generation of his line would at last see themselves as true members of the nobility, and they would have him to thank for it. No, he would not waver from his purpose. The very thought of his only child entering a convent instead of producing future heirs frightened him more than he cared to admit.

Sucking in his ample paunch, Squire Balfour squared his shoulders and assumed his gruffest manner. "Ye have no choice in the matter, daughter. I have already passed on half of yer dowry. The wedding is to take place the last week in May, and the duke shall host a ball at Lyndeforde in three weeks to make the announcement. One other thing, ye shall preside o'er the May Day this year to celebrate yer betrothal."

With that the squire turned on his heel and strode from the room. Mary collapsed weakly onto the gilt-edged sofa, her moment of strength gone. The vivid red of the upholstery contrasted oddly with the paleness of her features. For her part, Rorie wondered where Drumfielde would find the spirit to celebrate even though May Day was traditionally the biggest event of the year.

"Oh, Rorie, what am I to do?" cried Mary. "There's no sidestepping Father on this."

Rorie sat down beside her dispirited friend and put a comforting arm around the girl's trembling shoulders. Squire Balfour was indeed determined to see the matter of his daughter's marriage settled to his satisfaction.

"Perhaps it won't be as bad as you fear," she offered. "After all, the duke is in his forties. He can't live that much longer." Rorie hoped she sounded more convincing than she felt.

Mary looked at her friend in horror. "I should die at the man's first touch. It makes me shudder to think of it."

In truth, Rorie had to admit that were she in Mary's place, she would feel more than a moment's desperation, herself, and she chafed at her inability to help someone in need of her aid.

"I am so sorry, Mary," she said gently. "I don't know what I can do. In truth, 'tis I who had come to ask for your help."

"My help?" asked Mary in surprise. "What can I possibly do for you when I can do so little for myself?"

"I had hoped you might be able to convince your father to intercede with the duke on Drumfielde's behalf."

"Yes, I heard about the revolt, and I am so sorry, but you have seen the influence I carry with my father," replied Mary with a bitter laugh. "All those years I have strived to please him, and it has brought me to this end. I—I shall run away—to a convent," she suddenly declared, her eyes wild in her chalk-white face.

Rorie wished it were that easy, and she hated to dispel her friend's one glimmer of hope.

"Mary, with so much at stake, the squire would find you. And the embarrassment of the duke and your father would be such that the pressure they would bring to bear upon the order would be too great for the sisters to withstand. In the end, your father would have his way. As duchess of Lyndeforde, at least you will remain close to your home. Mayhaps you could find a way to convince the duke to better conditions for the village," added Rorie hopefully, appealing to Mary's social conscience.

"Yes, I suppose that is a thought," responded Mary, wiping her tears. "Perhaps some good can come of this nightmare. Would that I had your courage and spirit," she said with a tremulous smile.

Rorie gave Mary a reassuring hug. "You do, Mary. You just haven't realized it yet. Now I really must be going. If I can be of further help, you have only to ask," she reminded the distraught girl.

Suddenly, Mary brightened. "Rorie, wait! There is something you can do, and perhaps we can both benefit."

"What do you mean?" asked Rorie curiously. "You know that if it lies within my bounds, I shall surely accommodate you."

"In spite of your kind words, I haven't your strength and determination. I need you by me. I—I want you to act as my companion."

Rorie was dumbfounded. "Mary, I know it's customary for a companion to accompany a new wife on her wedding trip and to her new home, but 'tis usually a close relative. What will your father say to this?"

"He shan't deny me this," responded Mary with rare determination. "I harbor no further illusions of my father's concern for me, for all my efforts have moved him only to betray me with this vile betrothal. No longer will I act the pawn for anyone. Please, Rorie, you would be in a much better position to help Drumfielde as my companion."

Rorie hadn't counted on this new development, but after her vow to help Mary in any way possible, what could she say? How could she possibly let down her friend when all Mary asked for was her support? And Mary was right. What possibility did a village lass have of helping Drumfielde? But as a companion to the wife of the duke, perhaps, there was now a chance where none had existed before. She knew she had to grab onto it with both hands.

When Rorie nodded her assent, Mary breathed a deep sigh of relief. Already she felt a strength she had never known before.

Squire Balfour stared across the food-laden table in wonderment at his daughter's insanity. Choosing a village peasant for a companion over a dour-faced, respectable aunt was unheard of in his circles.

"After all," he expounded waving a drumstick in the air, "the position is not that of a servant. Your companion needs to be one of our class. The girl hath no polish, no manners, and she is not versed in the ways of the gentry. She will bring embarrassment upon this house. No, 'tis out of the question," the squire concluded, belching loudly.

"Nonsense," countered Mary, standing her ground for the first time in her life. "Rorie Shelbourne is as accomplished as any woman of class. She can read, write, and converse better than most nobles. Her needlework surpasses my own—and Rorie doesn't belch!" Mary glared at her father pointedly. "As for the ways of the gentry, the only difference between them and those of the villagers is that the gentry have titles to legitimize their actions."

Squire Balfour nearly choked on his mouthful of squab. He didn't know if he was more surprised by the treason she was spouting or by the fact that she had dared to spout it. Caught off-balance, he wasn't sure how to respond. In the end, he capitulated, murmuring thanks that his daughter, with this curious new streak of independence, would soon be off his hands. Let the problem then be her husband's, he mumbled sourly to himself.

Rorie's family wasn't so easily persuaded about the merits of her new position.

"Rorie, lass, do ye know what yer about?" Molly Fenton asked anxiously. "The duke hath little conscience an' willna think twice of dealin' with ye harshly should ye get in his way. Tell her, Will. There is still much unrest in the village—"

"But, Aunt Molly, that's why I *should* go. If there's the slightest chance that I can help Mary influence the duke—"

"I'll have no sister of mine beg," interrupted Terence angrily.

Rorie swung a level gaze on her hot-tempered brother. "I'll never beg," she replied evenly.

Molly's round, gentle features were creased with worry as she nervously wrung her hands on her apron. "I don't like it. If the villagers revolt again, ye'll be caught in the middle. They won't understand why yer under the duke's roof."

"If it comes to another rebellion, I can best serve by keeping a close eye on the scoundrel."

"No, 'tis too dangerous. I promised Sirena I'd care fer ye an' Terence. Rorie, lass, ye should be settlin' down with a nice village lad, a babe on yer hip and another in yer belly, not spying on some devil's spawn—" Molly's voice trailed off when she saw the familiar, stubborn set of her niece's chin. "Will, for the love of God, tell her," she pleaded desperately with her husband.

Will Fenton tapped out the clay pipe in the palm of his broad, calloused hand, his sole attention seemingly absorbed in the task.

"The lass is right, Molly," he said at last in a low, resolute tone. "We've lived too long with the duke's sword above our heads. He's taken the school, the land, and he willna rest until he has our dignity and pride. Rorie will go, for 'tis always best for a quarry to mark well his predator."

5

Steel blue eyes scanned the bustling London dock as the captain reflected upon the circumstances which had, at long last, brought him back to London. As had been expected, his grandfather had vehemently opposed the trip, but both had known this day would come, for Reed Delacroix would not rest in peace and the past would not be done until Cameron had finished it. The one-sided uprising he had observed in Drumfielde four days ago bore witness to that fact. And once again, he wondered about the muscular, stocky youth he had seen in the village crowd. The young man appeared to be working extra hard to bank the fire under an already boiling pot. If Deveraux had had any doubt of it, it was dissipated when the boy threw the first stone to mark the duke's emissary.

"You're thinking about the rebellion," said Rawlings, coming to stand beside Deveraux. It wasn't a question, for having observed the tense, distant look on the captain's face, he already knew the answer. "The lass could pose a danger to ye, sir, were ye to return to Drumfielde," he suggested offhandedly.

"The girl I removed from the path of the runaway horse?"

"Aye, she is certain to know you fer a stranger and wonder on yer presence. A newcomer in a small town is always suspect—especially in these times."

"Yes, it was rather unfortunate. I could have saved the child and still been assured of complete anonymity if that girl hadn't interfered. But I think 'tis doubtful, Rawlings, that she remembers any more of me than I of her in that turmoil."

"Jest the same, Cap'n, it may be wise to make some inquiries."

"Maybe so. 'Tis certain we can't afford any loose ends now. But have a care. Inquiries, however discreet, tend to raise only more suspicion."

Pushing himself away from the railing, then, Deveraux signaled to his first mate to meet him in his quarters.

The cabin was an extension of the captain himself—simply furnished but richly appointed. The detailed carvings of the polished, mahogany panelled walls, of the overlarge bunk which lay to one side, and of the huge hand-carved desk which dominated the center of the room were second to none. On the right side of the cabin stood a washstand, three large, worn, seaman's chests, and a low cabinet in which Cameron stored his maps and navigation tools.

Stripped to the waist, he was splashing water on his face and chest when Ian Hawkins appeared in the doorway.

"You wished to see me, sir?"

Taking a thick towel from one of the opened trunks and drying himself, Deveraux studied his first mate with a keen eye. Though not as tall or as muscularly built as his employer, Hawkins nevertheless cut a fine figure with his russet-colored hair, warm brown eyes, and boyish smile. At the age of twenty-three, he was still impetuous and not above getting into some tight spots, but he was a good, loyal, and trustworthy seaman, and Cameron valued him highly. As Rawlings was so fond of pointing out, the brash, young lad was Deveraux himself some years earlier. Cameron ran a hand through his thick, black hair. God, had he ever been that young? It seemed as though he had carried a heavy weight upon his shoulders for half his life, and now at twenty-seven, he sometimes felt as old as his grandfather's years. Once again, the pain of the past reflected briefly in his rugged features before he angrily shoved the memories back to the recesses of his mind.

"Sir," repeated Hawkins for the third time, his expression betraying the concern he felt, for it wasn't like the captain to be so preoccupied.

Deveraux silently castigated himself for having relaxed the iron control he had exercised over his mind for so many years. This part of his life was to remain locked away from his daily thoughts, but lately his mind seemed to display a will of its own, as it began to drag these memories more and more to the forefront of his attention. Without a doubt, the London newspaper notice had become the catalyst to a chain of events which would leave no one in its wake unchanged.

Observing the worried look on Ian's face,

Deveraux mentally shook himself.

"My pardon, Hawkins. It would seem that my past is demanding an audience. Come in. I have further instructions," he said, motioning his first mate over to the desk. "Rawlings and I shall be leaving the ship shortly for a stay in London, and I want you and the crew to set sail for Algiers in three days."

Ian looked at his captain in surprise. "Algiers! But sir, the Barbary Coast is a lair for the worst kind of thieves and cut throats."

"Your presence will be well protected. The Dey owes me his life."

"Beggin' your pardon, Captain?"

" 'Twas a long time ago, Ian. To shorten the story—I once saved a pirate from a pirate. Here is a letter of introduction. The Dey will honor it. Keep Richards by your side, as he alone understands their language and ways.

"Allow the men to have their pleasures, but be prepared to return by mid May, for I may have need of you. You are to weigh anchor in this inlet here off the coast," instructed Deveraux, pointing to a spot on the map. "Remain in secret until you have word from me. Is everything clear?"

"Yes, sir."

Hawkins wished he knew what was going on. First there was this unscheduled trip to England when the captain had always stood adamant against trade with the Mother Country. Then upon arrival, he and Rawlings disappeared for a few days without explanation. And now he was sending the crew off to Algiers. That the captain had his reasons, Ian never doubted, for the man never did anything without careful deliberation. But the mystery was killing him, and all attempts to wean information from Rawlings had proven in vain. That was another curiosity: the usually reserved Rawlings appeared years younger these days, radiating a sense of restrained energy and high excitement.

As though reading his first mate's mind, Deveraux relaxed his stern features.

"Rest assured, Hawkins, all will be known to you in due time. But until then, many lives may depend upon you, so take my instructions to heart."

Hawkins nodded and left more perplexed than when he had arrived.

Lord Dandridge, the earl of Marwynde, looked up from his dinner at the butler's approach. The unflappable Higgins had most assuredly been affected by something, and the earl wasn't sure he really wanted to know. It seemed as though his life had been unsettled for so long, each day bringing a new problem. He wondered how much longer he would have to endure. He was thinner, his face was more deeply lined, and his body was slightly stooped as though it had bowed to the weight of his sorrows—and shame. But he still carried about him the air of dignity and authority of a fair and noble man.

"What is it, Higgins?" he asked with a sigh of resignation.

"Milord, there be a gentleman to see you."

"What is his name?"

"I think you should see for yourself, milord—in the library."

Lord Dandridge walked haltingly into the

library to see a very tall, well turned young man
with a self-assured, almost arrogant, bearing that
made his presence impossible to ignore. He
apparently followed the new trend of the day,
shunning the traditional periwig, preferring
instead to wear his own dark hair unpowdered
and pulled back in the fashion. The earl judged
him to be a colonial by the cut of his clothes.
Although of a fine cloth and fit, they were
simply made, lacking the ridiculous fripperies of
the local dandies—and from the look of the man,
it wasn't from oversight. Taking further note of
the stranger's vigorous appearance, Lord
Dandridge was certain, then, that the young man
was not a member of the insipid gentry or
nobility. As he scanned the hard, angular
features—the patrician nose, the firm jawline,
and the clear silver-blue eyes further accentuated
beneath dark, heavy brows—the earl was left
with a strange feeling that he should know this
person.

"So, we meet at last, Lord Dandridge," said
the man in a deep, firm voice.

The earl's confusion was apparent. "My
apologies, sir, but I cannot seem to place you."

"There is no reason why you should, Lord
Dandridge."

A slight movement caught Lord Dandridge's
eye as a much smaller and older man emerged,
then, from the shadows. The earl's jaw dropped,
and a hand flew to his chest as his composure
faltered. He looked from one to the other until he
had resolved the reality of their presence in his
mind.

"Dear God, but it cannot be," he gasped.
" 'Tis surely you, Rawlings, but this cannot be—"

"I am Cameron Deveraux, milord, captain of the *Homeward Bound* newly arrived from the colonies. I am here to report that Reed Delacroix is dead."

Lord Dandridge stared incredulously at his visitors and collapsed into a chair. "B—But how can this be? Why wasn't I sent word?" he stammered.

"Why should it matter, milord?" asked Cameron, his eyes narrowing with interest.

After a few minutes, Lord Dandridge recovered himself. "You will have to excuse me, Captain Deveraux. This has come as quite a shock. You see, I failed the boy once. I had dared to hope that he would return one day to set things as they should be, and to allow me to redeem myself for a past action."

"Which was?"

Lord Dandridge shifted uneasily and his saddened eyes begged for understanding. He was still haunted by the image of that seventeen-year-old youth who had struggled so desperately with the news of his parents' deaths.

"I—I turned away from Reed at a time when he deserved my support. I should have used my authority to help him fight the injustice which had been done him. Instead, I was weak, using his youthful age for an excuse."

"I see. I'm sorry to have to impart news of this nature. I was well acquainted with Reed, and may I say that he never bore you any ill will or held you accountable for his past difficulties."

The earl seemed little relieved. "How did his death occur? And how come you to know of Reed?" he inquired anxiously.

"We met in the colonies and sailed together

for many years," began Cameron. "We became close due to similarities in our backgrounds. Nine months ago, he was taken ill aboard ship on a trip to the West Indies. His last request was that I come here in his stead, to complete unfinished business. Rawlings has continued to sail with me and to act as my valet. Indeed, his services have been invaluable to me. Mayhaps I can count on your aid, too, milord?"

"My aid? But for what, Captain?"

"To see that the duke of Lyndeforde receives his just due," Deveraux stated.

" 'Tis a tall order, Captain," warned the earl, more than a little surprised. "Roger Thornton is a dangerous man. Perhaps you could tell me more of yourself."

Cameron was reluctant, as always, to expose any part of himself, but he needed the earl's alliance. "There isn't much to tell, milord. My great-uncle is the Marquis de Sauvonnerie, and though my grandfather is next in line for the title, he has elected to seek his fortune in the colonies. Together we oversee a large shipping and trading concern between the southern colonies and the West Indies. Soon, we expect to expand into the China trade."

"I see," replied the earl. And he ran a second appraising eye over the virile young man. It would seem that the captain was an uncommon man, the noble blood in his veins accounting for his self-assurance and commanding presence. Unquestioningly, the lad appeared capable enough to undertake any task. For further confirmation, Lord Dandridge looked to Rawlings, who stood quietly in the shadows.

"The Cap'n can do wha' needs be done,"

Rawlings assured him tersely.

Lord Dandridge nodded, then, having made his decision. After all, he had nothing to lose, for he felt he had already lost his honor. Perhaps it could be regained if he were to avenge the Delacroix boy in death, and he waved Cameron to an opposite chair.

"You and Reed must have been close for you to risk so much."

Cameron nodded, seating himself. "Yes, one might even say kindred spirits. I owe him this. Aside from that, I've been known to enjoy an adventure or two."

"How much did Reed confide to you, Captain Deveraux?" the earl asked.

"Reed preferred not to talk of his past."

"Yes, that's understandable. There was much pain and misunderstanding all around. Did Reed tell you that his father was James Chard-wellende, the previous duke of Lyndeforde?"

Cameron nodded. "I was given to understand that his parents had never married."

"Quite right, though it wasn't from lack of desire to do so. James was already married when he met Claire Delacroix, but his marriage to the duchess was over in all but legal terms. There was nothing left between them but bitter animosity and family honor. You see, the duchess had never been able to conceive an heir, and she had always held James accountable. When news reached her of the duke's liaison with a beautiful French lady and of Reed's birth a year later, she went into an insane rage.

"She even went so far as to have Reed and his mother kidnapped once, but fortunately the duke found out in time to waylay the plan. He threatened to publicly declare the duchess insane if she or her nephew, Roger Thornton, ever took a hand against Reed or Claire again. In return, James had promised not to acknowledge Reed as his heir while the duchess lived. Then he moved Reed and Claire into Lyndeforde, the old family seat in Drumfielde Village, for better protection. The duchess couldn't abide the country life and rarely ever used the manor house. The estate was falling into disrepair, and the village needed a firmer hand, so 'twas the most practical solution."

Cameron's brow knit in deep thought as a myriad of questions flowed through his mind, but he said nothing. He didn't want to interrupt the earl's narrative, for he had the feeling that Lord Dandridge needed to purge himself of the story after all these years of silence.

"The duke sent Reed off to school in the north at the age of ten to prevent the boy from knowing that he was—ah—illegitimate until he and Claire had judged Reed able to handle the circumstances of his birth," the earl continued. "As it would happen, however, one of the older students, whose mother had been acquainted with the duchess, knew the full story. And he took devilish pleasure in relating the murky details—no doubt with certain embellishments— to a defenseless little boy. Reed felt betrayed and became bitterly estranged from his parents for seven years. James never recovered from that blow.

"The tragedy is that Reed had been on his way home to heal the rift between them, but he never got the chance. Ironically, the night that James and Claire were waylaid by highwaymen, they had just arrived from Lyndeforde and were on their way to the solicitor's office with a signed document which legitimized Reed's birth and named him heir to all of his father's estates. The duchess had died the previous year, and James was to have married Claire here in this very room at the week's end."

Cameron's brow shot up with sudden interest. "What happened to the document?"

"There had, in fact, been three such documents. All have vanished. One, an unsigned copy, was stolen from the solicitor's files, and the other was missing from the duke's personal effects following the murder. It is supposed that the third remains hidden somewhere. Rumor has it that Thornton does not rest easy and still seeks it, for if the document is signed—" The earl had no need to finish the sentence.

Lord Dandridge was exhausted, but he resisted Cameron's suggestion to put an end to the evening. It was about time the full story came out, and he needed to tell it. He had been weighted down by the awesome burden for too many years, and justice was long overdue, in spite of the possible consequences to himself. Shifting his weight once more, the earl resumed the narrative.

"Roger Thornton had managed to gamble away his inheritance from his parents' and aunt's estates. As James was the last of his line, legally speaking, Thornton was desperate to claim the Lyndeforde title and inheritance for himself. I knew Reed to be in grave danger, for Roger is not a man to leave loose ends. Illegitimate or not, Reed was a definite threat to that claim."

"So you had Reed waylaid on his journey

from the north and brought here," added Cameron, picking up the slack.

The earl nodded, nearly overwhelmed by the ten-year-old memory. "Yes. I knew Thornton was sending his henchmen to intercept Reed's coach. I was never privy to the exact nature of the scoundrel's plans for Reed, but 'twas fortunate, indeed, that my men had reached the boy first. 'Twas when Reed arrived here that the family's solicitor and I informed him of the inheritance from his mother's estate—a quite handsome fund which had been set up by the duke. And we both advised the boy to leave England for his own safety."

At this point, Higgins entered the room with a decanter of brandy and a tray of glasses.

"Milord, if I may stay?"

"Certainly, Higgins. By all means."

Catching Deveraux's looks of puzzlement and concern over the breach in security, Lord Dandridge hastened to allay his fears.

" 'Tis all right, Captain. Higgins was a part of this from the beginning."

Cameron looked to Rawlings. At a sign of confirmation from his trusted valet, he nodded for Lord Dandridge to continue.

"Reed had his suspicions regarding Thornton," resumed the earl. "When it appeared that Reed wasn't going to take our advice to leave England, Rawlings, Higgins, and I made plans to put him on a ship bound for the colonies. We then put forth rumors that the boy had been shanghaied," the old earl explained. "Reed was kept drugged until the ship was far enough out to sea for him to do nothing else save follow Rawlings's good counsel, until such time as he

was older, wiser, and strong enough to be able to
handle the likes of Roger Thornton. I'm sure
you're aware that Rawlings here was the stable
master at Lyndeforde. He served the family well,
transferring his allegiance to Reed following the
tragedy."

Lord Dandridge put his head in his hands. "I
thought the boy too young, so instead of using
what influence I had to help him fight for his
rightful claim, I had him kidnapped from his
own birthland."

Rawlings glanced uneasily at Deveraux, but
the captain's features had become inscrutable.

"Why should you stress yourself, Lord
Dandridge, when it was for Reed's own
protection that you acted?" Cameron questioned
curiously.

" 'Twas for more than Reed's welfare that I
bargained. 'Twas for my own as well," the earl
answered hoarsely. "You must understand that I
had invested heavily in improvements for
Marwynde, my country estate. I desperately
needed the revenues from the estate to pay the
debts incurred. Thornton had threatened to close
the Drumfielde market to my goods were I to
oppose his right to his uncle's inheritance. With
the next nearest market town being fifty miles
away, my perishable goods would have rotted on
the way. I would have lost most everything I
owned. It will be to my everlasting shame that I
sacrificed my dearest friend's son for my own
financial benefit, for my wealth has brought me
little comfort. Dear God, but I must be cursed!
Everyone whom I have held dear has been lost to
me—my wife, my daughter, James, Claire, and
now Reed."

"Take heart, Lord Dandridge. Given the circumstances, I am sure that Reed would have understood your plight. The past is past now, and we have only the present to concern ourselves."

"What are your plans, Captain? Roger Thornton is a blot on humanity whose black deeds would fill a book."

"Yes, I am well acquainted with the duke's handiwork," replied Cameron tightly. "And it is my intention to ruin him through his own vices."

"How may I be of assistance?" asked the earl with renewed hope.

"You can best serve our interests, milord, by way of an introduction to the infamous duke."

Lord Dandridge replied without hesitation. "Done," he said. "With your noble background and a basic knowledge of cards, it should pose little difficulty. And perhaps I can be of further assistance," he added mysteriously. "There were some papers which Reed was to have signed to claim his inheritance."

Cameron thought for a moment before recollecting the mention of some papers. "If I heard Reed correctly, the papers were never signed. And wasn't there some provision that if the inheritance remained unclaimed after one year, the sum reverted back to the government?"

" 'Tis true all that you said," replied Lord Dandridge, his eyes twinkling mischievously. "But as Reed's guardian appointed by his parents, I rightfully claimed the proceeds in his name. I also took the liberty of investing those funds. Turned a pretty penny, too, if I may say so. I was waiting until I thought it safe enough for Reed to return to England to claim his inheritance before telling him of his resources."

Cameron looked at the stately old gentleman in surprise. "And what does the solicitor know of this business?" he inquired.

"Only that Reed disappeared from my house before dawn, leaving behind a letter appointing me as administrator of his estate," Lord Dandridge replied with a wink. "Oh, he raised an eyebrow or two, but as he had no proof of Reed's handwriting for comparison, what could he do?"

"You would trust me with the whole of Reed's estate?" asked Deveraux, trying to mask his astonishment.

The earl shrugged. "Reed trusted you, and you're here. Somehow you have earned Rawlings's loyalty in the bargain. That is enough for me. Besides, who else should the monies go to—Roger Thornton?"

Cameron threw back his head and laughed deeply. He lifted his glass in salute, and the others followed suit.

Rawlings's brow furrowed with a new worry. "But, Cap'n, ken ye rightfully lay claim ta the money?"

Cameron was silent for the moment as he reflected on the matter. "Reed Delacroix is dead," he said at length. "What if I can produce a will signed by him stating that, in the event of his death, his sole possessions are to transfer to Cameron Deveraux?"

"We'll need a death certificate," said Lord Dandridge.

"That's no problem. I have a ship's surgeon who can produce the document. And Reed is logged in my book as having succumbed to fever aboard ship on July 7, 1749." He turned to his trusted valet. "Rawlings, you can see to that business before the *Homeward* leaves port."

Rawlings nodded eagerly, the promise of intrigue and adventure dancing in his veins.

"What is to be the stated nature of your business while in London? And what of your connection to me?" asked Lord Dandridge.

"I put out the word in the colonies before leaving that I would be here on a business venture," replied Deveraux. "I am seeking backers to expand my shipping line."

"Yes," agreed the earl. " 'Twill be credible, as everyone knows that I am searching for a new investment venture. Thornton has all but ruined the market fair in Drumfielde. But we must lose no time. The duke leaves at the end of the week to check on his other holdings before going onto Lyndeforde to marry Henry Balfour's daughter."

"Squire Balfour of Drumfielde?" questioned Deveraux in surprise.

"One in the same, Captain, but how did you know?"

"Although Reed talked little of the past, he carried a great fondness for Drumfielde, describing the village and its people often," Cameron covered smoothly. "But you were saying—"

"Oh, yes. I was saying that rumor has it that Balfour advanced Thornton half of quite a handsome dowry, with the promise of a large settlement upon the birth of his first grandson."

"Is the man blind to Thornton's true nature. He lives in the very village the duke has nearly destroyed!" Cameron exclaimed in disbelief.

The earl's mouth twisted into a grimace of disgust. "The squire sees nothing beyond the elevation of his lineage. The man would stop at nothing to bring a duke into the family—even to the sacrifice of his own daughter. More's the pity, too. Mary, though not what you would describe as a beauty, is a sweet, gentle girl and deserves better than this."

"When is the marriage to take place?"

"The end of May. There's to be a ball in three weeks at Lyndeforde, followed by the May Day celebration the first of that month."

"Good. That leaves me with four days to make his acquaintance and secure an invitation to the wedding."

"Why not attend as my guest?" suggested the earl. "As a business associate it would be perfectly acceptable."

"I think not, sir. The closer I can get to Thornton, the better."

"As you wish, Captain. He still keeps the Chardwellende town house on St. James Square, however, I think we would do better to catch him at his club this evening, where he'll no doubt be gambling away the dowry proceeds. One other thing," continued Lord Dandridge in afterthought, "I should like to suggest that you make contact with Captain Alan Hedrow at the Ministry. He has certain suspicions about the duke and Sir Perceival Osborn—"

Deveraux and Rawlings both jumped to attention. Perceival Osborn! It was a name they had never expected to hear. "What has he to do with Thornton?" Cameron inquired with deceptive calm.

" 'Tis common knowledge that the two

scoundrels have kept close company over the years," replied Lord Dandridge scornfully. "They make a ruthless pair; 'tis difficult to say who is the more dangerous."

But Cameron already knew, and it would make his task that much more difficult.

6

Roger Thornton dotted the perspiration on his forehead as he picked up his three cards. The game was set in motion, and hearts were laid all around. Thornton stared intently at his hand of clubs as though he thought himself capable of changing the face of the cards by concentration alone. But it was to no avail; he was forced to lay a club for his inability to follow suit. He had one chance. He had to control trump. If the top card of the deck, which would now be turned over to determine trump, reflected his suit of clubs and continued to do so for the remainder of the hand, the game would be his. The duke nervously licked his lips as he surveyed the twenty-thousand pounds in gold coins which laid upon the table. Reluctantly, he pushed forth the bulk of his funds. Slowly the card was turned to reveal diamonds as trump. Although trump had changed twice, clubs never appeared, and Thornton felt as though the air had been crushed from his body.

Lord Tewksbury coughed and impatiently tapped the top of a stack of coins. "Well, Your Grace, the turn comes to you."

Startled, Thornton glanced around in dismay to find all eyes on him as he reluctantly played his last card. Chortling with glee, Tewksbury took his third trick and raked in his winnings, including Thornton's vows for an additional three-thousand pounds.

"Outfoxed you again, ay, Your Grace? You ought to learn to play the game correctly."

Thornton thought he would choke on his anger as guffaws broke out among the observers. He blanched when Tewksbury leaned across the table, then, to deliver an ultimatum, his bantering tone now very serious. "That makes thirty-thousand pounds you owe me, Your Grace. I sincerely hope you can cover those drafts by the end of May."

The duke was casting about for excuses when he suddenly became conscious that the center of attention had pivoted from him to a newcomer who had just entered the club with Lord Dandridge. Osborn, coming to stand by Thornton, joined his cohort in appraising the tall, handsome stranger. Well dressed in a pearl-colored waistcoat and a blue silk coat embroidered in dull silver, the man seemed to command notice by just his presence alone. Ever curious, Thornton motioned Lord Dandridge and his guest to the gaming table. But Cameron Deveraux had no need of introductions, for he had never forgotten Roger Thornton or Perceival Osborn.

Sporting a bright blue velvet coat and yellow breeches that only accentuated the sickly pallor and the sunken features of his pockmarked face,

Osborn still dressed the peacock, Cameron noted. The heavily powdered and elaborately curled wig, he knew, camouflaged a bald head which had been another effect of the smallpox that had ravaged Percy's slight body as a youth. At thirty-three, Percy looked years older. And in overall appearance, he reminded Deveraux of a cadaver, save for the hard, little eyes which darted here and there with a malicious glint.

Cameron knew from experience that though Percy Osborn shunned the limelight, he effectively manipulated from behind the scenes. This, in his estimation, made Osborn exceedingly more dangerous, for it was easy to underestimate a man of his affected appearance. Cameron made a mental note not to make that mistake again, for this time it could be a fatal one. One didn't usually get a second chance with Percy.

The years had been kinder to Roger Thornton. At forty-two, he still cut a fine figure despite the mark of dissipation which was beginning to show in his hawklike features. Though undeniably ruthless, Thornton's evil lurked more on the surface of his emotions rather than in his cunning. It didn't make him any less dangerous, Cameron realized, just easier to handle. For a man like Thornton was predictable. Deveraux noticed with wry amusement that Thornton had abandoned his colorful dress and powdered wigs for severe suits of black and his own dark hair. Deveraux guessed that the new wardrobe was designed to further heighten the duke's power, for Thornton ruled through fear, while Osborn ruled through manipulation of such men as Thornton.

"You seem familiar to me, Captain

Deveraux," Osborn remarked after the introductions were made. His black eyes narrowed in thought. "Have I made your acquaintance before?"

Deveraux smiled easily, his strong white teeth a striking contrast to his deeply tanned face. "Anything is possible, sir."

"Captain Deveraux and his grandfather are leading members of the Charleston community. Their trading line is most important to the southern colonies. Until now the captain has never been in England, preferring to trade in the West Indies," interjected the earl.

"I think Captain Deveraux can speak for himself, milord," said Percy, continuing to hold his gaze on Cameron.

Deveraux returned Percy's stare measure for measure.

"Lord Dandridge speaks the truth, sir. My grandfather is the second son of a French marquis. He traveled to the colonies to seek his fortune. I joined him not long after the untimely deaths of my parents, and together we manage a quite successful trading and shipping line."

Osborn laughed bitterly, and his black eyes glittered with a deep-seated anger. "Yes, I understand only too well about not being the first born of a noble family in an age of primogeniture. And what is your business in England, if your trade is confined to the West Indies?"

"I seek backers to expand my shipping line into the East Indies," Cameron explained matter-of-factly. "As I was coming to England on a personal matter, I thought it expedient to address myself to this business as well. I prefer to see with whom I do business and to know the exact nature of the terms firsthand."

"Yes, I can see why your trade is successful, Captain. I admire a man who knows how to weigh opportunities and acts upon them accordingly," said Percy with approval. "Your ship is in port then?"

"Only for a few days," answered Deveraux. "My crew will be continuing onto Algiers, where they are to conduct trade. They'll return in six weeks time."

"Enough questions, Percy!" exclaimed Thornton impatiently. "Perhaps, Captain, you would join me in a game of cards. I seem to still have a few coins left in my pocket."

Cameron smiled. "It would be my pleasure, Your Grace."

Owing to drink, losses, and the strain of hours of play, only four of the six players remained. Deveraux played the next several hands, winning each deftly until he gauged that most of the players were ready to quit. To insure against the hangers-on, Cameron doubled the stakes until the game came down to Thornton and himself. His steel, blue gaze never wavered as his eyes issued a direct challenge.

Thorton chewed on his lip nervously and ran an anxious finger down the side of his face. If he won, the table stakes would pay off half his vows to Tewksbury. If he lost, he would be wiped out. There would be no more funds forthcoming from the squire until the wedding and the birth of a son. And worse yet, if the squire were to get wind of his finances, perhaps there'd be no wedding at all. Thornton soon became aware of all eyes on him, and he knew he could delay no longer. With a nod of his head, he shoved forth the rest of his coins and a vow for five-thousand pounds. Deveraux's luck couldn't hold forever, he decided. In the far corner of the room, Percy Osborn shook his head in vigorous disapproval as the cards were dealt.

Deveraux coolly consulted his hand one last time, and raked a considering eye over Thornton's anxious visage. Thornton led off the suit and took the first trick easily. But Deveraux took the second when the trump changed. Unable to follow suit, Thornton laid his last card—the eight of diamonds. A murmur sounded around the room as the trump turned over was in Thornton's favor. But Thornton was not home free yet. If Deveraux held a diamond higher than an eight, all would be lost to him. The tension was such that Thornton thought he would go mad, as more and more gentlemen crowded about the table in curiosity. Smiling, Deveraux played his final card—a seven of diamonds. Thornton nearly passed out in sheer relief. He was so stunned by his immense good luck, it was a few minutes before it dawned on him to collect his winnings.

After congratulations all around, Deveraux and Thornton played a few more hands, with Deveraux skillfully losing more than he had won.

"What a pity you are to leave the city in a few days. I had hoped to win back my losses," said Deveraux with a yawn. "May I offer my congratulations on your upcoming wedding, Your Grace."

"Thank you, Captain. But you still have some time left." Thornton smiled, well pleased with himself.

"I'm afraid not, Your Grace," replied

Deveraux casually. "My business won't permit me the time to gamble."

The duke looked at Cameron and seemed to be considering something. Never had he enjoyed such luck at cards—without sleight of hand. And that he would never dare run the risk of doing in the club. If caught, he would be ousted from British society forever and undoubtedly be called out to defend his honor. The captain, it would appear, brought him luck, and Thornton made up his mind that he wasn't going to lose this charm so readily.

"Perhaps you'll have your chance after all," said the duke, a slow smile spreading across his dark features.

"What do you propose?" questioned Deveraux, pretending a casual interest.

"That you be my guest at Lyndeforde until after the wedding festivities. It would not be untoward, as you do hail from a noble family. You did say that your grandfather is in direct line for a title?"

"Yes. My great-uncle is the Marquis de Sauvonnerie and has no living heirs, save my grandfather and me."

"Capital. Then you shall be my guest."

Deveraux stroked his chin thoughtfully, struggling to suppress a smile. "Perhaps. I am honored by the invitation, Your Grace, and should like to accept—if my other business can be concluded to my satisfaction."

Roger Thornton was not to be put off. "Lord Dandridge will be a guest also. Perhaps you can ride down from London to the country with him and discuss your business on the way."

"Yes, that might be arranged," agreed Deveraux. "But if you'll remember, I also have business of another nature. Perhaps you can be of some help to me."

"In what way, Captain?" broke in Percy, having approached the table unobtrusively to overhear snatches of the conversation.

"I am to collect an inheritance left to me by a good friend. I understand that you have a distant association with the deceased, Your Grace, so that perhaps you might be able to hasten the process a bit."

"And who might that be?" pressed Percy, curiosity reflected in his darting eyes.

Thornton glanced at Osborn in annoyance. "If you don't mind, Percy, I believe Captain Deveraux was addressing himself to me. Do go on, Captain. Of whom do we speak?"

"Reed Delacroix."

Cameron might have shot off a cannon for the stunned reactions he received. Thornton's jaw dropped and the coins, which he had been greedily collecting, rolled noisily to the floor. Percy's newly acquired monocle popped from his eye as though he had been slammed hard on the back, and his face became paler—if that were possible.

"I should hardly call it an association, Captain," Osborn responded indignantly. "Reed Delacroix was the bastard son of the duke's late uncle. You understand there has been no word of the lad in ten years. Indeed, he seemed to have vanished without a clue. How did you make his acquaintance?"

"We met in the colonies and sailed together for many years," Deveraux answered simply.

Thornton stared at Deveraux dazedly.

"Y—You say that he's dead?"

"Yes. He was taken ill aboard ship less than a year ago on a voyage to the Indies. It was most unfortunate."

"How do you come by his inheritance?" probed Osborn.

" 'Tis a common practice to make out a will at the journey's start, so there is no question as to wages and bounties in the event of unforeseen incidents. Reed was to become my partner in a ship-building venture at the journey's end, and, as he held no one else close, he bequeathed all that he owned to me. Of course, I had no idea that he had such a sizable fortune here in England until, in the course of my conversation with Lord Dandridge, Reed's name came up.

"What do you know of Delacroix's life?" Thornton questioned anxiously.

"Only that while enroute to his home from school, he was kidnapped and put on board a ship bound for the colonies."

Thornton fell silent, mentally recalling his own obsessive search for the boy. Following the deaths of his uncle and his uncle's paramour, he had sent men to the north under the pretense of informing Reed of the tragedy and to see that the boy "disappeared." Reed, however, had departed a few days earlier, having decided to reconcile with his parents. Thornton then arranged to have Reed's coach met enroute, only to discover that his men had been too late. According to the hysterical ravings of the coachmen, a host of highwaymen had descended upon them and absconded with their passenger. Thornton's rage had been great, as his network of spies and contacts all failed to turn up any concrete facts on the disposition of the boy's fate. He had even posted a reward which to this day still stood, but there was never any word. Perhaps now he could rest easier.

"Why did he never claim his inheritance?" Thornton finally asked when he had recovered himself.

"Evidently he had been estranged from his parents at the time of their deaths. If he was aware of the inheritance, I would guess that his past was too painful to permit him to return to England to claim it. Or perhaps it wasn't safe to do so," Cameron added so casually that only Osborn blinked at the veiled insinuation. "At any rate, I am to see the solicitor concerning the matter in the morning."

"Well, Captain," said Thornton, standing abruptly and hastily gathering the remainder of the coins, "if I can be of help in expediting matters, please inform me. Meanwhile, good-night to you." And he was gone, with Percy in his wake.

Deveraux signaled to Lord Dandridge that he was ready to leave and stood up to stretch his long legs. Flexing his shoulders, he smiled broadly as he imagined the scene which he knew would be soon unfolding.

Back in the privacy of his town house, Roger Thornton paced the floor angrily.

"How dare the solicitor withhold information of that inheritance from me! If I had known of it, I would have had Delacroix declared dead years ago and claimed the funds for myself. And I wouldn't be forced into this ridiculous marriage!" he screamed, flinging his brandy glass at the wall and shattering an oval mirror.

"Really Roger, let's not destroy this room before the library is renovated," remarked Percy dryly. "The servants are still hard put to set that room to rights after your last temper tantrum. People might begin to talk." Disregarding Thornton's glare, Osborn continued, "Do you believe Deveraux's story?"

"What's not to believe? Aside from the coincidence of the whole affair, his story much supports my own deductions. It would explain why the boy seemed to have vanished."

"Yes, the captain's story does appear to answer much. But yet—"

"What!" snapped Thornton irritably. "You suspect something in everything. What bothers you now?"

"The captain's eyes."

Thornton looked at Osborn as though he had lost his mind. "His eyes!" he shrieked. "God's blood, man, I'm talking about a lost fortune here, and you're babbling about a man's eyes! Well, what about them?"

"Didn't you notice?" persisted Percy vaguely. "They are the eyes of a man who hides much, yet draws from others their truths. I warn you, he bears close watching."

"Rubbish," snorted Thornton. "I think tomorrow I shall pay a call to the solicitor."

"And what good will that do? The inheritance is obviously from the mother's estate. As Delacroix's administrator, Lord Dandridge was completely within his rights to claim and to hold the money for the boy or for Delacroix's heirs as long as he cared to do so. Only he could have had the lad declared dead, in which case, the funds would have reverted to the government as un-claimed inheritance. Since Reed Delacroix was a bastard, you would have had no claim to the monies from his mother's estate, anyway."

"I need funds, Percy. The dowry the squire advanced me is gone, and Lord Tewksbury, the pompous ass, is calling in my vouchers at the end of May. The winnings from tonight and the rest of the dowry will not cover it all. God's blood, do you know what those animals would do to a duke in debtor's prison!" Thornton's eyes bulged in sheer horror at the thought as he saw himself being thrown into a dank, stench-filled, disease-ridden hole, crowded with dregs from all walks of life. "My God, Percy, you've got to help me!" he cried in sudden desperation.

Flicking the lace at his wrists and straightening his cuffs, Percy sighed in disgust. He had no use for human frailties. "You could give up gambling," he suggested dryly.

Thornton looked at his friend in disbelief. "Give up gambling! Don't be ridiculous! You know 'tis expected of me as a gentleman and a noble member of the peerage—"

"Yes, yes, I know," responded Percy, waving away the rest of Thornton's objection. "But not to worry, the boat from France will be in with our smuggled goods by then. Now that we will have full control of the village stores, you shall know more riches than the king."

Thornton's eyes lit up at the prospect. "Yes, I had quite forgotten. Your plan to place a man in the crowd to stir Drumfielde to riot worked beautifully. Now I shall have good reason to con-fiscate the stores for our purpose."

"The shops will provide the perfect hiding

place for the goods until they can be delivered to Portsmouth," agreed Percy. "What of the herald? Was his death seen to?"

The smile on Thornton's face lent his sharp features a more sinister appearance. "Aye. At long last this thorn in my side will be removed when I see Will Fenton hung for murder, and I will finally have that land my uncle so stupidly gave to him. Along with the common fields, it should increase my revenues considerably. Squire Balfour, the incompetent fool, has failed to punish anyone involved with the revolt, so this matter I shall see to myself after the ball."

Osborn laughed. "Two birds with one stone, ay, Your Grace? With Fenton out of the way, those wretches will have no one to rally them. And you can lay the gypsy hag's warning to rest, for who else would dare to raise a hand against the duke of Lyndeforde?"

But Thornton wasn't so certain. The smile died on his lips, and his mood turned suddenly sour at the thought of the gypsy fortune-teller. Next to gambling, superstition was his biggest weakness and his greatest fear. If only he could be certain that Fenton was the person about whom the woman had spoken.

7

"Word has reached me of a particular American ship just in to London port," the squire was saying as he drained his glass of port, "and I wish to speak with the captain concerning some investments I would make. It occurs to me, daughter, that 'twould provide an excellent opportunity for you to improve upon yer wardrobe with the best dressmakers at hand, though I trust ye will exercise discretion. I shall, therefore expect your company on this trip."

London! Mary could barely credit the thought. And she wondered if she had understood correctly. Not only was he insisting upon her company, but the penurious squire was also offering her a new wardrobe made by some of the most renowned courtieres in Europe! It would have meant a great deal to her earlier. She would have taken it as a long awaited token of her father's love, but now she knew better.

"No, thank you," Mary refused him politely. "I have a perfectly adequate wardrobe. And Mother's health is so deteriorated, I don't wish to leave her at this time."

"Humph," the squire said with a loud belch. "Your mother will be well cared for by the housekeeper. And as for your clothing, 'tis adequate for the village, but I shan't have it said that Squire Balfour sends his daughter to a duke's bed poorly clothed, No, sir, ye shall be presented to your husband dressed as the duchess ye'll be."

"But I don't wish to see the duke before 'tis absolutely necessary to do so," protested Mary.

The squire chuckled at what he mistook to be his daughter's maidenly shyness. "No need to concern yourself on tha' score, daughter. The duke be seeing to his other lands. He'll come straightaway to Drumfielde from the west. Now I'll hear no further argument."

"Yes, sir," responded Mary dispiritedly. "I'll tell Rorie to prepare herself for the journey."

Squire Balfour choked on his port, spewing the red liquid down over his snow-white linen cravat.

"What say ye, daughter!" he bellowed when he could speak again. "Can you be that addelpated to think that I, the future father-in-law of a duke, would play chaperone to a peasant! God's blood, 'tis bad enough that she must now live under my roof and partake of my food for all the village to see."

Mary flushed, hoping that Rorie had not overheard, for she knew that her friend and companion awaited her in the hall. But she hoped in vain.

"Must you fault your daughter for considering your comfort?" Rorie defended Mary from the doorway.

The squire eyed his daughter's companion

with suspicion, vastly irritated by her presence. "Explain yourself!" he demanded belligerently.

"Well, as a soon-to-be member of the higher nobility, Mary shall have to conduct herself accordingly. It will be necessary for someone to accompany her at all times in London," Rorie explained, undaunted. "As the future father-in-law of a duke," she mimicked the squire, "I am sure *you* don't wish to be seen accompanying your daughter to all the ladies' shops."

Clearly the squire had given no such thought to the matter, and it certainly wouldn't do for a man of his position to be seen in shops of various female fripperies.

"Oh, very well," he conceded begrudgingly. "But be ready by dawn."

As the squire's dust-coated coach entered the city of London three days later, the two girls were astounded by the noise and the traffic of people, carts, carriages, coaches, and wagons which thronged the narrow streets. Tradesmen shouted and bellmen announced their wares. As they passed by taverns, coffeehouses and shops, it seemed to Rorie as though noise issued from every corner of the streets. Hawkers called attention to their fruit, vegetables, meat, and pastries; oystermongers called out their seafood; and street criers sang their verses. At one point, a volley of oaths issued forth as their coach nearly overran a scavenger and his cart.

It was all so new that Rorie's head was spinning. And she noted with a bitter irony that while here, at last, was the adventure she had always yearned for, given the circumstances, she found it impossible to enjoy.

As the coach slowly turned onto fashionable Bedford Row and came to a halt in front of an attractive three story brick town house, the squire ordered, "Wait here. I would have a word with Lord Dandridge."

Without ceremony, he opened the door and lumbered to the ground. While Rorie and Mary looked on the curious amusement, the corpulent squire huffed and puffed his way up the short flight of brick steps. Once at the top, he paused long enough to mop his red, perspiring face before rapping on the heavy wooden door with his cane.

At the butler's discreet cough, Lord Dandridge and Cameron looked up from the plans they had been studying.

"Squire Balfour to see you, milord."

"Here? Now?" At the butler's nod, Lord Dandridge groaned in dismay. "The man never comes to London. What the devil could he want with me now?"

"There's but one way to find out," Cameron interjected, a bit curious himself.

The earl sighed. "Show him in, Higgins—but lock up the brandy first."

A few minutes later, Squire Balfour came bustling into the library. "How good of ye to see me and on such short notice." Without waiting for a reply, the squire rambled on, ignoring the other occupant of the room who was obviously not of their class. "I hear tha' ye hath an acquaintanceship with a certain colonial sea captain."

"And how did you come by such information, Henry?" inquired Lord Dandridge, exchanging surprised glances with Cameron.

"Oh, ye know how fast information travels in business circles," the squire extolled pompously. "A contact in the colonies with whom I've made investments told me of a most worthy Captain Deveraux who reportedly sails a tight ship. And as luck would have it, the good captain was preparing to sail for London. I've had a lookout on the docks for the past two weeks to sight his arrival, and he heard Captain Deveraux inquire after your residence. As 'tis no secret tha' ye been casting about for a venture—"

"How very astute of you, Henry," Lord Dandridge commented dryly. "What is the nature of your interest in the captain?"

The squire bristled. He liked to conduct his affairs as privately as possible, but as he sought the earl's cooperation in an introduction to the sea captain, he would have to acquiesce and state his business.

"Why I wish to back Deveraux's shipping fleet, of course," the squire answered, somewhat surprised that the earl hadn't guessed his intention. "I understand the man is a master at trade. With a fleet of ships at his disposal, I would guess the profits to be quite handsome. But surely you know all that."

Cameron was as taken aback as Lord Dandridge by this new development. The story of canvassing for backers for a new line of ships had been an excuse to make the trip and to establish contact with the earl. But if he could come away from this venture with backers in his pocket for his dream of expanding into the East

Indies and China markets, so much the better.
The idea began to germinate in his mind, and the
possibilities intrigued him. Standing behind the
squire, Cameron signaled to the earl.

"I take it then that you expect me to
introduce you to Captain Deveraux, Henry?"

"Well the thought did cross my mind,"
admitted the squire hesitantly, attributing the
earl's reluctance to cooperate to preferring to be
the sole investor. "With another partner, you
take half the risk, Robert—"

"My apologies for interrupting, sir," said a
deep, confident voice from behind, "but have
you any idea of the cost involved in under-
writing such a venture? I understood the captain
to be seeking a bevy of backers."

Squire Balfour whirled around to face the
stranger he had so summarily dismissed earlier.
Bronzed by the sun and simply dressed in brown
knee breeches and a loose-fitting shirt of white
cotton, the young man resembled a tradesman of
a sort. The squire was piqued that an outsider
should have been privy to his personal business.
It never occurred to Balfour that he, himself,
might be the one intruding.

"And who might ye be, young man, to
address yer betters in like manner?" the squire
demanded irritably.

Deveraux pushed himself away from the
desk against which he had been lounging in
silent amusement, and stood to his full height to
tower over the patronizing little man. The
squire's next words died in his throat as he
craned his neck up to stare in wonder at the
imposing figure before him.

Lord Dandridge could barely contain his

mirth as he said, "Henry, I should like you to make the acquaintance of one Captain Deveraux, the subject of your interest, and the grand-nephew of the Marquis de Sauvonnerie."

The squire desperately worked his mouth, but no words came forth at his bidding. He gave the appearance of a babbling idiot as he sputtered out an apology, all the while furiously dabbing his forehead with a soggy handkerchief. "My humblest apologies, Capteaux Devertain—er—Captain Deveraux. Had I but known yer identity, sir, I assure ye—" The rest of his words were lost as he stared into cold, silvery blue eyes.

"So you wish to limit my backers, sir," said Cameron, at last breaking the spell. "I daresay you had better have vast resources at hand."

His bravado gone, the squire could only nod. "I am pre—prepared to double Robert's offer for a slightly higher percentage," he stammered.

"And should Lord Dandridge not wish to invest, what then?"

"I shall finance the entire venture for half the profit, Captain," the squire finished timidly.

Captain Deveraux let out a low whistle at the little man's determination. "Perhaps we should talk further on this matter, gentlemen."

The squire brightened and beamed with satisfaction, having recovered a portion of his courage. He was hard put to contain his disappointment, though, when the earl rang for a bottle of port, instead of the excellent brandy he was known to keep on hand. Suddenly, Squire Balfour remembered his daughter and chafed at the delay it would mean to see her to an inn.

"My pardon, Robert, Captain, but I have left my daughter and her companion to await me in my coach. We have only just arrived from Drumfielde, and I must see about accommodations. May I return after they have been settled?"

·Forever the gentleman and observer of protocol, Lord Dandridge stared at the squire dumbfounded. "You've left two ladies of quality, one of whom is soon to be a duchess, to await you outside like common street people! Really, Henry, you go too far! Higgins, there are two ladies awaiting Squire Balfour outside in his coach. See to their comfort, posthaste, as they shall be my guests for the duration of their stay in London."

Squire Balfour looked decidedly ill-at-ease as he realized the enormity of his social blunder. Only ladies of dubious reputation or those who have fallen from societal favor were left to wait outside a residence for their escort's return—certainly never ladies of title or those above reproach. It had been so long since he had been to the city, he had quite forgotten such rules of etiquette, for life in the country was much less rigid. Should the duke catch wind of his negligence, there would be the piper to pay. Worse yet, the duke might break the betrothal for compromising the integrity of his title.

Deveraux looked on in obvious amusement as the squire downed his port in one nervous gulp, all the while babbling apologies for his gross negligence of social graces.

"How many guards have accompanied you, Henry?" inquired Lord Dandridge.

"Guards?" echoed the squire stupidly. "Why, there be just the driver."

"Good heavens, man!" thundered the earl.

"Are you so hidden in the country that you know nothing of the world! Highwaymen prey on every coach coming into and leaving the city on every route these days. No one is safe from these scoundrels—not even King George himself. It doesn't even bear thinking of the fate that could have befallen the ladies—and you. Luck was with you this time, Henry, but the next time—" Lord Dandridge shook his head, leaving the rest of the thought to the squire's active imagination.

Squire Balfour's jaw dropped, and his eyes bulged in sheer horror at his narrow escape. Dazedly, with shaking hands, he groped for the decanter of wine and filled his glass to the rim, with no thought to etiquette.

Out in the hall, feminine voices could be heard crescendoing and ultimately fading into the distance as the ladies were being shown to their rooms. Being the gentleman that he was, Lord Dandridge decided to formally welcome his guests at supper that evening, thus giving the ladies a chance to refresh themselves before meeting their host.

Shortly thereafter, Cameron excused himself, declaring that he had business to attend to which would carry him through the supper hour. Thinking that Cameron meant to seek out other backers for his shipping fleet, Squire Balfour leapt to his feet with some difficulty, nearly over-turning the small chair into which he had pressed his bulk.

"Er—let's not be hasty, my boy. I meant what I said. I shall finance any amount of money it takes to limit this partnership to the three of us."

"That's very generous, Squire, and I shall

think on it. However, I have other business which concerns me this day. Gentlemen." And Deveraux turned on his heel and left the room.

"But where shall I find ye, Captain?" the squire called after him, not trusting this young man far from his sight.

"Fear not, Henry, the captain is my guest also," said Lord Dandridge, smothering a chuckle, for he could sense Cameron's opinion of the squire. And, having come to know the captain over the past couple of days, he knew full well the captain's opinion of women as fey, fickle, empty-headed creatures from which to derive pleasure but to never give trust or allegiance. The earl rightly guessed that Deveraux's sudden business of the day was the avoidance of the earl's unexpected guests.

"Strange one, tha' one," Balfour muttered irritably, though he was relieved that they would be under the same roof. "Another man would have jumped at my offer, but Captain Deveraux has to think on it. And then he doesn't sit still long enou' to consider the possibilities."

"You'll have your chance, Henry. Captain Deveraux will be accompanying us to Drumfielde for your daughter's wedding at Roger Thornton's behest."

The squire's eyes widened in alarm. "God's teeth, the man hasn't already approached the duke about this business!"

Lord Dandridge waved the squire back into a more substantial chair for his bulk. " 'Twas on another matter that they met. Don't overly concern yourself. Now if you'll excuse me, I shall make ready for supper, and I suggest you do the same," advised the Earl, eyeing the squire's travel-worn appearance.

"Quite so, Robert." Balfour rose, his refilled glass in hand, and ambled from the room still mumbling to himself.

Lord Dandridge followed, shaking his head in wonder at the strange household he had suddenly collected.

8

Rorie stared in awe at the splendor of the room to which she had been shown. Never in all of her daydreams had she imagined such elegance, and for a moment she wondered if she were dreaming. The walls were panelled in a lovely blue and cream-colored damask silk which matched the drapes on the windows and bed. The four-poster bed, with its beautifully embroidered coverlet, was piled so high with feather mattresses that a commode had to be fashioned in the form of steps to gain access. The small writing desk, the washstand, the dressing table with its swing mirror, and the clothes press were all beautifully wrought of a light and graceful design that made the heavily gilded furniture at Balfour Grange appear gaudy by comparison.

Quickly, Rorie unpacked her meager belongings and was momentarily disconcerted to see how faded and shabby they appeared against the backdrop of her surroundings. Pooh, she chastised herself. Clothes do not the person make. But she wished she had heeded her aunt's advice to remake a few more of her mother's old gowns.

Rorie's brow puckered in bemusement then as she once again wondered why her mother had such a collection of fashionable clothes; she was painfully reminded of how little she actually knew of her parents' earlier years. All that she and Terence had ever been told was that their family had come to Drumfielde at the village's request for a schoolmaster—and to be near the Fentons. Her mother had sometimes made fleeting reference to a more illustrious past life, but all attempts to question her on the subject had always been cleverly diverted. Whether the Fentons had been privy to her parents' secret, Rorie had never been able to ascertain. In any case, they were no founts of information, and now, Rorie sadly noted, she would probably never know the past her mother and father had found too difficult to discuss.

If it hadn't been for the duke, Rorie thought angrily, her parents might be still alive. That they had died of a fever was incidental. The fact was that Richard Shelbourne, whose whole life had centered around teaching, lost the will to live when the duke had ordered the school closed. Her father had tried to turn his hand to farming, but things never seemed quite right after that. Although he attempted to cover his distress by throwing his academic energies into teaching his children and by taking a more scientific approach to farming, Richard Shelbourne was never the same. It was as though he had welcomed death as a release from the torment of living, for he seemingly did nothing to fight against it.

Her mother, Sirena, in a weakened state from fatigue and grief, had succumbed to the same illness without a fortnight, leaving behind a shocked daughter and an angry son, a trunkful of outdated but quite elegant gowns, four precious books, and a highly prized broach. Only the kindness of the Fentons and the other villagers had softened the blow of Rorie's devastating loss. Now it was Rorie's turn to help them in their need.

Reminded of the awesome obligation she had assumed, Rorie pushed the distressing thoughts of her parents to the back of her mind and selected apparel for the evening meal, her goal clear.

An hour later and in better spirits, Rorie surveyed her handiwork. An overgown of emerald-green ribbed silk flowed loosely over a bell-shaped lilac and deep purple striped undergown. The bodice was fitted and pointed, its oval decolletage showing the ridge of her creamy, white shoulders. Decidedly, the gown molded itself nicely to the curves of her young body and enhanced the slight blush of the sun upon her flawlessly carved features.

She had brushed her hair until it shone the color of spun gold, and pulled it loosely back from her face into a roll on top of her head. She had no time or patience for the elaborate hairstyles now coming into vogue, but she allowed the wisps of curls which escaped their pins to frame her oval face, giving her the deceiving image of a defenseless babe. All in all, she had to admit that she looked quite the lady. And for the first time in her life, she blessed her mother for having the fortitude, in the wave of strenuous opposition, to drill in her willful daughter the poise to match the present image. Rorie had never understood her mother's insistence that she learn to comport herself as a lady, but she was thankful now for Sirena's dogged determination. With a confident toss of her proud head, she hurried off to meet Mary.

The evening passed pleasantly enough, although conversation was somewhat stilted. The two course meal of twenty dishes each overwhelmed Rorie as she considered how many families in the village could have been fed from this feast, and she had difficulty eating. Still, Rorie was impressed by Lord Dandridge's humility and kindness, and inexplicably, she felt drawn to the stately gentleman. There seemed to be a sadness about him which softened his aristocratic features, making him appear touchingly vulnerable.

For his part, Lord Dandridge was quite taken with Mary Balfour's companion, and he was painfully reminded of the daughter he had lost so many years ago. He had been expecting a sour, old maid and was pleasantly surprised by the lovely, young woman who sat proud and tall before him. The girl was an enigma to the earl, however, as he noted her outmoded gown and work-roughened hands. Yet she walked with an easy grace and spoke in the soft, cultured voice of one born to wealth. After polite conversation with Mary concerning her wedding plans, the earl inquired after Rorie.

"Merely a distant relative, sir, whose family has fallen on hard times," the squire rushed to explain, for it certainly wouldn't do for anyone to know that his daughter's companion was a common peasant.

Mary smothered a giggle, enjoying her father's discomfiture, while Rorie gritted her teeth and shot Squire Balfour a withering stare. Unable to contain herself any longer as the squire made her out to be a poor, ignorant, long-suffering distant cousin, Rorie interceded brusquely.

"Actually, milord, my parents were quite enlightened. They believed that a liberal education could be as beneficial to a woman as to a man. Consequently, I was taught alongside my brother. I understand that you have an extensive library. Might I avail myself of it when time permits?"

The earl could not hide his surprise. It was rare, indeed, to encounter a young woman whose knowledge and interests encompassed more than the fashions of the day, matrimony, and childbearing. Without a doubt, there was more to this young woman than met the eye.

"Why, certainly, Miss Shelbourne. I would be most pleased to place my books at your disposal," he gladly assured her. "I must confess, though, that the room is more in use these days for business matters than for the reading pleasure it has to offer."

"Bloody waste of time 'tis, educatin' a female as a man," snorted the squire, stuffing his mouth with plum pudding until his cheeks bulged. "All a woman need concern herself with is how to run a house, converse, sew, and care for her family."

"Yes, I can see where you might think so," answered the earl with a hint of sarcasm. "For myself, I enjoy conversing with a woman who has an informed opinion on affairs other than domestic matters." And he turned his attention back to Rorie, much to the squire's annoyance and Mary's relief, for she didn't want her evening spoiled with continued references to her upcoming marriage.

"Miss Shelbourne, I have a clever friend, Dr. Samuel Johnson, who would prove to be of interest to you, I'm sure. I shall invite him to dine one of these evenings."

"Dr. Johnson!" exclaimed the squire, reaching for more scrod. "Humph, the man is one of those academic boors," he said with a disdainful sniff. "Talks incessantly. A body can't get a word in edgewise. He was a guest at the Grange once years ago. Came to see my library. Couldn't follow anything he said, though. And would ye believe, the man refused to observe the custom of tipping my servants!" the squire finished incredulously, filling his plate once again.

The earl chuckled, too much of a gentleman to point out that the squire was known to conveniently "forget" the custom, himself, upon many an occasion while a guest.

"Didn't Dr. Johnson write *'The Vanity of Human Wishes?'* " asked Rorie, searching the recesses of her mind. "You remember, Mary, 'twas a clever poem which we once read."

Mary nodded in agreement, while the squire eyed the girls sharply, wondering how they had come to be reading a poem.

"Yes," replied the earl. "He is currently engaged in writing a dictionary."

"Mary and I should be honored to meet Dr. Johnson," said Rorie, eager for some stimulating conversation.

The hour was late when the guests retired to their rooms. Accustomed to caring for herself, Rorie once again declined the services of the maid, whom the earl had placed at the ladies' disposal. After undressing herself and carefully hanging her gown in the huge armoire, she donned her worn muslin nightgown and tentatively bounced on the soft mattresses before slipping under the refreshing coolness of the clean bed linens. Never had she slept in such a bed. But after the high excitement of the day, sleep eluded her, and Rorie soon gave up trying.

Sliding off the bed, she threw open the French doors to breathe in the fragrant air of the flowering garden below before turning to restlessly pace the floor. After several minutes, she paused to tap on the door which connected her room to Mary's. But she was greeted only by silence. Rorie Shelbourne! she laughingly chided herself. Your wits must be addled indeed. There is a whole library at your fingertips and here you are pacing the room like some poor, crazed creature.

She quickly threw a shawl about her shoulders and eagerly emerged from the room. Shielding the flickering candle flame against the drafts, Rorie cautiously made her way down the long, narrow hallway and the winding stairs to the second floor. In the darkness, everything took on a different appearance. The eerie silence, broken only by the ticking of a clock at the head of the stairs, grated on her nerves, dampening her enthusiasm, as she tried to remember in which direction the library lay.

She was about to turn back when she noticed

a faint light coming from a half-closed door at the end of the hall. Perhaps a servant was about who could direct her. And she approached the door to peer uncertainly into the room. A very tall, young man stood off to the side with only his profile visible to her, his attention seemingly absorbed in the low, sputtering fire. One arm rested carelessly on the mantel, while the other held a brandy snifter. Rorie wondered who he was, for he didn't have the appearance of a servant, but nor did he affect the dress of the upper class.

Although totally engrossed in his thoughts, Cameron instinctively knew that he had a visitor. He turned, expecting to see Lord Dandridge and hoping not to see Squire Balfour. Instead, he was thunderstruck by the golden-haired creature who stood nervously before him in the doorway. The glow from her candle gave her an ethereal appearance and, for one insane moment, caught off-balance, his mind refused to register the vision as anything other than an angel.

The look on the man's face was so strange, Rorie began to believe that she had intruded into some part of the house where she didn't belong. Suddenly, she became frightened as she realized with blinding clarity her tenuous position. What right did she, a country lass, have to go traipsing through the house of a nobleman in the middle of the night? Exploring . . . it seemed to be a trait to which she was too often prone. Dear Lord, what if she were accused of stealing something! Many had gone to the gallows for less. Her eyes grew wide with fear as she edged through the doorway, poised for flight.

"Hold on there!" Cameron commanded. He was hardly aware that he had spoken. He only knew that this lovely intruder would not escape him before her identity was known.

The authoritative ring in his voice effectively brought Rorie to a halt. Painfully aware of her state of undress, she pulled her shawl closer around her, as Deveraux sternly beckoned her back into the room.

"I—I was looking for the library," she stammered. "I—I couldn't sleep. I thought perhaps if I read—" Her voice trailed off as Deveraux continued to stare at her.

She was both amazed and disturbed by the stature of the man, for her exposure to the male species had been limited to those of a slighter height and build in the village. This giant left her with a feeling of being quite insignificant and powerless, and Rorie shivered, more from nervousness than the chill in the air, as she prepared herself for a fierce tongue lashing—or worse.

Instead, Cameron burst out laughing. He felt like an idiot at his mind's foolishness. An angel, indeed, though the beauty of this girl could easily qualify her for one. Observing her confusion and ill-ease, he brought himself under control. With a sweep of his arm to indicate the book-lined walls, he smiled engagingly, his rugged features taking on an almost boyish charm.

"I would venture to say, miss, that you have found what you seek," he said with a slight bow.

But Rorie was not put at ease as the hangman's noose remained all too clear an image in her mind. "I'm sorry,' she whispered hoarsely. "I shouldn't be here at this hour. It's most indiscreet of me."

Cameron studied her for a moment before realizing the source of her distress. Setting his glass on the mantel, he approached Rorie with a slow, easy gait, calculated to be nonthreatening.

"I think you will find the door to Lord Dandridge's library open at whatever the hour," he said. "And if your fears are still not laid to rest, you may be assured that the earl shall not learn of your midnight foray from me."

Rorie nearly collapsed with relief, and she answered him with a smile of gratitude. The man didn't seem a bad sort, and she had no reason to doubt his word. Feeling that her future no longer hung in the balance, Rorie turned a more discerning eye upon him, taking careful stock of his stature and uncommon good looks. One certainly couldn't accuse him of being foppish, she had to concede. But the way his gaze so casually swept her made her feel uncomfortable. Self-consciously, she drew her shawl still tighter around her. The man was obviously a rake, but he seemed pleasant and courteous enough, she decided with some reserve.

Cameron was amused by her less than subtle perusal of him. "I trust that you find all to your liking," he challenged, though it mattered little to him. In affairs of the flesh, love played no part, and it was enough that he found her to his liking. Any other objection, he was confident, would take care of itself.

Rorie colored in spite of herself. "How confident you are, sir. But, alas, I fear 'tis more the case of one following the bad example of another," she countered baldly, referring to his own unabashed examination of her.

Deveraux cocked his head as though to give her her due, while the glimmer of a smile creased the sides of his full mouth, lending a strength to his features that was most decidedly masculine. The girl had spirit. He liked that in his women. And he decided that it was time to put an end to this cat and mouse game and to make the most of this pleasant and unexpected encounter.

The plain, patched gown and coarse shawl that she wore, and her fear of being discovered in the library at so late an hour told him that this lovely creature was undoubtedly a maid of sorts, though he was hard put to imagine her reading. Gauging her to be over sixteen, he was certain that a young lady of her looks and forthright manner would be well versed in the art of lovemaking. In any case, he was in need of a proper dalliance, and he couldn't imagine a more beautiful mate. Judging from her boldness, he figured her to need little coaxing.

"Now that your modesty has been compromised," he said, with a conspiratorial grin, indicating her nightclothes, "I daresay that introductions are in order. I am Captain Cameron Deveraux, at your service."

"Oh, yes, you're the colonial of whom Lord Dandridge spoke," Rorie replied with more ease. The man was outrageous, but she had to laugh at his engaging manner. The dimple in the corner of her mouth deepened as a friendly smile illuminated her striking features. Now here was her chance to know something of the outside world, she decided. "I'm very pleased to make your acquaintance, Captain. I am Mary

Balfour's—" Rorie had been about to say companion, but the word stuck in her throat at the instantaneous change in the captain's manner.

Taken aback for one of the few times in his life, a dark scowl distorted his handsome features, completely eradicating his rakish smile, and his warm, blue eyes turned suddenly cold and forbidding.

"If you'll excuse me, I shall take my leave," he ground out through clenched teeth. As though he found her very presence unendurable, he was past her and out of the door before Rorie could even speak.

Rorie could only stare after him in bewilderment. What was it she had said to offend him, she wondered, mentally reviewing every word of their conversation. Had she insulted the captain when she referred to him as a colonial? What a pity, and when she had so many questions to ask of his adventures. Since the captain was a guest of the earl, she supposed she should apologize for her blunder tomorrow, innocent though it was. She just hoped that he would hold to his promise not to disclose their late night encounter.

In his room, Cameron angrily paced the floor. It was stupid of him to have stalked out of the library like some rejected suitor, but when this lovely vision had introduced herself as Thornton's betrothed, he could no longer remain in the room with her.

"Damn!" he swore, at once angry that he had nearly jeopardized the mission and disappointed that his planned night of pleasure had been brought to a jolting halt. But underpinning his roiling emotions was a mounting rage that this woman belonged to his avowed enemy.

In light of her identity, Cameron charitably acknowledged that her right to be in the library at that hour was as legitimate as his own, and he allowed that his senses should have been alerted by her speech and graceful bearing. But she certainly didn't have the retiring manner of a future duchess, and what the bloody hell was she doing wrapped in those rags? He'd seen servant girls with better nightclothes than that!

Rawlings emerged then from his anteroom chamber, sleepily rubbing his eyes. "Thought I heard ye come in." Noting the fierce look on his captain's face, he eyed him worriedly. "Wha' be amiss, Cap'n? Have we been found out?"

"Damn the man's eyes!" snarled Deveraux.

"Who?" demanded Rawlings in a mixture of panic and confusion.

"Squire Balfour! The fool ought to be flogged for giving a woman like that to the likes of Roger Thornton!"

Rawlings breathed an audible sigh of relief. "Be tha' all wha' got ye in such a tizzy?"

"Be that all!" ranted Cameron, staring at Rawlings in amazement. "That a girl of her beauty should be wasted on a blackguard like Thornton, 'tis nothing less than a sin."

"Why should ye care? 'Tis none of yer concern, Cap'n. Besides if the girl is in agreement—"

Rawlings unknowingly hit a nerve. And Cameron halted his furious pacing to glare at his manservant, unable to answer. It was true, and therein lay the crux of the matter. The girl certainly hadn't appeared distraught. In fact, she looked quite the opposite—breathtakingly radiant, even in rags. The mere thought of Roger Thornton possessing such perfection sent Cameron into a white-hot rage.

Rawlings scratched his head in perplexity. A plain, timid, and very sensitive young woman was how Lord Dandridge had painted Mary Balfour. By that description, the lass wasn't even close to being Deveraux's type of woman, and, in so far as he knew, they had never even met. So why the devil was the cap'n carrying on so, wondered Rawlings, shaking his white mane and shuffling off to bed. The cap'n just wasn't to be figured at times, he concluded sleepily.

9

Cameron awoke the next morning in a fine temper. His head throbbed and his eyes ached as silent testimony to the restless sleep he had endured. As the beguilingly innocent, oval-shaped face with tilted green eyes framed in long sooty lashes continued to drift in and out of his consciousness, Cameron wanted to alternatively throttle the squire and take his sword to Thornton.

Rawlings regarded his captain sharply as Cameron stomped about the room, carelessly throwing on any clothes that came to hand. He had never seen him in such a state. The captain was usually so controlled, so clear-headed. And all this because of a woman to whom he would have never given a second glance in Charleston. Perhaps returning to England was a far greater shock to him than was anticipated, surmised Rawlings, more than a little concerned. The man-servant breathed a sigh of relief when Deveraux was at last ready to leave the disordered room to his capable hands.

When Cameron entered the dining room, he was surprised to find Lord Dandridge alone. Helping himself to an adequate plate from the sideboard, he took a seat across from the earl and raised one dark eyebrow in question.

"The ladies are making the rounds of the dressmakers, and the squire is off conferring with his banker," Lord Dandridge answered. "What a pity you just missed him. He is quite eager to have a word with you."

Cameron grimaced. "Were the man here, I'd thrash him within an inch of his worthless life," he barked savagely.

Now it was Lord Dandridge's turn to raise a questioning brow, but he refrained from commenting. Instead, he remarked, "Captain, I must tell you, I had quite a delightful supper last evening."

"With the squire?" asked Cameron in surprise.

"No, no. The man's a simpleton and always will be. I am referring to Mary Balfour's traveling companion, Miss Rorie Shelbourne. She is a young lady of many charms and great beauty. I should think you to find her of much interest."

Cameron stared at Lord Dandridge in disbelief. His room faced the street, and he had seen the two ladies departing earlier, appraising each at length. How could the man possibly consider that the plain, delicate little creature, who had preceded Mistress Balfour into the carriage, could possibly hold any interest for him? He liked his women full of fire and passion. For a moment, he wondered if the earl's eyesight might be failing.

"My mission hath no place for women,

Robert," he said at length. "But were either of the two ladies to hold my attention, 'twould be Mistress Balfour, and it fairs to make my blood boil to think that such a woman is to be handed over to the likes of Roger Thornton," Cameron thundered.

Lord Dandridge looked at his guest in ill-concealed amazement. Perhaps he didn't know the lad as well as he thought. "I quite agree with you on the latter observation," he finally allowed. "The poor child doesn't deserve such a fate. Her nature is better suited to a convent."

Cameron nearly choked on his food. God's blood, the mere thought of such flawless beauty cloistered behind sixteen-foot high granite walls was more than he could bear to imagine. Only the thought of her in Thornton's bed was worse. He pushed his plate of food away, having barely touched it, and strode quickly from the room, cursing roundly.

Minutes later, the earl heard the front door slam, and he stroked his chin thoughtfully. Never in all of his years would he have thought the demure Balfour girl to have such an affect on a rakehell like Deveraux. Life could certainly play strange tricks, he decided, hoping that the angry, young man wouldn't do anything foolish. For there was much at stake.

Deveraux followed the red-coated soldier into the plain and sparsely furnished office in the British Ministry.

"A Captain Cameron Deveraux to see you, sir," announced the soldier.

"Thank you, Reams. You may go," answered Captain Alan Hedrow mechanically, not bothering to even look up. His complete attention for the moment was absorbed in a particularly disturbing document.

Though the British captain was seated behind a cluttered desk, Cameron judged Hedrow to be a tall man, about thirty years old. His uniform was impeccably tailored to fit his lean, lanky form, and he wore a fashionable powdered wig with three rolled curls placed horizontally at the sides, with the back gathered by a black ribbon. His long, narrow features, while neither attractive nor homely, were rugged, and he carried about him an air of unquestioned authority. Cameron instinctively knew that this man was not to be trifled with. He could be either a valuable ally or a deadly adversary, and Cameron was hopeful of claiming him as the former.

Deveraux braced himself when Hedrow finally looked up to appraise him with shrewd, brown eyes, at once narrowed in puzzlement and suspicion. When he spoke it was in a firm, clipped tone. "Deveraux, you say."

Cameron nodded. "Yes, Captain. Just recently in from the colonies."

Captain Hedrow stroked his chin thoughtfully as he motioned Deveraux to a chair. "Yes, I saw Lord Dandridge a few days ago. He hinted that we might have use for each other as our goals are seemingly one and the same."

"If you are speaking of the exposure of a festering sore in the ranks of the nobility, 'tis truth."

The British captain seemed to be considering something as he studied Deveraux intently. Having made up his mind, he relaxed his stiff military bearing and took out a bottle. After pouring rum into two glasses, he handed one to Cameron and settled back to explain his position.

"As England, in all her wisdom, hath seen fit to raise taxes yet again," he said with a weary sigh of resignation, "smuggling has risen to alarming proportions. I have been charged with the nearly impossible task of putting an end to it. My men have been patrolling the coves, channels and inlets for nearly a year, and while our successes have been impressive, one gang still eludes us—the Warwicke Gang. They make their quarters at an inn in a town on the southeast coast. A more ruthless, brutal, and arrogant bunch we have yet to encounter. They control the town to the point that it is not safe for the king's men to pursue them beyond its limits. They make fools of us and laugh from the safety of their quarters. And there is nothing for it."

"Have you tried to infiltrate the group?"

"Yes—twice. Our last man lived just long enough to deliver this report." Hedrow frowned and tapped the paper on his desk, which he had been studying when Cameron arrived. "It would seem that the gang has joined forces with two men: one a nobleman, and one of a noble family. My man heard no names, but that we speak of Roger Thornton and Percy Osborn, I have no doubts. I've had my suspicions for several weeks. If I am correct, 'tis the job of Thornton and Osborn to see to the disposal of the goods. It is my understanding that the success of the operation rests with the bounty being moved to a safe station halfway to Portsmouth until buyers can be found. We need to find that station, Deveraux, before the goods are moved to Portsmouth. The port is so corrupt with townsmen and king's men of the Royal Navy alike that once there, both the goods and the moment are lost to us."

It was Cameron's turn to be surprised by the scope of the captain's information.

"From what I've heard of Thornton's gambling prowess, 'tis a natural conclusion that he would be involved in nefarious schemes," remarked Deveraux, downing the remaining contents of his glass.

" 'Tisn't difficult to believe of Osborn, either," Hedrow responded, watching Deveraux closely. "He and I go way back, and a more conniving, cunning rat I've never known. I daresay he is the brains behind their schemes."

"Having become acquainted with the man, I must say that I agree with you there," answered Deveraux casually.

Deep in the recesses of his mind, he remembered something Rawlings had mentioned once, and a plan began to take form. As he explained it to Hedrow, a grin spread across the British captain's narrow features.

"I like your ways, Captain Deveraux. But 'tis a dangerous plan. Tell me, just what is your interest in this?"

"I owe a friend a debt," Cameron replied evasively.

"Hmm, yes, I know of Reed Delacroix. A pity about his death. He, Osborn, and I attended the same school in the north. Rather odd, how Percy enjoyed tormenting the lad. Did Reed tell you that it was I who taught him how to defend himself against Percy's malicious gossip concerning his parentage? A born fighter he was, too."

"He remembered you with fondness and

gratitude," allowed Cameron. "He also remembered you to be a man of justice, which is why I am here now. I do not trust lightly, and I never forgive, forget, or overlook a betrayal."

Hedrow nodded. The colonial sea captain was a man after his own heart. "Well, Deveraux, I think we understand each other very well. I can't promise you or your men safe passage. You would in effect be smuggling and, if caught, well, you know the consequences. However, if you are successful, in the melee, some of the goods could be mislaid—if you catch my meaning."

Deveraux smiled knowingly. "One other thing, Captain Hedrow. I am expecting my ship to dock in a hidden cove off the southern coast in mid May. I would appreciate not having attention drawn to the *Homeward Bound* when she appears."

"I will see to it that your ship is not stopped."

Their business concluded, both men stood, each looking deeply into the other's eyes, each one taking the other man's measure and liking what he saw.

"I'll not establish contact again until our rendezvous next month," said Cameron.

"God be with you, Captain Deveraux."

Cameron emerged from the Ministry in a thoughtful mood as he mounted a horse from the Dandridge stable and rode into the center of London's exclusive shopping district. Although he detested the ridiculous flamboyant dress of the city's young men, he knew he would have to conform in order to attract less attention and suspicion. He turned toward Ludgate Hill in search of a draper-taylor recommended by the earl. He would stubbornly draw the line where wigs and ridiculous curls were concerned, though. His own dark, wavy hair would have to suffice, he told himself, no matter how barbaric he may appear. He couldn't abide wearing a puff of powder on his head for the sake of fashion.

Further ahead, Cameron spotted the Dandridge carriage which had been placed at the ladies' disposal, since the squire had need of his own vehicle for errands. Casting around, he saw Mistresses Balfour and Shelbourne laughingly emerging from a millinery shop. They were obviously enjoying themselves, he observed irritably. Mary Balfour certainly didn't give the impression of a woman facing a fate worse than death, which marriage to Roger Thornton could very well be. In fact, it rather galled him that she was accepting her future so well. He would have preferred to see her a bit more distressed. When his mission here was complete, and he had exposed and ruined her husband, would she hate him for it? And he wondered how he could spare her that humiliation? Suddenly, for the first time, his desire for revenge was threatened.

Without waiting to find his tailor, Deveraux abruptly wheeled the horse around and spurred it toward the dockside. This evening he would feel more at ease with sea-toughened sailors, for he had a lot of pent up frustration and anger, and he was just spoiling for a fight to release it.

It was well past the midnight hour when Cameron finaly stumbled into the town house. Somehow he had maneuvered the first flight of stairs and was about to negotiate the second when he noticed the light in the library. It was most likely Lord Dandridge seeing to business matters, he decided, and realized that he owed the earl an apology for missing the evening meal once again. He really was being a boor, but he wasn't up to sitting across from Mary Balfour for a whole evening making pleasant conversation about her upcoming wedding to Roger Thornton.

Drawing himself up, Cameron moved slowly and painfully toward the partially opened door. "My pardons, sir—" He cut himself short as a startled Rorie looked up from the book she had been reading. Her eyes grew wide, and she clasped a hand to her mouth as she took in his battered appearance. An ugly bruise was taking shape on his cheek, and a thin line of blood trickled from a cut on his lip.

"Captain Deveraux!" she exclaimed in shock. "What has happened to you?"

As he swayed unsteadily in the doorway, Rorie jumped up from the sofa and rushed to help him to a chair. Deveraux wasn't about to argue. Deciding that it would be distinctly ungentlemanly of him to refuse her help, he needed no encouragement to put an arm around her for support. The warmth of her slender body beneath the thin fabric of her robe and night-gown and the fresh, fragrant smell of her hair were intoxicating to his bruised senses. And ever so slowly, so as not to be readily noticeable, he let his hand drop to her small waist.

Her compassion always close to the surface, Rorie had rushed to his aid, fearing that he had been set upon by footpads. But catching a whiff of cheap perfume and liquor on his torn clothes, and feeling his hand now resting a little too intimately on her hip, Rorie angrily concluded that he had most likely been in a tavern brawl. She tried to shove him away from her then, but his arm tightened possessively around her, his long, sinewy fingers reaching out to caress the soft column of her neck.

"How nice to make your acquaintance again, m'lady, though I fear the circumstances to be somewhat lacking," Cameron said, his voice low and seductive.

As his gaze slowly traveled over her face and down the length of her figure, a half smile curved his lips, and his eyes turned dark with longing. It had been a long time since he had lain with a woman. Though many a female had made the offer, he could find none to his liking in London, and his virile body ached for release. In any case, it mattered little now, for having seen Rorie, he wanted only her—from the first moment that he had seen her standing in the doorway, bathed in candlelight. To hell with Roger Thornton, he thought savagely. The black-guard doesn't deserve this woman. Throwing caution to the wind, Deveraux lifted her face up to his.

Rorie saw the gleam in his eye and, in-experienced though she was, she wasn't ignorant in the ways of men. As he bent to taste her lips, Rorie's temper flared with a certain desperation. With all her might, she sent her small, balled fist crashing into his midsection, doubling him up and throwing him off-balance. Before he could gather himself together, she gave him a mighty shove into the chair behind him. Throwing him a look of utter contempt, she fled the room, this time leaving a shocked, bruised, and bewildered Deveraux to stare after her in disbelief.

Women never ran from him, he thought in amazement. In fact, it was quite often the case that he did the fleeing. Women! They couldn't be figured or trusted, he concluded, as he leaned back in the chair and fell asleep.

Safely back in her room, Rorie leaned against her closed door, unable to control the shaking in her legs. Panic welled up inside of her, fear and anger knotting her stomach. The man and his hugeness terrified her now. Though she had earlier pegged him as a rogue, she had thought him to be more of a gentleman. But she had no illusions about the fact that had he not been in his cups and half spent from a previous fight, she might never have escaped his determined grasp unscathed. She had felt the strength in those rock-hewn arms and the restrained power of his broad shoulders. At all costs, she resolved to avoid the man for the remainder of his or her stay, whichever came first. The captain was a bloody boor, and she no longer regretted having called him a colonial. It never occurred to her that the appellation might be a source of pride to Deveraux.

10

As bright rays of morning sun filtered through the crack in the drapes, Cameron opened his eyes in a state of confusion. His body was stiff and sore all over, and he winced with pain when he passed a hand across his bruised cheek. What the devil had happened to him! He tried to climb out of bed only to fall painfully back against the pillows. Glancing down at his chest, he saw that his ribs had been tightly wrapped with linen strips. He was shaking his head to clear his muddled senses when the door was kicked open with a bang, and Rawlings entered the room, balancing a heavy tray.

The manservant took a long look at Cameron, disapproval clearly stamped on his leathery face. "I only seen ye set on this path once afore, Cap'n, when ye wanted to take on the world. I understood then. I dinna know what's set ye off of late, but iffen ye don' have a care, laddie, we willna be much help ta those we come ta save. We'll be needin' savin' ourselves, we will," Rawlings warned severely. " 'Tis a dangerous trap we set an' ye be needin' a clear head from this day on."

Cameron smarted from Rawlings's stinging rebuke, but he had to acknowledge the truth of the words.

" 'Tis right you are, old friend," he admitted, flashing his valet a rueful smile. "I've no right to endanger you all by my folly. From this moment on, the mission has highest priority. Now tell me what the devil happened last night. I feel as though a carriage ran over me more than once."

Not knowing what to expect from his unpredictable captain these days, Rawlings grinned with relief, their comraderie reestablished.

"Found ye asleep in the library near to two in the morning," he explained. "Judging from the looks of ye, ye'd found yerself a grand brawl along the wharf somewheres."

Deveraux nodded as the fuzziness began to recede from his mind. Mary's frightened face drifted to the fore, and he was wondering how she had fit into his activities of the previous night, when something Rawlings was saying caught his attention.

"I wouldna found ye, but fer the Shelbourne gal comin' poundin' on the door as indignant as ye please. Said as how yer rude and boorish manner wouldna be overlooked upon further incident. An' she tol' me where ta find ye, she did. Whew! Aint' never wanna be on her bad side. Seems as how the squire's daughter chose her companion well."

Cameron massaged and flexed his shoulders thoughtfully. He remembered that he was about to taste the most inviting lips he'd ever known when—what?—his mind drew a blank. Then suddenly it all came flooding back to him and, painful though it was, he burst out laughing, as he again felt the wallop Mistress Balfour had delivered to his midsection. She must have lost no time in reporting the incident to the Shelbourne girl, who, in turn, took it upon herself to chastise poor Rawlings. Funny though, he couldn't imagine the colorless, little companion becoming transformed into a spitting tigress. Deveraux shrugged. What did it matter, anyway? He was done with them both, and he couldn't afford to waver from his goal.

Rorie had been more disturbed by the previous night's event than she cared to admit to herself. And she refused to leave her room until Mary reported that the captain had already left the premises.

London had lost its charm and adventure for her as she was forced to take note of the filth which shops and houses threw into the central gutters; of the ragged children who begged for alms; of the poor who lurched about the cramped and narrow streets with precious gin bottles tucked protectively under an arm. The air was fetid, the streets were unsafe, the water was barely drinkable. On the whole, Rorie had to conclude that London was not a healthy place for her to be—for more reasons than its lack of sanitation or safety. And she eagerly looked forward to their leave-taking in the next few days.

When Rorie finally emerged from her chambers to accompany Mary on a tour of Covent Garden, she found the squire, Mary, and Lord Dandridge in light conversation in the drawing room. When he caught sight of her standing in the doorway, the earl's face lit up, and he rose to escort Rorie to a chair near his own.

"The lad be most elusive, Robert," the squire was saying, a shadow of annoyance crossing his porcine features. "Always seems to be rushing off ne'er to return until a late hour."

"Captain Deveraux has much to attend to in so short a stay," replied Lord Dandridge in his defense. "I assure you, Henry, that he means not to affront you. In fact, he has promised to dine with us this evening and to make the ladies' acquaintance."

The smile on Rorie's face froze, and her youthful glow turned ashen so that the earl regarded her with concern. "My dear Miss Shelbourne, are you ill?"

Not at the moment, she thought desperately to herself, but tonight 'twill be a different tale. Aloud she said, "No Lord Dandridge, 'tis but a passing fancy."

Across the room, she could see Mary eyeing her curiously, and Rorie quickly lowered her long, dark lashes to hide her distress.

The day passed quickly and pleasantly for the girls, and it was only during the return to Lord Dandridge's residence that Rorie fell noticeably silent and withdrawn.

"What troubles you?" asked Mary solicitously, laying her hand on Rorie's arm. "You seem not to be yourself of late. Has my father offended you?"

Rorie squeezed Mary's hand reassuringly. "No, no, Mary. 'Tis of no concern. The excitement of the past days has conspired to put me off-balance a bit. If you don't mind, I should like to take the evening meal in my room and retire early."

"Why certainly, Rorie. You do look a bit pale. I shall make your apologies to Lord Dandridge. 'Tis a pity that you shall miss meeting Captain Deveraux."

"Yes, a pity, indeed!" replied Rorie more severely than she had intended, once again drawing Mary's curious eye.

When the girls arrived back at Bedford Row, Mary watched in further surprise as Rorie bounded past a stupefied Higgins, before he had even opened the door all the way, and swept up the staircase in an unladylike fashion, as fast as her hooped skirts would allow.

Mary and the butler continued to stare after Rorie's retreating back with open-mouthed astonishment, until Mary remembered her manners. "Ahem—ah—good afternoon, Higgins. I'm afraid Miss Shelbourne isn't herself today."

"Quite so, Miss Balfour," he agreed with a cocked eyebrow.

"Yes, well, please inform the cook that Miss Shelbourne will take her meal in her room this evening."

"Very good, Miss Balfour."

Mary made her way to her own room at a complete loss to explain her friend's odd behavior. This wasn't like Rorie at all, and Mary prayed that her companion wasn't going to break down just when she needed her support the most.

Meanwhile, down the hall in his room, Cameron Deveraux stepped irritably from the brass hip tub, sloshing water over the side onto the thick carpet. Damnation, he cursed, briskly drying himself off, this was the last place he had wanted to be this evening! But when Lord

Dandridge had approached him in the morning and diplomatically suggested his presence at supper, Cameron knew that he could no longer avoid his duty without further embarrassment to his host. He wondered for the hundredth time how the Balfour girl would receive him. He really ought to have apologized for his rude behavior, but their paths just never seemed to cross at the right moments. He broke into a grin, then, as he imagined her reaction to his invitation to her wedding.

When Cameron finally entered the drawing room, Lord Dandridge acknowledged him with obvious relief. "There you are, Captain. There was some concern that you might not be joining us, after all. I'm glad to see that it wasn't the case," he said pointedly. "I've already explained about your run-in with footpads last evening."

Deveraux took his cue, for the earl knew perfectly well the source of his bruises.

"Bloody shame it is when decent folk can't walk their own streets at night for fear of being set upon," thundered the squire.

A quick sweep about the room indicated that Miss Balfour was not in attendance, and Cameron's disappointment was such that he nearly missed his introduction to the other young lady. Although 'twas true the girl was plain, there was an air of compassion and benevolence about her, and a look of such gentle kindness in her eyes, that Cameron was nonplussed. This was the spitfire who had given Rawlings the dressing down of his life?

"Captain Deveraux," the earl was saying, "I wish you to meet Miss Mary Balfour."

Listening with half an ear, Deveraux took the

girl's hand and began the perfunctory reply. "I'm very pleased to make your acquaintance Miss Bal—" He stopped short when he realized what he was about to say. "You're Mary Balfour?" he asked in stunned amazement.

Mary nodded in bewilderment.

"But of course, Captain, whom did you take her to be?" inquired Lord Dandridge, a little surprised by Deveraux's reaction.

"My pardons, Miss Balfour," said Cameron, a strange glow lighting up his silvery blue eyes so that they appeared almost translucent. "I seem to have mistaken your—ah—companion's identity for your own. By the by, where is Miss—Shelbourne this evening?"

Mary smiled as her friend's strange behavior of late began to make some sense. So it would seem that Rorie had met the captain after all and, for some strange reason, had found him not at all to her liking. For the life of her, Mary couldn't figure it, for the man cut quite a dashing figure. His manner was forthright and charming, his attire impeccable. The ruby red, spotted silk coat, richly embroidered with silver stones and shades of silk, the form fitting dove gray breeches and the matching waistcoat were very fashionable, indeed, without stepping into the bounds of absurdity.

"I'm afraid Miss Shelbourne is not feeling well and is taking supper in her room this evening, Captain," Mary answered at last, satisfied with her appraisal of the situation. "I shall relay your regards to her."

"Thank you, Miss Balfour." As a warm smile lit up Mary's wide-set eyes, Cameron sensed he had an ally. But to what purpose?

Supper was long and tedious, as the squire expounded on everything from the mundane to the superficial, and it was with considerable effort that Cameron restrained himself from bolting from the table. Observing that "I-can't-be-held-accountable-for-my-actions-any-longer" look in Deveraux's eye, Lord Dandridge hastily moved to conclude the meal. Even so, it was nearly eleven o'clock, before Cameron was finally able to escape the squire's clutches.

Cameron didn't know why he didn't just give in and be done with the man's constant badgering. What started out as a clever cover story was turning into an ingenious financing venture, guaranteeing the realization of his dream if he would but let it. He decided that it was the devil in him that made him enjoy dangling the squire on a hook and watching the man squirm. Small payment for the life to which he was so cavalierly committing his daughter.

Having met the real Mary, Cameron had to agree with Lord Dandridge's assessment of the girl. In talking with her, Cameron was impressed by her compassion and desire to alleviate the suffering of others less fortunate. He found he liked the gentle, young woman very much, and vowed to spare her as much humiliation and pain as possible. As to the other girl, he asked himself again and again why she would introduce herself to him as Mary Balfour? What did she possibly have to gain? Suspicion ever present at the fore, this was one question which he intended to have answered.

As Mary perched on the edge of Rorie's bed, chattering on about the evening, Rorie sat at the

119

vanity brushing out her long hair. She was torn between wishing to hear all and wanting to know nothing. With a twinkle of devilry in her eyes, Mary purposely refrained from mentioning Captain Deveraux until Rorie could stand silent no longer.

Trying to sound as indifferent as possible, Rorie finally asked, "What of the captain? Was he present?"

But her nonchalance didn't fool Mary, and Mary was hard pressed to hide her amusement. "Indeed, he was, Rorie," she managed to answer in a normal tone.

"Well?" Rorie demanded impatiently.

"Well what, dear?" asked Mary innocently.

"Well, what manner of man did you find him to be?"

"Actually, he was quite nice, charming, and very handsome. I daresay I've never known such a man."

Rorie dropped her brush and turned to stare at her friend with incredulity. They couldn't possibly be talking about the same Captain Deveraux.

"Mary!" she exclaimed. "How can you say that. The man is a rake and a common brawler and, on top of that, exceedingly rude!"

Mary laughed. "Why Rorie, how could you know that? Have you two become otherwise acquainted?" she asked slyly.

Rorie was momentarily flustered. "I—I wouldn't say so. Actually we only met twice," she admitted reluctantly, "and 'twas for just a moment. But each time the man was a boorish clod. I don't wish to see him again."

"I'm sorry to hear that," replied Mary in

feigned regret.

"Why?" asked Rorie, one finely curved brow arched in suspicion.

"Well, it would seem that he is to accompany us to Drumfielde as an invited guest to my wedding."

"What! Who would do such a thing?"

"Apparently the captain has business dealings with both my father and the duke."

Rorie rose so abruptly from the dressing table, she nearly overturned the exquisitely embroidered bench. "Oh, no!" she cried, turning to pace the floor in obvious agitation. This was one development she had never expected. As though she didn't have troubles enough.

Aware of Mary's questioning gaze on her, she struggled to compose herself. "Mary, I'm afraid I still don't feel very well," she said, massaging her temples for emphasis. "Will you be so kind as to excuse me? I feel the need to retire now."

"But of course, dear. You really don't seem to have improved much from this afternoon. Perhaps more sleep is in order."

Rorie thought she detected a slightly patronizing edge to Mary's tone, but it was so out of character, she dismissed the notion immediately.

After Mary had left her room, all thought of sleep escaped Rorie. What was she to do, she wondered frantically? She simply couldn't face that man again, and certainly not for three days on the road. Maybe she could leave on the earlier wagon with the baggage and the few servants who were to accompany them. But she knew that the squire would not hear of an alleged relative, no matter how distant, riding with servants. She had to think of something. Perhaps some reading would help to calm her frayed nerves. It had always worked in the past. She turned to look for the book she had been reading. It was several minutes later, however, before she remembered that she had left it behind in the library last evening when she had fled from the captain.

"Damn!" she cursed aloud. "I'll not return there if I have to lay awake all night."

And she climbed into bed, only to toss and turn for what seemed an eternity. When she heard the little porcelain clock strike two, she decided to set aside her paranoia and retrieve the book from the library. The rake was undoubtedly passed out in a tavern somewhere, anyway. Just the same, she wouldn't make the mistake again of staying behind to read, no matter how much better the light was in the library. She'd go blind before she would risk another encounter with the captain, she concluded, stamping her foot in strong resolution.

Throwing a shawl around her, she cautiously peered out of her door and down the length of the dark, silent hall before quietly making her way to the second floor. Guided by the light of her candle and the sconces on the walls, Rorie moved hesitantly to her destination. She sighed with relief when she saw that the door was ajar and that the room stood wrapped in darkness.

Entering the library, she was setting the candlestick on the desk, when the door suddenly slammed shut behind her with a muffled bang. Raw nerves grating on her courage, she nearly jumped out of her skin and, with shaking hands, she struggled to keep the candle from spilling wax onto the lovely French desk.

"Silly goose! 'Twas naught but the wind," she scolded nervously when her attention was caught by the billowing curtains of an open window.

Now, where had she left the book? She thought she had set it on the desk, but a careful search yielded nothing. Maybe it had somehow been knocked on the floor. Tossing the cumbersome shawl aside, she bent down to examine the possibility, patting her hands across a large surface. Again, nothing. Perhaps a servant had replaced it on the shelf. She had fled the library in such a state last night, anything was possible. As she turned to examine the shelves, however, the breath caught in her throat, and she gasped as though the wind had been knocked from her body. Standing in the shadows, with his back against the door, was Captain Deveraux.

Cameron grinned at her wide-eyed astonishment. "I thought you would be along to collect this," he said, holding the book out to her. "I just hadn't figured on you arriving this late. Had the devil's own time keeping awake."

When she made no move, he shrugged negligently, laying the book on a nearby table. His expression, at first predatory, became implacably determined, then, as he openly studied her for the moment. His eyes coolly appraised her with an unnerving thoroughness, as though to mentally calculate her assets, and she anxiously eyed her shawl which laid just out of reach. Rorie swallowed hard. Resisting the impulse to shield herself with her hands, she lifted her chin to proudly and boldly meet his gaze. She would be damned if she would give him the edge by showing her embarrassment.

Cameron suppressed the urge to smile at her bravado. Her gesture of defiance—or had it been challenge?—had not been lost on him, for he had seen her glance at the shawl in dismay, and had easily guessed her discomfiture. At any other time he might have called her on it, but tonight he was concerned with a matter of far more importance to him than her modesty.

"Now, Miss Shelbourne, suppose you explain why you introduced yourself to me as Mary Balfour," he commanded firmly, his deep voice slashing through the tense silence.

Startled by the accusation, Rorie momentarily forgot her distress. "But why should I do that?" she asked, her brow furrowed in genuine perplexity. "I'm afraid you are mistaken, Captain."

"Come now, Miss Shelbourne, don't play games with me. You'll find that I'm a master at it. As far as I can tell, you had nothing to gain by the charade and everything to lose. So what was the purpose?"

As he moved toward her, Rorie retreated until the desk was at her back, her mind frantically working to recall the first encounter. She felt like a trapped animal. And then it came to her how he might have mistaken her identity. Her unruly temper took over as the injustice of the situation enflamed her, putting new life into her quivering body.

"I'm afraid the error is of your own making, Captain!" she spat furiously. "If you hadn't so rudely vacated the room before I had finished my introduction, you would have heard me to say I was Mary Balfour's *companion*. As it happened, the minute I mentioned Mary's name, your mood turned black and you were gone. And just who the bloody devil do you think you are, accusing me of playing games! Why, we've only just met. What possible consequence could it be to you, anyway!"

Cameron halted his stride, astounded by Rorie's outburst. He had expected tears of denial and, at best, a meek confession, but certainly not this passionate tirade shifting the blame to him. He had to admit that she made a good case for herself and decided to give her the benefit of the doubt—for the time being.

The tension in the room crackled. Watching her stand there with the candlelight illuminating the sweet curves of her body through the thin material of her nightgown, her high, firm breasts heaving with anger, and those emerald cat eyes flashing with fury, Cameron would not be denied any longer.

In three quick strides, he was across the room before Rorie could react. Gripping her by the shoulders, he pulled her to him and pressed his lips against the petal softness of her own, his edict to Rawlings but a fleeting memory. There was something about this girl he found impossible to ignore. His kiss, at first hard and demanding, became slow and masterful, as his mouth moved surely across hers with a sensuality that drained Rorie of any strength. Feeling her go limp in his arms, he took it for submission, and his ardor was fanned. Unbeknownst to him, however, Rorie was, in fact, experiencing a hell partially of her own making, as images of a long ago event once again replayed themselves in her frightened mind.

When Cameron lifted his head, he was shocked to see a vacant look of terror reflected in the amber-flecked depths of her eyes, where he had expected to read an invitation. Momentarily perplexed, he loosened his hold on her. Then, in a lightning flash, the palm of her hand delivered a resounding blow to his cheek.

"Now you have a bruise to match the other one, you arrogant cur!" she hissed and ran from the room, sobbing.

Cameron rubbed his stinging cheek in absolute confusion. His touch had elicited many reactions from women over the years, but never fear. Perhaps he had overestimated her experience in such matters, he surmised. But just as quickly, he dismissed the thought, for it was difficult to imagine a woman of her beauty, spirit and maturity never having known at least one man's hand.

His eyes narrowed in speculation. Was it all a clever ruse to lead him on a chase with marriage being the payment demanded for her favors? It was commonly known that men enjoyed the hunt more than the bagging, and it wouldn't be the first time that a besotted man had been slyly led into matrimony by a scheming woman.

Cameron smiled. He would play her little game to see where it led, he decided, for it most certainly would prove a pleasant diversion from the tedium of Squire Balfour. And the lovely lady would find him a most worthy opponent.

11

Amid a bustle of activity, the coaches were readied for the trip to Drumfielde. A wagon had left earlier that morning, heavily loaded with trunks and servants. As predicted, when Rorie had suggested that she accompany the wagon, the squire bellowed with indignation and informed her roundly that so long as he was affording her the honor of recognizing her as a member of his family, she was to conduct herself accordingly. Rorie bristled with helpless rage. After all, it wasn't her idea to be a distant relative. And yet, she held her tongue.

Thank heavens they would be in separate coaches, and she wouldn't have to face the insolence of that rogue captain. She had managed to avoid him during the last days of her stay here, but she had had to endure his gaze on her throughout the evening meals. The man positively unnerved her with his hypnotic eyes, so clear and blue one minute, so inscrutable the next. At times, she felt as though he could see straight into her very soul. There was something else about the captain that she couldn't quite put her finger on—something familiar. Yet how could that be, when they had never met before this visit?

The saving grace of the last evening was that Dr. Johnson had dined with them, and that Deveraux had not. Although Johnson's puffy, pockmarked face—an effect of infant scrofula —was drawn into a perpetual scowl, and the greasy ill-kempt wig, the worn coat and the ink-stained fingers made for an appearance which was shabby at best, Rorie had loved the man's keen wit and often sardonic humor. Beneath the surly and, at first, repulsive exterior, Rorie sensed a kind and charitable man, though she had known better than to say so, for it was obvious that Johnson enjoyed his infamous reputation for eccentricity.

"And how is the squire with the unread library?" Johnson had asked when introductions had been made.

To all appearances Johnson's manner was gruff, but Rorie had caught the twinkle of devilry in his eye when the expression on the squire's face had turned thunderous. Although it was rumored that society matrons vied for the privilege of being insulted by the witty Dr. Johnson, Squire Balfour decidedly did not share their enthusiasm, and he bristled whenever the lexicographer had chanced to look his way. At one point during the meal Rorie had looked up, startled, to find Dr. Johnson's shrewd, dark eyes on her.

"Well, Miss Shelbourne, I understand you to be a woman of some intelligence and insight. Shelbourne. I was acquainted once with a

Richard Shelbourne. Brilliant young man. Could use him at work on my dictionary. You remember, Robert, he taught in the surrounding areas of your country estate. Had a school in the village there."

Lord Dandridge had thought for a moment. "Yes, I remember now. The village was sorry to see him leave. Something about relatives in a neighboring village."

"Yes," said Rorie. "My father moved us to Drumfielde to be near my aunt and uncle. Both of my parents were taken by the fever last March."

Squire Balfour had shifted uneasily in his seat as Johnson eyed him with keen amusement. "Miss Shelbourne is a relative did you say, Squire?"

Rorie had to suppress a giggle then, as the squire had turned red and choked on his scrod. "Distant—quite distant," he had mumbled at long last.

All in all, Rorie had found the evening delightfully stimulating as Johnson offered brilliant and insightful observations on a wide range of topics and sparred mercilessly with the squire like a cat playing with a mouse. She would have preferred, however, to see Deveraux impaled on the end of Dr. Johnson's sharp wit. Now she chuckled, entertaining images to that effect as she climbed into the coach behind Mary.

While the ladies settled themselves, the men remained inside the house, discussing the last points of the trip. Since the squire had inflicted his company upon them, Lord Dandridge and Deveraux devilishly decided to pinch him where it hurt—in his pocketbook. And it was with great relish that Lord Dandridge informed Squire

Balfour that they would all be stopping at the best inns along the way for bed and board. The squire paled when he mentally figured the expenses, but ever conscious of his future social standing, he forewent argument.

"By the by, Squire," added Cameron off-handedly, "before you and I discuss our business venture, you had best lay out your rules of partnership with Lord Dandridge."

The squire brightened. "Why, yes, that's a capital idea. I shall ride the day with you, Sir Robert." At this, Lord Dandridge barely managed to suppress the moan on the tip of his tongue. Sixty miles with Squire Balfour was more than any man should have to endure. "And might I impose upon you, Captain, to take my place in my coach to watch over the ladies' safety?" continued the squire.

"If that is your wish, sir." Deveraux grinned as he caught sight of the chilling look the earl shot him.

On edge all morning from too many sleepless nights, Rorie was relieved to see Lord Dandridge's guards take their places and the claret and black, gold crested coach pulling out at last. All that remained was for the squire to join them, and they would be on their way, too.

"What is keeping your father, Mary?"

"I have no idea, Rorie, less perhaps some last minute details with Captain Deveraux."

"Oooh!" shrieked Rorie. "Unless you wish to endure this journey in silence, Mary, take heed and speak naught of that odious man to me again!"

Startled, Mary stumbled over an apology. At that point, the door opened, and Rorie's jaw dropped to her knees as the subject of her wrath lithely swung himself into the seat next to her. This was too much, and her first thought was to quit the coach.

"Settle yourself, Miss Shelbourne," ordered Cameron, as though reading her thoughts. The steady, deep timbre of his voice left her in no doubt that there would be consequences should she disobey him.

Mary looked from one to the other, hoping that someone would volunteer to clear up her confusion. She had a myriad of questions, but watching the daggers which Rorie's flashing eyes shot at the captain, Mary wisely decided that her curiosity could be appeased at a later date.

After a tense moment of a silent battle of wills, Rorie uttered a sigh of exasperation and leaned back heavily against the cushioned seat. The earl's coach had already pulled out. She couldn't very well stay behind, and there was nothing to be gained from a confrontation with the captain at this point, she decided. She was instantly dismayed to find, however, that the hoop of her travel gown allowed her to put no further distance between her and her antagonist. And the half smile of amusement which Cameron flashed her, as he watched her struggle unsuccessfully with her skirt, galled her to no end.

As the coach lurched forward, Deveraux swung his attention to Mary to relieve the tenseness in the air. "And how did you find London, Miss Balfour?" he asked politely.

"Well, Captain," Mary replied hesitantly, "as a country dweller, I must confess that on the surface, I find it very colorful and exciting. However, in my heart, I fear that I must ally myself with Hogarth in finding it sadly wanting."

"I quite agree with you, Miss Balfour. The deprivation in this country is appalling. And how might you set it to rights?"

Mary's eyes were wide with amazement. Nobody had ever consulted her for an opinion before, and she found that not only did she have one, but that she very much liked being asked for it. Casting an uneasy eye on Rorie's scowling face, Mary soon overcame her feelings of disloyalty as she warmed to the topic and became immersed in conversation with the captain.

The dog, thought Rorie angrily. Somehow he knew that this subject lay dear to Mary's heart. Did no one see through that rogue but Rorie herself?

After two hours of traveling, the heat of the day, the jouncing rhythms of the coach, overwrought emotions, and restless nights all conspired to overcome Rorie's stubborn resistance to sleep. Soon she was nodding off, in spite of herself. Only the banging of her head, when she was thrown against the side, kept her from succumbing to the exhaustion which plainly marked her face. Mary nodded in agreement as Cameron gently eased Rorie against him. Too fatigued to be completely aware of her surroundings, Rorie put up no struggle when he cushioned her head against his broad shoulder. She only knew that she had found comfort and gave in to blissful slumber.

She stirred a few hours later, to the barking of dogs and the playful cries of children as the coach pulled into the courtyard of the Hawk and Dove Inn. Feeling comfortable and secure, Rorie was loathe to come fully awake. Instead, she burrowed deeper until a familiar, masculine scent wafted to her senses, bringing her to full consciousness with a jolt.

Realizing where she was, Rorie twisted around to discover that Cameron had shifted his long body so that she lay cradled against his chest, his one arm encircling her waist to keep her from falling. Fury flooded her features as he greeted her with a leisurely grin. Jerking herself to an upright position, she moved as far away from him as the coach and her skirt would allow, the twinkle in his eyes incensing her all the more.

"I trust you had a good sleep, Miss Shelbourne," Deveraux said, his deep voice tinged with a measure of triumph. And on a note of dismissal, he opened the door to step out of the coach.

As the heat traveled up Rorie's neck to spread across her face, she rounded on her friend in a fit of anger. "Mary, how could you have allowed it!"

"You needed the rest, Rorie. You were quite on edge," Mary answered simply. "Captain Deveraux kindly saw that you got it. I should think you would be grateful to him."

Rorie's eyes flew open in astonishment. Mary had changed of late. She seemed to have a newfound confidence or purpose and was speaking her mind more and more. At another time, Rorie would have been pleased, but she didn't like this new alliance which seemed to have sprung up between the captain and her friend. Suddenly, she felt quite isolated.

Ignoring the hand Deveraux so smugly

extended to her from the ground, Rorie bounded out of the coach past him only to land in a mud hole, which could more appropriately be termed a quagmire. She would have fallen face down had not Cameron laughingly grabbed her arm and scooped her up by the waist. She had to be grateful to him for that, but when he neatly tucked her under his one arm and carried her to the inn to deposit her on the doorstep like a sack of flour, it was too much.

"I—how dare you." She started to berate Cameron, but her humiliation was so great that she only ended up sputtering in helpless indignation.

"First time I've ever known that wench to be at a loss for words," roared Squire Balfour, descending from the other coach and slapping his thigh in glee.

Cameron knew better than to say anything, but the trace of a grin and the cock of his brow said, "Next time don't be so arrogant, my dear."

Rorie didn't know whom she wanted to strangle most—the captain or Squire Balfour. Squaring her shoulders and presenting her stiff back to the men, she marched into the inn with her head held high, leaving a trail of mud behind her. The only evidence of the mortification she felt was in the bright spot high on each cheekbone and in the fiery snap of her eyes.

After lunching on a palatable meal of boiled fowl, oysters and woodcock, Rorie felt her spirit returning. She decided to turn the tables on the good captain.

"Lord Dandridge," she inquired with interest, "I should enjoy hearing of the new farming methods you are in the process of implementing on your estate. Perhaps they might prove beneficial to the village. Would you mind if Mary and I rode with you in your coach, so that we might converse more fully?"

Lord Dandridge beamed with pleasure as he saw a most charming way of ridding himself of the squire. "My dear, 'twould be a pleasure to have your company. I believe that the squire and I have concluded our business."

"Quite so, Robert," Balfour agreed affably, now looking forward to having the captain as his captive audience.

Cameron could barely contain himself as he caught the earl and Rorie smiling at him in benign amusement. He lifted his tankard in salute to them, then rose slowly and unenthusiastically to follow the squire to his coach, not unlike one being led to the gallows on Tyburn Hill.

12

By the time they had arrived at an inn for the night, darkness had fallen. The rest of the day had passed very pleasantly for Rorie, Mary and Lord Dandridge, and they entered the inn in high spirits. Squire Balfour's coach had preceded them, and, with a glance of thunderous reproach to the earl upon his appearance, Cameron quickly downed a second tankard of ale.

"My but you're looking a bit worn, Captain Deveraux," Rorie remarked, the amusement in her thickly lashed eyes belying the concern in her voice. "The trip did not pass well for you?" She ignored the empty seat on the bench next to him and seated herself at the far end of the table.

"On the contrary, we've managed to conclude a handy bit of business, ay, Captain?" boomed the squire, heartily slapping Deveraux on the back. Cameron grimaced and once against signaled to the barmaid for a refill.

With a toss of her flaming red hair, her broad hips swaying suggestively, the barmaid sidled up to Cameron. She had already decided to give this handsome man her very special attention.

" 'Ello mate, me name's Annie. What's yer pleasure?" She winked saucily, looking Deveraux straight in the eye, careful to leave nothing to his imagination.

Rorie's eyes narrowed as the captain nodded lustily at the barmaid. She wanted to leap across the table and slap that lopsided grin right off Deveraux's face. Men! she fumed. They seemed to have but one thought!

Annie tore her attention away from Deveraux long enough to reach behind her and soundly cuff a toothless old man on the side of his head. The patrons roared with laughter as the hapless little fellow held his ringing ear and howled with unexpected pain. Rorie and Mary jumped at the sudden violence.

"Don't ye go feelin' sorry fer tha' old fool, missies. The man had his filthy hand up me arse," Annie stated matter-of-factly. "I only lets certain gentlemen do tha'," she added throatily, shooting Cameron a meaningful glance.

Once again, Rorie could feel the heat of anger and embarrassment start up her neck and spread across her dumbfounded features, as she caught Deveraux's amused grin and heard the squire's unrestrained guffaws. With more dignity than she felt, Rorie stood up and announced, "If you'll excuse us gentlemen, I think perhaps it more fitting that Mary and I take our meals in our room."

"I don't think it necessary for you to enclose yourselves in your room, Miss Shelbourne, to avoid the baser elements," contradicted the captain smoothly. "I'm sure Annie, here, can find a private dining room in which to serve us.

How about it, Annie?"

Annie giggled as Cameron raked an appreciative eye over her buxom figure. "Right ye be, Cap'n. Oi gots jest the room fer yer party. The Rose Room it be. Reserved fer gentry loik yerselves."

"Now, now, Captain," interrupted the squire in alarm as he mentally calculated the added expense of a private dining room. "I'm sure the ladies are quite done in after the day's journey and would prefer to dine in their room."

For once Rorie looked at the squire in gratitude for his timely support, but her hopes were soon dashed by Lord Dandridge.

"Nonsense!" the earl exclaimed. "I have much I would like to discuss with the ladies. I find Miss Balfour and Miss Shelbourne to be refreshing conversationalists. A private dining room is an excellent suggestion, Captain Deveraux."

Like a bird freed from her cage, Mary eagerly embraced Lord Dandridge's decision, while the squire groaned and Rorie fumed.

Although their supper of roast beef, potatoes, potted trout, melon and apple pudding, was more than adequate, Rorie barely touched her food and spoke only in monosyllables. Rubbing her throbbing temples, she wanted only the comfort of her bed where she could block out the annoyances of the day—namely, one arrogant sea captain.

The dining room was small and stuffy, and the nearness of the captain's presence directly across from her affected her more than she wanted to admit. The anger she felt, as she watched him flirt openly with the agreeable barmaid, was beyond her comprehension. She despised the insolent rogue, so why should she care what actions he took? It was all very puzzling and frightening to her. She usually ignored circumstances which defied logic. But Captain Deveraux simply refused to be ignored.

As though willed to do so, Rorie looked up into his riveting blue eyes and was taken aback by the sheer intensity of their power to hold her gaze. When she finally broke his hold and turned away, she was alarmingly pale and shaky.

"Are you well, my dear?" asked the earl solicitously, his dignified features drawn up in concern.

Rorie smiled weakly. "I'll be fine, milord, after a night's rest. I've had a rather exhausting day. If you will excuse me, I should like to retire for the evening. No, no, Mary. There's no need for you to accompany me. Stay and finish your meal. I can make my way."

As she stood up to leave, Rorie swayed slightly, and a strong hand clamped over her arm to steady her. She turned to express her thanks, startled to find Catpain Deveraux towering above her. Somehow he had made his way to her side undetected, and she jerked her arm free from his grasp.

In a low, authoritative tone which brooked no argument, he said, "If you gentlemen will excuse me, I shall see Miss Shelbourne to her room as I have business upstairs myself."

Rorie could well imagine what kind of business he had, as she glanced at the giggling Annie. She opened her mouth to protest, enraged that Deveraux should dare to use her as an excuse to leave the table for his baser pursuits, when she felt his hand tighten on her elbow, as though warning her to hold her tongue.

Clamping her mouth shut, she smiled tightly and shrugged him off. "That won't be necessary, Captain. I can find my own way."

She turned abruptly, intending to leave him in the wake of a dignified departure. Instead, she caught her heel in a knothole in the floorboard and cruelly twisted her ankle, falling heavily against Deveraux.

Gathering her wits about her, she attempted to pull away. But as she put her weight on her injured foot, searing pain shot up through her ankle, and she would have pitched forward had Cameron not grabbed for her. She moaned as he forced her back into a chair and gently removed her shoe. When he began to massage and manipulate her ankle, Rorie cried aloud and nearly shot out of her seat from the excruciating pain.

"What is it?" cried Mary in alarm.

'I think it to be a bad sprain, for I can feel no broken bones," Cameron responded. "I'm afraid you'll have to accept my assistance now, Miss Shelbourne. I have much experience in dealing with broken bones and sprains, having assisted my ship's doctor on numerous occasions."

Rorie thought the confident smile he flashed her bordered on smugness. She grimaced with both pain and helpless rage, as he swung her up in his arms to carry her effortlessly through the tavern and up the stairs to her room, amidst the snickers and bawdy cheers of curious gawkers. Mary followed close behind.

"Miss Balfour, would you be good enough to fetch a leather satchel from my room? It contains a balm I shall have need of," he called over his shoulder as he entered the bed chamber.

When Mary quickly left to do his bidding, Rorie became uncomfortably aware that she was once again left alone with the captain and was most certainly at a disadvantage. Acutely cognizant of the pressure of his hands where they touched her body, she began to wiggle uneasily in his arms when he made no move to set her down.

"I think you had best release me now, Captain," she said crisply. "Your mission is ended."

"You think so, Miss Shelbourne?" he replied, settling her on a chair. "We shall see. Now, kindly remove your stocking."

Rorie's jaw dropped. Why the impudence of the cad. "How dare you!" she sputtered. "You seem always to assume liberties where they have not been offered. Now get out of this room!"

"You mistake my intentions, Miss Shelbourne," Deveraux responded coolly. "I mean only to better inspect your injury. Now shall you do the honors, or shall I?"

As he moved toward her, Rorie hastily decided to yield. After all, she was no match for this rogue, incapacitated as she was.

"Oh, very well. Turn around!" she commanded petulantly. She had just finished removing her stocking when Mary burst breathlessly into the room, holding out a small jar.

Deveraux chuckled. "Easy now, Miss Balfour. You needn't have rushed so. 'Twasn't a matter of life or death."

"I'll be the judge of that," snapped Rorie, ruefully surveying the swelling, purple mass, which had once been a rather well-turned ankle. "Now if you please, hand me the liniment and be gone from my room."

Deveraux shrugged. "Be my guest, Miss Shelbourne, but be forewarned. If the ankle is not properly cared for, you could very well feel the effects of your injury for years to come. And from your position, I do not think you can sufficiently address the task."

"But 'tis only a sprain, you said."

"Sprains can sometimes be more debilitating than an actual break."

"Well, then, Mary can administer the liniment and dressing."

"Oh, no, Rorie, I shouldn't want to accept that risk. Let the captain care for your ankle, as he alone has done this before," pleaded Mary.

Rorie bit her lip thoughtfully. This certainly was a quandary. She obviously had no wish to be lame for the remainder of her years, but yet the thought of the captain's hands on her person once again was more than she could tolerate.

"Oh, all right, administer the ointment," she relented in a less than gracious tone. "Well!" she demanded when he made no move to return to his ministrations.

"I don't accept orders, Miss Shelbourne, I give them," he replied curtly. "What I do accept are courteous requests."

Rorie could feel the red blush of anger stain her face as she rose and grabbed the edge of the table for support. "The devil take ye then!" she shouted. "I would take my chances of being lame to groveling at your feet."

Cameron shot her a long, considering look. "You know, if a fire spit as much as you, one might be forced to damper it. You had best take care, Miss Shelbourne."

As he turned to leave the room, Rorie grabbed the candlestick from the table and hurled it past him, narrowly missing his head. She regretted her action immediately and sank back into her chair wide-eyed as his startled features turned thunderous, and she imagined this bronzed giant suddenly swooping down on her to choke the very life from her body. Instead, chilling blue eyes regarded her steadily, demanding her full attention.

"I will remember never to turn my back on a tigress," he said. His voice was low and sure, the warning unmistakable. And with that, he exited the room.

Mary could only stare incredulously from Rorie to the empty doorway.

That night, Rorie pitched feverishly on her bed, writhing in agony. Faces loomed before her in and out of focus, and she moaned and whimpered as someone seemingly twisted her ankle again and again, until she thought she could no longer bear the pain. Snatches of conversation drifted about her consciousness, and she felt herself restrained each time she struggled to throw off the covers. At last she fell into blissful slumber, untormented by fleeting images or hollow voices.

As a door opened and closed, part of Rorie struggled to awaken, but she felt so much at peace she fought the urge. When a cool hand touched her forehead and cheek, she could no longer delay the inevitable. Thick, dark lashes fluttered against colorless cheeks, as she slowly opened her eyes to discover Captain Deveraux leaning over her and regarding her with grave concern.

"Well, the beauty has at last awakened from her slumber," he observed with a weary grin.

She searched his eyes, but in place of the mockery she had expected to find, she saw only relief. "What are you doing in my room?" she demanded weakly, trying to rise. But the effort was too much, and she fell back against the pillow, wincing with pain as she was rudely reminded of her ankle.

Ignoring her temper, Deveraux lifted the covers and began to examine her ankle with an easy familiarity which made Rorie blush to the roots of her hair.

"What do you think you are doing!" she croaked hotly, her spirit returning.

Deveraux chuckled. "Easy Miss Shelbourne. Over the past two days I've become quite accustomed to this swollen, purple mass you call an ankle—and nothing more. So don't throw yourself into a tizzy over it. You'll need to gather your strength."

Rorie looked at Deveraux in disbelief. "I've been ill for two days? What happened? A person doesn't fall ill from a twisted ankle."

"One does when she has gone without proper food or sleep for the previous week," Deveraux answered pointedly. "You were already in a weakened state. Twisting your ankle was the final shock to your body."

At that moment, Mary entered the room with a tray loaded with biscuits, oat cakes, and tea. "Rorie! Thank heaven you're awake. We were all so worried about you, but Captain Deveraux, here, knew you would recover." She smiled shyly, as Cameron took the heavy tray from her.

"Oh, and just how did Catptain Deveraux know that?" croaked Rorie, her brow arched in question.

Mary giggled. "He said you were so contrary, neither heaven nor hell would claim you."

Deveraux merely winked and stuffed a cake in his mouth, as Rorie shot him an indignant glare.

"Miss Balfour, I believe you can handle our patient from this point. If you ladies will excuse me, I shall see to some preparations. Miss Shelbourne should be able to travel the day after tomorrow if we take it easy."

"I don't want that man in this room again, Mary," Rorie whispered hoarsely when Deveraux had left.

The smile left Mary's face, and she looked down at Rorie with a mixture of dismay and anger. Her hands on her hips, Mary spoke quietly and evenly. "Rorie, you owe Captain Deveraux more than you know. That night when I helped you into bed, I knew you felt too warm to the touch and decided to check on you throughout the night. Before midnight, your ankle was grossly swollen, and you were being consumed by fever. I went to Captain Deveraux for help."

"Oh, that must have been a trick. No doubt you had to pry him from that hussy's arms," interjected Rorie sarcastically.

"Whether I did or not is not the issue. What matters is that he came without a moment's hesitation. One of the travelers here was a surgeon, who upon consultation wanted to amputate your leg below the knee. I shudder to think where you'd be had the captain not intervened. He threw the quack out on his ear and took over your care himself—with my help," Mary added quickly, when she saw the blush that stained Rorie's cheeks. "Don't worry," she said, softening her tone. "Everything was done according to convention. The captain was the soul of propriety. He touched nothing more than your leg. I did everything else with his instruction. At night we took turns watching over you while the other slept."

Mary thought it best not to mention how, upon waking for her shift of duty, she found Deveraux gently cradling a thrashing, hysterical Rorie, in the throes of some imagined terror. In the end, he had succumbed to his own exhaustion and stretched out alongside her on the bed for a few hours.

Rorie felt ashamed of herself, noticing for the first time the dark circles under her friend's eyes, the tired droop of her shoulders, and the dishevelment of her usually fastidious attire. She reached out to take Mary's hand. "Dear Mary. I am so sorry to have been such a burden to you."

"Rorie, you must take better care of yourself. I couldn't bear to lose you."

"Promise." The old Rorie winked. "Now please convey my apologies to the squire and Lord Dandridge for delaying their departure."

"Oh, but they've left," said Mary. "Father was carrying on about needing more time to prepare for the wedding, and Lord Dandridge was so worried about you, he was constantly underfoot—"

"So Captain Deveraux suggested that they go

on ahead. How very convenient," finished Rorie sardonically.

"No," said Mary, plumping Rorie's pillow and placing a plate of cakes on her lap, "I did." At the look of surprise on her friend's face, Mary hastened to explain, "I thought you and the captain should have some time to settle your differences." She eyed her patient keenly. "I don't know what's between you and Captain Deveraux, Rorie, but it needs be settled."

13

The next day of the journey passed pleasantly enough and without incident. Rorie and the captain agreed to an uneasy truce for Mary's sake, and, though it was difficult to keep quiet as his powerful arms carried Rorie to and from the coach and her room at the inn, she held a civil tongue. In fact, had she been honest with herself, she would have had to admit that the feeling of his arms around her was not a wholly unpleasant experience. But she found the idea so disturbing to her that she ignored it as best she could.

It had rained the previous night, rendering the roads nearly impassable the following day, and their progress was slow. The setting of the sun still found them ten miles outside of Drumfielde and, although Lord Dandridge had left them a guard of three men, Deveraux knew that they would be easy pickings for highwaymen at the rate of speed the were forced to travel. Casually, he shifted his pistol to within easy reach.

Rorie's ankle throbbed unbearably from the

constant jarring of the coach upon the muddy ruts. She bit her lip and dug her nails into the palms of her hands, stoically refusing to say a word. But the distress was plain in her face each time she winced when the coach struck yet another hole. At Mary's nod of agreement, Cameron tapped on the roof.

"Driver, put in at the next inn," he ordered. "We won't be going on to Drumfielde tonight."

Rorie opened her mouth to remonstrate, but the set look on Cameron's face dared her to defy the truth of her discomfort. Helplessly, she turned to Mary for support, but finding none in that corner either, she slumped back against the cushioned seat in resignation. So close and yet so far, she sighed irritably. She was anxious for the trip to be done so that she could be free of Deveraux's presence, which she found to be a most disturbing force at best.

A half hour later, as they pulled off the main road and followed the sign down a narrow lane to the Houndstooth Inn, Rorie was secretly grateful that the decision had been made to stop. The stone structure had a homey appearance from the outside, but the moment that Deveraux had settled her on the bench in the taproom, Rorie felt it. Something wasn't right. The tavern was empty and ominously silent, and she knew that Deveraux felt it, too.

A buxom serving maiden, her hair dull and matted and her clothes dirty and torn, appeared uncertainly from the back room, obviously startled to find guests. She had the appearance of one abused beyond the point of feeling or caring. Rorie had seen that vacant, hunted look before in her nightmare of the past, and she shifted uneasily in her seat. As Deveraux ordered their meals, the servant girl's eyes darted nervously to the window. And when he asked for two rooms for the night, the stark fear which shadowed her face, totally unnerved Rorie.

"Ye kenna stay here," the maid whispered desperately. "Eat yer meal an' be gone—"

"Betty!" bellowed a voice sharply from the doorway. "Get ye in the kitchen an' sees ta our guests' food."

Betty jumped and skittered into the back room like a frightened rabbit, carefully edging her way past the bulky man in the doorway. Of small stature, barrel-chested and long-armed, the man reminded Rorie of some pictures of apes she had seen.

"Me name's Bigelow. I be the innkeeper here. Welcome to the Houndstooth." He smiled broadly. "Pay Betty no mind. She was handled pretty rough by a gang of ruffians what come through here a while back and ain't been the same since."

That would account for the maid's strange behavior, and, as the group found nothing threatening in the man's rather obsequious manner, they relaxed somewhat.

"How can I helps ye? I sees tha' yer coach be crested. Ye'll have nothin' but the best here."

"We desire accommodations for the night," Cameron replied shortly, refusing to satisfy the man's obvious curiosity about his illustrious guests.

Undaunted, Bigelow fairly beamed. "We don't gets many travelers of quality, bein' off the main road a ways. Ye ken have the best rooms in the inn." And with a last backward glance, he went off to see to the preparations.

Presently, Betty entered with their food, careful to keep her eyes averted. She passed out the tankards of ale, and when she came to Deveraux, she kept her hand on the mug and lifted her eyes to stare at him full in the face. The maiden said nothing, but Rorie had the feeling that an exchange had taken place, and her temper was roused as she interpreted it be an invitation. Irritably, she jabbed at her meat pie. It was greasy and tough, the bread stale. Her stomach turned over with the first bite, and she shoved the remainder away in disgust, reaching for the ale instead. Deveraux was strangely quiet, and the meal passed in awkward silence. Rorie didn't know which she found more irritating— his bantering or his silence—and she was relieved when he finally suggested that they all retire for the evening.

When the girls entered their room, Rorie's lips curled in disgust, and Mary gasped in dismay. The room looked and smelled as though it hadn't been aired or cleaned in a year. A thick layer of dust covered everything, and, without even checking, Rorie knew that the straw mattress would be infested with bugs and ticks.

"I suggest that we sleep in the chairs," said Rorie with a weary sigh. "If we clean off the table, perhaps we can stretch out and lay our heads on our arms. I wonder what the worst rooms in the inn are like," she added wryly.

Mary could only nod in vigorous agreement. Although the squire held his coins in a tight fist, never had she encountered such vile accommodations. "I can see why the inn doesn't get many travelers," she responded at length. " 'Tis more doubtful that it ever sees any returns, for one visit is experience enough."

Too exhausted from the long day's travel to change to their nightgowns, the ladies removed their hoops and loosened the stays of their bodices. Slumped in the hard, uncomfortable wooden chairs, their heads pillowed in their arms on the table, Rorie and Mary drifted into uneasy slumber.

Rorie had no idea what time it was when she first became aware of raucous laughter drifting up from the taproom below. The candle had gone out, and the room was shrouded in blackness. For a moment she didn't know where she was, for the waning moon provided very little light.

"Mary," she called.

"I hear them," Mary responded uneasily. "Who do you think they are?"

"Most likely a constable and his band patrolling for highwaymen," Rorie concluded, hoping that she sounded more convincing than she felt. " 'Tis a likely place hereabouts with all the woods—"

Both girls jumped, then, as Deveraux suddenly burst into the room. "Mary, get under the bed and don't make a sound, no matter what you hear," he ordered tersely.

Mary nodded dumbly and flew underneath the wood frame and low slung ropes. Rorie gasped as she felt herself being lifted up and shoved roughly onto the bed. It flashed through her mind that the captain had gone mad, and when his hand reached out to tumble her hair and to tear the top of her dress down the middle, she knew it for certain. It was the last straw, however, when he stripped off his vest and shirt, pushed her back against the dirty mattress, and fell on top of her.

Her rage knew no bounds as she thrashed and railed against this gross indignity. She had known the captain wasn't to be trusted, but that he was capable of this vile deed was something she had never credited to him. Momentarily nonplussed, she ceased her thrashing when he whispered low in her ear, "That's right, keep fighting." She was galvanized into action again, however, as he brought his mouth down hard against hers to smother her shrieks of unparalleled anger.

Just then the door was flung open, so hard, it crashed against the wall. A squat, ugly man appeared unsteadily in the doorway. Holding a dimly lit rush stick high, his eyes became glazed as they traveled from Rorie's pretty face alight with anger, fear, and astonishment, down to the creamy fullness of her breasts which peaked out from the torn bodice.

"Hey, Browne, how'd ye git here?" he demanded, his manner surly. "Thought Patrick sent ye up ta take care of the gent."

In a low, guttural tone, affecting the crude English drawl of the man, Deveraux said, "Oi did. Slit his throat, oi did, an' found this morsel in the bargain. Now leave off. Ye gits her when oi'm done."

Cameron held his breath, hoping the room was too dark and the thug too drunk to notice that aside from his dark hair and lean body, Deveraux bore little resemblance to the man's comrade. In fact, the thing's friend, Browne, lay dead in Deveraux's bed. In the end, it was Rorie who was the deciding factor. From the moment the robber had spotted her, his eyes never left her, and his dull mind, besotted with liquor, held no room for any other thoughts except the obvious.

Swaying precariously, holding onto the doorframe for support, the man grinned lewdly with great expectations. "When ye be done, Browne?"

Cameron shrugged, carefully averting his face. "Oi'm done when oi'm done."

Disgruntled, the thief turned to leave when a thought suddenly came to him. "Hey, Bigelow says there was two women up here." He lifted the light high to survey the room. "Where's the other one?"

"Purdy has her," mumbled Deveraux, praying that he had overheard the man's name correctly during his eavesdropping.

"Purdy!" exploded the thug. "That bloody bastard. He promised me first crack hereon. The wenches ain't good fer nothin' when he's had done with 'em. Near ta kills 'em he does. Waits 'til oi gets me hands on tha' bloody liar. Oi'll shows 'im tha' Billy Smyte be one ta reckon with."

Smyte's colorful expletives followed him down the hallway as he staggered off in search of Purdy, all thoughts of Rorie forgotten with the vile infraction of a robber's code.

Immediately Cameron jumped up and closed the door, as Mary rolled out from under the bed, dirty and frightened.

When Cameron reached over and yanked Rorie to her feet, she blustered. "What the devil do you think you're doing—"

"Trying to save your bloody life, though I can't think why," he snapped impatiently.

"Who are these men?" Mary asked fearfully, as renewed shouts and laughter reached their ears.

" 'Tis Patrick O'Malley and his band of cut-throats." Deveraux had decided that the ladies might move faster if they knew the truth of the situation. "They use this inn as a way station on their travels throughout the countryside."

The color drained from both girls' faces. They had read about the shocking Strowbridge incident in the London papers. After brutally raping the young daughter of a prominent family, the band had slit her throat, as well as those of the other family members, and burned the house to the ground. Among the highwaymen of the day, O'Malley was by far the most callous and feared.

"We must be quick now, before that drunken fool finds his friend, Purdy," warned Deveraux slipping on his shirt and vest.

Rorie mentally grasped for straws. "What about the guards? They can help us."

"The driver is dead, and I earlier sent the guards on to Drumfielde to raise the alarm."

"All three of them!" exclaimed Rorie with a hint of censure in her voice.

"This is an area rich with highwaymen, Miss Shelbourne," Cameron responded curtly. "I figure three men have a better chance than one of getting through."

"What shall we do, Captain?" asked Mary in alarm.

"You'll have to ride a horse, so take off the petticoats."

Rorie watched in wide-eyed astonishment, as the usually demure Mary scrambled to do his bidding without question and with no thought to modesty. Biting her lip uncertainly, Rorie looked up, then, to find Cameron glaring at her.

"Well, turn around," she said crossly. If this was a trick, she would see the knave drawn and quartered.

"Get moving, Miss Shelbourne!" barked Cameron. "Or I shall see the job done myself."

Rorie flinched. In the darkness she couldn't see his face that clearly, but she knew by the tone of his voice that he meant it. Her fingers flew under her skirt and fumbled to untie the myriad of strings which secured the undergarments. With an exasperated curse, Cameron whirled Rorie around. Throwing her skirt over her head, he unsheathed a knife from his waist and cut the offending ties with two quick swipes of the blade. When a mound of white satin and lace fell about her feet, Cameron lifted her up, kicked the garments out of the way, and propelled her to the door. A low gasp of indignation escaped her lips, but she said nothing.

Deveraux peered cautiously out the door before motioning for the girls to follow. "This way—down the back stairs."

As they slowly descended the narrow stairs, the din of ribaldry grew louder. The band, well plied with liquor, was now clearly out of control. The little group had to pass by the opening to the taproom to get to the back door, and Cameron quickly calculated their chances. Timing would be everything, and heaven knows they didn't have much of that left. Any moment now, Browne's body might be discovered, or the ladies could be found missing. In spite of the seriousness of the moment, Deveraux allowed himself the luxury of a smile as he imagined the confrontation between Purdy and the drunken

Smyte. Judging the moment to be right then, he shoved Mary across the opening so forcefully, she fell in a heap on the other side, unmindful of the bruises and grateful that she hadn't been detected.

As Rorie awaited her turn, high pitched screams caught her attention, and, in spite of Deveraux's warnings, she looked into the room to see Betty being passed from one degrading brute to another, her clothes in such tatters as to afford no covering at all. Rorie's heart went out to the maiden, and, once again, the past which had haunted her consciousness for so many years became intertwined with the present. Rorie was aware of nothing else except that this time she had to act.

"Stop!" she screamed, hardly aware that she had even spoken, and she struggled against Deveraux's tightened grasp to run to Betty's aid.

Deveraux yanked her out of sight, scarcely able to believe what had just happened and praying that no one had seen or heard her above the noisy confusion. But he hoped in vain. The room grew deathly silent as the cutthroats glanced up in stunned amazement to catch sight of Rorie in the doorway.

"Hey, 'tis the woman. Browne must be done with her," shouted one. And the men, roughly ten in number, bolted toward them.

As Rorie snapped out of her daze, suddenly realizing the consequence of her actions, Deveraux scooped her up and shouted for Mary to run for the back door. Out in the yard, a boy nervously held two bridled horses. Without ceremony, Cameron threw Rorie up on one and Mary up on the other.

"Cap'n—" The boy's eyes begged more eloquently than any words.

Cameron nodded. "Get on behind her," he said, indicating Mary, and he jumped up behind Rorie.

A frenzy of shots rang out as the robbers spilled out of the inn and ran for their horses to give hot pursuit.

"Circle around from the west," Deveraux shouted to the boy. "I'll come round from the east."

Her ankle throbbed as it dangled in midair and crashed against the side of the horse, but Rorie was barely conscious of the pain as they raced at breakneck speed to outdistance the gang. They seemed to ride forever, but in fact, were only minutes away from the inn as they circled completely around.

Presently they came to a mound covered with branches, ferns, and moss, deep in the woods. Rorie watched in curiosity as Deveraux climbed down from the horse and parted fronds, revealing the opening of a cleverly concealed hut. When he reached up to pull her roughly to the ground, she winced as her full weight fell upon the injured foot, and she pitched forward against him. He paid scant notice to her discomfort, though he took the time to steady her before driving off the horse. Rorie knew he was angry. She had felt it in the tenseness of his muscles and in the icy silence, but she didn't care.

As she turned to hobble into the hut, Cameron caught her by the arm and whirled her around to face him. "What the hell were you trying to do back there—get us killed?" he demanded. "If you don't care about yourself or me, have a care for Mary. Do you know how she would have faired in those cutthroats' hands!" His voice, although low, was edged with rage.

"You don't understand," said Rorie dispiritedly, slumping to the ground.

Deveraux was stupefied. The wench nearly spelled certain death for them all, and all she could offer by way of excuse or apology was that he didn't understand. His emotions running high as his mind freely imagined her at O'Malley's mercy, he furiously jerked Rorie to her feet, his hands firmly gripping her shoulders. He found her so exasperating, he wanted to throttle her. Instead, he kissed her with a savage intensity which stunned them both.

When Rorie stopped fighting him, the kiss became more a pleasure than a punishment. Remembering her reaction to their last encounter, however, Deveraux moved slowly with her, the master of seduction. And instead of the revulsion and fear that she had expected to feel, Rorie knew only a delightful, heady sensation as his lips trailed a fiery course down the column of her neck to linger teasingly in the hollow between her breasts. Indeed, she was only dimly aware when he lowered her to the pine-covered ground.

As his lips returned to capture her mouth and his tongue began to explore its sweet inner recesses, Rorie gasped. Her last defense crumbled when his hand unobtrusively brushed aside the tatters of her torn gown to cup a soft, rounded breast, and to rhythmically rub a taut nipple between his thumb and forefinger. She had never been kissed or touched like this before, and, floating upon a gentle wave of oblivion, Rorie was powerless to resist the force of his desire or the strength of his virility.

As his hand then moved slowly down her leg and under her skirt with exacting thoroughness and exquisite torment, Rorie began to respond with an urgency of her own. Suddenly, the crackle of underbrush catapulted them both to reality, shattering the magic of the moment.

"Captain—Rorie?" Mary called softly through the night.

Deveraux's tensed body relaxed, and he cursed under his breath as he reluctantly released Rorie and helped her to her feet. "Next time, Rorie—" he murmured huskily, cupping her chin and kissing her lightly. "And there *will be* a next time." It wasn't merely a statement, but a promise.

Dazedly, Rorie straightened her clothing as Mary and the boy materialized from the shadows. She was deeply thankful for the darkness that hid the shame and guilt now flooding her consciousness. What had come over her? How could she have let him touch her like that and, worse yet, respond like some common harlot? The question which haunted her most, however, was why hadn't she fought him? If they hadn't been interrupted, only a fool would have to guess what might have followed. Never again, she vowed grimly. Never again would she allow herself to be placed to that disadvantage, for she would never consent to be ruled by any man's hand, emotionally or otherwise.

"Captain, thank God you found out about those men in time. Rorie and I owe you a great debt," Mary cried breathlessly as she stumbled toward the couple. She attributed the tension in the air to the danger of their plight.

"The debt belongs to Robin, here, and Betty," Cameron replied, hurriedly ushering everyone into the small hut.

"Betty?" questioned Rorie softly, unable to stop thinking of the poor girl.

"She is Robin's sister. She warned me that the ale was drugged."

"But Rorie and I drank it," said Mary.

" 'Twas me Bigelow wanted out of the way. You ladies he wanted full of spirit for his 'guests,' " Deveraux said tightly, his anger still close to the surface. "When we retired for the evening, Robin was waiting for me in my room to explain the whole situation. He showed me the hut, and we planned to hide everyone here, but by the time Robin and I had returned to the inn, it was too late. O'Malley and his band were arriving, and our driver was already dead. 'Twas luck that we had dispatched the guards to Drumfielde beforehand. While I was making my way to you ladies, Browne came upon on me, and my intended fate became his own."

Rorie was instantly contrite as she shamefully recalled how she had misinterpreted poor Betty's warning as an invitation of pleasure to Deveraux.

"Robin, why haven't you and Betty left?" Mary asked gently.

Robin cast his eyes to the floor. "Beggin' yer pardon, miss, we've tried to run away, but Bigelow always found us an' the beatin's was worse each time."

"You could have approached one of the passengers for help and left with one of the coaches," suggested Rorie.

"I think Robin is trying to tell us that no one leaves the Houndstooth—alive," Deveraux broke in solemnly. "Isn't that right, Robin?"

Robin nodded, struggling to choke back the tears of a young boy who had lived with fear, death, and violence for far too long. His thin shoulders trembled, and he sniffed audibly, wiping his nose with the back of his hand. "Betty an' me tried ta warn the others, but none would listen. Betty said as how ye was our last hope."

"How old are you and Betty?" Cameron prodded quietly.

"Fourteen, sir. Betty be eighteen."

"Why don't you tell us everything, Robin."

With tears coursing down his cheeks, Robin recounted a tale of horror. He told of how coaches were lured to the inn, how the men were drugged while the women were beaten and raped. All "guests" were finally murdered and buried on the grounds. The coaches were then burned as the robbers split up the passengers' belongings.

"Our pa was dead an' ma was dyin', so she was sendin' Betty an' me ta a uncle in the north. Our stage put in here for the night an—" His voice broke, and it was few minutes before he was able to continue. "Betty was real purty then, an' O'Malley liked her. Bigelow needed a serving wench an' an ostler he could control, or else we'd a been killed, too. I wished we had been. We been waitin' fer someone like you, Cap'n, to come along fer four years." Robin sniffed again and self-consciously brushed some tears away. "When O'Malley, Bigelow and the others is full enou' of drink, Betty slips a powder inta their cups an' we come here til they all leaves in the morn. This be an ol' poacher's hut. I found it a few years back. 'Tis where we dress our wounds an' dream of leavin' this hell. We thought ta swallow a poison once, but Betty said as how we had ta stay alive long enou' ta see tha' Bigelow pays fer his deeds."

Mary and Rorie were aghast, and they shuddered as the full realization of what their fate might have been, and could still very well be, preyed upon their minds. Robin reminded Rorie of Terence, so young and vulnerable, and she moved to comfort him, but Cameron put a hand on her arm, forestalling her. She understood then that even young boys had their pride and most especially those who have experienced the horrors that Robin had, for pride was all that was left to him.

"Upon my word, Robin, you and your sister shall see this business ended soon," Deveraux said firmly.

Suddenly, Rorie and Mary started. They sucked in their breaths as they heard the beating of bushes nearby. The pounding of horses hooves upon the ground soon matched the pounding of their hearts, as shouts went up and pistols were discharged.

Deveraux and Robin glanced at each other. "They must have found our horses," Cameron surmised quietly.

"Cap'n, the ground still be soft from the rains. They'll find our tracks for certain at the first light." Robin tried to keep the panic from his voice, but had little success.

Deveraux nodded, his brow furrowed in consternation and thought. Taking note of the lanterns winking in the distance as the gang moved back toward the Houndstooth, he observed, "They'll more than likely return to the inn until dawn. We'll have to make our move before then." They no longer had the time to wait for reinforcements from Drumfielde. Besides, there was no guarantee that the guards had made it through, and there was every possibility that they might have run into O'Malley on the way. "Come with me, Robin. We'll have to return to the tavern to see what can be done." Drawing out a pistol, Cameron handed it to Rorie. "Can you use this?"

Rorie had never held a pistol in her life and the metal felt cold, heavy, and awkward in her hand, but she nodded with no hint of uncertainty. She would do what she had to do.

"Good. If you need to use it, hold it at arm's length, and don't forget to cock the bloody thing. And stay here!" he warned severely, fully acquainted with Rorie's willful character.

"Captain," Mary called, "God be with you."

There was the sound of brush being pushed aside and carefully replaced, and then Rorie and Mary were alone in the dark cavelike dwelling.

Time dragged on, seemingly endless, though in fact, only one hour had passed. Rorie and Mary sat huddled together upon the hard, dirt floor, slumped against the earthern wall, their emotions drained, but every sense alert to the slightest sound. Their nerves were stretched to the breaking point, and they were much too frightened to even speculate. Indeed, it was too much of an effort to speak. Why was it so quiet?

Another half hour had passed, when Rorie suddenly jumped to her feet as a faint rumbling sound reached her ears.

"Mary, do you hear it?" she cried. Both girls nearly jumped out of their skin when there followed an outbreak of blood curdling screams, shouts, and pistol shots. They covered their ears and shut their eyes tightly against the din which raged just a hundred and fifty feet away.

When the noise had subsided, Rorie peered through an opening in the brush, but could see nothing. "Mary, I've got to see what's happening."

"No! Captain Deveraux said to wait here," insisted Mary, grabbing Rorie by the arm.

"He and Robin are just two against ten. The gang could be following our tracks to this hut right now. We'd be trapped, Mary—"

Rorie's voice trailed off, and Mary's eyes flew open in alarm. They both heard it. Masculine voices and the snap of twigs under heavy boots punctuated the blackness of the night.

"Oh, Rorie, what will we do?" whispered Mary, panic-stricken. "You know what those men will do if they catch us."

"Not without a fight," Rorie responded fiercely. "Here take this." And she shoved a length of board, which Robin and his sister had been using for a table, into Mary's trembling hands. Dear God, what had happened to Deveraux!

Rorie had no idea how she had gotten there, but she found herself positioned squarely in front of the opening of the hut. Mary gasped. And at the sound of brush being pushed aside, Rorie cocked the pistol and raised her arm in readiness to shoot. Her knees were shaking and her heart fluttered wildly, but as she caught sight of a figure bending to enter, Rorie shut her eyes and squeezed the trigger.

The blast was deafening, and the pistol recoiled over her head, nearly throwing her backwards. In the next instant, as she struggled to regain her balance, the weapon was knocked from her grasp with a force that sent a numbing sensation from her hand up to her shoulder. Before she could react, her back was crushed against a rock hard chest, a heavy arm looped tightly around her throat.

"Captain Deveraux, 'tis you!" Mary sobbed, collapsing against a wall with relief.

Rorie stiffened, the weakness in her knees evaporating as her anger overrode her fear for the moment. Breaking free of his grasp, Rorie rounded on Cameron in a furious flash of temper.

"What the devil are you trying to do! Scare us to death?" she shrieked, rubbing her bruised neck.

"*Me!*" he exploded. "You nearly blew my damned head off!"

"Well, why didn't you announce yourself!"

"This isn't exactly a soiree, Miss Shelbourne! How was I to know if, in the confusion, one of the robbers had escaped to find his way here."

"Captain Deveraux, what has happened?" called Lord Dandridge anxiously from outside.

Rorie and Mary looked at each other in shocked surprise when they recognized the earl's voice.

"It's over," Cameron explained to the girls as he waved an all clear sign to the rescue party. "The guards I dispatched ran into Lord Dandridge as he was leaving Balfour Grange for Marwynde. He gathered together some men and arrived just in time to lend Robin and me a hand. Bigelow and O'Malley are dead, and we think we've gotten the rest, as well."

"What of Robin and Betty?" asked Rorie.

"Lord Dandridge has taken charge and sent them ahead to Marwynde to recover. They've both been sorely used and shall require a physician's hand for a time."

As the little group was anxious to leave the Houndstooth Inn far behind, horses were quickly hitched to the coach, which had been hidden behind the stable. Drained of strength and spirit, Rorie and Mary stretched out on the cushioned seats and soon fell into deep slumber. Rorie had wanted adventure in her life, but this, this went well beyond the bounds of reasonable expectations. She was ready to submit to the quietude of Drumfielde—at least for the time being.

14

Rorie stared at herself in the floor length mirror, unable to believe that the image reflected there was really her. She studied the graceful lines of her gown, as she ran her hand reverently over the deep green figured silk which was trimmed in pale green and silvery-gray ribbon. The decolletage, she noted with some discomfort, was very wide and deep, exposing an enticing amount of creamy flesh above high, rounded breasts. However, the close fitting, long-waisted bodice which accentuated her tiny waist, made even smaller by the stiff, uncomfortable whalebone stays, met with her distinct approval. At the back of the gown, full lengths of pale green, pleated silk flowed from shoulder to hem, and the green, silk ruched ribbon edged with silver satin and lace added just the right touch to her elbow-length sleeves. A ruff of peach-colored frilling and silver satin ribbon encircled her long, lovely neck to complete the striking portrait.

She would never be comfortable in these

ridiculous hoops and stays and, once again, cursed the conventions of a society which demanded them. But she could certainly become accustomed to the richly made gowns, she conceded. Never in all her dreams had she ever considered a wardrobe of such splendor. And she couldn't resist fingering the lush, delicate material of her gown. It was simply made by the standards of the day, but as the dressmaker had pointed out, it was the very simplicity of the gown which accentuated and complemented her natural beauty. The color was chosen to reflect the deep emerald-green of her eyes and to heighten the golden sheen of her hair, which had been styled into a small pompadour and set off with a pompon of peach-colored flowers with silver leaves.

As tonight was the betrothal ball at Lyndeforde, Rorie was in a festive mood. Laughingly she twirled about the room in the arms of an imaginary dance partner, stopping only to lift her voluminous skirts to view the exquisite court slippers of silver brocade. She mustn't forget her reason for being here, she instantly chided herself, remembering Drumfielde's plight. But she couldn't resist wiggling her toes in childish delight, grateful that Madame du Vronnet's many assistants had been able to complete the gown before Rorie had left London. A shadow crossed her face at the thought of London. It was a memory that she was anxious to leave behind. She still had nightmares of the Houndstooth Inn, and Captain Cameron Deveraux was definitely one person she wanted to forget. Impatiently, she picked up her matching fan and cloak and swept from the room to join Mary in her chambers.

The maid was putting the finishing touches to Mary's hair when Rorie entered the room. Mary's eyes grew wide with admiration.

"Oh, Rorie, you look so lovely! You shall surely be the most beautiful woman there. Perhaps the duke shall marry you, instead."

"Nonsense." Rorie laughed. "You have a beauty all your own. I see you have chosen the purple and lavender gown. It is very becoming."

"Yes, you were right. 'Tis a color better suited to me, and I like the new hairstyle you have suggested. Rorie, I must tell you what a godsend you have been to me these past weeks—and to mother. She looks forward to your visits each day. You are like a sister to me. These weeks have been the loveliest days of my life, in spite of our one misadventure." She shuddered slightly at the still-fresh memory of their narrow escape from the highwaymen. Mary was so thankful to be alive that not even marriage to the duke could dim her newfound enthusiasm for life.

"You and the squire have been most generous to me, Mary."

Mary giggled. "Even if Father doesn't yet know the extent of his generosity. But no matter, with you by my side, I no longer fear the future."

The two girls descended the stairs arm in arm. Waiting impatiently at the bottom, wearing a bright blue suit which only served to emphasize his ever expanding waistline, the squire bellowed the arrival of the carriage.

It was a lovely evening, one made for magic and fantasy, and the girls felt their excitement rise as the carriage covered the short distance to Lyndeforde. The squire did not cease his obvious gaping of the young ladies. He had not paid much attention to his daughter over the years, and, though she would never be a beauty in the sense of the word as he understood it, there was, nevertheless, a new dimension to her which he had never noticed before.

It was the Shelbourne girl, however, who really gave him a turn. Appropriately dressed and coiffed, she presented an arresting picture of a proper lady of breeding. The tilt of her head gave her an air of assurance, which he knew to be genuine, and her classic features were at once commanding and alluring from the pert, upturned nose to the sensuality of her full, pink lips. Indeed, he might think of marrying the chit himself, once his own ailing wife has succumbed, he concluded in amazement. For an old dog, he still had a few tricks left.

Rorie was mesmerized by the grandeur of the grounds as the carriage wended its way up the hill along a broad, gently curving corridor of towering oaks. They passed stylized trees and a symmetrical waterfall, surrounded by lovely alabaster statues inspired by Greek mythology, before coming to a halt beneath a stone arched entryway. Footmen in powdered wigs and gold satin suits met them with torches held aloft to light the way up the steps.

Although she had never been inside Lyndeforde, Rorie had always admired its majestic beauty from the road as it set proudly on the hill. But she had never expected the opulent splendor that presented itself to her eyes. She drew in her breath at the huge, white columns and the large gold-framed landscapes which lined the walls. And she was captivated by centuries of ancestoral portraits, their eyes seeming to follow her progress through the wide, marble hallway to the ballroom. All of the chandelier candles had been lit, and each room was alive in a blaze of light, so that the high, beautifully painted ceilings and delicate plasterwork were well displayed. Doors and windows had been opened wide to catch the gentle, spring breeze and to stir the refreshing fragrance of the hundreds of fresh-cut flowers placed strategically throughout.

Etiquette called for the duke to greet his guests. Given the circumstances, however, everyone forgave his absence, for the duke was preparing to have his first meeting with his betrothed in a private parlor off the ballroom prior to the start of the ball.

As the squire, Rorie, and Mary approached the ballroom, a servant arrived to escort Mary to the prearranged meeting. Rorie gave her a reassuring squeeze and, with a baleful look, Mary followed the servant down the hall. The few guests who were not staying at Lyndeforde were arriving from neighboring estates, each matron casting Rorie a suspicious eye after noticing the direction of her husband's gaze. Uncomfortably aware of the interest she was stirring, Rorie gratefully accepted Squire Balfour's arm.

As she was led into the ballroom, the splendor of the room with its hundreds of lighted candles, its huge floral arrangements, and its food-laden tables of every delicacy rendered her speechless. The musicians began to play, and Rorie was struck by the vivid array of every color of the spectrum as guests, dressed in all of their splendid finery, mingled freely about.

She felt as though she were in a dream.

The squire had assumed an air of importance and the demeanor of a protective bulldog, as he strutted about the room with Rorie on his arm, making introductions. While Rorie was immensely enjoying the moment, she decidedly was not enjoying Squire Balfour's advances. Clumsy though they were, the intent was not to be mistaken. She particularly resented the way he discouraged other young men from approaching her. She didn't know what information he was giving out, but it was enough to turn the young gentlemen on their heels in the opposite direction. Several times she cast uneasy glances toward the entrance, praying for Mary's quick return. At last she was able to divert the squire's attention to the food. He had been reluctant to leave her, but eventually the growling of his belly and the temptation of the vast delicacies conspired to weaken his resolve, and he ambled off to one of the tables. Rorie was beginning to feel a little out of place, when she saw a familiar figure approaching.

"Miss Shelbourne, I could scarce believe my eyes 'twas you," said Lord Dandridge with a smile of genuine affection. "You are so lovely, I daresay you are the envy of every woman here."

"Not every woman, Robert," came a low, sultry voice from behind.

Rorie turned to see that a stunning woman, some years older than herself, had joined them. Her stylish and daringly low cut gown of gold and rose silk brocade further heightened the exotic features. Although her hair was powdered and swept up into a very high pompadour, Rorie guessed that the woman's tresses were as dark as her black, kohl-rimmed eyes.

A shadow of aversion crossed the earl's noble features as he regarded his wife. Two years after his beloved first wife had died, he had married Eleanora—much to his everlasting regret. Perhaps it had been too much to hope that Eleanora would be the mother that his little daughter had needed. In any case, after three-year-old Aurora had disappeared from Marwynde one day so many years ago, and he could no longer bear to remain on the estate, Eleanora had made her position quite clear. She would remain at Marwynde, where she had free rein to entertain her gentlemen friends without censure, the earl had later bitterly ascertained. But what did it matter? Without his Aurora, he was a sad and broken old man with nothing to offer a young and vibrantly beautiful wife. Theirs was a marriage of convenience now, and it was quite enough that he saw her only when he made his quarterly inspection of the estate.

"Miss Shelbourne," said the earl tensely, "I should like you to make the acquaintance of my wife, Lady Eleanora Dandridge."

"I am pleased to make your acquain—" Rorie started to say when Lady Dandridge cut her off abruptly.

"So this is the sickly young woman you were carrying on about, Robert. I'm afraid my husband did not paint an accurate portrait of you, Miss Shelbourne. By his account, you were much the worse for your harrowing experiences." Eleanora's glittering eyes raked Rorie from head to toe, noting the healthy glow of youth and envying the lovely, flattering folds of her exquisite gown. "Wherever did you find that unfortunate gown, my dear? I'm sorry to say that it doesn't suit you at all, much too plain. You really ought to see a couturiere in London or Paris." She smiled slyly.

"Eleanora!" exclaimed Lord Dandridge, astounded by his wife's rudeness.

But Rorie was not to be outdone. "How unfortunate, Lady Dandridge, that you so seldom leave the countryside you don't recognize a gown of the latest fashion when you stand before one," she interjected smoothly, while inwardly she smoldered with rage at the older woman's audacity. "You see, Madame du Vronnet, herself, designed this gown for me."

Lady Eleanora nearly gagged on the snide retort she was about to make. Madame du Vronnet was London's leading couturiere, with an inside line to the latest fashions in Paris. Her clientele was as illustrious as her outlandish prices, and Eleanora had tried unsuccessfully for several months to secure an appointment with the imperious designer. She looked at Rorie in amazement, forgetting her animosity for the moment.

"Pray tell, Miss Shelbourne, how is it that the untitled companion to a squire's daughter managed to secure an appointment with Madame du Vronnet, when the wife of an earl could not?"

Rorie shrugged matter-of-factly. "I suppose the fact that Miss Balfour is betrothed to the duke carries some privilege. And then, of course, Lord Dandridge graciously lent his support."

Eleanora swung snapping, black eyes upon her husband. "Robert!" she cried shrilly. "How could you speak to Madame du Vronnet on *her* behalf, only to say nothing for your own wife.

You know how I have tried to secure an interview with that woman!"

"You never asked, Eleanora," Lord Dandridge replied simply.

Eleanor looked as though she wanted to claw her husband's eyes out. Seeking to discharge the potentially explosive atmosphere of the moment, Lord Dandridge turned to Rorie. "You will be interested to know, Miss Shelbourne, that Robin and Betty are recovering nicely and shall soon be traveling to their uncle in the north. He is a leading merchant in the town and, by all accounts, will do well by them. I mean to see that they get there this time."

Lady Eleanora turned away, her features twisted with anger. It was bad enough that he had brought those two common brats back to Marwynde to recover, ruining her social life for weeks. But this—failing to intercede on her behalf to the famed seamstress—was his greatest injustice to date.

She fanned herself furiously while scanning the guests for possible conquests. Her fluttering motion came to an abrupt halt, however, as her eyes came to rest on a tall, dark man on the far side of the room. Plainly but strikingly attired in blue and gray silk, his black, wavy hair pulled back in the fashion of the day, the man seemed oblivious to the surrounding throng of admiring females as instead, he studied her little group as intently as she studied him. Even in a crowd his presence commanded notice, and a thrill of excitement coursed through Eleanora as she noted the breadth of his shoulders and could well imagine the strength of his muscular thighs beneath the close fitting breeches.

She tapped her husband on the shoulder with her fan, interrupting him yet again. "Robert, who is that man over there near the fruit table? The very tall one?" she asked, throwing the stranger a coquettish smile.

"Oh, that is Captain Deveraux," Lord Dandridge said. As Rorie looked up, she found her eyes locked with Cameron's hypnotic gaze. He nodded, and that infuriating half grin on his face told her that he was remembering the intimacy they had shared on that desperate night when they had fled the highwaymen. She flushed crimson at the memory of his touch, which was still all too vivid, in spite of her determination to forget it.

The smile faded from Eleanora's rouged lips as she realized that it was not she who was eliciting a response from this handsome stranger. Her eyes narrowed in suspicion when she turned to see the disconcerted look on Rorie's blushing face. "Are you two acquainted?" she demanded curtly.

" 'Twas the captain who treated Miss Shelbourne's injury and who rescued her and Miss Balfour from those cutthroats, my dear," explained the earl.

Lady Dandridge looked from the captain to Rorie once again, before hastily excusing herself and making her way across the room. Immediately thereafter, Rorie was beseiged by her own group of admirers when the young men noted the absence of her protector. Her attention was soon captured as she wittily paried their double entendres and laughed along with them at their ridiculous posturings and outlandish antics. All thought of Deveraux and Lady Dandridge faded away.

At length, the duke entered the room with Mary on his arm to the blasting of trumpets and a round of vigorous applause. Nervousness and uncertainty flitted across Mary's pale, delicate features as she bravely sought to meet the moment, and Rorie's heart went out to her. She was reminded of a lamb being led to the wolf's den. Rorie tried to infuse some of her strength into Mary with a broad, reassuring grin when their eyes met, but Mary could only answer her with a wan smile. Rorie could easily guess her friend's misery.

This was the first glimpse of the duke that Rorie had ever had, for he never showed himself in the village, usually preferring to have others do his dirty work, she thought, struggling to hide her anger. Fairly tall and lean, still possessed of his teeth, when viewed objectively, he wasn't a bad looking sort. But his manner of dress was severe, bringing to mind a stern, ill-humored schoolmaster. Anyone with half an eye could see that the smile was forced, a mockery of sincerity, barely softening the lines of his dark, hawklike features; the platitudes practiced, a thin veneer of deceit. And it positively infuriated her how he moved among his guests, demanding and receiving a fawning respect when all knew his true nature. It was as though by their presence alone, they all condoned his actions—she among them—and it was all Rorie could do to keep her silence.

In a far corner of the room, Cameron Deveraux was also fighting an overwhelming anger borne of his inability to act, as he, too, observed the grand entrance of the duke and his betrothed. Here he stood, expected to join the crowd in spewing accolades to a man upon whom he had sworn vengeance. Instead, he wanted to jump to the fore and denounce him for the thieving murderer that he was.

"Hold fast, Cap'n, we'll get our chance."

Startled, Deveraux looked down to see his valet and friend by his side. Due to a shortage of servants, Rawlings had been pressed into service. He had been circulating through the crowd with platters of hors d'oeuvres, when he'd recognized that familiar, intense look upon the captain's face and hurried to his side.

Cameron flashed a grin to the little man "You know me too well, Rawlings. But have no fear, for I've come too far to tip my hand now." His eyes returned to canvass the milling crowd with renewed interest, his temper defused for the moment.

"The li'l lady be off ter yer right now, Cap'n," Rawlings said with a chuckle before sidling off to move among the guests.

"Ye be too big for yer britches, mate," Deveraux called after him good-naturedly, affecting Rawlings's brogue. And he looked to that direction in time to catch a flash of golden hair and a cloud of green silk behind a wall of young dandies. As a few of the men moved aside, Cameron was once again afforded a full view of Rorie's breathtaking loveliness. He couldn't help but smile, as he noted the haughty tilt of her head and the fixed, indulgent smile on her lips which had become so familiar to him in the last days of their journey from London. Since coming to Lyndeforde, he had seen nothing of Rorie and had forgotten how truly beautiful she was.

Deveraux was about to cross the room to her, when he was intercepted by feminine wiles practiced at its best.

"Captain," said Eleanora, "I understand you are a hero."

"I fear, madam, then 'tis your understanding alone," replied Deveraux brusquely, eager to be on his way.

"Modest and handsome, too. Well, Captain, I can greatly appreciate the latter, but I have no use for the former."

"The lady is short on words and long on actions," observed Cameron, amusement lifting the corners of his mouth.

Eleanora shrugged. "For an action to take place, it needs be begun. You'll find, sir, that this lady does not wait patiently by."

Looking down into her dark, almond-shaped eyes, Cameron could easily read the invitation there. "And does this lady have a name?" he inquired, running his gaze over her in the way that Rorie always found so disconcerting.

Eleanora laughed throatily. "I fear you'll find the lady is a lady in title only. I am Lady Eleanora Dandridge."

"I see. Well, Lady Dandridge, there are those who will tell you that I am guilty of many dastardly acts, but I've made it a rule to never betray a friend or a man I respect. And I regard your husband in both lights. So I'm afraid that I cannot avail myself of your—charms. Now, if you'll excuse me, I have another matter to attend to across the room."

Eleanora felt as though she had been dashed with cold water and, seeing the dismissal in his silvery blue eyes as she followed his gaze to

Rorie, it took every ounce of her fortitude to mask her rage and indignation.

"Then perhaps you would sign my dance card, Captain," she asked with forced casualness.

Absently, Cameron signed her card, and Eleanora departed with decorum, playing her most difficult role. We shall see, Captain, she thought to herself, we shall see who has the greater strength.

Deveraux was nearly across the floor when Roger Thornton and Mary approached Rorie. He knew Rorie was being formally acknowledged as companion to the future duchess, a mere formality, and so it was with astonishment that he observed her shocked reaction when the duke spoke to her. The duke, however, appeared to find nothing unusual in her response, and the entourage soon moved on.

With grave curiosity, Deveraux then watched Rorie skirt the crowd to slip away unnoticed to the balcony. And he slowly wended his own way through the throng of gaily clad guests to follow her.

He had nearly reached the French doors leading to the balcony, when Lady Peprell descended upon him in all her generous bulk and jewels. She twittered on about her travels until he thought he would go mad, his one eye on the door watching for Rorie. At last, Lady Peprell reluctantly released her victim, but not before Cameron had promised to lead her out for the next minuet. When Cameron finally reached the open doorway to the balcony, he was surprised to hear weeping.

Rorie's mind was a jumble of torturous memories revived by a voice from the past she had vowed never to forget. When the duke had spoken to her, recognition had dawned, and she had been conscious of nothing but a sickness in the pit of her stomach and an overwhelming need to escape his presence. And now, scenes of that brutal past event she had so desperately sought to forget, scrolled freely across her consciousness in ugly, vivid detail. She felt powerless to do anything but sob amid her misery.

She had been thirteen at the time and was gathering berries and nuts in the woods, when she heard a horse crashing through the underbrush and the frenzied approach of baying hounds. Frightened, she had just hidden herself behind a fallen log when a young maiden broke into the clearing, screaming hysterically. Within seconds, the hounds had been upon the terrified girl, and Rorie had been about to leave her hiding place to help when a nobleman arrived to beat back the dogs.

Realizing how defenseless she would have been against a pack of dogs with the scent of bloodlust in their nostrils, Rorie was blessing his timely arrival when a high-pitched, piercing scream and raucous, masculine laughter brought her attention back to the scene. Shocked beyond her senses, unable to move, she had watched in helpless revulsion as the man grabbed the girl and ripped the clothes from her body. Rorie had covered her ears, but it hadn't shut out the maid's heartrending pleas for help as the man then threw her to the ground and fell on top of her.

Never had she witnessed or ever imagined such a violent, callous disregard of a woman by a man before, and Rorie could stand no more. Picking up a log, she ran from her cover to beat the stunned assailant about the back and shoulders. But instead of discouraging the man, she only succeeded in enraging him, and, with a backward lash of his arm, he had sent Rorie crashing against a tree. She had lost consciousness to shrill screams and bawdy jeers as the man continued to ruthlessly sate his lust on the young servant girl.

When Rorie had opened her eyes again, the man was gone from the clearing, and the girl was staring sightlessly up at the sky. She was so still that, for a moment, Rorie had feared her dead. Slowly and painfully, her head aching abominably, Rorie had crept to the maiden. The girl's cheek was discolored and would soon be swollen, and Rorie recoiled in horror at the ugly purple bruises, teeth marks and welts which covered the girl's neck and breasts. Unmindful of the cold, she had taken her own worn cloak from about her shoulders and gently covered the poor maiden. Suddenly, the girl's entire body had begun to shake and heave with deep, soulful sobs. Not knowing what else to do, Rorie had put her arms around the maiden and held her until she had quieted. No words had been spoken. None were needed. At length the girl, grimacing with pain and clutching the cloak tightly about her, had slowly moved to stand with Rorie's help.

"What is yer name, li'l one?" she had asked hoarsely.

"Rorie. Rorie Shelbourne."

"Thank ye, Rorie. I shall ne'er forget yer kindness."

Rorie had never seen the girl again, nor had she ever spoken of the incident to anyone. So great had been her guilt at not being able to help the maiden, she had withdrawn into a confused and angry state. Those who knew her ebullient and free-spirited nature had become quite alarmed by her sober manner. Several months later, when she had finally been able to come to grips with her inner turmoil, Rorie had emerged from her cocoon with an unshakable and fiery determination to relinquish control to no man.

Rorie had not clearly seen the face of the assailant, but never would she forget the chilling nasal voice of the man who had committed that dastardly deed. And now, he had an identity. He was the duke of Lyndeforde. Oh, dear God, how could she let Mary become tied to that monster, knowing what foul deeds he was capable of? But what could she do? To tell Mary the truth would only cause the girl more needless heartache, for servant girls were taken advantage of by their employers every day, and it was doubtful that it would be considered an offense great enough for the squire to break the betrothal. Besides, it would be the word of a village peasant against that of a duke on an incident that had occurred over six years ago. What could she do?

"May I offer some assistance?"

Rorie jumped at the low, all too familiar voice from behind. Quickly she wiped the tears from her cheeks with the back of her hand. The oddly vulnerable childlike action, moved Deveraux to take her in his arms and console her. But the tone of her voice checked him.

"I don't remember requesting your company," she said tartly.

"And I don't remember asking you," he shot back crisply. "Truth is, I saw that you were distressed, and I came out here to offer my assistance. But—"

"Psst, Rorie, Rorie!"

Both Cameron and Rorie looked over to the balcony doors in surprise to find Mary frantically signaling Rorie's attention.

"I believe you are being beckoned, Miss Shelbourne," remarked Cameron dryly. He leaned back against the balcony wall, obviously of no mind to leave.

With an indignant huff at the rude man, Rorie stormed over to her friend.

"Mary, what is it?" she asked as Mary pulled her into the shadows.

"Oh, Rorie, I overheard the duke and his friend, Osborn, discussing plans. The duke is having your uncle arrested within the hour. The guards are to be ready to leave after the betrothal announcement."

"What! But why? Mary, are you sure you heard correctly?"

"Yes! He's being charged with the murder of the duke's emissary at the rebellion. Rorie, I think he means to hang your uncle."

The blow couldn't have been any more debilitating if it had been physical in nature, and Rorie reeled with the shock of it.

"There must be some mistake," she finally heard herself say. "The emissary was pelted by a few rocks, but he left the village alive. Oh, Mary, I must warn Uncle Will," she whispered urgently.

"I'll tell the duke that you aren't feeling well and had to return home," suggested Mary.

"I shall leave at once, then."

"No, wait!" cried Mary, yanking Rorie back. "You must have an escort," she said, lowering her voice as both became aware of Cameron's curious gaze on them. " 'Twill arouse less suspicion."

"But whom will I ask? I don't know anyone." As Rorie followed Mary's eye to Deveraux, she shook her head vehemently. "No!" she exclaimed flatly. "Never!"

" 'Tis either the captain or my father—"

"All right, all right. I'll ask the captain."

"Good. Now I must go, lest I arouse suspicion, myself. Luck be with you."

As Mary slipped away, Rorie struggled with the task at hand. "Captain," she began anxiously, "as it so happens, I am feeling unwell and do have a need to return to Balfour Grange forthwith."

"But of course. I'll convey your sentiments to the squire immediately, Miss Shelbourne," Cameron responded with deliberate obtusity.

"No, no!" she exclaimed hastily. "I—I don't wish to intrude upon the squire's evening."

Rorie bit her lip uncertainly, obviously fighting a battle within herself. If Deveraux was one of the last men she wanted to seek help from, the squire was absolutely *the* last person she wanted to be alone with in a dark carriage.

Deveraux smiled to himself as he readily guessed her quandary, but he refused to make it easy for her. And seeing that he wasn't about to volunteer his services, Rorie at last swallowed her pride.

"Wou—would you see me to the Grange, Captain?" she finally blurted out.

Looking down into her clear, luminous eyes, Deveraux could see the anxiety there. Likewise, the urgency in her voice hadn't escaped him. He bit back the sarcastic retort on the tip of his tongue. Her sweet vulnerability had pierced his hard shell, however slightly, and he could guess what it had cost her to make such a request of him. Suddenly, laughter and applause burst from the room. The betrothal announcement had been made.

"Please, please, you must help me to leave here—now!" she pleaded desperately.

Deveraux stared at her in bemusement. Was this the iron-willed chit who had given him such a fit for over a week in London, daring to spurn his every advance as though he were some callow country youth?

Just then the musicians broke into a minuet. Deveraux groaned as he heard Lady Peprell's loud, shrill voice seeking him out. Glancing through the doorway, he saw her approaching the balcony at a fast trot, nearly colliding with Lady Dandridge. As the two became engaged in heated debate, Deveraux remembered that he had also promised the first dance, though a minuet was not specified, to Lady Dandridge.

"God's teeth," he mumbled under his breath. Scooping up a shocked Rorie in his arms, he bounded down the stairs leading to the gardens and around to the front of the house. When a surprised liveryman had returned with the Balfour carriage, Rorie was shoved inside before she had time to protest her cavalier treatment.

"Was all that necessary?" she fumed, settling her wide skirts. "I requested an escort and a dignified departure, not a brigand and a hasty retreat. Why, I shall be regarded with great suspic—rudness now."

"Mary would never think ill of you, whatever the offense," retorted Deveraux as he swung himself in beside her. "And as to the others, I have the impression that you couldn't care a fig what any of them thought. And yes, you would think it necessary, were it you about to be caught between a whey-faced cow and a sharp-nailed siren."

Rorie had to laugh in spite of the anxiety she was feeling. It was a needed outlet, and her high, clear laughter reverberated musically throughout the carriage, as distinct images of Lady Peprell and Lady Dandridge stalking the hapless Captain Deveraux appeared in her mind's eye. She knew of whom he was speaking, for it was a very accurate description of those two ladies, and one which she had entertained herself. In any event, Rorie had no doubts as to the captain's ability to fend off enamored women.

Cameron had never heard her laugh before and found it to be delightful, but he couldn't help feeling a little indignant that it was at his expense. The arrogant, little chit could be a bit more understanding of his plight, he thought in annoyance. Almost as quickly as her infectious laughter had rung out, however, her mood changed, and she grew still and quiet, careful to keep her face averted from his searching eyes.

Cameron noted the way the light from the carriage lantern played upon her profile. The dimple at the corner of her mouth, the slightly up-turned nose, and tilted eyes lent her a certain impish charm, while the firm set of her chin and the proud cock of her golden head fought to give her an air of demure sophistication. Possessed of an earthy spirit and yet a noble grace, this lovely creature of such quick temper and quicksilver moods was a dichotomy unto herself. And she intrigued him as no other woman had. Suddenly, he was seized with the need to know everything about her. As he reached out to cup her chin, forcing her to meet his eyes, he was surprised by the raw tension he saw so vividly defined in every detail of her features before she knocked his hand away.

"Don't touch me!" she whispered in a desperate tone which further puzzled him. After that night at the hut, he thought he had stirred something in her—or had that all been just a part of her game?

The air had turned cooler, and, as Rorie began to shiver, she looked at Cameron accusingly.

"I know," he said, reading her thoughts. "If I had been more of a gentleman, I would have remembered your cloak."

He took off his coat and held it out to her, never even presuming to put it around her shoulders himself. As she looked from him to the coat uncertainly, Deveraux barked, "If you don't move to warm yourself with it, I shall do it for you. Unless you wish to lie abed with fever again—at the mercy of the squire," he added slyly.

Cameron chuckled, knowing that his remark had hit home, when Rorie suddenly grabbed the coat from him and hastily placed it around her shoulders.

"All right, Rorie, do you want to tell me what set you off back at Lyndeforde? I saw you fall apart after meeting the duke."

Rorie looked up at Deveraux sharply. Only once, at the hut, had he addressed her so familiarly, and she shifted uncomfortably beneath his shrewd and assessing gaze. Damn the man's eyes, she thought. They see everything.

"I don't know what you mean," she finally answered with an innocence that didn't ring true. "I am just not feeling well. And don't address me so intimately."

Deveraux gave a short, annoyed laugh. "Damn it, Rorie, after all we've been through, I deserve that much."

"You deserve my thanks, which you now have, and nothing more. After all, 'twas you who was the cause of my illness in the first place. If I hadn't had to worry myself over your boorish actions, I should never have twisted my ankle and fallen ill. And we wouldn't have had to put in at that horrible inn!"

At this point, the carriage had pulled up in front of Balfour Grange and Rorie, throwing Deveraux's coat at him, bounded from the carriage. Cameron had been so flabbergasted by her convoluted logic that he could only watch as she rushed up the stairs and into the house. She was positively the most contrary person he had ever encountered—with the possible exception of his grandfather. The deuced wench had to have a strong line of French in her ancestry, he concluded. He was equally as certain that her anxious reactions to the duke and to her whispered conversation with Mary on the balcony were related to two different events, and he meant to know of them both.

15

Rorie squirmed impatiently as the chambermaid, standing on a stool, slowly and carefully lifted the exquisite gown above her head, followed by the bell hoop.

"Hurry up, Mandy!" Rorie pleaded, already pulling at the multitudinous fastenings of petticoats and stays with a hopeless frustration. "Get me out of these things."

"Iffen we goes any faster, we'll jest end up with knots," the servant reminded her, stifling a yawn. "See here, we gots two already."

As the clock struck twelve, Rorie's patience was strained enough without the woman flitting about her. She had thought she would be able to change faster if she had some help and had awakened the maid allotted to her, but Mandy had four thumbs and, too late, Rorie realized her mistake. With one eye anxiously on the timepiece, she bit back a scream of sheer exasperation as the process seemed to go on forever.

"There ye be. 'Tis the last tie," stated Mandy triumphantly, standing back to survey her handiwork. And Rorie breathed a deep sigh of relief when the satin undergarments dropped to her ankles.

"No, no, Mandy, just leave the clothes."

"But, Miss—"

"I'll take care of them! I—I'm sorry, Mandy, I didn't mean to snap, but I'm not feeling well and want to be alone. You understand," said Rorie, taking the woman firmly by the arm and leading her to the door. "And, Mandy, I don't wish to be disturbed for any reason until tomorrow morning."

"Yes, Miss."

When Rorie was finally alone, she hurriedly pulled on a muslin shift, a dark-colored bodice and skirt, and a pair of worn shoes. She had no time for petticoats and stockings which would only hinder her progress anyway.

It was late and the servants would all be abed until the squire and Mary returned from the ball, so Rorie had no trouble sneaking out of the Grange unseen. Guided only by the moonlight, she stumbled several times on the deep ruts in the road, once tearing her skirt and scraping her knee. In the darkness, images and sounds took on a sinister hue, playing havoc with her frayed nerves. And at one point, she was certain she was being followed, but she refused to indulge in silly fantasies, determined to see her task done. When the Fenton farm came into view, Rorie laughed with relief and picked up her speed for the remaining distance.

"Terence, let me in!" she shouted, pounding on the door. Her knuckles were raw and bleeding from the splinters before she saw a light under the crack.

"Rorie! What the devil—" cried her brother in astonishment when he had opened the door and Rorie fell into his arms. Helping her inside, Terence stared at her in disbelief. Her hair had half escaped its pins and hung in a chaotic tangle of ringlets around her head, her face was smudged with dirt, and her torn skirt was stained with blood from the cut on her knee. "Dear God, what has happened to you!" he exclaimed in alarm. "Who did this to you!"

"No, I have not been attacked," Rorie gasped out breathlessly. "Terence, listen to me. The duke is sending guards to arrest Uncle Will. We've got to get him away. They'll be here any minute."

"What's that you say, lass?" demanded her uncle, suddenly appearing in the kitchen with Molly standing wide-eyed behind him.

Quickly, Rorie recounted the facts as she had heard them.

"I'll not run out like a fox from a hound!" declared Will resolutely. "I'm guilty of no such act, and my innocence will be proved."

"Will, ye must go," protested Molly. "Don't ye see, 'tis not a question of yer innocence. The duke means to hang ye pure and simple—"

"If he has to make his own truths to do it," finished Rorie soberly.

"I fear the lass is right, Will. Besides ye'll be no good to those who be countin' on ye with a rope 'round yer neck."

As he saw the truth in what Molly said, Will nodded his head in resignation. "Then 'tis done. I'll go. Terence, ready the horse."

While Molly threw food and clothes into an old sack, Will turned to Rorie.

"Ye've risked too much already comin' here tonight, lass. I don't want ye ta come 'round no more until things is settled."

"But Uncle Will—"

" 'Tain't likely that the duke knows of yer and Terence's connection ta me, an' 'tis safer fer ye ta keep it this way. If ye should be found out, ye must forsake us all."

"I can't denounce my family and friends!" exclaimed Rorie incredulously. "I won't! How could you ask me to do such a thing?"

"Heed my words, lass," her uncle warned sternly. "The duke's fury will be second to none when he learns I've made good an escape. If he kenna take a hand, he'll look ta the fingers. The squire has already claimed ye fer his relative, so he kenna say nothin' without riskin' his own hide, an' I'll wager tha' the knowledge lies safe enough with his daughter. The need may never arise, but ye must protect yourself as best ye ken."

Rorie nodded slowly in agreement, knowing in her heart that he was right. Suddenly Terence burst through the door.

"Uncle Will, I hear horses in the distance!"

Hastily, Will made his goodbyes. "Get word ta Rawlings tha' I ken be reached through the innkeep," he whispered to Molly.

In the next instant, he was gone. Minutes later they heard the clamor of horses and masculine voices outside, followed by a resounding pounding on the door.

" 'Tis the guards! Hurry, you must leave," whispered Molly, hustling Rorie through the dairy room."

"But what about you and Terence?" Rorie

asked frantically.

"They'll think nothing of an old woman and a 'foreman' in the house, but they kenna find you here. They'll know someone warned Will off, and 'twouldn't take the duke long ta remember ye was a guest in his house this night."

"Hurry!" called Terence from the kitchen. "They're about ready to break through the door."

Molly's quick embrace seemed so final, and Rorie fought the wave of emotions which threatened to tear them both apart as her aunt propelled her out the door. And with a last backward glance, Rorie was seized with a terrible sense of foreboding. Something told her that the storm had yet to wage its full force.

Rorie pressed herself tightly against the side of the cottage until she was sure that the way was clear. Then she darted into the barn. She had just closed the door and climbed up to the loft when she heard shouting and a pounding of feet in every direction. She guessed that her uncle's absence had been discovered, and that the guards were now searching the grounds.

Her heart suddenly jumped to her throat when the barn door squeaked open. Lowering herself on her stomach, she looked over the edge to see that a man suitably attired in the duke's crimson and black colors had entered.

"Can't see a bloody thing in here. Someone fetch a light," he yelled out impatiently. Picking up a pitchfork, he began to fork threw the hay. Before long, three others had arrived with a lantern.

"Hastings, you search the loft," ordered one.

Rorie scrambled back from the edge as she

heard a foot on the step. Why oh why hadn't she remembered to pull up the ladder! She was trapped, and the palms of her hands grew sweaty as she waited for a head to peer over the top to discover her.

Just then a shout went up from outside. "He's over here!" And there was a mad scramble as the man jumped off the ladder and the guards ran out of the barn.

Rorie's knees buckled under her, and she slid to the floor in relief. When she had marshaled her courage, she prayed that the sighting of her uncle was a false report. And realizing that the guards might return, she quickly descended the ladder. Her hands shook so much, she could barely hold on. Toward the bottom, her foot slipped, and she slid past the last four rungs. Bruised and bleeding, her hands full of splinters, Rorie was numb to all but the fear that drove her as she picked herself up off the ground. Peering through the door, she saw that the guards were on the other side of the cottage. Carefully, she inched her way out the front of the barn and around to the back.

If she could just cross the field, she thought, she would be able to skirt the village and return to the Grange unnoticed. Rorie was hitching up her skirt, preparing to run, when a hand clamped over her mouth, and she was dragged into a clump of bushes a few yards away. Full blown terror seized her as she struggled in vain. Her captor held her closely. Her heart beat a wild tattoo against her chest.

"Be quiet," whispered Deveraux, slowly releasing his hand from her mouth.

Rorie's eyes were huge with shock as she

slowly sat up. "What are you doing here!" she finally gasped, trying to catch her strangled breath.

"Following you."

"How dare you! You nearly scared the bejesus out of me!"

" 'Tis lucky for you I did," said Cameron, indicating the two guard just emerging from the fields.

Rorie shivered when she realized that she would have run right into them had Deveraux not stopped her.

"I would have managed," she replied stubbornly.

"Just as you did in the barn?"

"What do you mean?"

"Who do you think drew the guards away from there long enough for you to get out? It would seem that rescuing you is becoming an occupation, Miss Shelbourne," he added dryly.

"Your gall, Captain, is—"

"Later, Rorie. We've got to get out of here. The fields have all been searched now, so 'tis safe to go."

Rorie grimaced with pain when he grabbed her battered hand, and it was all she could do to keep from crying out as he pulled her after him across the field.

"Stop, I've got to rest," called Rorie breathlessly when they had emerged on the other side.

Deveraux nodded and led her over to the safety of a copse, where she slid gratefully to the ground.

"Why did you follow me?" demanded Rorie, her spirit reviving somewhat.

"To see what trouble you were getting yourself into next," Cameron replied with such assurance that she wanted to reach up and slap him. "I knew you were up to something when you left the ball. What was going on there, Rorie?"

When Rorie made no move to answer, Cameron pulled her to her feet to face him. "Answer me! Who was the man I saw running away from the farm?"

Rorie was too weary to argue. "All right," she relented, "I suppose you'll find out sooner or later, anyway. 'Twas Will Fenton, though I don't know of what concern—"

"Will Fenton, you say?" interrupted Deveraux brusquely.

Now it was Rorie's turn to be curious. "Do you know of him? But, of course, as a guest at Lyndeforde, you would know that he is sought on some trumped up murder charge, no doubt conceived by the duke," she spat heatedly.

"What is your part in all of this?" Deveraux demanded, ignoring her temper. "And who was that boy you went to meet?"

"Terence is—a friend," replied Rorie, remembering her uncle's warning and not quite understanding the captain's line of questioning. "He works for the Fentons. They're good people."

"I see," said Deveraux tightly, having mistaken the greeting he had seen between them for a lover's embrace. It all made sense now to him, and he didn't like the conclusion he was drawing.

"Look, Captain, I would prefer that you make no mention of having seen me tonight."

"Yes, I can understand where it might prove

awkward for you, having left the duke's betrothal ball pleading illness, only to be found at the dwelling of an outlaw. One might even surmise that you were there to warn him—as a friend of the family, of course."

Rorie glanced up at Deveraux sharply. "And how would I have known of his intended arrest?"

"Funny thing about women, Miss Shelbourne, they have a unique talent for becoming an invisible presence and an underestimated force. They sometimes hear things one doesn't realize they hear and are quite happy to pass along to—interested companions on balconies."

Deveraux had been guessing, but now he knew he was on target as Rorie fell uncharacteristically silent.

"Well, until you have facts, Captain," she said at length, "I don't think it prudent to spread theories."

"Perhaps upon occasion, you will remember your own advice, Miss Shelbourne."

"I must be getting back to the Grange now, Captain." Deveraux's insight had unnerved her to the point that she didn't know what to deny and what to admit, especially when she wasn't sure how far she could trust him.

As they walked back to Balfour Grange, Rorie's mind was a whirl of activity trying to figure the captain's own part in all of this. He was an ally of the duke by virtue of having accepted the scoundrel's hospitality, but was he a cohort or merely a curious observer?

"Captain," she finally blurted out, "if you think that I warned Will Fenton of the duke's intentions, why should you work against the duke's interests by helping me escape the guards?"

Cameron smiled. "It's quite simple, Miss Shelbourne. My interests come first, and my business with you is not yet done," he promised. "Though you present more the picture of a bedraggled street urchin than of a lady of worth at the moment, I find you rather intriguing. How well I keep your confidence will depend upon you."

Rorie came to an abrupt stop and stared up at him in disbelief.

"You bargain my favors for your silence?" she shrieked. "Why you arrogant blatherskite!"

Cameron caught her hand in midair, on the way to his face, and the moment was suspended as he looked into her eyes and held her gaze. "The middle is a dangerous place to be, Rorie," he murmured huskily, lowering his head to brush his lips across hers.

Without the stiff undergarments, he could feel the soft curves of her body as she leaned against him, and he released her arm to draw her closer. Rorie shuddered as one hand played lightly across her shoulders, traveling up her neck into her hair, while the other tightened around her waist. When his kiss deepened and fingers came to rest on the swell of her breast, Rorie began to panic.

"No, stop it!" she cried, breaking away from him in sudden desperation, her voice cracking with tension. "Why can't you leave me alone!"

Cameron frowned as he watched her run down the lane to Balfour Grange. Every time he thought he had broken through her reserve, something happened to Rorie he had yet to understand. Was it perhaps her conscience reminding her that she was betraying this Terence? Or did she still play a game with him? In either case, he was tiring of this cat and mouse play and was determined to force the issue.

16

"Ouch, be careful!" cried Rorie, as Mary picked out the remaining splinters from her badly bruised hands.

"Rorie, whatever did you do last night? Slide down a board?" ·

"Close," responded Rorie irritably, recalling her slip on the ladder.

"Well, you should see an apothecary. Your hands are so raw, they may well become infected, not to mention your knee. To my eye it could use a stitch or two."

"No, 'twould only raise questions," Rorie insisted firmly.

"The captain has that liniment he used on your ankle—" Mary's voice trailed off as she caught Rorie's steely-gray glare on her. "Sorry, I was only trying to help. You know, the captain didn't return to the ball last night for quite some time," she ventured casually.

"I don't wish to discuss the man," Rorie snapped.

Mary sighed in exasperation. "Really, Rorie, I

simply don't understand why you find the captain so objectionable."

"The man is a rogue of the lowest level and not to be trusted. Do you forget he is a guest of Lyndeforde by the duke's own invitation?"

"No, but he doesn't seem a bad sort."

"Ha! Then you don't know him."

"And you do?" asked Mary coyly, smiling to herself.

"I—he—that is, you—I don't want to talk about him," a flushed Rorie finally stammered out.

"I see. Well then, if you won't let the captain help you, how about your brother? He was apprenticed to the apothecary for a time. He would know how to dress your wounds."

"No! Mary, I told you, I must have no contact with my family so long as my uncle is being sought."

"Yes, Father is in rather a snit, himself, worrying about the consequences should the duke learn that you are not only not a relative, but the niece of Will Fenton as well."

Mary and Rorie looked at each other and suddenly burst into gales of laughter as each imagined the scene. "Yes, I should like to see the squire explain his way out of that one," said Rorie, wiping the tears from her eyes.

As it had been such a long time since the girls had been able to laugh at anything, they enjoyed the moment for as long as they could. But as always, the shadow of the duke stood ever ready to intrude upon their slightest amusement.

Mary's smile faded as anxiety suddenly clouded her pale features. "Oh, Rorie, I must confess that if I thought the matter would end

my betrothal to the duke and bring you no harm,
I would expose the lie myself. He was so angry
when the guards arrived empty-handed last
night."

"What did he say?"

"Oh, it wasn't what he said. He managed to
remain civil, but his eyes . . . they were so cold
and unfeeling." Mary shuddered at the memory.
"Rorie, had he but dared, I fear he would like to
have taken his displeasure out on me. There is
something evil about that man. I can feel it in his
presence, in his touch."

"Mary, don't think about it," said Rorie
gently. "Somehow everything will work out for
the better. You'll see."

"Will it? I heard the housekeeper telling cook
that all the village shops were seized this
morning."

"Why?" asked Rorie in stunned amazement.

"As punishment for the rebellion and for the
villagers' refusal to come forth with any information on your uncle. I fear there is no hope for
Drumfielde—or for me," Mary added with quiet
resignation.

Deep down, Rorie had already acknowledged
that truth, but her spirit refused to allow her to
accept it.

"Don't say that!" she admonished Mary. "So
long as there is life, there is hope. If the duke has
no heart to appeal to, then we shall find something else he values more."

"Yes, of course we will," replied Mary with a
wan smile. "You mustn't mind me. Now I must
go. Mother is not well, and I will be spending the
day with her."

Rorie nodded. "I could do with a walk myself

to clear the mind. Please give my greetings to Mistress Balfour."

Though the day had dawned clear and bright, Rorie was in a somber mood as she walked down the lane. It seemed that problems were compounding steadily, each day giving rise to a new one. They seemed so insurmountable, she was at a loss as to how to solve any of them. And she felt so cornered and woefully inadequate, she found herself lashing out at everyone. In spite of her confident words to Mary, she had no idea how to help her friend or her village, and she wished she had some source of strength to draw from.

At this, her thoughts drifted to Captain Deveraux. If only she could trust him. After all, he did help her out of a few difficult situations. But just as quickly, she dismissed the thought. The man was an unprincipled rogue! And she had plenty of evidence to that end, she thought angrily, recalling his proposition of last night! Nor could she overlook the fact that he was a personal guest of the duke, which was a dubious honor in and of itself.

Still, the captain remained an enigma to her. He could be gentle, charming, courteous, and witty, as she had witnessed him to be with Mary, or he could be a mean, cutting, ill-mannered lout, as he was with her. They seemed to bring out the worst in each other, yet she could not deny the strange sensations that he stirred in her each time he touched her. Aside from being roguishly handsome, the captain emitted a virility that disturbed her mightily. And she was vastly irritated by that lazy smile—or more correctly, the smirk—which tugged at the corners of his mouth, while his eyes roamed boldly over her body, as though assessing what pleasures laid beneath the wrappings. Worse, he was at once totally unpredictable, yet so damned sure of himself. He never made excuses for his actions because he cared not a fig for anyone's opinion of him, least of all hers. It would have astounded her to know that Deveraux viewed her in the same light.

But what disturbed her most was the way he had of eliciting a response from her body, despite her mind's refusal. Rorie could feel the heat start up her neck and suffuse into her face at the memory of that night at the poacher's hut. She still could not believe the liberties she had allowed that man. Oh, she had permitted hugs and kisses from the village lads before, for they were harmless, and she remained unmoved by their clumsy, inexperienced touch. In truth, she had decided that she was quite revolted by the feeling of a wet mouth moving sloppily against her own like some overly friendly dog, and she most certainly had no intentions of suffering the degrading intimacies which she knew men to expect in the marriage bed. But the captain, it would seem, was not just any man. He was the devil's own spawn, Rorie decided angrily, venting her frustration upon a stone in her path.

"Ho there, I hope the wrath ye feel fer tha' stone willna apply ta me as well," came a voice silkily from behind.

Totally absorbed in her thoughts, Rorie jumped at the undetected presence so near at hand and twirled about to see Wiley Pate emerging from the trees.

"Are you making it your occupation to catch me unawares? For you seem to have none other," she retorted heatedly.

"No more than ye seem ta make it yers ta daydream," he countered easily.

And for a fleeting moment, his careful smile was replaced by a hard, appraising look which made Rorie want to back away. She stood her ground, however, and the look had come and gone so quickly, she began to wonder if she had imagined it. Just the same, she was left with an undeniable feeling of mistrust for her brother's friend.

Wiley noted the narrow look of suspicion in her gold-flecked eyes, and he cursed his lack of control. Carefully composing himself, he tried again.

"Come now, Rorie, I have no wish ta quarrel with ye. I want only ta know ye better. I've been waiting fer ye ta come by this way fer days."

He wondered if she knew how charming she looked standing there, her thickly lashed eyes spitting green sparks of fire. His taste normally didn't run to highly spirited women, but the end reward that this one promised would be worth the exception.

"How 'bout it, Rorie?" he asked huskily, running a hand caressingly over her shoulder and down her arm. "I know a place where we won't be disturbed."

Mistaking her shudder of revulsion for acquiescence, his arm suddenly snaked tightly around her, and he pulled her to him. Although Wiley stood but a half head taller, Rorie knew that his strength was more than she could handle. Seeing the look in his eyes and feeling the hardening in his loins as he drew her even closer, she knew he was beyond reasoning, and, for a moment, she was paralyzed with fear.

Grasping her chin tightly in his hand, Wiley smiled victoriously as he lowered his head, expecting to conquer her soft lips and to plunder the sweetness of her trembling mouth. Instead, he was greeted by a searing pain through his vitals, a pain so intense that tears sprang to his eyes. He dropped to his knees writhing and groaning in agony. Acting through blind instinct, Rorie had brought her knee up to connect sharply with his crotch and was delighted with the results. She knew she should flee for her life. Without a doubt, Wiley would try to kill her if he could get his hands on her. But Rorie couldn't resist a parting shot.

"Do you wish to know me now, Wiley?" she asked sweetly.

"You li'l bitch!" he ground out between spasms of pain. "Ye'll pay fer this!"

Rorie felt truly frightened now, for she sensed his was no idle threat. She had injured the man's most treasured possession: his ego. And for men like Wiley, ego was all they had. Picking up her skirts, she raced into the village.

When Rorie came to the square, she slowed her pace. Wiley was forgotten as she passed by the charred, skeletal remains of the cottages which stood as a poignant memorial to the tragedy that had occurred here. She had been unprepared for the impact it had on her. But aside from the harsh memory, there was an unnatural silence. Something wasn't right; no one stirred. Then Rorie realized that it was just as Mary had said, the shops were closed. A knot of injustice twisted her insides unmercifully, and she was so consumed with rage that she lifted her skirts and bolted, running off her frustration and anger until she thought her lungs would burst. She didn't want to think; she didn't want to feel. She just wanted to escape.

At length, Rorie found herself at a little known lagoon, which she and her brother had discovered one day while exploring. It was so well hidden from prying eyes that they had come to regard it as their own private domain. Just the sight of the lagoon's unspoiled beauty and the thought of the cool, clear blue water against her hot skin already seemed to ease her worries. Well, why not? she thought. It was only midmorning, and she had the whole day to herself. Quickly, she shed her clothes to partake of the serenity the still waters offered.

17

That same morning, though it was a bright midmorn, all traces of sunlight were obscured by tangled underbrush, scrub trees and huge, towering pines as three men slipped furtively into the dark marsh. They made a quick check of their weapons before proceeding, for those who moved on Romney Marsh always went armed. Robbery and murder were the norm in this lair of desperate thieves, murderers, smugglers and deserters. Survival definitely belonged to the fittest and to those with the sharpest senses. With the howling of stray dogs, the quavering cries of curlews, and the hooting of owls in the mist, it was nearly impossible to detect a man's predatory footsteps in the miasma of the swamp. The three men made slow progress along the narrow path concealed by overgrowth. Keeping a close eye out for snakes and cutthroats, they hacked at the vines which seemingly reached out and entangled their legs.

" 'Tis doubtful tha' this path be known to any who frequent the marsh," said the heavier set man, as the other two stopped to listen now and then, their bodies tensed to fight. "They mostly stays on the other side of the marsh where the smugglers do their business. Ain't no good outlet ta the sea from here."

"I recollect tha' Will be right about tha', sir," responded Rawlings. Cameron nodded soberly, and they continued on. Eventually the path gave way to a small clearing where rays of sunlight were able to find their way through the less dense growth.

"Here be where the pack trains was loaded. The hut is up there," the stockier Will Fenton said, pointing to the side of a rocky bluff overlooking the sea. Seeing the look of doubt which flitted across the young captain's face, he laughed. "It ain't as high as it looks. Look closely an' ye'll see steps cut into the hill. 'Tis to the sides of 'em where the grade be more gradual tha' we cut a path an' rolled the hogsheads ta the bottom. Come, let's have a look at the hut."

The men carefully climbed single file up the side of the steep hill, coming to a halt on a small ledge. There, Will pushed aside a tangle of vines to reveal a crude, wooden door. Weathered and warped by age and the briny sea air, the door refused to give admittance until Will threw the bulk of his weight against it. With a groan, it grudgingly gave way to allow entrance. Dank, musty smells filled their nostrils as the three men entered the black cavity.

When their eyes had adjusted to the darkness, Rawlings gave a whoop of laughter upon noticing the rough, wooden table strewn with crude maps of the area. It was as though the dwelling had been awaiting their arrival. "She be all set up fer business, sir," he quipped proudly.

Cameron waved aside the cobwebs and surveyed the room with cool detachment. It was more of a cave cut into the side of the bluff with a wooden floor and rotting timber supports than a hut. "Where is the access to the tunnels?" he asked.

"Under the table, 'neath those rushes," answered Fenton with a tilt of his red head.

As Deveraux made a further study of the hut, he caught his companions' questioning glances. " 'Twill do nicely, once we've replaced the timbers," he announced. "Now let us see to the maps." He had to smile as the older men let out an audible sigh of relief.

The maps, although thirty-years-old, were still amazingly accurate in their detail of the marsh. Fenton's calloused finger pointed to a spot on one map, a quarter league to the northeast of the hut.

"Tha' be the cave where the owlers puts in their cargo," he explained, stabbing at the mark again. "The tunnels below this hut connect here an' here with the owlers cave, but this tunnel collapsed some thirty years ago. The cargo is usually stored in the cave 'til the pack train is brought ta the beach fer loadin'. Ye'll have a few hours ta move the goods through this tunnel."

Cameron nodded. "How is it that the tunnels have never been discovered?" he asked.

The older man shrugged. " 'Twas a well guarded secret from the old days. Our band dug the tunnels so we never had ta worry 'bout bein' caught on the open beach while loadin'. 'Twas safer ta transfer the goods ta the pack train from the hut. So far as I know, the word was never broken."

"When the band broke up," chimed in Rawlings, "most of us went on ta other lives an' had no wish fer our past ta be found out. The others be dead."

"Aye," agreed Fenton. "And from inside the cave, the tunnels are carefully hidden by thick vines. Ta my way of thinkin' a man kenna see what he ain't lookin' fer. As 'tis always night when the goods is moved an' time is short, the tunnel be easy ta overlook. Besides, smugglers nowadays think with their weapons rather than their heads."

At this, the burly Will Fenton paused to look doubtfully at the young man beside him. Although the lad was tall and powerfully built, he looked to be untried, and much was at stake here. There could be no mistakes.

"Smugglers have been doin' business fer generations in the marsh," Fenton continued. "Me and Rawlings here was a part of it once. Livin' along the coast as we did, 'twas the only chance we had against the taxes. But we was respectable, mind ye. We married local women, provided work for men who could make naught but a poor living, and we spent the money we made in the area. But as profits grew, vicious men took over the trade. 'Twas then that I took Molly further inland to set up a farm in Drumfielde. And Rawlings followed shortly after, taking a position as head groom in the stables of the late duke of Lyndeforde. No sir, we wasn't anything like these bloodthirsty brigands now what give smugglin' a black name. And the Warwicke Gang be the biggest an' best organized in all of England. They deal in dear cargo, laddie, an' willna think twice 'bout killin' ta keep their goods or their freedom. Smugglin' be a hangin' offense now," Fenton warned.

"Don't be a worryin' none 'bout the cap'n," Rawlings assured his old friend. "He be knowin' wha' he's about."

Will shot Deveraux an appraising look, borne more of curiosity than uncertainty this time. When Rawlings had first approached him about the scheme several days ago, he hadn't expected a leader so young, but neither then had he expected his old smuggling partner to turn up on his doorstep after ten years, nor to be accused of murder. So be it. His lot was cast, and there was no turning back. If Thomas Rawlings vouched for the lad, 'twas good enough for him.

And now that he stood with them, he had several questions on his tongue. For one, why would this stranger from the colonies choose to risk his life for a village and people he knew naught of? For another, how had this young pup won Rawling's loyalty, for his longtime friend did not give his allegiance easily? Once won, however, 'twas for life. The admiration and respect which Rawlings and the lad shared for one another did not go unnoticed by Will.

Feeling Will's questioning gaze on him, Cameron straightened to his full height and leveled his gaze on the older man. The steely blue eyes had such intensity, they reminded Fenton of a storm at sea. Deveraux's angular features were hard and inscrutable as though carved in stone, but Fenton could feel the energy of his resolve and the strength of his presence. The captain was like a sleek, deadly predator, coiled and ready to strike at the heart of his prey. This man gave no quarter. For one fleeting moment, Fenton actually felt pity for Roger Thornton. He could see now that the captain was clearly an opponent to be reckoned with, and the power of his strength was not to be underestimated because of his youthful good looks. Suddenly, Fenton knew more confidence than he had known in several years, and he extended a huge, rough hand in friendship. Perhaps now he could feel like a man again.

A smile slowly played at the corners of Deveraux's mouth, and he readily accepted Fenton's hand in a strong, firm handshake. Rawlings sighed with relief, as he watched the two men he held in highest regard accept each other with unquestioned faith.

"In time, my friend, all your questions will be answered," said Deveraux, reading the startled Fenton's mind. "But for now 'twill be safer for us all if you know nothing of me and protect the secrecy of my part in this plan."

Fenton nodded soberly. "As you wish, Cap'n. I don't know the whole of your game, but ye ken count on me. I've a score of my own ta settle with the duke."

"So I've heard," remarked Cameron. It was on the tip of his tongue to inquire about Rorie's part in this man's escape, but he thought better of it for the moment. "How can I contact you?" he asked.

"The tavern keep'll know how ta get a message to me."

"You are certain he is trustworthy?" questioned Deveraux guardedly.

"Aye, Cap'n," broke in Rawlings. "Jacobs

was one of our band. So long as 'tis fer me and Will, he'll do our business, no questions asked."

"Good. Now, Will, tell me more of the Warwicke Gang, for 'tis with them that I suspect lays the allegiance of Thornton and Osborn."

Fenton gave a long, low whistle. "Then 'tis a handful we have, Cap'n. Our steps must be surer than ever, fer Davey Billings be a cunning, merciless leader an' his men be all the more cruel fer it. They take their name from the small inland village from whence they come, an' they make their headquarters in the old inn at Rye. Took over the whole town they did. They knows every street, back lane and alleyway. A worse nest of vipers I never knowed. They be a hard lot, Cap'n. They murder anyone who crosses 'em an' ain't 'bove robbin' an' torturin' ta gain their ends."

"Yes, we shall have to work fast," replied Deveraux, understanding Will's underlying concern for the villagers in the face of Billings's wrath, once the smuggler began to miss his booty. "When is the next shipment expected, Will?"

"Iffen they run true ta nature, Cap'n, 'twill be with the new moon."

"That would be in about three and half weeks. Rawlings, have you heard anything of the *Homeward Bound*?"

"None, Cap'n. She ain't due ta the end of the week leastwise."

"Let's hope she's sailing a true course, gentlemen. Our lives may depend on it."

As the men emerged from the fetid marsh, each took a different route. Deveraux traveled slowly to reacquaint himself with the countryside. If memory served him correctly, there was a little known lagoon to the east where a man could enjoy some well deserved solitude.

Hot, dusty and tired, Cameron began to savor the idea of a swim more and more as he drew closer to this hidden paradise. And it was with dismay that he greeted the sounds of splashing water in the distance. His mounting irritation that he would not be alone, as he dismounted and stealthily approached the lagoon on foot, immediately gave way to pleasure when he glimpsed a young woman, in all of her grace and natural beauty, swimming and diving like a playful otter. He wondered on the identity of this sea nymph as she emerged to stand waist deep in water, with her back to him. It had to be a lass from the village, for a woman of distinction would certainly never be caught at such a disadvantage, let alone exposing her milk-white skin to the sun's rays. He smiled as another thought crossed his mind. Perhaps a romp with this enchanting creature would rid his mind of that annoying Shelbourne girl. He approached the bank with an eager step and a telling gleam in his eye.

"One shouldn't swim alone. Perhaps I should join you," he called out in a deep, lazy drawl.

Rorie went rigid in the water and quickly ducked own to her shoulders at the sound of the low, caressing voice she recognized all too well. She couldn't believe her ears. The wind was calm, but as she slowly turned to face her nemesis, the air took on an electrifying charge. The look of astonishment on Deveraux's face was almost worth the embarrassment Rorie was feeling. But then as he threw back his head and roared with laughter, the last of her composure slipped.

" 'Twould seem, madam," he said with obvious relish, "that you are a woman of many accomplishments. Where did you learn to swim like that? I've men in my service who have yet to stay afloat in bath water."

Rorie flushed hotly, and she crouched still lower. "If you must know, 'twas my broth—'twas a friend," she amended quickly. "How did you find your way here? No one knows of this place!"

" 'Tis a question I thought to ask of you, my dear. But to answer yours, a man I knew once lived in Drumfielde as a small boy. He used to speak often of this lagoon."

"Well, you have seen it. Now leave!" Rorie snapped with exasperation.

Deveraux leaned casually against a broad tree trunk, his arms folded, the smile, which Rorie always found so infuriating, playing around his mouth.

"I had thought to partake of the cooling waters, myself. Were I to defer to your wishes, Miss Shelbourne, how shall you recompense me for my disappointment?"

"Another proposition, Captain?" she spat caustically.

"Perhaps."

"And what shall you bargain with this time?"

"Why, my silence, of course," replied Cameron matter-of-factly. "You seem to have a talent for being caught in rather compromising situations. It might lead one to almost think they were planned."

Advancing to the water's edge, he slipped off his shirt to display a hard, muscular chest which tapered down to a slim waist.

"Shall we proceed?" he asked as one consummating a business deal.

His smile broadened into a grin as Rorie's jaw dropped. Although no words were coming forth, he knew her well enough by now to know that she was sputtering. And he was enjoying the moment immensely. He was done now with letting her have the upperhand, leading him in a merry chase. The game had just changed, and from here on, he decided, he would set the rules.

As he surveyed her meaningfully, she clearly understood the message. He had told her that night at the hut there would be a "next time." And now the look in his eye coolly warned her that if he chose to avail himself of this or any other situation in the future, he would do so. She smoldered with indignation and apprehension, for if that time at the hut and last night were any indication of the power his touch had over her, she would be surely lost—and he knew it. Somehow, he always managed to catch her at her weakest moments. And she resolved to cut him a wide berth.

"Miss Shelbourne, shall we proceed?" he repeated.

The man's gall was unbelievable. "No, damn you!" shrieked Rorie. "If you were a gentleman, you would allow a lady her privacy."

Deveraux laughed. "I've never alluded to being a gentleman. And I wasn't aware that there was a lady present," he said pointedly, referring to her lapse of polite language and her unfortunate position.

Rorie turned crimson. It was true that while she had no use for the trappings of ladyhood and disdained the shallow, simpering, tea serving, empty-headed fools who answered to that honor, the remark, nevertheless, rankled—especially coming from him. It positively infuriated her how he could render her so helpless with rage.

Wisely, Deveraux decided to withdraw. He had served her notice. The rest would have to wait, for there was something about this girl that always brought him up short, and he was damned if he knew what it was. Retrieving his shirt, he called, "Another time, Miss Shelbourne. I fear the hour is short today."

"Deveraux," she screamed after him, "if you tell anyone of this, I'll tear your heart out!"

He halted and half turned, a devilish grin splitting his darkly handsome features. "Don't you know, madam? I haven't any heart."

18

Cameron had just climbed out of the bronze hip tub and wrapped a thick towel about his waist when Rawlings entered the room to lay out his master's evening clothes.

"The squire's carriage ha' jest arrived fer ye, Cap'n," he announced casually, holding out Deveraux's dove gray knee breeches.

Deveraux groaned as he could well imagine the evening which stretched before him. It was a dining invitation he had been loathe to accept but thought better of declining, for the squire unknowingly protected his cover as a man of business, thereby, enabling Cameron to move freely about, above suspicion. The only thing which would make the long, tedious meal bearable was seeing Rorie again. He smiled as he recalled how a furious Rorie had crouched in the crystal, clear water, when he had come upon her the other day. He hadn't the heart to tell her that the positioning of the sun had made every delicious curve of her desirable body clearly visible to his sharp eye.

He slipped on a white shirt and was arranging the lawn neckcloth, when Rawlings approached to assist him with his gray waistcoat and puce-colored coat. The little man looked furtively about and lowered his voice.

"Cap'n, the *Homeward* jest docked in the cove an hour ago. The men await your orders."

Deveraux nodded. "Any problems?"

Rawlings shook his head. "All went well, sir."

"Excellent. Tell Hawkins, James, and Richards to meet me at midnight in the glade at the edge of the woods, two miles east of Drumfielde. And get word to Fenton to appraise them beforehand of the situation here."

"Aye, sir."

As Rawlings continued to hover about him, Deveraux looked at his valet curiously. "Is there something else, Rawlings?"

Again, the old salt cast a covert glance over his shoulder as he brushed imaginary lint from Deveraux's coat. "Watch out fer Osborn, Cap'n. He ain't a man of ordinary tastes, iffen ye catch my meanin'."

Cameron nodded, the muscles in his jaw working furiously. "I think I know that better than most," he answered in a strangely remote and bitter tone.

"Yes, sir. It's jest that he watches ye with too close an eye fer my comfort."

"He searches for a weakness he can use to manipulate me. But this is not yer concern, Rawlings. I shall deal with Percy Osborn in my own way."

Rawlings looked up at Deveraux sharply, surprised by the harsh edge to his captain's voice. There was an undertone here he didn't like and obviously some information he hadn't been privy to. But he respected the captain enough to defer to his wishes.

With a shrug of his shoulders, he said, "Yer business is yer own, sir."

"Has there been any notice of the girl from the revolt?"

"Rawlings scratched his head in perplexity. "None, sir. Most of the servants here was hired from another village since no one in Drumfielde would pledge a day's work to Thornton. And Jacobs says the town is bound tighter than a virgin's chastity belt. Some sort of vow of silence, he says."

"Jacobs knows nothing?" inquired Cameron thoughtfully.

"Amid all the confusion during the rebellion, he did not see the event. And nothing was later said. He has no idea whom we seek. But don't ye worry none, sir, Jacobs'll find the girl if anyone ken."

"Well, Rawlings, let's just hope that the lass, whoever she may be, has no more recollection of me than I have of her."

"Yes, sir."

Cameron arrived at Balfour Grange in a heavy moon, which became still heavier when he found that Rorie was not to be present, for she always provided a pleasant distraction for him. To Cameron, the meal seemed interminable, as dish after dish was removed, only to be replaced by something more filling and tasteless than the one preceeding it. The squire had miraculously spared no expense, Deveraux thought wryly, wishing he had an appetite for the bland English cooking. Having become accustomed to the more seasoned French dishes, however, he found English cuisine barely palatable.

From time to time, he caught Mary's curious gaze on him as he half-heartedly joined in the conversation. In truth, his mind was on the secret meeting he had arranged for later with his ship's officers. Fortunately, the squire was too busy stuffing himself to take note of his guest's inattention.

At ten o'clock, Mary rose to withdraw to her chambers and leave the men to their after-dinner port. "It was a pleasure to have you here, Captain, but I fear that you missed the company of another far more," she said with a knowing smile. "I'm sorry that Miss Shelbourne didn't want to—ah—wasn't feeling well enough to join us," she amended sheepishly, ill-at-ease with the lie. But she couldn't very well tell the captain that Rorie had refused his company, and she certainly couldn't repeat Rorie's words.

"The dashed female is always having a vapor!" declared the squire petulantly, considering his own unsuccessful attempts to woo Rorie's favor.

Having guessed the truth of the matter though, Cameron suppressed the urge to laugh as he took Mary's hand. " 'Tis quite all right, Miss Balfour," he assured her with a smile. "You were company enough. Please tell Miss Shelbourne that, in the future, she should take better care not to expose herself so much to the elements."

"Yes, Captain, I shall convey your concern," Mary replied, taking his words at face value.

Again, Cameron had to smile as he could well imagine Rorie's reaction to his seemingly well-intentioned comment. And his mind drifted back for a moment to their encounter at the lagoon.

The squire waved his hand impatiently. "Off with ye now, lass. The Captain and I have matters to discuss," he ordered, dabbing at the grease which drooled down his chin and refilling his glass. When they were alone and Deveraux had reluctantly returned to his seat, the squire leaned forward conspiratorially. "Nasty bit of business, this Will Fenton, ay?"

"Yes, His Grace's temper is something to be avoided these days," admitted Cameron.

The squire snorted peevishly. "Well, if the duke hadn't seen fit to ignore my authority and so foolishly attempted to arrest the man himself, Fenton would been caught. It takes a man who knows his business, don't ye know," he added self importantly, leaning back in his chair until it was precariously balanced on two legs.

"I shall relay your sentiments to the duke, sir."

The squire paled. His mouth worked wordlessly, and he nearly pitched over backwards. "No, no, Captain," he sputtered. "I don't think our—I mean the duke's interests are best served by throwing salt in the wound, so to speak. 'Twas but an observation better kept between us, you understand. And we most certainly don't wish to upset the groom before the wedding now, do we?"

"As you wish, sir."

Cameron was hard pressed to hide his amusement as the squire retrieved the napkin from under his chin to dot the perspiration on his brow in relief.

"Thank you, Captain. Your confidence would

better serve Miss Shelbourne as well."

Cameron's surprise turned to curiosity. "Miss Shelbourne? How?" he inquired with forced nonchalance. He was continually amazed by how little he knew about this girl.

"Wha-what?" stammered the squire.

"What has your daughter's companion to do with this matter?" Deveraux pressed.

Squire Balfour blanched when he realized he had opened a can of worms. He had meant only to stress to the Captain that his silence benefitted many people but, instead, had succeeded in drawing attention to the very person he sought to hide. God help him if the duke ever got wind that his own daughter's companion and a girl whom he had claimed as a relative was, in fact, the niece of the most wanted man in the county. Damn the lass anyway! He took her under his roof, fed her his food and even clothed the chit, and this was how she repaid him, he thought irrationally.

Cameron leaned back in his chair and continued to observe the squire with interest. "Well, sir?" he demanded.

Balfour roused himself with difficulty. "What, oh, I—I only meant, Captain, that Miss Shelbourne's compassion for these village people lies too close to the surface for her own good," he explained with a nervous laugh. "The girl is so headstrong there's no telling what she'll do, and I don't wish to invite the duke's scrutiny at this point."

Cameron's eyes narrowed in suspicion. "Is there something in Miss Shelbourne's background which won't stand up to examination?"

The squire groaned inwardly. He seemed

only to be making matters worse, and for some reason the captain was like a dog with a bone. "Of course not," he denied hastily, nearly tripping over his tongue, and he firmly changed the subject. "Now, about *our* business, Captain."

It was after midnight when Cameron was finally able to make his way to the glade. It had not been easy to take his leave of the squire. The man was something of an octopus. Every time Cameron had started to leave, Balfour had found a reason to draw him back. His path became clear only after the Squire had dozed off after consuming a prodigious quantity of port.

As Deveraux broke from the protection of the trees into the open clearing before him, he showed the squire's horse for which he had freely exchanged the carriage. Every sense was alert to the sounds of his environment. At last, the signal issued forth from a stand of pine trees about fifty yards to his left. Cautiously, he made his way in that direction. As he approached, Ian Hawkins, his first mate, Thomas James, his second mate, and George Richards, his boatswain, emerged from the shadows.

Cameron greeted each heartily before assuming a serious air. "How went the trip to Algiers, Hawkins?" he asked in a lowered tone.

"All went as it should, Captain."

"Good. Can I assume that you are all acquainted with the situation here?"

"Aye, sir. A Will Fenton has told us about the village," spoke up Hawkins, his brow furrowed in puzzlement. "But what has that to do with us, sir?"

"It means, Ian, that I have a personal stake in

seeing these people freed from the likes of one Roger Thornton, duke of Lyndeforde, and I need your help."

Deveraux ignored the quizzical looks of his men and continued. "The plan I have in mind to achieve this end is extremely dangerous. Although others of high rank in London have pledged their aid, if caught 'twould mean the gibbets on Tyburn Hill for us all. For this reason, I offer you the choice of sailing the *Homeward Bound* back to Charleston under Ian's leadership, or following me. I'll think none the worse of any man who chooses to return, for I can offer you naught but danger and perhaps a share of some booty. But know this, I shall deal fairly by you and your families at the conclusion. If only but a few elect to return, I'll arrange passage for them on the next ship to the colonies."

A low murmur passed among the three hearty seamen before Ian stepped forward to speak. "Captain, sir, we've sailed with you long enough to know you to be a man of your word, fair and honorable. And you've showed us all a kindness at one time or another. I think I can speak for all the crew when I say that whatever score you have to settle, you can count on us to stand with you."

James' gruff voice boomed out, "Aye, Cap'n. The men could do with a spot of adventure. Gettin' soft we was, laid up in port fer tha' long."

"Didna hear ye complain overloud, James," snorted Richards. "Disappeared with a wench on each arm fer four days. Near ta gave ye up fer dead."

"Those wenches *were* nearly my death," James responded with a chuckle.

Deveraux laughed, joining in the ribaldry for it served to cover the emotionally charged atmosphere of the moment. Though he would never show it, the blind loyalty of his men had moved him. They had been together through many voyages, and there wasn't a man in his crew, whom he didn't trust with his very life.

The men quieted as Deveraux's tone became serious once again. "Thank you for your confidence, but I wish the choice to be put to every man. You can communicate the results to me through Fenton. In the meantime, stay on the ship, and let no one see you. I wish no word of your presence to escape. I will relay all instructions through Fenton as well."

With that, he bid them all a hasty goodnight and departed for Lyndeforde.

When Cameron rode into the Lyndeforde stables a half hour later, his thoughts were on Rorie as he wondered what secrets she kept. Owing to the squire's slip of the tongue, the captain was now certain she was hiding something. Flexing his shoulders as he handed his mount to the livery boy, Deveraux finally acknowledged his weariness. Quietly, he slipped into the stone fortress of the manor, hoping to remain undetected.

"Ah, Captain Deveraux, so you have returned," Percy Osborn greeted him smoothly, standing in the doorway of the gaming room.

Deveraux had the uneasy feeling that the pristine fop had been laying in wait for him, and he struggled to keep his features devoid of the revulsion he felt for the man as he forced himself to join the guests.

"The squire's company must be improving,

as the hour is so late," commented Thornton snidely, not tearing his gaze from the cards he held in his hand. Cameron could see he was still in an ugly mood.

Most of the guests who had arrived for the prenuptial ball were remaining for the May Day celebrations and the wedding. The card games were a nightly event for both men and women, with Thornton remaining true to form and losing heavily. Tonight was no exception and only fueled his simmering rage over Fenton's escape. Thus far, Cameron had managed to stay clear of the gaming, but as he knew that it was the underlying reason for his being there, Deveraux realized he could no longer ignore the invitations to play. Anger bred suspicion, and Cameron couldn't afford to arouse the duke's ire at this time.

Coolly, Deveraux surveyed the scene before him. The women had all retired. Six men including Thornton sat around the table, engaged in a game of loo. From their rumpled appearance, the glaze of their eyes, and the stale smell of liquor, it was obvious the games had started early.

Percy lounged against the doorjamb, seemingly absorbed in picking lint from his chartreuse coat. "Could it be, Captain," he began lazily, "that someone besides the good squire held your attention for so long, keeping your company from us?" At this he looked up and cocked a brow questioningly.

Although Deveraux's features were closed and unreadable when he met Percy's gaze, for a moment, he felt unnerved. Could this little weasel have been privy to his meeting this night?

Just as quickly, he discarded the notion as an impossibility and decided to take Percy's insinuation at face value. He became aware of the sensitive nature of Percy's seemingly innocent remark, however, when he caught sight of the suspicious look which the duke now threw his way.

Thornton's eyes had narrowed to dark slits and his voice shook with barely suppressed fury. "Well, Captain, pray tell us. Who was the object of your attention this evening? Mistress Mary was in attendance, was she not?"

Cameron could sense the uneasiness in the room as the others shifted nervously in their seats. He shrugged his shoulders in feigned amusement. "I had no idea that a supper of rabbit and sole, aspic and tarts—as we are all accustomed to the squire's 'generosity'—and an evening spent in listening to a lovestruck young lady sing the exalted praises of her fiance, could be of such interest to so many. If you are so desirous of an invitation, I'm sure I could arrange it with the squire."

At this, the duke burst into unrestrained laughter and loud guffaws resounded through the room as each man was quick to assure Cameron that he had no need of an invitation.

"No doubt, your pockets are picked clean from all the vails you were obliged to pay Henry's servants," offered one of the guests wryly.

Indeed, the Squire's parsimony was legion among all who had the misfortune to sit at his table, where the only givens were plain fares, hours of dull conversation and heavy vails. As wages were so low, it had become customary for guests to tip their host's servants. The vails were meant to be an added incentive for extra service, but at Balfour Grange guests complained that they were in fact paying the servants' wages.

" 'Tis truth." Deveraux groaned with exaggeration as he turned an empty pocket inside out, much to the everyone's amusement. "To be sure, the brightest part of the evening retired with Miss Balfour at ten o'clock, the remainder being spent in idle business chatter."

"And what of the other young lady?" pressed Percy, slowly crossing the room to Cameron, for he had not been blind to the captain's interest in the chit.

"If you are referring to Miss Shelbourne, sir, she was not in attendance this evening," replied Cameron succinctly.

Percy's stride faltered as he felt the intensity of the hard gaze that Cameron leveled on him. He searched the captain's bronzed face for telltale signs of love, hate, aversion, fear, weakness—anything which would explain the sudden flash in those strangely hypnotic, blue eyes. But he could read nothing in the strong features. Somewhere in time he had experienced this same sensation, but he couldn't, for the life of him, recall the circumstances. A careful search of the captain's room had yielded nothing. Deveraux was just as he represented himself—nothing more, nothing less. But yet there was something . . .

Slowly Deveraux turned his attention back to the table, looking pointedly at Lord Dandridge who was having a poor night of it. "Perhaps a fresh hand might improve your game, Your Grace."

The earl, tired and drawn, took his cue and gratefully relinguished his chair to the captain. As Cameron accepted it and deftly engineered the duke into several winning hands, Thornton's temper was mitigated and a precarious balance restored. Only Osborn remained outside the circle, continuing to regard the captain with a curious intensity.

19

The sun had just peeped above the horizon when everyone turned out to go a-Maying. The townspeople scampered about the countryside, collecting branches for the evening bonfire and spring flowers for crowns for the royal procession.

But though the women chattered and the children gamboled, their actions were guarded. Thoughtfully seating herself upon a bed of fragrant clover to weave her crown of gilly flowers, Rorie could feel the tension. There was a certain wariness in the air that couldn't be surmounted by even the most celebrated event of the year.

The news of the arrest warrant on her uncle had reverberated throughout the village like a bolt of lightning, shattering the very foundations of hope and scattering their courage to the four winds. Now, no one took a step without first looking over his shoulder.

What of her uncle? Where was he, and was he well? And what would happen to her family should her background become known to the duke? What was to become of Mary?

Suddenly, Rorie felt weary and trapped beneath the weight of worries she knew not to be groundless. If only she had someone to turn to . . .

Rorie took a deep breath and squared her shoulders; she couldn't fall apart now! She was angrily chiding her weakness, when a plump, red-haired lass flopped down beside her.

"Lucy," she greeted, managing a smile, "how happy you look." She and Lucy Finley had grown up together and had shared many an adventure as well as some well-earned paddlings. If anyone could ease her heavy mood, thought Rorie, the effervescent Lucy could.

"Oh, Rorie," the girl cried, "I have a secret I must share with someone, or I shall surely burst from happiness."

Rorie ceased the weaving of her flower crown and looked into her friend's smiling, freckled face. "I'm glad someone is to know happiness. What is your secret, Lucy?"

"I'm to be married," the girl announced proudly.

Rorie couldn't hide her surprise. Although she hadn't seen her friend for some time, she wasn't aware that Lucy had been serious about any of the local boys.

"Who is the lucky one?" asked Rorie curiously. "Is it Matthew?"

"Matthew! Heavens no!" Lucy exclaimed. "Matthew be but a boy. I've got me a man."

Rorie put up a hand to stem the excited flow of Lucy's words. "Enough already," she said with a laugh. "Who is your intended?"

"It be Wiley Pate."

The congratulations died on Rorie's lips, and the smile froze on her face. Lucy was good-hearted and a dear friend, but she wasn't a pretty girl. Rorie knew with a certainty that Wiley was using her, and she felt sick at heart. All too soon, Lucy would know it, too.

"Are you sure that you understood his words?" asked Rorie.

"Well, he dinna say it in so many words," declared Lucy stoutly, disappointed in her friend's reaction, "but when he finds out I'm carryin' his babe—"

"Oh, Lucy, do you know what you have done?" cried Rorie in consternation. "Men like Wiley care nothing for anyone but themselves. Don't you see? He's just using you. He's no good to anyone." Rorie hadn't intended to express her reservations, but her fury at Pate's bold-faced lie and fear for her friend's future loosened her tongue.

Lucy rose abruptly, her plain, round face flushed with anger.

"Lucy, I—"

"We ain't friends no more, Rorie. Ye jest stay away from me. Talk is ye've gotten too big fer yer britches anyhow, runnin' ta Londontown, rubbin' elbows with the gentry. And soon you'll be keepin' house with the very man who hunts yer uncle down."

"Lucy, how can you say that! You know very well the circumstances of my position."

"I thought I did, but now some of us is beginnin' ta wonder."

"Wonder what?"

" 'Tis funny how ye no sooner become

companion to the future duchess of Lyndeforde and your uncle is accused of murder, the stores are seized . . . What was the price—a few fancy gowns?"

Rorie was stunned. "Lucy, you know me better than that. How can you think I would betray you all?"

"Look around, Rorie. There be plenty what think it."

Rorie reeled under the unexpected verbal attack and before she could recover, Lucy was gone. It must be true, she thought with a sinking heart, remembering the guarded looks and mumbled greetings she had received from fellow villagers. She had laid it to the oppressive atmosphere, but now she knew the truth: they thought her a spy in the duke's service! Her aunt had warned her that people might not understand her living under the roof of the very man who persecuted them. Rorie laughed at the bitter irony. She no longer had to worry about repudiating them, for they had already ostracized her.

Dazedly she rose, her crown of gilly flowers sliding unnoticed to the ground, and began to walk. Heedless of direction, oblivious to her surroundings, she was unaware of anything but the pain and shock of Lucy's accusations. At length she came to a stop before a vine-covered cottage, the pathway overgrown with weeds and vines. Rorie would have turned back, but some inner force propelled her on, forcing her to open the protesting weathered door and to step inside.

She walked slowly about the room—the room where she had known so many happy hours with her parents and brother. It was such a simple time, then. Her finger traced lines in the thick dust on the smooth table and chairs. Everything was as she and Terence had left it the day they had moved in with the Fentons. The huge, black kettle still hung in the fireplace; the rushsticks were still upon the table which her mother had always kept polished to a high sheen; and her father's high-back chair remained by the hearth where he had spent long hours reading. Only his few books were gone—the only items from which Rorie and her brother had derived any comfort and could bring themselves to remove.

She looked up the steep stairway to the loft rooms, but could not force herself to climb the stairs. She had laid enough ghosts to rest for one day, she decided, and turned to slump wearily into a chair by the table. Bowing to the anger, uncertainty, and frustration of the past days, Rorie laid her head on her arms on the cool table and gave vent to great, racking sobs. She felt so confused and unsure of herself. "Damn Wiley Pate! And to hell with anyone who would dare think me in league with—with—" Wrenching sobs overwhelmed her. Why did she have to be alone at a time when she most needed gentle guidance and wise counsel?

As if in answer, she felt herself being gently lifted and enfolded in the security of strong, comforting arms, where she continued to cry and babble incoherently until there were no more tears left to fall. She didn't know how Terence had found her, but she was so very grateful that he had.

"Thank you Terence, I—"

Immediately feeling his body stiffen, Rorie

looked up in puzzlement. Instead of the mischievous, brown eyes of her brother, she stared
up into the cool, appraising, blue eyes of Captain
Deveraux.

It was a bittersweet moment for them both.
Rorie had never felt so safe and comfortable. And
though she repeatedly told herself that she
detested and feared this man's touch, she made
no attempt to move away when Cameron's hands
dropped to rest lightly on her hips.

For Cameron, it was an uncomfortable
moment of truth as he faced the realization that
Rorie might possibly stir something more in him
than lust. And as he felt the sweet curves of her
body fitted so neatly to his own, his desire to
make love to this beautiful young woman was
checked by his wish to protect the innocent waif
in her. Lost in the shimmery green and amber
depths of her incredible eyes, he struggled with
his impulses before reluctantly releasing her.
What spell did this little witch weave on him, he
wondered in amazement? He was supposed to be
making the rules, yet she still seemed to be
calling the moves.

Sensing the change in him, Rorie quickly
backed away, struggling to control her own
rioting emotions. Shamefacedly, she realized that
she might have surrendered to him had he but
pressed the advantage. And the knowledge
frightened her badly, for her only exposure to
lovemaking had been one of violence and
degradation.

"I thought the Rorie Shelbournes of this
world never cried," Cameron teased lightly in an
effort to break the uneasy tension between them.
"What is this place, anyway?"

Rorie's fingers plucked nervously at her skirt. "This was my home before my parents died. I knew many happy moments here," she answered quietly. Noting the puzzlement on Cameron's face as he surveyed the simple dwelling, her pride was pricked, and she found herself explaining. "I'm not related to Squire Balfour. 'Twas but a story he contrived to shield himself from embarrassment when Mary insisted that I act as her companion."

So that was what the squire sought to hide, thought Deveraux, and he threw back his head in a burst of laughter. "Well, 'tis a relief to find that you and the squire are not cut from the same cloth after all."

Rorie instantly wished that she had cut out her tongue and prayed that he wouldn't look for further truths. As she wiped away the last trace of tears with the back of her hand, she reminded him of a child caught with her hand in the cookie jar.

"What are you doing here?" Rorie demanded, with a flash of her old spirit.

"The procession begins in an hour, and Mary became worried when she couldn't find you. Someone told her you were headed this way, so she asked me to seek you out. Come on, I have a horse outside. I'll take you back to the Grange where you could do with a bit of soap and water."

Rorie looked down at the dirt on her hands and clothes and nodded in agreement.

"Here, wipe the smudges from your face. Can't have anyone thinking we took a tumble in the hay," Cameron said with an amused wink as he tossed her a handkerchief.

Rorie wanted to slap his arrogant face, but he was out the door before she had time to react.

As she reluctantly followed after him, he waved his hand in the direction of the horse. "Front or back, milady?"

Recalling his rude insult at the lagoon, Rorie responded tartly, "A *lady* does neither, thank you. I shall walk."

"Then as a gentleman, I shall be compelled to walk also."

It was in Rorie's mind to debate that issue, but she let the moment pass, for she was in no mood to spar with him. Instead, she made a face which left him in no doubt how she felt about his company, but he chose to ignore it.

In the course of her tearful unburdening, Cameron recalled her mention of a Wiley somebody. And then, of course, there was this Terence. Good Lord, how many men was she involved with anyway? he wondered, suddenly angry at the thought of her involvement with any other man. After a half mile, the tension between them had built to such a peak that Cameron finally broke the silence.

"Tell me, Miss Shelbourne," he asked suspiciously, "what has cast you so low? Could it be a lover's spat?"

Rorie heard the brittle edge to his tone and wondered what she had done to warrant his ill-humor this time. "Things are not always what they seem, Captain Deveraux," she snapped, her own temper rising in response to his. "You of all people should know that."

Cameron raised a questioning brow. "Oh, and how should I know that, Miss Shelbourne?"

Rorie bit her lip, as she debated the wisdom

of blurting out her suspicions to a stranger she told herself that she disliked and distrusted. But his snide arrogance got the better of her cautious nature.

"Oh, come now, Captain, as a friend of the duke, you of all people would know that the enclosure is just an excuse for him to increase his holdings without expense."

"The circumstances are unfortunate," Deveraux agreed, ignoring her sarcasm. "But one can't escape the fact that the land has been so overworked here, the soil can no longer support the populace in its present condition."

Rorie looked up at Cameron sharply. "Are you condoning the stealing of one's birthright, Captain?"

"No, Miss Shelbourne. Total enclosure is a bitter cure. The same results can be achieved with crop rotation and the putting aside of your damnable practice of sowing broadcast. Scattering a handful of seed for every two strides is wasteful and impractical. Why, two-thirds of the ground goes unplanted while the rest grows so thick with seed, the land doesn't prosper. If the growth were confined to a particular area, I'm bound you would save five pounds of seed to the acre.

"Similarly, if you people planted a field of turnips for the herds to feed on instead of only hay, you wouldn't have to kill and salt down so many animals when the spring grass didn't come in or if the hay failed. That way the flocks and herds could increase, which would mean more meat, butter, milk—and manure to improve impoverished soils."

Rorie stared at Deveraux in surprise. "And

just how does a sea captain know so much about farming?" she asked crisply.

"My business is trade, Miss Shelbourne. It behooves me to familiarize myself with the latest techniques and inventions in all areas of life."

"Bah, you sound like Terence and my father."

"Then this Terence will eat, while those too stubborn or foolish to change will starve," replied Cameron stiffly.

"Do you call us fools?"

"That depends. Sometimes one forgets that just as a person must grow and change, so does the world. It's only the fools who refuse to accept it. Are you a fool, Miss Shelbourne?"

For one of the few times in her life, Rorie found no ready retort on her lips. She could only glare up at Cameron as she realized the wisdom in his words. He was right, of course, but she would rather swallow her tongue than to tell him so.

"It still doesn't excuse the duke's actions," Rorie argued stubbornly. "The man has no intentions of enriching the soil. Once more, I know that the rebellion was staged to seize the shops and the emissary murdered as reason to persecute and even hang our villagers. I don't know the why of it yet, but, Captain, I promise you, I will. One other thing I would know, sir, is what part a colonial sea captain plays in this nasty business. And not just an ordinary sea captain, I would warrant, for ordinary sea captains aren't taken into the confidences of the nobility and invited to be their guests, ay, Captain? I mean to know your interest, who you are, and what you are—"

Rorie was shocked into silence when Cameron's large hands suddenly shot out to grasp her upper arms in a bruising grip, lifting her off her feet. She shrank from the cold anger she saw reflected in his steely eyes.

"If you value your person and the lives of your friends, you will raise no question of me nor stick that pretty little nose into places it doesn't belong," he warned slowly, punctuating each word. "There is more at stake here than you know. Let it lie, or you'll bring naught but harm to the very people you wish to help. You said it yourself, Rorie, things may not be as they seem."

He released her so abruptly, she would have fallen had it not been for the support of his hand on her arm. Rorie pulled away from him in wide-eyed alarm, massaging her forearms and struggling to keep the tears in her eyes from spilling onto her cheeks. Instantly, Cameron regretted his harsh actions, but, before he could make a conciliatory move toward her, Rorie turned on her heel like a startled deer and ran off across the field in a cloud of petticoats.

"Damn!" Cameron cursed aloud. He knew his rashness would only serve to heighten her distrust and curiosity of him. He would have to watch her closely now. And judging by the look in her eyes, he would have a damnable time getting close to her again.

20

Rorie arrived back at the clearing just as the procession was starting. Scrubbed and clothed in the customary white gown, her frame of mind had slightly improved. She waved a greeting to Mary as the young woman stepped into a flower bedecked chariot to be escorted down country lanes to begin her reign as queen. Rorie was struck by the pale tenseness of her friend. Indeed the sobriety of the crowd brought to mind more a funeral procession than a celebration, she thought, as she took her place behind the chariot.

Two little boys, gaily clad in jesters' costumes, and each carrying a large hoop decorated with spring blossoms, gay ribbon streamers, bells, and shiny trinkets headed the parade. Numerous children walked and skipped along the lane, carrying sprigs gathered from hedgerows, or small baskets filled with spring flowers. Others touted hooked canes festooned with nosegays and ribbons, or rolled flower-covered hoops along the way. But even their impish antics could not dispel the anxious gloom which wove through the village like a spider's web.

As the parade wound its way to the village green, a young boy who was designated the herald and dressed in an overlarge red coat and black hat, cried out, "Silence! Silence! Make way for the queen who has come to be crowned!"

Children scattered rose petals in her path as Mary left the chariot to walk to the dais, followed by Rorie and the rest of the attendants carrying flower banners. A hush descended over the crowd as the duke of Lyndeforde, dressed in his usual black attire, stepped forward then, to place a crown of fresh flowers upon Mary's head and to pronounce the festivities open. There was forced applause and restrained cheering as the Maypole, twelve feet high and brightly painted in stripes with colored ribbons hanging from a garlanded top, was dragged in by a group of men and youngsters happily blowing on whistles made from willow branches.

The tree was set in the center of the green. About two feet below the decorated top, there was an even number of streamers of alternating pink and blue cheesecloth securely attached and left dangling loosely about the pole. When the pole was in place, the Jack-in-the-Green stepped in front of the dancers and loudly proclaimed:

Come all ye lads and lassies,
Join in the festival scene,
Come dance around the Maypole
That 'twill stand upon the Green.

Rorie looked on as boys and girls approached

the Maypole in an orderly fashion to claim their streamers and go through the motions of wrapping the pole—always with a watchful eye to the duke. When the pole was wound, the dancers then skipped once more around the pole and off the field, signaling that the games were to begin.

As sports seemed to provide an outlet for anxieties, the games were more animated than the rest of the festivities had been. Rorie was glad to see that even Mary managed a smile or two, though the duke continued to look on in apathetic boredom. But for her part, Rorie felt as though the villagers were puppets in a performance, forced to entertain, and she longed for the sham to be over. She had searched for Terence and her aunt, but, given the circumstances, she knew they would not be present. Rorie was seized by a pressing loneliness in the midst of a crowd.

Finally, the duke stood up to release the queen and her court to their own devices, and Rorie could almost feel the sigh of relief sweep through the crowd when he withdrew his presence. With no more stomach for games, the villagers were also about to disperse when gypsies, clad in brightly colored costumes and announcing their presence with a lively tune, suddenly strode to the fore. After several minutes at the subtle coaxing of fiddles, people seemed to come alive and even Rorie couldn't resist swaying to the wildly sensuous music.

"Rorie," said Mary, joining her friend, "I'm going to return to the Grange. The housekeeper has just sent word that Mother is worsening."

"Oh, I am so sorry, Mary. I shall come with you."

"No, there is nothing you can do. I want you to stay here and enjoy the festivities, for it would seem that Drumfielde is at last to receive the celebration due it."

"In any case, 'tis a fitting death knell," observed Rorie cynically. "You know, you have only to send word if you need me."

Mary smiled gratefully. "I know."

As Mary melted into the crowd, Rorie turned to watch the young gypsy women dance. Long, black hair fanned out from their shoulders, and skirts of brilliant hues swirled around trim ankles as their bodies writhed provocatively in tempo to the erotic rhythm of tambourines and fiddles. It was intoxicating to the senses, and soon Rorie found herself under the gypsies' spell, yearning to share their freedom of spirit. It was then that her eyes were drawn unwillingly, irrevocably to the tall sea captain, and her mood turned sour when she recognized the comely Lady Dandridge draped across his arm, their dark heads seemingly bowed in shared secrets.

It inflamed her to think how close she, herself, had come to submitting to his advances, and Rorie's face suffused with shame as she recalled how easily he had manipulated her at his every whim. At last, she had to admit it. She and Lucy Finley were no match for the Cameron Deverauxs and the Wiley Pates. Men like that thrived on seduction; it was a game they played all too well. And, for the first time, she could understand Lucy's lapse in common sense. It was too late for Lucy, but Rorie angrily resolved that she would not be the captain's next conquest.

Dusk had long since fallen. The children were sent to their beds, but the adults, buoyed with ale, mead, and mulled wine showed no inclination to draw the festivities to an end. Young lovers fought for secluded spots, while others joined in the dancing or games of chance. Freely imbibing along with the rest, the squire uninhibitedly pinched the rumps of nubile lasses when he thought he could get away with it. Indeed, he worked the crowd as though he had generously funded the festivities, when, in fact, he hadn't contributed a penny. The largess of food and drink came from the scant resources of the villagers. There was such gay, almost frenzied, abandonment as the gypsies fiddled even livelier tunes that it appeared to Rorie as though the people thought this their last merriment.

She wished she could join in, but she was no longer one of them. Although nothing had been said aside from Lucy's outburst, the looks and actions were unmistakable; she was being shunned. Not even Wiley approached her, though he continually watched her movements with a nasty smile on his face that dispelled any relief she would have felt at his distance. And with a certainty that sent a shiver of apprehension up her spine, Rorie knew he was laying in wait for her—even as she watched him disappear into the bushes with Lucy. Suddenly, the festivities lost their appeal for her, and she wished only for the solitude of her bed to forget the captain, to forget Wiley Pate, and to bury her warring emotions beneath the soft, downy coverlet.

As she turned to leave, Rorie became uncomfortably aware of an old gypsy crone intently studying her from the side. The woman was seated on a chair near the fire, her black eyes never wavering in their gaze until Rorie felt compelled to approach her.

"Is there a debt that I owe you, gypsy woman?" she asked brusquely. "Else why do you look at me so? Pray tell me your name." As the old woman continued to stare at her, Rorie shifted uneasily beneath the gypsy's unswerving scrutiny. "Well!" she demanded impatiently, her temper already tried dangerously close to the breaking point.

"I am called Magda, queen of the gypsies," responded the woman in her own good time. " 'Tis not what ye owe me, my pretty, but 'tis what ye owe ta yerself—and ta another."

"I don't know what you mean," declared Rorie, a mixture of bewilderment, curiosity, and anxiety creeping into her tone.

"Ye will," the old gypsy assured her mysteriously. "There be two forces afoot, my dearie. One ye must avoid an' t'other ye must not fight. Flow with the tide an' ye shall know rewards. Flow agin it an' ye shall reap sorrow."

"And just what are these forces?"

"Love and pride, dearie. It remains for ye ta discover which to embrace and which to cast off. Now leave me, fer I will soon have done with my job an' would know peace."

The woman leaned back and closed her eyes then, in obvious dismissal, and Rorie backed away, perplexed and unnerved by the old crone's strange warning.

As Cameron watched Rorie leave, he noticed the dejected slump of her shoulders. She seemed to carry many weights on her, and he wondered what new burden she had just added. He knew that she was angry with him. The withering glares she had shot him the few times that he had managed to catch her eye told him so in no uncertain terms. He suspected though that her ire stemmed more from the identity of his companion for the day than from their earlier confrontation.

'Twas true. The lovely Lady Dandridge was proving to be more of a problem than he had anticipated. The lady was provocative and obvious if she was anything, and Cameron was finding it inceasingly difficult to ignore her sensuality. But he would never jeopardize a valued friendship, least of all Lord Dandridge's, over any woman. Besides, Rorie was constantly on his mind these days. She possessed none of the sophistication or air of experience he was used to in his women, but yet something about her impetuous spirit and spontaneous nature both intrigued and challenged him. And he couldn't help wondering how she might compare with his other conquests. He knew he could have had her this morning at the cottage, but for reasons he still couldn't fathom, he hadn't been able to cross that line—not yet.

Handing an indignant Eleanora off to her husband, Cameron started to follow Rorie in hopes of making whatever amends were necessary. As he pressed through the crowd, however, he felt a tug on his arm and looked down into the blackest eyes he had ever seen.

"What is it old woman?" he asked with a flash of annoyance. "You see that I am on my way."

The old gypsy cackled, undeterred by his manner, and motioned him down to her level.

"I am Magda. Remember me, for ye've come full circle, lad. Prepare yerself well an' ye shall be the victor; overlook wha' be before yer eyes an' ye shall be the fallen." And as if in afterthought, she added, "Take not that what be not freely given, for 'twill be yers soon enou'. Temper time with patience."

And she pressed something small and hard into his hand.

A flood of memories assailed his consciousness as he stared down at the object.

"Where did you come by this ring!" he demanded hoarsely.

But when he looked up for the answer, the old crone had disappeared. He searched for her amid the crowd, but all his inquiries were met only with hostile response. Finally he returned to Lyndeforde.

When Deveraux entered the manor, he could feel that something was wrong. The place was too quiet, and the servants he encountered met him with downcast eyes and a manner more nervous and sullen than usual.

"Has something happened?" inquired Cameron with a cautious curiosity.

"In a manner of speaking, sir," the butler informed him guardedly.

"Is the duke about?"

"Yes, sir, but may I say that to intrude upon the duke at this time would be to trespass upon a hornet's nest," replied the butler meaningfully.

"I see. Well, then, I think we shall leave the hornet's nest in peace." Deveraux wasn't anxious to encounter Thornton in such a foul mood, and he was confident that Rawlings would know the full measure of the story anyway.

The butler wiped his brow in obvious relief. "Thank you, sir."

In the master suite, the duke refilled his brandy glass for the fourth time, covertly glancing at the note on the desk, hoping that it had been a figment of his imagination. But each time he looked, it was still there, bringing a reality now to his nightmares.

"Roger, what's happened?" cried Osborn, hurrying anxiously into the bed chamber.

"Percy! Where the bloody devil have you been!" screamed Thornton, rounding on his cohort in a fit of blinding fury.

Percy stiffened. "I've been seeing to a few details," he replied coldly as he eyed Thornton's rumpled, liquor-stained apparel with disgust. "What's gotten into you?" he demanded. "It smells like a whore's den in here, and the whole house is in an uproar. It seems you've been abusing the servant maids from the chamber-maid to the scullery girl—"

"This! This is what!" shrieked the duke, jabbing at the folded parchment on the desk.

Osborn crossed the room, sidestepping the shards of smashed liquor glasses, and picked up the note. "Atonement is near. Soon your judge shall appear to demand his due," he read aloud. "What the devil is this?"

" 'Tis the gypsy's curse," mumbled Thornton, quaffing the brandy in a single gulp.

"The gypsy you strangled? Don't be ridiculous," scoffed Percy. "Get a hold of yourself, man, you're babbling like an idiot."

"No, no listen. The butler said an old woman delivered this message, and when I looked out the window, she was down there, standing by the tree, staring up at me as though she were waiting for me to look."

"Roger, it is dark out—"

"It was her, I tell you! I saw her. She had some kind of a light around her."

"So you think her a spirit?" Osborn inquired with scornful amusement. "Really, Roger, you take this superstitious nonsense too far."

"Well, what would you think!" snapped Thornton. "The guards searched the grounds. The woman just disappeared."

Osborn snickered. "Spirits don't write notes, Your Grace, and even less do gypsies."

"She didn't write it!"

Percy looked at Thornton in confusion. "But I thought you said the woman—"

"The butler wrote it for her, you boob! He wrote what she told him to write."

"I see. Well, did you search the gypsy camp?"

"The guards just reported that they've gone, leaving behind not so much as a wagon track. I have men out scouring the countryside now, but so far nothing."

"Yes, those people always could conveniently disappear into thin air."

"I've got to capture Fenton, Percy!" Thornton's voice rose hysterically. "He is the judge in that note. I'm certain of it, and I must find him before—"

"Calm yourself, Roger, you're drunk. 'Tis all a coincidence. By the light of day and a clearer head, you will see that there is a logical explanation. The note probably means that one of your magistrates is demanding payment for a service. Now get some sleep so you'll be presentable for the picnic tomorrow. We shall discuss our plans when you're in a better frame of mind."

As he led Thornton to the bed, Osborn began to wonder if he had chosen his partnership wisely.

21

The next morning, Cameron shrugged into a loose fitting shirt of white lawn and tucked it into the top of his fawn-colored breeches, as his valet continued to ponder the mystery.

" 'Pon my soul, Cap'n, wha' da ye be supposin' the old hag meant by them words last night?"

"Your guess is as good as mine," Cameron answered, pulling on his high-glossed jackboots.

Rawlings laughed. "Well, whoever she was, she sure put the duke into a tizzy. He's had guards out combing the countryside for her all night."

Cameron's eyes narrowed in contemplation as he took the ring from his pocket. "I believe the woman called herself Magda. She gave me this," he said quietly. "It once belonged to my mother, and she valued it most highly."

"Magda?" repeated Rawlings in a tone rendered barely audible by his astonishment.

"The old crone must have stolen the ring years ago and had a twinge of conscience," continued Deveraux, so locked in his own thoughts that he had taken no notice of his man-servant's reaction. "I don't know how she recognized my identity or knows of my business—"

"She didna steal it, Cap'n."

"What?"

"The ring. She didna steal it. Yer mother give it to Magda fer—well—safekeeping." As the stunned expression on Cameron's face demanded further explanation, Rawlings swallowed hard. "Please, Cap'n, this ain't the time ta open up old wounds. Ye don't need no more ta think about now. Let it go 'til later, sir. It'll keep jest as well, fer the woman be a friend and poses no threat ta ye."

Cameron stared at the valet long and hard before comprehension dawned. "Is she the one to whom I was sold as a child?"

Rawlings nodded his shaggy, white mane slowly. "Aye, sir, she be the one, though I kenna think 'twas Magda ye seen last night."

"Why?"

"Well, sir, Lord Dandridge told me she was found strangled to death on All Hallows' E'en outside of Drumfielde. There was a gypsy funeral an' all."

"Then Lord Dandridge is mistaken," insisted Cameron firmly. "I saw and talked to the woman myself." But even as he said it, Deveraux couldn't help thinking about the expressions of shock and anger on the gypsies' faces and the moody silence with which they had greeted his questions about Magda. "We'll talk of this later," he said abruptly. "Now what word have you had on our other matter?"

" " 'Tis as ye suspected, Cap'n," responded Rawlings, likewise eager to change the subject. "Looks like a pack train is ta be loaded an' readied ta move the day of the weddin'."

"That means the ship will drop anchor before midnight the night before, and the train will be loaded by dawn. The smugglers will have the protection of the fen through the daylight hours. By the time they can move the wagons to the edge of the marsh, the night will hide their travels across the open road."

"Aye, Cap'n, an' 'tis like ye thought, too. The goods is ta be stored in the village shops what the duke seized until the next night. Jacobs overheard the Lyndeforde bailiff in the tavern the other day, tellin' some young rowdy."

Cameron ran a hand across his face in restless irritation. "But where are the goods being hidden on the way to Portsmouth?" he wondered aloud.

"I don't be knowin' that, sir. Jacobs only heard the Lyndeforde bailiff tellin' this Wiley fellow 'bout the shops—"

"Did you say Wiley?" demanded Cameron sharply.

Rawlings blinked in surprise at the captain's sudden reaction. "Aye, sir, do ye know of him?"

"I heard the name once," replied Cameron tightly, recalling Rorie's mention of him.

"Well, Jacobs says ye should watch yer back with this one. Shall I pass the word ta Will and the men ta stand ready?" asked Rawlings hopefully, his face alight with the prospect of action at last.

"No, I will do it. I don't want to take the chance of any villagers recognizing you from the past and making a connection between us. Osborn is suspicious enough, and he and

Thornton have spies everywhere since Fenton's escape. From here on, I think it best that you not show yourself outside of Lyndeforde. I'll be back within the hour."

"As ye say, sir."

Cameron's height was such that he had to duck as he entered the White Swan Inn. At his sudden appearance, all talking ceased as the customers turned to peruse the black-haired stranger. Cameron raked the crowd, in turn, with eyes that dared anyone to challenge him. The room was full. Some of the patrons were locals, while others were passengers on a stage passing through to London. Walking with a deliberate step, Cameron moved confidently through the center of the room to a table in the far corner. Animated chatter began anew as the patrons' interest in the newcomer waned, and they resumed their regular activities of dart throwing and wagering.

"Oooee, have ye ever seen such a man as tha'?" cooed one of the barmaids, patting her hair and yanking her blouse lower. "Oi'll wager he be a frisky one in the sack." As she moved off to approach Cameron, she felt a restraining hand on her arm.

"Leave off, Sally," warned the other barmaid threateningly. "Oi seed 'im first. Oi'll serve the gent."

Both girls suddenly shrieked as they each received a resounding smack on the rump.

"Neither of ye be servin' the gent," shouted the stout innkeeper. "Ye knows the rules abou' fightin' o'er the customers. We got plenty enou' ta serve asides him. Now get yer arse movin'."

As the girls made an indignant face and moved off in opposite directions, the innkeeper approached Deveraux, studying his patron with a keen eye.

"Wha'll it be gent?" he asked gruffly. He didn't cater much to the local gentry or strangers—unless they stepped off a stage with full pockets.

"Ale," Cameron answered, looking the proprietor square in the eye. "Are you Jacobs?" he asked in a lowered voice.

"Who wants to know?"

"I understand you have an owler's special for a midnight rider."

The innkeeper's eyes narrowed in suspicion. "How know ye this, stranger?"

"Mutual friends from Romney Marsh," returned Deveraux.

The man nodded, satisfied with the answer. "How soon do ye ride?"

"Midnight of the twenty-ninth."

"I'll see ta yer order, myself," he assured Cameron.

When the innkeeper returned with a full tankard fifteen minutes later, Cameron caught the imperceptible nod of the man's head which assured him that all would be ready, and he acknowledged it in kind, both being careful to make no noticeable contact.

Then Cameron swiveled his attention to the other patrons, studying them as he slowly drank his ale. He recognized no one—save one. It was Terence, the lanky youth whom Rorie had embraced at the Fenton farm the night he had followed her. Deveraux's features drew taut, as he wondered what attraction the lad held for the headstrong wench who so disrupted his thoughts of late. He was a mere boy, barely Rorie's age, as fresh and untried as a young pup. Yet she didn't shrink from *his* touch.

Suddenly the barmaid shrieked in righteous anger, dislodging a searching hand from under her skirts. "Leave off, Wiley Pate! I tol' ye before if ye kenna be a gentleman like Terence here—"

Cameron's eye was immediately drawn to Terence's companion. So this was Wiley. A few years older and shorter in stature than Terence, the young man was well muscled and attractive enough in a brooding sort of way. But whereas Terence looked the innocent, there was a swaggering unconscionable air about this Wiley which put Deveraux on his guard. Cameron had dealt enough with Pate's kind to know the danger they represented. Aside from that, there was a familiarity about the boy that continued to nag at Cameron's mind. Then it came to him—this was the youth who had instigated the pelting of the duke's emissary at the rebellion.

The two boys were such an unlikely pair, Deveraux couldn't help wondering about the connection between them and Rorie. If Pate was involved in the duke's smuggling network, where did Rorie and Terence fit in? Did he unjustly brand them guilty by association, or was there a basis for his suspicions? Perhaps he was jumping to conclusions, Cameron allowed, but in the next moment, his doubts were dispelled when he heard Rorie's name being discussed between the two youths. And once again, Cameron was struck by how little he actually knew of this girl. As Rawlings had once asked him, what difference should it make? He'd had women in his bed where not even a name mattered to him. But Rorie was different somehow, and everything about her mattered. He didn't know why; it just did. And the thought that she might be intimate with one or both of these boys—whatever their game—tore him apart.

Deveraux quaffed the remainder of his ale, impatient to be off, and left without undue notice. A picnic had been arranged as part of the prenuptial celebration. He was late already and was not anxious to raise the duke's suspicions after going to so much trouble to cultivate his trust. Aside from that, there were questions to which Rorie was going to provide a few answers, he decided grimly.

Rorie stared in dismay at the purple smudges beneath her tired, aching eyes as she looked into the vanity mirror. She had passed the night in sleepless confusion, trying to decipher the meaning behind the old gypsy's words, but nothing presented itself, and she ended by attributing the message to the ravings of senility. Then there was Deveraux. Just how did he figure into the scheme of things? she wondered over and over. That he was hiding something was evident to her by his brutish manner of the day before.

"Rorie, you aren't ready!"

Rorie started as Mary burst into the room. "Ready? Ready for what?" she asked in surprise.

"Why, the duke's picnic, of course," Mary reminded her with a grimace, flopping mournfully into a chair. " 'Tis in half an hour. Don't tell me you've forgotten."

Rorie groaned as she recalled the invitation.

She was tired, her whole body ached, and her temples throbbed incessantly. She clearly wasn't up to facing the world today, least of all Captain Deveraux.

"I'm sorry, Mary, but I can't possibly go. The pounding in my head leaves me no relief."

Mary regarded her friend with suspicion for a moment before her thin face crumpled into the more characteristic consternation. "You really don't look well," she admitted. "Perhaps a day in bed would be far more advantageous to you." Suddenly Mary's face lit up. "I know, I shall stay with you."

"No, Mary, you mustn't," protested Rorie. "If you don't go—"

"Who's not going where?" boomed the squire, his bulk filling the open doorway.

"Rorie isn't feeling well, Father. She has decided to forego the picnic and stay behind to rest."

"That so?" replied the squire, rubbing his paunch, thoughtfully.

"Yes, and I think that I should remain to look after her."

"You will do nothing of the kind, daughter. The duke's temper has been tried enough by this girl's uncle, and you'll not add fuel to the fire. You go ahead, and I shall see that Miss Shelbourne receives all that she requires," the squire added slyly.

Rorie detected a glow in his small, piglike eyes, which made her distinctly uneasy. Of late, the squire seemed to be very solicitous of her, touching her hand, taking her by the arm, moving his chair nearer to her own, and brushing against her thigh. Once when she had turned suddenly and caught him unawares, he was looking at her oddly, as though mentally stripping her of her clothes. At first she chided her overworked imagination, but as he began to become bolder in his advances, Rorie could no longer ignore his intentions. And, once again, she cursed the nature of men.

"How kind of you to offer, sir," she replied curtly, "but it suddenly comes to me that the fresh air would be a far better tonic for my ills after all."

The squire's heavy jowls fell in clear disappointment. "Oh—yes, quite, if that is your wish," he stammered, hastily vacating the room.

Mary, nursing her own disappointment, seemingly took no notice of the awkward tension in the chamber, as she, too, dispiritedly rose to return to her room to wait for Rorie.

"I'll send in Mandy to help you dress," she called over her shoulder.

"No, I can do just as well myself," replied Rorie. "Just allow me a few minutes."

When Rorie, at last, had the chamber to herself, she carelessly yanked on an oval hoop, a white satin petticoat elaborately quilted with tiny purple and pink flowers, and a simple lavender overgrown of lace and figured silk. Attacking her snarled mass of hair, she deftly plaited it into one braid and twisted it on top of her head. Then, she jammed on a bonnet of white straw with lavender ribbons and stomped out to do battle with the day.

Although Rorie had contrived to share her seat with Mary in the open carriage, placing the squire opposite them, it was impossible to escape his seemingly accidental brushings against her leg as they were jostled along country lanes. She thanked providence when they finally pulled into the meadow beneath gray, cloudy skies.

As the duke stepped forward to help Mary out of the carriage, both girls looked at each other in surprise at his appearance. Though there was no fault to be found with his dress, his features looked drawn and his eyes were red and puffy, fixating almost maniacally on points for moments at a time. His attention was definitely lacking, and there was a certain high-strung edge to his manner that made the girls distinctly uneasy as they struggled to contain their revulsion.

After Mary had vacated the carriage, Rorie moved to step down, but the squire quickly maneuvered to precede her so that she was forced to suffer his clammy touch as he reached up to help her down from the conveyance. When he reluctantly released his hold, Rorie fled into the crowd, leaving the squire in her dust, his mouth hanging open in surprise.

"Miss Shelbourne, is anything amiss? You look a bit peaked?"

Rorie jumped and turned to face the speaker. "Lord Dandridge, how nice to see you again," she gasped in genuine relief, struggling to catch her breath. "I'm fine, but I fear I'm a bit more piqued than peaked. Overzealous admirer one might say."

" 'Tis not difficult to understand. You look lovely, my dear, doesn't she, Eleanora?"

"Hmmm, what, Robert?" Lady Dandridge's attention had strayed to the crowd where her dark eyes avidly searched for the darkly handsome Captain Deveraux. At the light pressure, which her husband subtly exerted on her arm, she forced her attention back to the lovely, young woman who stood proud and tall before her.

Eleanora's eyes turned hard and cold as they missed nothing in their scrutiny. Taking in Rorie's creamy complexion, the incredible green of her dark, thickly lashed eyes, and the sensuous curves of her young body, Lady Dandridge was awash with envy. At thirty-eight, Eleanora was still quite desirable, but she was very conscious of her own thickening waistline and the fine lines which were networking around her eyes and mouth. The years of overindulgences were indeed taking their toll. Suddenly she knew an all consuming hatred for the girl, and though a smile remained on her face, it held little warmth.

Rorie refused to lower her eyes and show her unease under the older woman's glittering perusal. Instead, she returned Eleanora's stare measure for measure until Lord Dandridge nervously coughed to relieve the tension.

Ahem, I was saying, Eleanora, how fresh and pretty Miss Shelbourne looks," he repeated.

"Yes, Robert, but then children rarely appear otherwise," Lady Dandridge replied in a stilted voice, the furious waving of her fan betraying her agitation.

Rorie smiled her most charming smile. So the lines have been drawn, she thought to herself. Aloud, she responded sweetly, "I suppose to a woman of your age and experience I might appear a child, but I assure you, Lady Dandridge, I am very much a woman—as I am sure Captain Deveraux will attest."

No one had ever dared to speak to her in such a way before, and Lady Dandridge's face could only register shock which immediately changed to envy and dismay upon Rorie's casual allusion to the captain.

As Rorie politely excused herself from their company, she could barely contain her mirth. The look on Eleanora's face had been worth a thousand words, and a dimpled smile hovered about Rorie's lips as she wondered how Deveraux would react to being *her* pawn. Perhaps this day would wax satisfactory after all, she thought with a triumphant smile. Milling through the crowd, Rorie was wondering what to do with herself next, when the growling of her stomach reminded her that she had eaten nothing since rising that morning. With an eager step, she approached the food table.

Set beneath a sprawling oak tree, the table had been attractively set with linen, china, and crystal, and was heavily laden with every food stuff from cod, mutton, and veal to gooseberries, tarts, and puddings. In the center was a pyramid of syllabubs and jellies to dazzle the eye and to tease the palate. Rorie was hungrily reaching for a plate when, out the corner of her eye, she saw Squire Balfour bearing down on her as fast as his short, bandy legs would carry him. Two birds with one stone . . . Damnation, but she should have known better than to venture within a hundred yards of food! she chastised herself. Muttering a distinctly unladylike oath and casting a last wistful glance over the tempting fare, Rorie edged into a group of matrons who were exchanging the latest gossip.

"But my dear, 'tis truth," one pinch-faced old

dowager was declaring stoutly. "Horace Walpole's coach was halted by robbers in Hyde Park. Bold as you please. Nearly lost his head, don't you know. Mr. Walpole placed an advertisement in the paper offering twenty pounds for the return of his goods. And what do you think? The scoundrels had the audacity to answer—demanding forty pounds!"

"No!" shrieked another. "I just don't know what's to come of us. Getting so a body isn't safe on the streets or the roads anymore. Why, I was just telling Lady Swarthington the other day that—"

The women broke off their conversation in midsentence to stare in bewilderment at Rorie as she crouched low in their midst, her eyes darting anxiously in all directions. The ladies then turned to glance askance at each other. One by one, each astonished matron shrugged her shoulders, and the lull in their conversation soon penetrated Rorie's brain. She flushed in embarrassment when she realized that she was the object of their curiosity. Attempting to flash them a charming smile, she ended by stammering apologies and awkwardly backing out of the group. She was uncomfortably aware all the while that curious eyes continued to stare after her as she quickly moved into a secluded stand of trees.

Rorie had just hidden herself from view beneath low hanging branches when the sound of voices reached her ears. Tall oaks and pine trees shielded the interior from sunlight. And peering closely through the darkness, it was a few minutes before she recognized the two figures who stood several yards away, conversing in lowered tones. Wondering what they could be up to, Rorie moved closer, pressing herself against the trunk of a broad oak tree and pulling her skirts as tight about her legs as the hoop would allow. Her heart beat loudly in her ears as she strained to catch snatches of their conversation.

"I've spoken to certain officials," Roger Thornton was saying to a little man, whom Rorie recalled to be Percy Osborn.

In spite of his outlandish dress and affected air, Osborn presented to Rorie's mind the very image of a cutthroat with his shifty, close-set eyes, his sallow, pitted face, and cruel, thin lips. Suddenly, she felt nervous. How dangerous were these two?

"Good. Matthews is getting impatient," responded Osborn, taking out his snuff box. Thornton looked on in disgust as his companion put a pinch to each nostril and let out a healthy sneeze. "Clears the head. You ought to try it sometime," Osborn suggested pointedly. "Now, to business at hand. It occurs to me, Roger, that had we our own ships, we wouldn't need to pay Matthews' outrageous fee to broker the goods out of Portsmouth. As it is, we take all the risks dealing with that cutthroat Billings, and Matthews pockets most of the profit."

"And just how would we protect these ships from search?" asked Thornton with a derisive snort. "I can't lend my name and title to such a venture. At least Captain Matthews has the benefit of cover. Who is going to stop and search a ship of the Royal Navy?"

Percy smiled craftily. "No one. And neither would the nephew of the Marquis de Sauvonnerie and the grandson of a respected colonial French merchant invite scrutiny."

Thornton's jaw dropped in surprise. "Captain Deveraux?"

"Captain Deveraux," Percy reaffirmed. "And who more perfect? Everyone knows he is here seeking a backer to expand his line. We'll simply become his very silent partners."

"Good God, Percy, I haven't the means to cover my gambling vows. How am I to finance a fleet of ships!" Thornton demanded in ill humor.

"The captain is a businessman. I'm sure that he will understand that the funds will be forthcoming."

"Do you think that he would agree to that?"

"Oh, I think so," Percy assured the duke confidently. "Captain Deveraux strikes me as a man of adventure who would be willing to take risks when balanced against high profits. Certain goods would fetch a nice sum in the colonies, don't you think? If he is agreeable, we can broker the third shipment due soon from Calais with him. Just think of the wealth we'll have if the captain is later successful in expanding his line to the China trade?"

Thorton ran a finger along his nose as he considered the matter, and his eyes began to glitter darkly at the prospect of greater riches.

"You know, Roger, there might be another way by which we can profit," continued Osborn, rearranging his full, powdered wig after another hearty, snuff-induced sneeze. "With the enclosure, the peasants no longer have a field in which to graze their sheep. Offer to buy their herds at a fraction of their worth. We can then 'export' the wool to the colonies through Captain Deveraux, bypassing England's tax on wool in the bargain. The wool in this section of the country is of the finest in the world. What do you think?"

Thornton answered with a slow, upward curve of his lips. "I shall speak to the captain at first opportunity," he said. "I believe that his ship will be docking in three weeks. Perhaps now something shall be done right," he added in disgust.

"Come, now, dear boy. Don't tell me you still think about that gypsy woman," teased Percy with a hint of scorn in his tone.

Thornton grabbed a startled Osborn by the neck of his coat, pulling him up until they were almost nose to nose. "Listen, Percy," he hissed, "the old crone said someone seeks my fall at the end of May, and Fenton is still free. I'll not rest until his head is brought to me on a platter. Is that clear?"

"What's clear is that there is no reasoning with you on this matter. Fenton will be caught, but until then, I suggest you put your mind to this plan," declared Percy, disdainfully disengaging himself from Thornton's grasp. "We should return to the picnic now, before our absence is noted."

Rorie's mind was a jumble of thoughts at the scope of the information she had overheard. And as she realized the danger she would be in if her presence was detected, she held her breath and fought to control the quivering in her legs when the men passed by her.

As Thornton and Osborn emerged separately from the small, wooded area, Deveraux's eyes narrowed in speculation—only to widen again in sudden surprise when Rorie followed behind them a few minutes later. In his mind, everything seemed to fit now. That lying, little bitch, he thought savagely. Pretending such concern for the fate of Drumfielde and, all the while, she was just a part of Roger's and Percy's schemes. That would account for her connection with Wiley, but what of this Terence? The boy just didn't fit into this nefarious scheme. Was Rorie using him, playing on his innocence, to get to Will Fenton? He had thought her at the Fenton farm that night to warn Will, but was she, in fact, part of the plan to frame him? Cameron cursed his stupidity for nearly having allowed himself to fall under her spell. That scene yesterday, when he had come upon her crying in the cottage, had no doubt been a well staged plan to gain information from him, as well. Did that mean that Thornton and Osborn were suspicious of him, too?

He shuddered to think how close he had come to taking her into his confidence when she had confronted him. And he wondered how much of himself he had given away. The girl was a sorceress. By God, but she had played him for the fool! And it only fanned his anger to consider how easily she had done so, as though he were some naive country boy. He would uncover the part she played in this business, if he had to beat it out of her! No more gloves, he smiled grimly, no more gentlemanly overtures. She was playing in rough waters, and he resolved to see her drown along with the rest.

As though on cue, the thunder clashed and the heavens opened up in a sudden, drenching downpour. Cameron lost sight of Rorie, as screeching women darted about for the shelter of their carriages. In spite of his anger, he took devilish delight in the comical sight of Squire Balfour sitting in the open carriage, drenched from head to toe, angrily shouting conflicting orders to his confused footman. Mounting his horse, Cameron carefully searched the retreating coaches and carriages, but there was still no sign of Rorie. Soon the meadow was empty with only the remains of the picnic left behind for Lynde-forde servants to reclaim at a more propitious time.

His efforts frustrated, Deveraux swore, un-mindful of the rain as he continued to scan the horizon. His determination was rewarded at last when he caught sight of a lone figure, struggling against the force of the driving storm. And a slow smile spread across his stern features as he readily guessed Rorie's destination.

22

Rorie's hands shook as she worked the steel and flint to strike a spark in the tinderbox. When the tinder was at last glowing, she thrust in a thin match tipped with brimstone. There ought to be an easier way to strike the fire, she muttered irritably, touching the flaming match to the kindling in the fireplace. She then jabbed furiously at the small sparks which struggled to take hold, thankful that the wood bin and tinderbox had been full when she and Terence had abandoned their old home. When the red and orange flames finally leapt to life, she dragged the worn coverlets from the beds to make a pallet on the warming hearth.

The downpour had done nothing to dampen her anger. Soaked through to the skin, she shivered as much from cold as she did from fury, as her mind replayed the conversation she had chanced to overhear. Captain Deveraux was an unprincipled scoundrel, and she had been right about him from the start, she fumed, savagely pulling off her soggy gown and hoop. It was bad enough that he might be involved in smuggling for the likes of the duke of Lyndeforde, but that the captain would aid in the downfall of her village by smuggling out the wool stolen from her people was the final straw. 'Twas simply not to be borne. And her inner voice screamed out for justice, as she angrily kicked at the stale rushes which littered the earthern floor.

What could she do? The squire was the magistrate for Drumfielde, but she knew better than to expect him to move against a member of the nobility and his own future son-in-law. Besides, the duke legislated the local ordinances and would no doubt find a way to protect his part in this nerfarious scheme. What then? she desperately asked herself. Who could help her? Lord Dandridge? Yes, that was it. Lord Dandridge was also a member of the peerage with influential contacts—and he was an honorable man. She would speak to him, she decided, feeling an enormous flood of relief.

Suddenly, the door burst open to crash against the whitewashed wall. Rorie started violently, trembling from head to toe. Deveraux's large, muscular frame filled the room. She blinked incredulously. The tension was explosive. Narrowed ice-blue eyes connected joltingly with astonished fiery green orbs as each antagonist gave vent to the fury of his emotions, neither stopping to wonder at the anger of the other. Standing menacingly before her, his rain-soaked breeches tight against his thighs, his shirt open to the chest, and his black hair curling damply about his hard, angular features, the captain looked like the devil incarnate to her. And Rorie stood spellbound, her surprise and anger beginning to turn to fear.

" 'Twould seem, madam, that you are to have a visitor—or were you perhaps expecting someone else? I see that you are all dressed for the occasion." He mocked her huskily, raking an insultingly bold eye over her person.

Cameron's words made no sense to Rorie, but a bright spot appeared at the top of her cheekbones as she became painfully aware of her bedraggled and scantily clothed appearance. Clad only in a wet chemise and limp petticoat, which clung enticingly to the curves of her body, she grabbed for a coverlet.

Deveraux laughed mirthlessly, the smile not reaching his eyes, as he slowly advanced on her like a predator stalking his prey.

Her rage and indignation taking root, Rorie found her voice and stopped backing away from him to defiantly stand her ground. "You low, lying, thieving bastard. What gives you the right to burst into my dwelling and act the cad? If you are looking for shelter from the elements, I wouldn't offer it to a self-serving knave of your ilk if he were drowning outside my door. Now be gone with you before I—"

Her voice trailed off as Cameron continued to stare at her accusingly. And she gasped as his hand suddenly shot out to encase her wrist. Although his eyes were dark and inscrutable, Rorie didn't miss the all too familiar glint as he pulled her roughly to him, steel-like fingers beneath her chin forcing her face up to his.

Seeing the fury in her face once again turn to fear, Deveraux's anger ignited, and he was moved to comment sneeringly, "May I congratulate you on a well played part, Miss Shelbourne.

You may have pulled the curtain, but I've one more act to play out."

And his lips swiftly possessed hers with a singular purpose. As his mouth moved firmly and surely across her soft lips, his kiss demanded a response. A myriad of conflicting emotions assaulted Rorie's dazed mind, but she stood frozen, fearful that the slightest movement would feed his lustful fury. She relaxed slightly as he slowly stroked her neck and shoulders, sending a warming sensation through her body. But when his hand slipped inside of her chemise to caress a full, round breast, she remembered her resolve not to allow him to manipulate her, and her mind and body sprang to life, at last pulling together in a common effort.

Struggling against a rising passion, she drew her arm back, intending to land a well-aimed blow to Cameron's jaw, but he managed to intercept her balled fist. In one quick movement, he bent her backwards before releasing his grip to swoop her up into his arms. Striding purposefully to the makeshift bed before the hearth, impervious to Rorie's shrieks of protest and the fists which pounded against his rock-hard chest, he deposited her roughly upon the pile of quilts. The look on his face told her that this little game was over.

Rorie's eyes grew wide, then, as he immodestly pulled off his boots and stripped off his soddened clothing to reveal a magnificent physique. But when Cameron reached out to so handily relieve her of her own undergarments with a few quick jerks of a sure hand, a paralyzing panic began to overtake her.

Cameron sucked in his breath sharply when

her soft, creamy body in all of its splendor—long, lithe, perfectly proportioned—was exposed to his eye. And for a moment, the expression on his face softened as he lowered himself to lie alongside her. But just as quickly, his features turned hard and unyielding, when he reminded himself that her wide-eyed innocence was all a charade.

"Now we shall see just how good an actress you really are, Miss Shelbourne," he said huskily, his voice taking on a cutting edge. "How far were you willing to go for information? I'll wager you're getting more than you bargained for, ay?" He chose to attribute the quizzical look on her face to more theatrics.

Rorie's heart raced and thudded against her chest, as he shoved her back further against the coverlets. The gross indignity of it all suddenly exploded upon her brain, and, marshalling her strength, Rorie angrily struck down his hand. Rolling away from him and scrambling to her feet, she had thought herself free when his arm reached out to pull her struggling and screaming beneath him. Laying one heavy leg across her to impede further movements, Cameron easily captured her flailing fists in one large hand and raised them high above her head. His lips once again took hers with an electrifying intensity that numbed her senses and smothered her protests, while his free hand caressed the length of her body until he felt her once again begin to yield. Releasing her mouth, he moved lower to continue the assault, his hands playing erotically over her sensitive skin.

Rorie gasped as his mouth then imprisoned one taut nipple, teasing it with his tongue, while his fingers explored her inner thigh, sending bursts of exquisite torment pulsating through her body until she thought she would go mad. She felt apart from herself. Her mind and body seemed to be two separate entities, neither responding to the commands of the other. Her mind screamed out for the cessation of this indignity, while her body arched and quivered for the release of the tension that the skillful plying of his hands and lips were creating. The feverish intensity of the feelings which rocked her heaving body was a shock to her senses, and just when she thought she could endure no more, Cameron separated her legs to lower himself on top of her.

Try as she might, Rorie's body refused to fight him, seeking only selfish satisfaction. She was capable of little thought, save one—she wanted him. And ruled completely by her emotions now, she answered Cameron's continued caresses with reckless abandon. She stiffened, then, fear suddenly gripping her emotions as she felt Cameron begin to enter her. The mind of reason stepped in to take control over physical gratification, and Rorie desperately tried to pull back. But it was too late. Everything was moving too fast. In the next instant, a tearing, searing pain between her legs completely blotted out the enjoyment of an earlier moment, and agonizing sobs escaped her throat at the full import of what was happening. Cameron slowed his driving thrusts to regard her questioningly for a moment. But the rage of being the imagined dupe for a scheming woman drove him on with no further regard to her pleasure, refusing to allow him to accurately assess the situation.

When he had spent himself and moved off of her, Rorie buried her face in her arms, horrified by her initial acquiescence to what was now an obvious and calculated seduction of her. Feeling as debased as the young servant maiden of her nightmare, she cried for her own humiliation and lost innocence with heart-rending sobs which issued from the depths of her being.

As Cameron fastened his breeches and pulled on his boots, he stared down at the sobbing, young woman. A bewildered frown marred his strong features as he mentally recounted the event. Something did not ring true, and he wasn't relishing the revenge he had exacted. This girl did not have the feel or experience of the skilled seductress he had imagined her to be, and he felt certain now that the hysterics were no act. He picked up a coverlet, and, as he moved to cover her shaking form, he saw the telltale stains where she had lain beneath him. It impacted upon his brain like a thunderbolt, and his conscience had to accept what his brain had been trying to tell him all along: he had seduced and humiliated an untried, young woman.

Ever since his grandfather's mistress had first introduced him to the pleasures of sexual pursuits, he had steadfastly avoided virgins. To his mind, the rewards of the experienced far outweighed those of the innocent. Suddenly, for the first time in many years, he felt helpless. He bent to put a comforting hand on Rorie's shoulder, but she angrily shrugged it off, as though it had scalded her.

"Look, Rorie," he began feebly, "I didn't know. I—I thought you to be Thornton's mistress and that you had played me false."

The sobbing stopped, and clasping the quilt tightly to her, Rorie slowly sat up to face

Deveraux, staring at him as though he had lost his mind. Quick as a whip, the palm of her hand slammed against his cheek with a resounding crack, leaving behind the perfect imprint of her fingers. Her whole arm ached from the force of the blow, and, for a fleeting moment, she wondered if she had broken her hand.

As if he were cast in stone, Deveraux barely flinched, though he wasn't able to conceal the shock in his eyes.

"I deserved that, Rorie, but don't ever try it again," he warned in a low, deliberate tone.

"You deserve more than that, you unspeakable louse!" she spat, her eyes glistening with tears, her face flushed from crying.

He wasn't used to being rebuked, and the truth of her words was such that he struck back angrily. "What is your connection with Thornton and Osborn? Before you deny anything, I saw you leave the woods with them during the picnic."

Again, she fixed him with a stare of such incredulity that, for a moment, Cameron questioned what he had seen with his own eyes. She startled him further, when she broke into high, shrill laughter. Just as suddenly it stopped, and her tone was harsh and brittle.

"You dare to question my motives? You, who has allied yourself with the duke and no doubt his smuggling activities; you, who cuckholds the very man who counts you a trusted and valued friend. Don't make me laugh, Captain. If there be a traitor in our midst, look to yourself."

Cameron was still reeling from her stinging indictment as he watched Rorie hastily don her rumpled, water-stained gown, gather the remainder of her garments and walk stiffly but proudly in the direction of the lagoon. Deveraux cursed himself roundly. This certainly hadn't been the plan, and his first inclination was to follow after her, but something told him that Rorie needed to be alone. This time, he heeded his instincts.

The storm had ceased, dispersing the clouds and leaving a fresh, clean smell in its wake. As the sun was beginning its descent behind the hills, Cameron judged it to be late afternoon. He jerked on his shirt. Mounting his horse, he impulsively turned toward the village tavern. What he needed was a bottle for company this night, not Roger Thornton and his silly guests.

As he rode, he considered Rorie's angry words. How did she know of the smuggling if she wasn't in league with Thornton and Osborn? After all, she hadn't actually denied the charges. She may not be Thornton's mistress, but the lass knew too much for her not to be a party to the duke's plans, he decided, seeking to rationalize his harsh behavior toward her. As for Lady Dandridge, Rorie was right, he couldn't let the earl look the fool. The man didn't deserve that. Unleashing a volley of oaths, he spurred his horse to breakneck speed.

Safely back at Balfour Grange, the squire bemoaned his own fate between sneezes, as he leaned back in the comfortable chair into which he had stuffed his bulk. Despite the warmth of the evening, he sat before a roaring fire, his feet soaking in a tub of hot water, and a mustard plaster on his chest. It had taken considerable finesse—and courage—for the squire to arrange for the duke to see Mary home following the afternoon picnic. This was supposed to leave him alone in the carriage with Rorie, but Mother Nature hadn't seen fit to cooperate.

"Did the lass come in yet?" he demanded hopefully of the housekeeper, as she entered to present him with another glass of port.

"No, sir. I suspect that Miss Rorie sought shelter at the Fenton farm, it bein' the closest. Miss Mary be askin' after ye fer supper, sir."

The squire sneezed again, sloshing wine over his paunch. "Tell her ta take a tray in her room this night. I be doin' the same," he instructed, wiping his nose on his coat sleeve.

23

A few days later, an event occurred which solved one man's problem while compounding another's. As Roger Thornton read the squire's message, announcing the regrettable passing of his wife and the necessary postponement of his daughter's marriage for a period of six month's mourning, Thornton became more and more enraged. He kicked a chair across the room and turned eyes of such blazing wrath upon the messenger, that the Balfour footman fled the manor in fear for his life.

"I heard," said Percy, entering the room soon after the departure of the terrified messenger.

"You heard," mimicked Thornton nastily. "Well, did you also hear how I'm to repay the rest of my debt to Tewksbury in two weeks time? The estates are nearly bankrupt, and I have no funds in the coffer. My God, Percy, he could have me sent to debtor's prison!"

Thorton suddenly paled at the thought of the stench-filled, disease-ridden hole jammed with thieving mongrels who were reduced to little more than animals. Oh, how those wretches would love to get their hands on a duke! "What am I to do?" he cried shrilly. "I can't have someone of Tewksbury's peerage dispatched, especially when the crown still glances askance at me over my uncle's death. My God, do you believe that after all these years, I'm still regarded with suspicion?"

Percy snorted. "What do you expect, Roger? Your uncle was a great friend of the king's, and you claimed the title before his body was even in the ground."

"Never mind!" snapped Thornton. "The fact remains, I must have the balance of that chit's dowry now. The girl could be dead herself in a few month's time by any one of the dozens of maladies which plague this populace. Look what almost happened with those highwaymen. Then where would I be?"

"Yes, Mistress Balfour's demise does come at a most inopportune time—just nineteen days before the wedding," agreed Osborn. "And with that outlaw still evading your guards—"

'Shut up, Percy!" Roger screamed in exasperation. "I need answers, not more problems!"

"Dear Roger," smirked Percy, "wherever would you be without me? My advice to you would be to play the dutiful mourning son-in-law-to-be for a few weeks. Then suggest a quiet, very private ceremony."

Thornton snorted. "And why should the fat fool agree to that?"

"Unless my eyes play tricks, the squire is not the bereaved man he pretends to be. I do believe he is quite besotted by Miss Balfour's companion."

Thornton's eyes grew wide in amazement. "Miss Shelbourne? How do you know that?"

"My dear Roger, one of us has to be observant. Unless I miss my guess, at this very moment, he's calculating how to get the lass to the altar and into his bed. I daresay that, were you to promise to deliver the young lady into his hands, he would be quite amenable to a shorter mourning period."

"But how do we get Miss Shelbourne to agree? Unless she goes willingly, the squire will never give his consent."

A sly smile spread across Osborn's crafty features. "Information has come to me that the lass is not the distant relative the squire purports her to be. She is, in fact, a local farm girl and the niece of that troublesome Will Fenton."

Thornton stared at Osborn incredulously. "The devil you say!"

"Think about it, Roger. Miss Shelbourne was at the ball that night. She left early, pleading illness, and a short while later, her uncle disappeared just before the guards arrived."

"You mean she warned him!"

Percy nodded. "I have it on the best authority."

"Dare you to tell me that the squire has had the audacity to place not only a mere peasant, but the niece of an outlaw in my bosom!" he shrieked. "I shall see the man flayed alive. Those villagers are a ruthless lot. Why, the girl could have slit my throat in the night," the duke screamed in wild-eyed fury.

"Roger, you are missing the point," snapped Osborn. "If you use your head, you will see that the squire has done us a favor. This girl has value to us in a number of ways."

"How?"

Osborn smiled complacently. "You shall see."

"But what of my debts?" persisted Thornton. "My vows must be redeemed soon, and Lord Tewksbury has made it plain there are to be no extensions."

"Not to worry, Roger. Two ships from Calais and one from Bordeaux are due to arrive with plenty of wine, brandy, tobacco, tea, and coffee to satisfy your debts—for now."

At the sound of a muffled thump outside the door, Roger and Percy looked at each other in alarm before racing out into the hall. Nothing appeared amiss, however, as the two men conducted a careful search of every darkened corner.

Thornton was about to open the door to a small compartment under the stairs when Percy suddenly exclaimed in relief, "Ho, there! 'Tis only a piece of fruit that has fallen from the tureen here on the side table."

Shakened by the danger of sudden exposure, both men laughed in relief and returned to the library for some needed spirits.

When Deveraux stumbled into his chambers at Lyndeforde much later that night, Rawlings was waiting, arms folded, disapproval stamped all over his wizened face.

"What be the devil on yer back this time, Cap'n?" he asked in a hushed, angry tone. "Ye ain't been yerself fer nigh on two weeks, wha' with yer broodin' and dark moods. Ain't had a civil tongue fer no one. Even Lady Dandridge is beginnin' ta wonder 'bout ye, as besotted as she be."

Deveraux angrily waved his servant away. "Don't concern yourself, Rawlings. Leave me be."

"God's teeth, laddie, someone had better be concerned cause it sure ain't ye. Much is amiss this night. Where ye been—ye smells like ye been drinkin' an' a whorin' in the stables. Here, drink this coffee an' gets inta the tub of water there. Fetched it up meself."

His head somewhat clearer from the coffee, Cameron sank into the tub only to bolt upright again. "God's blood, man!" he roared. "This water is as cold as a stream in midwinter."

"Well, 'twasn't when I fetched it up two hours ago!" Rawlings retorted hotly.

"Never mind. What's the news?"

When Rawlings had finished relaying the squire's message about the death of his wife, Cameron remarked solemnly, " 'Twould appear that fate is lending us a hand. How know you all of this?"

"I was listenin' at the door. Nearly got caught, I did, when I knocked a piece of fruit ta the floor. Jest had time enou' ta hide meself in tha' compartment under the stairs."

"Good work, but have a care," admonished Cameron. "We can't show our hand yet."

"There be more, Cap'n. It concerns Miss Shelbourne."

Deveraux groaned and braced himself. He was in no mood to discuss that wench. "Well, out with it!" he demanded impatiently.

"The squire has had an eye on the young miss. Thornton is goin' ta force her ta offer herself ta the fat lout iffen the squire agrees ta lay aside the postponement of his daughter's marriage."

"And why should I care? She's part of their schemes. She nearly played me for the fool," Cameron said with a bitter laugh, trying to justify his actions of that day.

Rawlings looked at his captain in surprise. "With all due respect, sir, I kenna think ye know the miss as well ye thought. It seems that the blackguards intend ta force her ta their will."

"No one forces that wench to anyone's will so easily," declared Cameron dryly. "Just how do they propose to do it?"

"I didna hear, but I think I can guess. Cap'n, Jacobs found the girl we was seeking . . . from the revolt?"

"What's that have to do with this?"

Rawlings pulled nervously on his chin. "Well, sir, the lass be Will Fenton's niece."

"I see," remarked Cameron, surprise and confusion evident in his voice as he tried to unravel the point Rawlings was attempting to make. "Then we have nothing to worry about on that score, do we?"

"Ah—well—ye don't see, sir. Fenton's niece is Miss Shelbourne," Rawlings finally blurted out.

Cameron's eyes turned a tumultous blue as he half rose from the tub in shocked amazement. "What!" he exclaimed. "What did you say!"

" 'Tis truth, Cap'n," said Rawlings, rushing forward with a towel. "I checked it out with Will himself. As it turns out, Molly Fenton an' Miss Rorie's mother was sisters. The Fentons took the lass an' her brother in when their parents died—"

"Rorie has a brother?" interrupted Cameron.

"Aye, Terence be his name, and he manages

the farm now—"

Rawlings voice trailed off as Deveraux suddenly threw back his head in deep, rich laughter. There it was, the mystery suitor, and he turned out to be Rorie's brother. The joke was on him, Cameron had to acknowledge. He had played the fool—all by himself—with no one's prompting but his own arrogance.

"Cap'n? Cap'n!" called Rawlings, eyeing his captain worriedly.

"No need to concern yourself," Cameron assured his valet, sobering quickly as he considered this new turn of events.

Rorie had said she wasn't related to the squire, but he had never dreamed she was Will Fenton's niece. She must have been spying on Thornton and Osborn when he saw her follow them from the woods. The silly wench might have gotten herself killed, he thought angrily, notwithstanding what he, himself, had done to her. Now the pieces were beginning to fit an entirely different puzzle. Rorie had been innocent all along.

"Yes, I can see how Thornton and Osborn can use her to their advantage," said Deveraux, thinking aloud. He ran a hand wearily across his face and across the back of his neck, his brows knit in consternation. "The question is, how do we protect her against Thornton's blackmail? And how do we contrive to stay on at Lyndeforde, with all the guests leaving now that the wedding has been postponed?"

Rawlings grinned. "No need ta worry on that, sir. Osborn tol' me as how the duke wants ye ta stay on until yer ship docks. He has important business ta discuss with ye."

24

The misery of the incident after the picnic still haunted Rorie. She ached with an inner pain, her sense of loss beyond tears, as she tried to shove her own emotional turmoil to the back of her mind in order to comfort Mary in her grief. But Rorie slept little, ate less, and passed the days in a haze of anguish, quietly withdrawing a little more each day from a memory she found too intolerable to bear.

At the burial sight of Mistress Balfour, both Cameron and Lord Dandridge were shocked by Rorie's appearance. Gone was the feisty, exuberance of youth, and in its place was a wrenching sadness which made her appear all the more vulnerable. She was thinner, and the sun-kissed glow of her skin had paled to the point of transparency, all the more evident by the dark hollows beneath her eyes and the prominence of her cheekbones.

Deveraux felt his chest constrict with remorse, for he suspected that he alone was responsible for her precarious state. He also knew that Rorie was in no condition to fend off Thornton's blackmail plot; in fact, the scheme could break her down completely. He firmly made up his mind to one course of action. It would take some doing to convince Rorie, but she would soon see that she had little choice. Deveraux took Lord Dandridge aside for a hasty conference.

The earl nodded in agreement, his face a mixture of disbelief, anger, concern, and surprise as Cameron explained the situation, carefully avoiding any mention of his own shameful actions.

"I shall see that Miss Shelbourne accompanies me to my estate and has the best of care at Marwynde, Captain Deveraux. Don't worry about Eleanora," he interjected, noting Cameron's hesitation. "She'll be accompanying the Asquiths to their estate nearby for the next several days."

"I'm sorry, sir."

Lord Dandridge smiled ruefully. "Don't be, my boy. I have no illusions where Eleanora is concerned. In fact, you're to be commended for your restraint."

And the two men parted company, each to do his bidding.

For the next few days at Marwynde, Rorie drifted in and out of consciousness in a state of exhaustion, her nightmares of the past intermingling with realities of the present. Several times she cried out in delirium, only to have soothing hands calm her fears and place cool cloths upon her forehead. Voices—loud, soft, high, low—prodded her to consciousness, and she opened her eyes once to see unrecognizable images floating in and out of her vision.

"Highly irregular, Captain—"

". . . Serious matter . . . her safety at stake—"

". . . Family notified?"

"The poor lass doesn't seem to care—"

Rorie wanted to scream for them all to stop, the constant murmur made her head ache, and she only wanted to sleep. Someone took her hand as a soothing voice intoned passages of a sort. Was she dying? If so, she would gladly welcome the peace. And she allowed herself to drift even deeper into the welcoming blackness. At this point, she became dimly aware of a flurry of activity. Someone was shouting orders, and huge hands were shaking her roughly by the shoulders.

"Fight, damn you, Rorie, fight! I won't let you take the coward's way out!"

Coward! She had never been a coward in her life! And as the word penetrated her subconscious, Rorie finally began the struggle up from the depths of oblivion to full awareness. She awoke the next day, dazed and confused, in a strange, though pleasant, sun-filled room. Raising herself to a sitting position, she found that she was so weak, the effort made her head swim. She fell back limply onto the pillows.

A door opened quietly to admit a gentleman of middle years, medium height, and slight build. When he found her awake, his anxious visage broke into a pleased smile, which lent a certain charm to his otherwise ordinary features. The premature graying around his temples gave him a distinguished air, inviting respect, and his seemingly easy manner made Rorie think of her father.

"So you decided to come back to us, ay?" he

greeted amiably.

"Who are you, and where am I?" Rorie's feeble voice sounded hollow and strange to her own ears, and for a moment, she wondered if it were she who had, in fact, spoken.

"You are at Marwynde, Lord Dandridge's estate, some twenty miles from Drumfielde, and I am Dr. Farley, at your service." He smiled kindly. "Do you remember anything?"

Her winged brows were knit in perplexity as she tried to sort out her thoughts. "I remember Lord Dandridge approaching me at the funeral and saying that I was to ride with him in his coach," she began hesitantly. "I can remember being helped in, but nothing more."

The doctor nodded with satisfaction. "You collapsed from exhaustion, and Lord Dandridge thought it best for you to recover here, in view of the tragedy at Balfour Grange. You've been catching up on your rest these five days. Your spirit was at such a low ebb, we thought we had lost you once. I understand that this isn't the first time you have neglected your health, Miss Shelbourne. You must take better care of yourself," he scolded.

"Five days! I've been here for five days!" cried Rorie in disbelief. "Mary will be worried. I must return to the Grange at once."

"Easy, lass," admonished Dr. Farley as she struggled once more to sit up. "Miss Balfour has been notified of the situation and bades that you stay until fully recovered."

"But she needs me."

"You're no good to anyone in your state, least of all to yourself," the doctor warned sternly.

Realizing the truth in his words, Rorie

allowed him to settle her back against the pillows. She soon became lost in thought, however, as something niggled at the back of her mind. Massaging her forehead, she tried to recapture the days she had lost in her memory, but all her thoughts seemed to be in a jumble. And her frustration only increased with the effort. She didn't know how much was real and how much she had imagined in her dream state. She knew she had a hundred questions, but didn't know what they should be.

The doctor forestalled her. "There'll be time for questions later, my dear. For now you need rest and nourishment. I'll have a tray sent up."

A short while later, a heavyset servant girl, whom Rorie thought to be a few years older than herself, entered the room bearing a silver tray of broth, juice, tea and oat cakes. For a moment, she stared at Rorie oddly before breaking into a smile of such warmth, Rorie couldn't help but return it.

"Me name be Eloise, miss. 'Tis glad I am ta see ye well," she said shyly. " 'Twas worried, we was, specially the cap'n. Why, when they thought ye nearly dead, the cap'n shook the very life back into ye."

As the maid turned to set the tray on a nearby table, she missed the stunned look on Rorie's face. So it wasn't all a dream. The blaterskite had been present!

"Was the captain always here?" asked Rorie, striving to keep her voice steady.

"No, miss, he arrived a few days later with the Reverend Wickersham. Stayed by yer side night an' day, he did. Ye kept callin' his name."

"I was more than likely cursing it,"

responded Rorie sharply.

Eloise blinked in surprise. "Beg yer pardon, miss?"

"Nothing, Eloise."

Rorie turned her face away to hide the tears which threatened to spill down her cheeks and onto the pillows. She began to shake from the intensity of her raw emotions, for her collapse had done nothing to dull her earlier memory. The humiliation she had suffered at Deveraux's experienced hands was still too close to the surface. She started as a timid hand stroked her hair, and she offered no resistance when Eloise enfolded her in compassionate arms.

"Let it go, miss. It does no good ta keep all tha' misery an' hate inside ye."

Eloise's wise counsel and gentle voice was the breaking point for Rorie, and she sobbed out her heart until there were no tears left to cry. All the while, Eloise held her tightly and rocked her, soothing her as best she could.

"There, there, miss," she crooned softly. " 'Tis the lot of women to bear a man's attentions whether invited or not, and there be nothing fer it. But sometimes it has a way of working itself out again."

Rorie lifted her golden head, her teary eyes wide with surprise. "You know?"

"Yes, miss. Ye talked much in yer sleep. Most of it was gibberish, but I could guess the nature of yer torment. Ye see, I've had the same nightmare. Happened ta me some years ago, an' I was so full of hate, I didna want ta live no more. But 'tis not the way of all men. My Jemmy—he be the stable master here—he come along an' made things right fer me, jest like the cap'n 'll do for ye."

"The captain," spat Rorie contemptuously, "is a cur with no more conscience than the blackest knave!"

Eloise looked at Rorie closely, "Beggin' yer pardon, miss, but Cap'n Deveraux dinna strike me as a man who would have ta force his attentions on any woman."

Rorie flushed as she recalled how her body had shamelessly responded to his practiced hand. "Though the circumstance may have been forced, I can't say that the act was, in the truest sense of the word," Rorie finally admitted slowly. "But it was humiliating just the same, with no end reward to justify the misery. I shall never suffer it again."

Eloise smiled. "The first taste is sometimes not as sweet as the second, miss. Did the cap'n not prepare you?"

"The captain thought I was someone's mistress," Rorie replied bitterly.

"Ah, I see," said Eloise with new understanding. "Some men don't always think with their heads, don't ye know. The cap'n is a man of too much pride."

"In any case, I never want to see that bastard again! If he ever comes near me, I'll kill him!"

"I'm afraid, miss, things have gone beyond that point, an' 'tis out of yer hands."

"What do you mean?" Rorie demanded, a knot of apprehension twisting inside of her.

Eloise looked thoughtful for a moment. "I mean," she said at last, having considered the matter, "the Cap'n is not the black-hearted villain he seems. Until ye started turnin' to, he was like a man possessed, pacin' abou' here. The doctor had ta finally bar him from the room. The two of ye got off ta a bad start, I'm guessin', and now 'tis time ta put it behind ye an' go on from there—like Jemmy an' me. Give the man a chance, miss, for I feel there to be more of a bond between ye than either of you are willing to admit." She patted Rorie's hand with confident assurance. "He'll be by here in a few days."

Rorie could only stare at the little maid in stunned amazement. First Mary, and now Eloise. There seemed to be no defense against Deveraux's silver tongue.

25

At Lyndeforde, Roger Thornton rode into the yard with such speed, he nearly ran down the stable boy. Jumping from his mount and throwing the reins to the shakened boy, he ran into the house, oblivious of the curious stares from his staff. He flew up the wide, oaken staircase and burst into Percy's room, frightening his alter ego badly.

"Good God, man!" yelled Percy angrily, jumping up and dabbing at the spilled liquid spreading across the front of his pants. "Can't you see I'm having my tea? You might have scalded me—ruined me for life! What is so urgent that you must come bursting in here like a madman, shortening my years by half?"

"I've found the girl, Percy!" exclaimed Thornton collapsing into a chair. "I went to pay my respects to the squire and—"

Percy waved him on irritably. "Get to the point, man!"

"Lord Dandridge has her at Marwynde."

"Dandridge! What's he doing with the

wench?"

"Seems she took ill at the funeral, and the earl took her away to recover. Fact is, she nearly died. He even had that fool, Wickersham, over there. Mistress Mary just sent a trunk of clothes to her. No telling how long the girl will be there."

"Hmmm, Captain Deveraux spent a few days at Marwynde," reflected Percy. "Why didn't he mention Lord Dandridge's houseguest upon his return?"

"Why should he? How's he to know of our interest in the chit?"

"Yes, quite right, Roger. But still, one would think he'd have mentioned it in passing."

"Don't be so bloody suspicious of everything," retorted Thornton in annoyance, as he restlessly paced the floor. "It doesn't appear to have been a well kept secret. The girl took sick, Balfour Grange is in mourning—Marwynde would seem likely enough."

"Yes, one might think so. However, all that aside, we are now presented with a new problem. If you'll remember, the earl was supposed to be returning to London."

Thornton whirled around in alarm. "Good God, I'd forgotten. Percy, we've got to get him out of there!"

Percy stroked his chin thoughtfully. "With the girl gone, he would have no reason to remain. Did you speak with the squire?"

Thornton nodded. "The old fool is so anxious to get his hands on the wench, he'd agree to anything."

"Good, then we simply go and claim Miss Shelbourne. We'll tell her that—that Miss Balfour has need of her."

"Capital, I'll see to the coach. With any luck, we shall make Marwynde before the night."

Thanks to Eloise's careful ministrations, Rorie had rapidly recovered her strength, and her emotional wounds were healing, too. An easy friendship had grown between the girls, and a special bond was forged, transcending any class barriers or social distinctions. Though their cases differed widely, they were, first and foremost, women who shared a common hurt.

When the doctor pronounced Rorie fit enough to leave her room, she sent word to Lord Dandridge that she would join him in the drawing room for tea that evening. Her hair was freshly washed and swept high on her head with two ringlets of curls left to dangle saucily over one shoulder.

From the clothes press, Eloise drew out a claret-colored velvet gown which parted in the front to reveal a pale pink, satin petticoat. Highlighted with gold piping and white lace around the sleeves and low oval neckline, the gown would heighten Rorie's pale features. Seeing the question on her charge's face, Eloise laughed and explained that a few of her clothes had been brought from Balfour Grange while she was ill. Rorie nodded, agreeable to the choice, and allowed Eloise to finish dressing her.

At last, Eloise stood back to survey her handiwork. She cocked her head sideways and frowned. "There be somethin' lackin', Miss."

Eloise's small, round face suddenly brightened as a thought came to her. Rummaging around on the dressing table, she at last held up the broach which had belonged to

Rorie's mother. Rorie was startled until she remembered that she had been wearing it the day of Mistress Balfour's funeral.

Beaming, Eloise pinned the broach to the gown in the hollow between Rorie's breasts. "There ye go, miss. Ye be ready now. Ah, but ye be a beauty." And she led Rorie to the cheval glass.

Rorie couldn't believe that the young woman who stared back at her from the mirror was she, herself. She was shocked by her sunken appearance. Her face was so pale that her eyes were huge, like two green, sparkling jewels in her small, oval face.

"Oh, Eloise," she cried, "I might just as well be dead, for well I look it. I'm so pale."

"Here now, miss, don't ye take on so. 'Tain't good fer ye. I knows jest the thin', and I'll return straightaway."

A short while later, Eloise bustled back into the room with an array of small jars on a tray. "Lady Dandridge would have me neck if she know'd I touched her jars. As luck would have it, her ain't due back 'til mornin'."

"I couldn't use this," protested Rorie, more preoccupied with the thought of Lady Dandridge's impending arrival than she wanted to admit. "Besides, I can't put you at risk for your livelihood."

Eloise airily waved aside all of Rorie's arguments, and Rorie finally relented, allowing Eloise to dab a touch of rouge to her cheeks and a bit of color to her lips.

"With eyelashes tha' dark an' thick, ye dinna need this kohl around yer eyes," pronounced Eloise, at last satisfied.

Rorie had to admit that her coloring now looked healthier than her previous stark paleness. "Thank you, Eloise. You've been most kind." And she gave the maid an affectionate hug.

" 'Tain't nothin', miss." Eloise smiled, hastily wiping a tear away, for it was rare for a member of the upper class to show her any appreciation.

At the sound of a knock on the door, Rorie jumped, and Eloise hastily hid the makeup jars under the dressing table.

"Easy, miss. Tha' jest be Mrs. Winton come ta show ye the way ta the drawing room."

With the exception of Mrs. Simmons, the Balfour housekeeper, and now Eloise, Rorie had never felt comfortable with servants. The maids were either too silly or too sullen. Mrs. Winton was of the latter group. Tall, thin, forbidding, her gray hair pulled back severely into a bun at the back of her head, Mrs. Winton ruled her efficient household with an iron hand. Her black clad form was everywhere, and her eyes were all-knowing as she moved about the house, issuing orders with military precision.

When Mrs. Winton entered the room, Rorie felt as though she were an object of scrutiny as the dour, long-faced housekeeper surveyed her from head to toe. When Mrs. Winton's gaze fell upon the broach, Rorie thought she detected a flicker in the woman's eyes, but of what?

Her emotions still close to the surface, Rorie found the examination unnerving. "What is it, Mrs. Winton!" she demanded at last. "Why do you inspect me thusly?"

Mrs. Winton's eyes were unfathomable, but her stern features relaxed ever so slightly, and

303

her tone was strangely wistful. "Beggin' yer pardon, miss. Ye remind me of someone I once held dear."

Before Rorie could respond, the housekeeper had assumed her familiar air of authority. "If you are ready, I shall direct ye to the drawing room," she said stiffly.

Rorie nodded, and smiling nervously over her shoulder at Eloise, she followed Mrs. Winton out of the door. As they proceeded down a long, candlelit hallway, Rorie regarded the portraits of the Dandridge ancestors lining the panelled walls. Of the faces that stared back at her, some very ignoble, some vainglorious, some imperious, but all very illustrious.

The portrait of a young woman, in particular, caught her attention, and she stopped. The woman was very pretty and fair in color, with delicate, contoured features. But what had caught Rorie's eye was the happiness which radiated from the portrait. Unlike the dour expressions of the others, this woman smiled enchantingly, her eyes filled with laughter, love, and humor. There was something else about the portrait which nudged at Rorie's memory, but she couldn't put her finger on it. She would like to have studied the painting more thoroughly, but Mrs. Winton hurried her on.

When she entered the comfortable drawing room, she found Lord Dandridge anxiously awaiting her.

"Miss Shelbourne, how well you look," declared the kindly old earl, solicitously escorting her to a chair near the fire. "Gave us all a turn, I don't mind telling you, ay Charles?"

Doctor Farley nodded in somber agreement,

as he raked a professional eye over his patient. "Glad to see you up and about, Miss Shelbourne. I see Eloise is holding to my instructions."

"Yes, Eloise has been most capable. I owe you all so much. I'm sorry to have been such a nuisance," responded Rorie gratefully. "I can be ready to leave tomorrow."

"Capital idea, Miss Shelbourne. I was about to suggest the same," broke in Roger Thornton, striding into the room with Percy and a very displeased butler on his heels.

"I'm sorry, Lord Dandridge," said the butler indignantly with an audible sniff. "The duke and his—companion wouldn't allow themselves to be properly introduced at this late hour."

"That's quite all right, Edmonds. Please convey to Mrs. Winton that more tea, port, and brandy shall be required."

Edmonds took his leave, but not before casting a disapproving eye over the unexpected guests.

"To what do I owe this pleasure, Your Grace?" inquired the earl with little enthusiasm.

Undaunted, Thornton and Osborn settled themselves comfortably. "The deuced roads make nighttime travel a menace," complained the duke, slapping the dust from his breeches. "But to answer your question, Percy and I have come to escort Miss Shelbourne back to Balfour Grange."

"That's totally out of the question," retorted Lord Dandridge brusquely. "Miss Shelbourne has only just left her bed this night. Such a journey would invite a relapse, as I'm sure Dr. Farley, here, will tell you."

Dr. Farley regarded the newcomers

suspiciously. "I must agree with Lord Dandridge, gentlemen. I cannot allow Miss Shelbourne to make such an arduous journey so soon after her illness."

Thornton's composure slipped for a moment, and a swift shadow of anger swept across his face. A hot retort was on his lips, when Percy interrupted smoothly.

"Gentlemen, we certainly aren't discounting your concern for Miss Shelbourne's welfare, but His Grace is likewise concerned for the welfare of his betrothed. You see, Miss Balfour is in need of the comfort of her companion in this most grievous of times, and she has entrusted us with Miss Shelbourne's safe—and speedy—return."

"Is Mary ill? If so, I must go to her," Rorie cried in alarm, forgetting her own state of health as her concern for Mary overode her distrust of Thornton.

Dr. Farley snorted. "Miss Balfour is physically and emotionally fit, given the circumstances. I have it on Reverend Wickersham's authority, having seen the man just yesterday in the village." His brow was furrowed in mock confusion. " 'Tis my report, gentlemen, that Miss Balfour wishes Miss Shelbourne to remain until fully recovered, which to my best estimate should be another week."

Thornton choked on the brandy, which had just been passed to him, and the pretense of the smile on Osborn's pinched face began to fade.

"Perhaps if we were to have a private word with Miss Shelbourne," suggested Percy tightly. "This matter does concern her alone."

"Miss Shelbourne's health concerns us all," protested Lord Dandridge.

Rorie felt sidelined as the debate swirled about her. She felt torn between her duty to Mary and the peace she was loathe to leave in these new surroundings. But most of all, she resented being bandied about and excluded as though she had no mind of her own. She opened her mouth to speak, willing her voice to be steady and unyielding.

"Gentlemen! I believe I can speak for myself," she said tersely. "If you please, Lord Dandridge, Dr. Farley, I will see our visitors alone."

All argument ceased as everyone turned to stare at Rorie as though she had suddenly materialized out of the air. Lord Dandridge started to protest, but Rorie effectively quelled him with a stern look which brooked no argument. The earl finally threw up his arms in defeat, and he and Dr. Farley reluctantly vacated the room.

Thornton and Osborn were smiling at each other smugly, when Rorie turned to look them straight in the eye.

"Now gentlemen, presupposing Dr. Farley's report to be authentic concerning Mary's well-being, suppose you tell me what exactly you are doing here. Why is it so urgent for me to return with you?"

Assuming that they would be dealing with the usual silly, impressionable female, Thornton and Osborn were totally unprepared for the forthright, well spoken young woman who stood so coolly and confidently before them. Catching the look of surprise on their faces, Rorie's soft tone took on an edge of heavy sarcasm. "We're not all the illiterate, easily led fools you think us to be, Your Grace. Though we seem to have few rights, some of us do exercise our minds."

"I—ah—well—" Thornton could only stammer and stare as he saw Rorie in a new light. It was Osborn who stepped in to seize control of the situation.

" 'Twould seem, Miss Shelbourne, we've underestimated you. I think we can drop the pretenses here, Roger," he said, not shifting his hard, ferretlike eyes from Rorie. "The truth is, Miss Shelbourne, we have a proposition to put to you."

"I'm listening."

"It seems that Squire Balfour has taken a strong liking to you. As a widower, he is in need of a wife and could do quite nicely by you, I daresay. If you're agreeable, the squire will agree to waive the mourning period for his daughter's wedding, providing the ceremony is small and private, of course."

Rorie laughed mirthlessly. "Either you've lost your minds or His Grace is in that much of a hurry to lay his hands on Mary's dowry."

By the look on their faces, Rorie knew that she had guessed right, and she silently recalled her last visit with Mary's mother. The kindly woman, aged and shrunken from her long and debilitating illness, had been unusually alert and perceptive that day, as she questioned Rorie about her daughter's upcoming marriage. Not wishing to distress the ailing woman, Rorie had thought she had been skillfully evasive. However, as she rose to leave, Mistress Balfour had smiled and firmly assured her that the wedding would not occur as planned. Rorie had thought that Mistress Balfour intended to exercise some influence over her husband, but when the gentle lady had passed away two days later, it came to Rorie with a certain insight that Mistress Balfour was protecting Mary in the only way that she had known—by hastening her own death. Rorie couldn't allow that unselfish sacrifice to account for nothing.

Aloud she said, "Aside from the fact that I shall never let that pig so much as touch me, I'm certainly not going to hasten Mary's unhappiness when she has only just been reprieved."

Thornton's face turned livid with fury, but Percy was undaunted. "If you don't agree to our proposition, Miss Shelbourne, we have one of two options. We can draw out the rat by using you as the cheese—"

"I'm afraid that I don't understand," interrupted Rorie.

"We know now that you are Will Fenton's niece."

Rorie quickly masked her surprise and alarm. She knew the information would surface at some point, but she had never counted on being held ransom for her uncle. And her mind raced for a solution. Suddenly, she recalled her uncle's advice.

"Well, then, gentlemen," she said smartly, "you must also know that I have been shunned by my family and the villagers because I have chosen to remain Mary's companion. Nor do I have any use for the lot of them. They think me a traitor to their cause. I fear you'll get no satisfaction from this course of action, for my uncle will not come forth to aid my case."

"Percy, I fear she may be right on that

score," affirmed Thornton anxiously. "I saw for myself at the May Day how people turned from her as though she had the pox. I thought it rather peculiar at the time."

But Osborn just smiled. "Then we shall move to our second alternative, Roger."

Rorie had the uneasy feeling that her victory was a hollow one, as she waited for the odious, little man to reveal his next plan of action.

"I believe you have a brother, Miss Shelbourne," continued Percy. "Were he to be brought up on poaching charges, I'm sure your uncle could be coaxed out of hiding—"

"My brother would never do such a thing!" protested Rorie. "And you have no evidence to that fact."

"Come now, if you're as astute as you appear to be, you must know these things can be arranged—unless you persuade us otherwise."

Rorie felt as though her stomach had leapt to her throat, as she realized what they were purporting. Her favors for the lives of her brother and uncle. She grasped the back of the chair for support, her thought processes at a complete standstill.

"So you see, Miss Shelbourne, you don't actually have a choice in the matter," Percy concluded triumphantly, feeling the full measure of his control and enjoying it immensely.

"I'm afraid, gentlemen, that the lady does very much have a choice," came a clear, firm voice from the side.

All three turned in amazement to find Cameron Deveraux lounging against the doorjamb, a frown deepening the creases of his rugged features. The conversation had been so intense that none of them had observed the captain's ill-timed arrival.

"Captain Deveraux, what a surprise to see you here. I thought your business with Lord Dandridge concluded," said Thornton trying to hide his annoyance. "If you'll excuse us, Captain, we are resolving a private matter of no concern to you."

"You stand correct, Your Grace. My business with Lord Dandridge is concluded, however 'tis only beginning with Miss Shelbourne." Cameron smiled with easy assurance, as he casually crossed the room to stand behind Rorie. When he placed his hands—strong, firm, and protective—on her smooth shoulders, Rorie inhaled sharply at the contact. One part of her wanted to flay him, while the other wanted to seek his protection. His closeness was so compelling, so bracing that she had to close her eyes against the onslaught of conflicting emotions which ripped through her body like a well-edged sword.

"And this matter *is* of concern to me," Deveraux continued, "for you see, Miss Shelbourne became my wife some days ago."

The shock felt by all, was evident by the open mouths and wide eyes. Rorie started to protest, but said nothing as she felt the increased pressure of Cameron's hands on her. Thornton and Osborn were so astounded by the news, they failed to notice the strange tenseness between the newlywed couple.

"I don't believe it," whispered Thornton. The color drained from his face when he suddenly recalled that Reverend Wickersham had been sent for last week.

"Pray do believe it, Your Grace, for if you

gentlemen ever put forth a prosposition of any kind to my wife again, I shall call you out. I think you will find my dueling record formidable," Cameron finished with cold, deadly resolution. "And one other thing: Rorie's brother is now my charge."

Rorie's own mind was so staggered that only the continued pressure of Deveraux's hands on her shoulders held her steady. And she was but dimly aware of the others in the room, as she fought the disturbing magnetism which was building between her and the man who had stolen her innocence; the man she had vowed always to despise; the man to whom she now owed her brother's and uncle's lives. Through her haze, Rorie clearly saw the rage reflected in Thornton's and Osborn's faces before fainting away into Deveraux's arms.

26

Rorie awoke with a start in her room. A candle sputtering beside the bed, cast the only illumination. Her stays, hoop and gown had been removed, and she was clad only in her chemise.

"Had the devil's own time of it removing that cage you ladies insist upon lacing yourselves in," said Deveraux, from the corner of the room. "Finally had to cut the damned thing off of you. 'Tis no secret why you fool women suffer from the vapors—you can't breathe properly in that contraption."

Furious at her vulnerability, Rorie jerked the coverlet about her and jumped shakily to her feet. "How dare you touch me again!" she ground out with mounting rage. "Get out of my room before I summon Lord Dandridge to have you thrown out."

"It might appear a bit awkward for a husband to be ejected from his bride's chambers," Cameron pointed out with mock concern.

"All right, I admit you helped me out of an

uncomfortable situation. God knows you owed me that. But you can drop the charade now. Get out!" she yelled, her voice breaking with the fury of her emotions.

Calmly, Cameron stood up and moved toward her. His tone was low, firm, and implacable, with no hint of mockery, as he explained to her reeling mind, "Rorie, you are my wife, there is no mistaking that. And, however much you want to deny it, 'tis upon this very fact that your safety and the safety of your brother and uncle depend. So don't act the fool. There's more to consider here than your pride."

Rorie searched his face for any trace of chicanery. The sincerity in his features and the tone of his deep voice convinced her that he spoke the truth. "But how?" she cried, desperate to make some sense from all of her confusion. "I was no party to a ceremony."

Quickly he told how he had heard of Thornton and Osborn's scheme, and how, upon observing her physical state at the Balfour funeral, he had arranged for Lord Dandridge to spirit her away to Marwynde until arrangements could be made for the marriage.

"Marrying you was the only way I could think of to save you from their scheme. I hadn't counted on you being near death's door when I arrived with Reverend Wickersham," he commented dryly. "It took a bit of persuading to convince the Reverend to marry a half-conscious bride."

Rorie searched her memory. Dimly she remembered a curious intoning of passages and someone lifting her hand.

"Why should you want to help me or my

family?" she questioned suspiciously.

Cameron shrugged. "As you said, I owe it to you, and I always pay my debts. I also told you once before, Rorie, that we haven't yet finished. Here, I believe this belongs to you," he added, holding out an exquisitely engraved gold band dotted with rubies and slipping it on her finger. His tone became oddly distant then. "It was once my mother's ring. She was about your size. All that remains now is for you to sign this document to be recorded with the church."

Rorie stared from the ring to the document. "I won't sign it. I shan't be forced into such a detestable union to ease your conscience," she declared, angrily flinging the parchment aside. Once again, she was feeling manipulated. "There must be another way."

Cameron's voice hardened. "Squire Balfour, your brother's death—or me, Rorie. 'Tis simple as that, and the choice is yours. I think you'll find my bed much more pleasant than the squire's. There's another side to be considered here, my dear, before you so hastily discard my offer. Should the afternoon we spent together come to light, your brother might feel duty bound to call me out. I've come to know Terence, and I like the boy. I would hate for him to be injured or killed while defending your honor, for I never lose, Rorie."

"You despicable bastard," breathed Rorie. "You're no better than that fop who calls himself a duke. 'Tis blackmail by whatever reasoning."

"Perhaps, but mine is the better offer, my dear wife," Cameron replied, smiling with confident assurance as he stripped off his shirt and unfastened his breeches. "Now let's get some sleep. Chasing Thornton here from Drumfielde was no easy chore by half."

He yawned, falling naked upon the bed, and patted the place next to him. Though the marriage had been at his instigation, he had yet to figure out if he was the spider or the fly. In any case, that afternoon at the cottage had been a mistake that he was now eager to rectify.

"Your gall is unbelievable!" sputtered Rorie, stamping her foot in outrage. "If you won't leave, then I shall!"

She turned, intending to stomp out of the room in full-blown indignation. But before she could take a step, Cameron reached out and yanked hard on her trailing coverlet, catapulting Rorie off her feet and bringing her to land on the bed beside him.

"Be still, Rorie," he commanded gruffly, laying a restraining arm across her struggling body and pulling her closer.

Conscious of where his warm flesh touched hers, her breathing became uneven, and Rorie closed her eyes tightly against his closeness. No, this couldn't be happening again! Her mind screamed out, as his hand slid down her taut stomach to the swell of her hips and his lips planted feathery light kisses on her neck. She couldn't bear that humiliation yet a second time. Tears trembled on her eyelashes to trickle down her cheeks. She wanted desperately to fight with all her might, but the illness had taken its toll and left her too weak. Even with all of her strength, she would be no match for this huge, black-haired devil.

Cameron fell back from her, cursing himself as he ran a hand through his dark hair in frustration. He hated the fear that he seemed to inspire in her. Women had always been instruments of pleasure to him, and he gave as good as he got, but this girl was different. Not only did she dare to spurn his advances, which was a new experience in and of itself for him, but she also lacked the calculating ways of the women he knew, which had always rendered him insensitive to all but their physical needs. He was at a loss as to how to handle Rorie. Aside from that, he couldn't have Thornton and Osborn suspecting that he had married her to keep her from their clutches when he was supposed to be allying himself with their interests. For both their sakes, it was important that Rorie appear to be in communion with him.

"Look, Rorie," said Cameron, trying again and holding her trembling form gently, "I know I hurt you before, and you have good reason to fear me, but I don't intend to earn the ire of the duke and Osborn for snaring you from their trap. They're too important to my pla—business of trade," he quickly amended. "I need you to put your ill feelings for me aside for the time being and cooperate, and for that reason, I make you this promise. I won't lay a hand to you unless you come to me first. At the conclusion of this business, I'll instruct Reverend Wickersham to file for an annulment."

Rorie swallowed hard and bit back her tears. "Y—you would agree to this?" she stammered in wide-eyed amazement.

"If it insured your cooperation."

"What must I do?"

"To begin with, you can sign the document. From there, just follow my lead and try to play the loving wife."

"For how long?"

"For however long as it takes," Deveraux snapped, a bit ruffled that she should regard their union as such an ordeal.

Rorie fell silent as she tried to absorb everything that had happened this evening. Casting sidelong glances at him, she wondered what his scheme was. He was practically blackmailing her into this marriage, yet he agreed not to force her submission. He had placed Terence under his protection, but he was unprincipled enough to smuggle, for she had no doubts that he had accepted the offer she had overheard the duke and Osborn discussing. Trade business my foot! she thought. What manner of man was he, anyway? Clearly there was more here than met the eye. And 'twould seem that the only way she would ever find out for certain was to go along with the marriage. After all, she had no alternative, and if Deveraux held to his bargain, she would have nothing to lose and perhaps the security of her family to gain.

"I shall agree," she said at long last. "But on one condition: that you refuse to smuggle wool from the village."

Cameron regarded her sharply, noting the firm set of her features. He wondered how she had found out about the smuggling and the wool, for she had cleverly placed him in an uncomfortable position. To refuse Rorie invited an expose on the truth of their marriage, and to refuse such a part of Thornton and Osborn's proposition now would only raise suspicion, certain to end with the withdrawal of their trust.

Having considered the matter at length,

Deveraux answered carefully, "Whatever else may reach your ears, Rorie, know that the village will be protected."

Rorie's eyes narrowed in suspicion. "I give you fair warning, Captain, don't mock me with riddles for answers. Either you give me a straightforward answer or the bargain is off."

"I don't think that you are in a position to barter, madam," he pointed out succinctly. "I can only say that you have no need to fear for Drumfielde on this score, whatever the word. And while we are extracting conditions, I have one of my own to put forth. If you are ever found inquiring after me, your half of the bargain is forfeit, and I shall use you as I please."

The look in his eye told her that he wasn't joking, and Rorie bristled at his arrogance. She knew she had no choice but to agree to his condition. Now, how would she ever know just where his allegiance lay?

"Good," said Cameron as she nodded her grudging consent. "Since we understand each other, let's get some sleep."

Whether it was from the exhaustion of the day or the secure warmth of the man beside her, Rorie fell into a deep, restful sleep. The next morning she awoke refreshed to find herself snuggled against a broad, muscular chest, her head fitting perfectly in the hollow between Cameron's shoulder and neck. Disoriented for the moment, Rorie lifted her head to find Cameron regarding her with a twinkle of amusement dancing in his silver-blue eyes.

"Madam, unless you care to begin something that you may well not wish to finish, I suggest that you remove your leg, or I shan't be held accountable for my actions," he murmured huskily.

Rorie blinked in confusion. His tone had been so low and caressing that it was a moment before her groggy senses had grasped his meaning. A blush flooded over her features, and she abruptly came wide awake, however, as the full import of Deveraux's words sank in. Feeling the nature and depth of his discomfort, she jerked her leg away, which had inadvertently become positioned across his lower midsection, and jumped from the bed.

"I—I'm sorry," she stammered with profound embarrassment. "I must have gotten chilled in the night."

Her voice faded to a whisper and her green eyes flew open in astonishment then, as Deveraux rose to his full height, naked and tanned. Rorie struggled to maintain what little composure she had left, but when he stretched, forcing her gaze to travel the entire length of his superb form, a strangled cry escaped her throat, and she fled into the anteroom.

Damn the man and his arrogant smugness, Rorie fumed, as his laughter followed her every step into the dressing chamber. She certainly wasn't in the habit of gawking at unclothed men, and she cursed the curiosity which got the better of her dignity. Everything about him disturbed her, from his powerfully built body to his hypnotic eyes which assessed, studied, and stripped her of her defenses. But most of all, she was troubled by the intensity of feelings that his slightest touch was able to spark.

Deveraux crawled back into bed beneath the cool linen and put his hands behind his head, wondering how to break through Rorie's reserve.

When Edmonds opened the front door, his jaw twitched imperceptively. "Good morning, milady," he greeted with prim austerity as befitted his position. Only the tautness of his features betrayed his true feelings. But all went unnoticed as a preoccupied Lady Dandridge swept through the hallway, ignoring his greeting.

"I saw my husband's coach outside. Why hasn't he left for London?" she demanded.

"I believe his delay in leaving is due to the presence of guests—"

"Guests?" she questioned, cutting him off curtly. "We have guests here? Who?"

"His Grace, duke of Lyndeforde and Sir Osborn—"

"What are Roger and that little worm doing here?" she wondered aloud.

"Captain Deveraux and—"

"Captain Deveraux!" She whirled on Edmonds, her kohl-rimmed eyes aglow with imagined pleasures. "In which room? The guestroom in the east wing?"

Edmonds nodded. "But Lady Dandridge, there is something ye should know."

"Later Edmonds." She dismissed him summarily with a wave of her hand as she started briskly up the stairs. "And don't tell Robert I've returned. I'll tell him myself—later," she shouted over her shoulder.

As Lady Dandridge hurried up the stairs as fast as her full skirts would allow, Mrs. Winton joined Edmonds at the foot of the staircase.

"I should like to be a little mouse in that room when her ladyship makes her discovery," she said grimly.

"I only hope our young lady is strong enough to meet the challenge," responded Edmonds.

" 'Tis true, Lady Dandridge is a viper, but instinct tells me she hath met her equal."

As the butler and the housekeeper looked at each other, the ghost of a smile crossed their usually staid features. Perhaps the old house would know some life yet.

Rorie frowned in perplexity as she tried to arrange the bodice of her blue linen day dress across the increased fullness of her bosom. Her illness must have somehow affected the proportions of her body, she decided. As she struggled with the fastenings, she heard the door of the chamber burst open, and a sultry voice, which grated familiarily on her ears, cooed seductively, "Cameron, darling, had I but known of your presence here, I would have returned earlier."

Quickly, Rorie tumbled her hair, loosened the bodice and set aside the hoop and petticoat.

"Lady Eleanora," Cameron replied coolly, striving to control his surprise and dismay. What would Rorie do now? he worried. For he had no doubts that she was listening to every word. "Do you always burst into a guest's bedchamber unannounced?"

"Only when it holds certain promise, darling," she replied with a sly wink. "Still abed, I see. Shall I join you?"

"I wouldn't advise it, Lady Dandridge," said Rorie crisply from the doorway of the anteroom. "You may make light of *your* wedding vows, but

I assure you that I do not." The privileged class
never failed to amaze her. While strict observation of etiquette and protocol was demanded,
apparently morality was not.

Lady Dandridge whirled about to stare at
Rorie in such shocked dismay, she missed the
import of the younger woman's words. Her eyes
took in Rorie's unfastened bodice which exposed
a handsome cleavage to the eye. And together
with the disheveled hair tumbling bewitchingly
about her shoulders, without a doubt, the girl
presented an arresting picture of awakened sensuality. All totaled, the nature of Rorie's presence
struck Eleanora all too clearly.

"What are you doing here!" she hissed, her
eyes blazing with fury. But with a sinking heart,
she thought she already knew, and Rorie's next
words only served to confirm her fears.

"I believe the answer is rather obvious, Lady
Dandridge," replied Rorie sweetly, moving
across the room to sit possessively beside
Cameron on the bed. As she leaned her head on
his shoulder and ran her fingers through the
dark hair on his chest, she could hear Lady
Dandridge's sharp intake of breath. And she
noted with great satisfaction that the smug grin
on Cameron's face was slowly fading. Had she
but known how he struggled to control himself,
she might not have been so free with her
playacting.

"Now, Lady Dandridge, why don't you run
down the hall to your husband's chambers—if
you remember the way—and leave my husband
to me," Rorie concluded in lofty dismissal.

Eleanor's mouth dropped open, as she nearly
choked on her own words. "You—your

husband!" she finally blurted out, her dark eyes swiveling from Rorie to Cameron. "Cameron, is this true? You would take a child to wed, when 'tis a woman you desire?"

Cameron merely shrugged, but Rorie returned Eleanora's scathing look measure for measure.

"Lady Dandridge, when a man is hungry and the table full, he will always choose the freshest food while discarding that which is aged and soon to be spoiled."

Eleanora turned on Rorie with a look of such intense hatred, that Rorie was at great pains to keep her body from trembling from the force of it. After Lady Dandridge had fled the room, Rorie turned on Cameron angrily and gave him a shove that nearly tumbled him from the bed.

"You conceited lout! Instead of lying here, grinning like a well fed tom cat, why didn't you stand up to her!" she shouted.

Cameron threw back his head in laughter. "My dear, you seemed to be doing just fine all by yourself. I never saw Eleanora at such a loss for words."

His fingers played lightly across the swell of her bosom above the open bodice, sending impulses through her body, impulses that weren't entirely unpleasant. Then swift as a cat, he pulled her to him and pressed his mouth to hers, moving his lips slowly, masterfully, possessively across her own. She felt her defenses weakening and her thoughts fragmenting, as he then slipped the chemise off her shoulders and slid his hand inside to caress her breasts. Bursts of arousing sensations exploded when his mouth soon followed to massage the rose-tipped aureoles. His actions were light and smooth with deadly accuracy, calculated to introduce pleasure and dissolve suspicion and fear. And Rorie was succumbing to his spell.

She was dimly aware when he brought her under the sheet with him and raised her skirt. In a minute he would have her beneath him. With a certain desperation, Rorie struggled against her instincts and rising passion, but as his mouth reclaimed hers and his hand played lightly between her legs, her protests died on her lips.

Sensing a response deep within her as her arms encircled his neck, Cameron prepared to enter her when Eloise loudly announced her presence.

"Lord Dandridge thought as how ye newlyweds would prefer yer breakfast here, where it be private like," she called out from the hallway. She smiled knowingly then as she entered the room and took in Rorie's dazed face and disheveled appearance.

"Damn it, Eloise," growled Deveraux, "next time, knock before you burst in."

"I did, sir, but I guess ye was too busy ta hear." Eloise winked and broke into merry laughter as she set the tray on a table and quickly left the room.

Struggling free of Cameron and leaping from the bed, Rorie's eyes smoldered with rage. What was wrong with her! The rogue had already won over Mary and Eloise. Was she to be betrayed by her body and mind, too? Damn him! She would fight him with the one thing he had little control over—her temper.

"If you try that again, Captain, our bargain is off," Rorie warned, in a low voice, tight with anger. The glint in her emerald eyes told Deveraux in no uncertain terms that she meant what she said.

Cameron frowned, studying her intently as she yanked the gown into place and struggled to fasten the bodice. Rising from the bed, he slipped on his breeches and went to stand behind her. Rorie jumped when his strong fingers brushed against her neck, sending shivers up her spine, as he pushed aside her trembling hands and began to hook the garment. Although she didn't protest his help, her back remained stiff and unyielding.

"Why don't you admit it to yourself, Rorie?" he said, breaking the awkward silence.

"Admit what?" she asked warily.

"That if you gave yourself half a chance, you might enjoy submitting to my hand." Angrily, he whirled her around to face him, taking her roughly by the shoulders. "Damn it, Rorie, look at me. What has happened to make you so rigid?"

"You dare to ask me that!" she shot back hotly, breaking free of his grasp. "You, who took that which was only mine to give. Bah! You're no different from any other man. You take, but never give—or ask!"

"I'll admit I didn't help matters overmuch," Cameron retorted with a twinge of conscience. "But this aversion you have to lovemaking didn't start with me. Now tell me! It's not just my hand you object to. It's any man, isn't it?"

Rorie refused to massage his ego. "I'll tell you nothing, Captain, save this—I'll never willingly submit to any man, nor will any man control my life!"

Cameron was thunderstruck by the vehemence of her declaration and could only stare after her as she swept into the anteroom, her tousled head held high. His jaw tightened, and he banged his fist against the bed post when he heard the door slam and the lock click into place.

Suddenly the words of the old gypsy woman sprang to his mind: "Take not that what not be freely given, for 'twill be yers soon enough. Temper time with patience."

All along he had thought the old woman was making reference to his plans for Roger Thornton, but as though a light had flashed on in his mind, he suddenly understood the true meaning of her words.

"Damn!" he cursed. "What a blundering fool I have been!"

27

"You fool!" shrieked Lady Dandridge, bursting in upon the duke in his allotted chamber, completely indifferent to his state of dishabille.

Thornton jumped and turned a cold eye on Lady Dandridge. "I think you forget to whom you speak, Eleanora."

"Don't pull class rank on me, Roger. We've shared too many beds for that. How could you let this happen!" she screamed, rounding on Percy, who had just entered the room.

Percy regarded Lady Dandridge with ill-concealed distaste for a moment, before nonchalantly straightening the lace at his cuffs and assuming his subservient demeanor. "If you are speaking of the captain and Miss Shelbourne's marriage, milady, I assure you, we were taken just as unawares. Roger, here, stands to lose a handsome dowry, his prestige in the peerage, and quite possibly his freedom."

Thornton blanched at hearing his future laid out so simplistically, as though he were about to embark upon a mere tiresome journey.

"But you, Lady Dandridge," Percy continued snidely, "have lost only a—tentative bed partner, at best."

"How dare you!" Eleanora breathed.

She would have raised a hand to strike the insolence from Percy's face, but something in his eyes made her think better of the idea. She hated the pasty-faced little weasel. She couldn't abide physical imperfections in men, however much she welcomed them in women. But aside from that, there was something else about Osborn, something dark and sinister. She wasn't fooled by the whiny self-effacing front he presented. And she never once discounted the rumors that he had twice tried to engineer his brother's death, so that he could succeed to the title.

"We'll do no better by fighting amongst ourselves," snapped Thornton. "Unfortunately, the Shelbourne girl is lost to us. The squire is not going to be pleased by this, and we shall have to force the wedding—not to mention Fenton out of hiding—by some other means."

"Yes, but it does seem rather a coincidence, though, don't you think, Roger?" mused Osborn aloud. "The captain, by all appearances, is not the marrying type, and 'tis rather odd that he never mentioned his interest in the chit beforehand. Indeed, if Captain Deveraux weren't so necessary to our plans, I might find his actions suspect. In any case, I think this merits a closer eye."

"Perhaps, but we do have a more immediate problem that needs to be addressed," Thornton reminded him.

"Yes, quite," agreed Percy. "Lord Dandridge, Dr. Farley, the captain and his—wife must be persuaded to leave the estate within the next few days." Percy purposely stressed the word "wife," knowing how it rankled Lady Dandridge.

"Well, what do you suggest—short of kidnapping?" Eleanora demanded snidely. "You can't exactly host a ball with your betrothed in mourning, Roger."

Osborn smiled craftily. "Perhaps not a ball. But a hunt with Lord Dandridge, the good doctor and Captain Deveraux would not be outside the realm of propriety at this time."

"Excellent idea," applauded Thornton, his flagging spirit reviving. "I shall suggest it at supper tonight.

The evening meal was constrained, with Rorie refusing to rise to Eleanora's spiteful baiting. Lord Dandridge was decidedly uncomfortable with his wife's ill manners, and he unsuccessfully attempted to cut her off more than once. And Thornton and Osborn were ever watchful of the newlyweds, waiting for the chink in their vows to manifest itself. Only the doctor and Cameron seemed impervious to the tension in the room as they discussed a myriad of subjects between them pausing now and again to throw out a question to the group or to look intently at Rorie—for different reasons.

The serenity of the old manor had disappeared with Lady Dandridge's return. Thus, it was with great relief that Rorie found Thornton's suggestion for a hunt well received by all. She was eager to return to Drumfielde to check on her family and Mary—and to escape her husband's attentions. She was beginning to feel so stifled here, having to walk a tightrope between Cameron and Lady Dandridge, that she feared she would soon go mad. She needed to strip off her cares and plunge into the wonderfully cooling waters of her private paradise. As she looked down at the variety of dishes before her, Rorie suddenly felt her stomach constrict, and the room began to swirl about her.

"Mrs. Deveraux . . . Mrs. Deveraux." Somewhere in the distance someone was calling her name. She felt a supportive arm go round her shoulders, but she could only close her eyes tightly against the rising tide of nausea which threatened to engulf her. When she was able to open them again, her eyes were a startling green against the paleness of her face. Aware that everyone's attention was on her, Rorie smiled wanly.

"Please excuse me, Lord Dandridge, but I seem to have overestimated my recovery."

As she stood to leave, Cameron moved to help her, but the doctor laid a restraining hand on his arm. "I'll see to the lady, Captain," he said firmly. And as Dr. Farley escorted Rorie to her chambers, Cameron frowned after them, his mood pensive.

"Well, Captain," Lady Dandridge snickered, "your fresh flower appears to be wilting. What a pity you haven't realized that some things are better with age."

For a moment Eleanora felt a glimmer of hope when Cameron turned a considering gaze upon her, but in the next instant, it died when he looked away as though he had assessed her charms and found them lacking. He was more interested in what was transpiring upstairs.

* * *

Having examined his patient more closely, Dr. Farley stepped back from the bed. "Well, Mrs. Deveraux, how do you feel?"

" 'Tis only the tension of the day, Doctor. I'll be fine after a good night's rest and shall be ready to leave for Drumfielde with the others."

"I'm not sure that's wise, madam," said the doctor, watching her carefully. " 'Tis a hard trip. The roads are some of the worst in all England. In your weakened state, a baby could be at risk."

Rorie started to wave aside his protests, when her hand stopped in midair. "Are you telling me that I may be—" As Dr. Farley nodded, her pretty face registered an array of emotions from shock to dismay. "Oh, dear God, no," she cried. That was the one thing she had never considered. It was beyond the realm of possibilities alongside her other difficulties. And her expressive features began to crumble in total defeat.

"The thought never occurred to you?" inquired Farley.

Rorie shook her head miserably.

"Truth to tell, 'twas Eloise who first raised the possibility," he admitted. "You must have suspected something, though, when your time had come and gone to no avail."

"I thought 'twas the exhaustion," she replied dispiritedly, suddenly remembering the new fullness to her breasts. "Can you be that certain?"

"Well, 'tis a mite early," Dr. Farley agreed, "but the signs appear to be present. Another week or two should tell the truth of the matter." He smiled reassuringly and gently patted her hand. "There now, these things happen. 'Tis natural to be frightened with the first. When the shock wears off, you will feel differently. I'll wager the captain will be pleased to hear."

Rorie's downcast eyes flew open in sudden alarm, and she grasped his hand in desperation. "Dr. Farley, please, don't say anything to—to my husband. You see, ours is not a conventional marriage," she hastened to explain. " 'Tis more an arrangement that is to be dissolved in a few months time."

The doctor frowned and stroked his chin thoughtfully, not certain that he understood the situation at all. "Although the circumstances surrounding your marriage, Mrs. Deveraux, were a bit bizarre," he allowed, "I hadn't counted on the union being likewise. Still, you don't beget a child by yourself. Captain Deveraux would be the father, would he not?" he asked in sudden consternation.

Rorie flushed to the roots of her hair. "Yes, yes," she responded impatiently, not wanting to dwell on her relationship with the captain. "What has that to do with anything?"

The doctor sighed with obvious relief. "Well, Mrs. Devervaux, a man has a right to know if he has fathered a child, whatever the circumstances."

"If there is to be a child, I had no say in the conception," Rorie snapped bitterly. "Captain Deveraux shall have no say in the child's future. I give you fair warning, Dr. Farley, my husband is never to know unless I choose to tell him. Is that clear?"

Farley was taken aback by the flash in her eyes and the forcefulness of her tone. So that was the way of it, he thought, nodding his head slowly. It would certainly explain her attitude.

Aloud he said, "I understand your feelings, Mrs. Deveraux, but I think you underestimate your husband. True, he can be a hard man, but I believe he truly cares for you in his own way. He was quite concerned when you appeared to be on the decline."

"He cares for no one and nothing, Doctor, save his own pleasures."

"How do you propose to keep it from him? If the diagnosis is correct, within a few months your condition will be obvious."

"In all likelihood, my husband will have returned to the colonies by then," she responded in a brittle tone.

"I see," said the doctor, clearly disturbed by the young lady's bitter disclosures.

As he prepared to leave, Rorie called after him. "Doctor, in light of the circumstances, I wish the captain to have other sleeping accommodations—for the time being," she hastily amended at the look of protest on his face. "The marriage, itself, comes as an unexpected shock and now together with the possibility of a baby, I feel the need for some time alone to gather my thoughts."

"The situation does appear to be causing you undue stress which is most certainly ill-advised at this point," agreed Farley, noting the set of her features and the conviction of her tone. "Very well, I shall inform your husband that you are still convalescing and that he is to make his bed in the anteroom—for the time being," he warned, repeating her own words.

"I would prefer to have him in another chamber."

"I'm afraid a bed in the anteroom is the best

we can do, Mrs. Deveraux. The captain will be difficult enough to handle as it is, and you'll only arouse speculation by casting the bridegroom from his rightful chambers."

For the next few days, Rorie kept to her room, recapturing her strength and spirit. Thornton and Osborn had departed earlier to ready Lyndeforde for guests once again. And she saw very little of her husband or Lord and Lady Dandridge. When she and Cameron did meet, each was too busy wrestling with his inner emotions to speak. But she was acutely aware when he entered the chamber late at night. Even though she pretended to be asleep, he always stopped by the side of the bed to peer down at her, before continuing on into the anteroom. At first she had been filled with dread that he would touch her, but then she began to trust that he would hold to his bargain.

For his part, Deveraux was torn between frustration at his helplessness to make things right between him and the need to keep a clear head for the business he was about. Later, he told himself, when this dastardly work was done, he would mend fences, for she had touched something in him—something he couldn't explain or define.

When Dr. Farley had told him that Rorie was at a crucial point in her recovery and that he would have to make his bed in the anteroom, Cameron stared in disbelief. If his ego hadn't been so bruised he would have laughed at the irony of the situation. All of his adult life he had access to any woman's bed he desired, except that of his own wife. He had agreed to the damnable bargain Rorie had struck, thinking he could charm his way around her in due time. But then he hadn't counted on her not only holding him to the terms, but throwing him out of her bed as well.

Although he didn't believe the story of her convalescence in the least, he went along with it. In the meantime, by staying away from Rorie, he wryly noted, he was shielding her from Lady Dandridge, for the woman dogged him mercilessly, complacent in the knowledge that all was not well with the newlyweds.

28

The trip back to Drumfielde passed slowly for Rorie. The coach was well sprung and comfortable, the gently sloping countryside was awash with bright colors, and the air had an invigorating freshness to it. But Rorie was only aware of the pressure of Cameron's arm on her shoulder and side whenever they were jostled against each other.

The few times he spoke he was stiffly polite beneath Dr. Farley's watchful eyes, and Rorie wondered what he was thinking each time he turned a frowning gaze upon her. Her feelings were in such a state of confusion, she no longer knew how she felt about him. She despised him for the way he had shamed her—or was it her own weakness she deplored? In all fairness, she had to admit that his slightest touch had the capacity to break through her defenses, and on more than one occasion, she painfully reminded herself, she had succumbed to his caresses. Neither could Rorie discount the fact that in her greatest hours of need, he seemed always to be there for her, so that she unconsciously sought safety in his strength. Or was it more the case that his presence set the stage for these misfortunes?

Rorie covertly glanced at the strong lines of his profile, as though trying to divine his innermost secrets. That he had some, she didn't doubt, for the few times they had shared an intimate moment, she felt a barrier go up between them. Outside the realm of the physical, he seemed unwilling or unable to commune with a woman. How typical, she thought disparagingly, and swiftly concluded that as with all men, he simply wasn't to be trusted. Yet, she couldn't deny the magnetism of his masculinity, and she firmly resolved to stay beyond his reach. If the flesh was weak, her mind wasn't!

For Cameron the journey was agony. To be so close to Rorie, to smell her fragrance, to know how she looked and felt beneath those clothes and not be able to feel or touch her was almost more than he could bear. The damnable hoops, he decided irritably, had to be the contrivance of either a woman scorned or a protective father to keep men at arm's length. And he wondered if he wouldn't have been better off riding with Lord Dandridge and Eleanora. If his temper wasn't being so sorely tried, he might have found the circumstances amusing. He thought he had been setting the rules, calling the moves, but Rorie had been in control all along. What strange power did she have over him that he found himself married to her and still unable to avail himself of her pleasures? She was like a thorny rose—beautiful but untouchable. And from time to time he would gaze at her in genuine perplexity, as if to unravel her mysteries.

A slight smile wreathed the doctor's mouth as he observed the couple from under lowered eyelids. Although Rorie and the captain were silent, the nervous tension reflected by the set of their features and the restlessness of their bodies spoke louder than any words. Whether these two wanted to admit it or not, there was much unfinished business between them, Farley decided. He was confident that, in time, they would be powerless to resist the force which bound them together.

As the coach pulled up to the stone fortress of Lyndeforde directly behind that of Lord and Lady Dandridge, Rorie moved to flee the conveyance the moment it stopped, but the sound of Cameron's deep voice, rending the unnatural silence of the last few hours, startled her into immobility. "Madam," he said. His brow raised in stern admonition reminded her of the role she must play, and she dutifully waited for him to help her out. Neither was prepared for the jolt each received, however, when his large hand reached up to encase her slender fingers. In the next instant the moment was gone as fast as it had appeared when Rorie jerked her hand free, and Cameron quickly rearranged his startled features into an inscrutable mask.

"How jolly good to have you all here again to liven up these old walls," called Roger Thornton from the steps. "Let us all retire to the drawing room for refreshments.

The duke greeted his guests with such exuberance—and not without a modicum of relief—that Cameron couldn't help feeling there was more to the invitation than they knew. He resolved to watch the situation closely. At least Rorie couldn't escape him here. She would have to share his bed now, he thought smugly, a smile of anticipation relaxing her from the coach told him that he could still reach her.

As the group moved into the house, Rorie started when she felt Cameron's hand rest lightly on the small of her back. To her mind he was staking out his territory, and she fairly bristled at his arrogance.

"I hope you shall find your accommodations satisfactory,' Thornton was saying as brandy was passed among the men and tea among the ladies. "You will all be in the west wing. And as per Dr. Farley's instructions, Captain, Mrs. Deveraux shall occupy the room next to yours until her convalescence is completed."

Eleanora snickered. Standing across the room with the other men, Cameron's smile faded as he noticed the look of gratitude that Rorie threw the doctor. When he caught Rorie's eye, his gaze was steady, betraying none of the disappointment, frustration, and anger he was feeling, as he raised his glass in mock salute.

By the time the guests had retired to the rooms to rest and dress for supper, Cameron was in a black mood.

"How did the li'l lady take the marriage, Cap'n?" Rawlings asked eagerly when Cameron stomped into the chamber. The minute the words were out of his mouth, he regretted his curiosity, for, in answer, Deveraux turned upon him the most thunderous look that the man-servant had ever seen.

The men rose early the next morning for the

hunt. Leaving Eleanora still abed, Rorie had a chaise hooked up for her use. Though she was supposed to be denying her family, she couldn't stay away any longer. She had to see her aunt and brother, to know of their well-being, to hear of her uncle.

On the way, she stopped by Balfour Grange to see Mary. Although drawn and paler than usual, Mary was as well as could be expected. For the moment, the news of Rorie's marriage had transcended her sadness, and she was so full of tearful congratulations that Rorie didn't have the heart to explain the true circumstances, for she had always been uncomfortably aware of her friend's matchmaking attempts. Mercifully, the squire had not been at home.

When she surreptitiously entered the Fenton farmyard a few hours later, Terence and her aunt hurried in from the field.

"Oh, Rorie, 'tis glad I am ta see ye, but ye shouldna come," said Molly, casting anxious glances around her. " 'Tis too dangerous. Someone may be watching."

" 'Tis truth, Rorie. You must leave before you're seen," agreed Terence.

"I know, but I had to see that you are well," replied Rorie, struggling to hide her emotional distress.

Molly hugged her niece tightly. "Bless ye child. But this'll soon pass an' we'll be a family again. Ye'll see. Come, I don't s'ppose it could hurt to talk fer a few minutes. and then ye'll feel better."

Gathered around the familiar kitchen table once more, surrounded by her family, Rorie felt more at ease than she had in the past several weeks. As she hesitantly relayed the news of her marriage, omitting any mention of a baby, Molly and Terence burst into smiles of approval.

"Ah, Rorie, 'tis a good man ye have there. 'Tis proud we are ta have him in the family," said Molly, her eyes dancing merrily. " 'Twas worried we've been fer ye, lass, but with the cap'n ta protect ye, we know ye'll be safe."

"Aye," agreed Terence with hearty enthusiasm. "I had a few doubts when I knew him to be a guest of the duke's, but then we came to terms. The captain be just what you need, Rorie, to handle that rebellious streak in you. He'll keep you out of trouble," Terence added with a mischievous wink.

Rorie was stunned by their reactions and her serenity dissolved. "You knew of the marriage?" she asked in astonishment.

"Aye, 'tis tha' we did," replied Molly.

"How?"

Terence's freckled features turned dark. "The captain told us of the duke's scheme to marry you off to Squire Balfour, Rorie. He asked permission to marry you instead."

"And you gave it!" exploded Rorie, her eyes wide in disbelief. She didn't know what she had expected. Grudging consent perhaps, but certainly not this rousing ovation. She felt as though she had lost her last allies.

Terence and Molly looked at each other in surprise at her outburst.

"Easy lass," said Molly, gently patting Rorie's arm. "Ye've been ill and under a strain. The cap'n said ye was well acquainted, an' there was no other way. The man seemed a fair minded sort."

"How can you be so sure!" she demanded. "You don't really know Cameron Deveraux. Why he's a colonial, for heaven's sake!"

"I don't know what all the fuss is about. You should be grateful. God's teeth, one would think the man was taking advantage of you," declared Terence impatiently. At this, Rorie turned a sharp gaze on her brother, but said nothing. " 'Tis you who obviously doesn't know the captain," he went on. "You owe him much more than you think."

"What do you mean?" asked Rorie suspiciously.

"Terence, that's enough!"

"No, Aunt Molly, she should know that not only does she owe him this favor, but she owes him her life as well."

Rorie exploded with anxious curiosity. "What are you talking about, Terence!"

"The horse that almost ran you down last month, well 'twas the captain who pulled you from its path."

Shocked into silence, Rorie, stared from her brother to her aunt. "How do you know this?" she asked in a hoarse whisper.

"Will sent word of it so'd we know to trust Captain Deveraux about your marriage," confirmed Molly.

Rorie sensed that her aunt was holding something back, and her eyes narrowed in determination. "What aren't you telling me, Aunt Molly? You might just as well confide everything, for I won't leave until I know," she threatened.

Molly Fenton hesitated for a moment before giving in. "Rorie, what I tell ye must go no further than this house," she warned soberly. "Ye must be special careful now tha' ye be livin' at Lyndeforde."

Rorie nodded and braced herself. She couldn't imagine what would be any worse than losing her family's allegiance to her husband. When her aunt had finished recounting the daring smuggling scheme to trap the duke, however, Rorie could only stare in further disbelief.

"How did Uncle Will get involved in this?" she asked.

"It seems tha' Will knows of some hut in the marsh wha' be important ta the plan," answered Molly. "That's where he's been hidin'."

"How could he do it! 'Tis enough he's sought for murder."

"Will can't run forever, lass, an' the duke will ne'er allow him ta clear his name. 'Tis the only chance he and Drumfielde has. The duke must be ruined before he can do any more harm. With the harsh winter we had and now the enclosure claiming the common land and crops, we'll be fortunate enough to feed ourselves, much less others in the coming months."

"Open your eyes to what's around you, Rorie," her brother admonished impatiently. "The duke blocks us at every turn. What men we don't lose to further bloodshed, we'll lose to the tin mines. If we're to survive, we must act now. A ship is due in tonight, and I'm to have a part," he added proudly.

A small cry escaped Rorie's lips, and her hand flew to her mouth. "Terence, you can't! You are too young. Aunt Molly, tell him he can't go," she pleaded desperately.

"I'm tha' sorry, lass," said Molly with gentle

firmness. "Terence is a man now an' has earned the right to go. Besides, he is needed. There be too many spies about the village fer yer uncle to be able to place his trust in anyone else. There'll be no need to fear, lass," her aunt continued, attempting to assuage Rorie's anxiety. "A man named Rawlings is an old friend of Will's, and has promise ta look after Terence as much as possible."

Rawlings! Rorie's head shot up. "Rawlings is Uncle Will's friend!" she exclaimed, when at last she could speak. A sudden panic began well up in her stomach.

"Aye, they go back many years," answered Molly in surprise. "Do you know him?"

"Apparently not. Is he at the head of the plot?" Rorie persisted urgently.

"No," said Terence, looking at her with unveiled curiosity. "He's just one of the contacts I'm to meet along with a group of men in the clearing tonight before midnight. Only this Rawlings and Uncle Will know who sits at the head. Why?"

"Nothing," she murmured, knowing all too well who lead them. Rorie stood up abruptly. "I should leave now, as I have a matter to look into," she said determinedly.

Rorie climbed into the chaise and whipped the horse into a breakneck pace. Damn the sod! How dare he worm his way into the midst of her own family and place them at risk! And why had he been present at the rebellion, if not to spy? Why did she alone stand against him? Although Terence might be easily led, her aunt and uncle were no fools. Her mind was a chaotic jumble of thoughts as she whipped the horse still faster.

Suddenly a thought struck Rorie, and she shivered in spite of the evening warmth. Dear God, what if this was another trick to help the duke trap her uncle. If caught in the act of smuggling, the charge would be much more creditable than this silly trumped up murder charge, and her uncle's and brother's blood would be on the hands of the King's Court. Her thoughts were so ponderous that she had entered the stable yard without realizing it until her horse was brought abruptly to a stop.

"What the hell are you trying to do—break your damned neck!" yelled Deveraux furiously, struggling to bring both of their horses under control. "If you have no regard for your own life, have a care for good horseflesh," he railed. "It's bad enough that you're riding around the countryside by yourself at night, but you nearly ran me over in the bargain just as I was starting out to search for you."

When Rorie gave no indication that she was listening to his tirade, Cameron swung himself down from the horse and walked over to the carriage, anger echoing from every step. He had long ago concluded that the wench was positively the most frustrating female he had ever encountered, and tonight's incident only reaffirmed it. "Well, are you going to sit there all night?" he demanded, extending a hand.

Rorie started and looked at Deveraux as though he had grown two heads. "Don't you dare touch me, you miserable swine!" she screamed, stumbling out of the chaise and running into the house.

Deveraux stared after her in amazement. What the hell was that all about? he wondered.

What had he done now? Without a doubt, life had been far simpler before he had met this girl. Well, he had more important things on his mind this night, and would deal with her later, he vowed with stern commitment.

The others were gathered in the drawing room, drinking brandy and port, and Rorie knew she wouldn't be able to escape their notice. She was hesitating outside the doorway, trying to regain her composure and wondering how to make an entrance, when Cameron came alongside. Scowling down at her, he wordlessly offered her his arm. Glaring up at him with a mixture of contempt and wariness, she reluctantly took it.

"Well, well, the lovebirds are together at last," sneered Lady Dandridge, her dark eyes glittering with envy as they entered the room. Noting the tense anger between the couple, however, she began to preen and glow with obvious satisfaction.

On the other side of the room, Percy Osborn stroked his chin in thoughtful meditation as he, too, took careful stock of the newlyweds. For the life of him, he couldn't figure their relationship.

"Really, Cameron, I am beginning to wonder if you have imagined this wedding business," Eleanora was saying sardonically. "After all, it doesn't seem to be agreeing with either one of you." She arched a dark brow as her gaze then swept critically over Rorie's attire. "You appear to have enjoyed your ride, Miss Shel—Mrs. Deveraux."

Rorie almost groaned aloud as she realized how disheveled she must look alongside this neatly coiffed and seductively attired siren.

"Some of us have interests which go beyond the drawing room, Lady Eleanora," Cameron cut in smoothly with a yawn. "It has been a long day for us early risers. I think that my wife and I shall say goodnight."

"Excellent idea," joined in Thornton. "Tomorrow is another hunt. We could all do with a bit of rest."

"By all means," agreed Lord Dandridge, extending a hand to his wife. "Eleanora?"

Lady Dandridge smiled pointedly at Cameron, ignoring her husband. "Must you so soon, Captain? I thought perhaps we might pass a hand of pharoah. I'm sure your . . . wife can find her own way."

Lord Dandridge cleared his throat. "Eleanora, mayhaps if you retired at a more conventional hour, you might be able to rise before the setting of the sun," he said firmly.

"Possibly the ladies would like to join us tomorrow," suggested Cameron casually.

Thornton and Osborn shrugged indifferently. "I shall be leaving before the hunt anyway as I have business in Portsmouth," said Percy, glancing meaningfully at Thornton.

"Capital idea, Captain," agreed Lord Dandridge. "What say you, ladies?"

Lady Eleanora looked decidedly displeased with the suggestion and cast a withering glance at her husband. She was not at her best in the early morning hours, and the harsh sunlight only seemed to accentuate the tiny lines and wrinkles she sought to keep hidden behind more subdued light.

Although Rorie had never ridden to the hounds before, she had always enjoyed riding her uncle's mare about the farm. Her eyes shone as she imagined the wind whipping through her hair and the cool morning mist upon her face. 'Twas just what she needed to clear the cobwebs from her brain, and it was on the tip of her tongue to gratefully accept when, with sudden clarity, she realized the trap Cameron had set. To accept the invitation would be to admit that her convalesence was complete, and Cameron would have her moved into his room before the hour was out. Helplessly, she floundered for an excuse when Dr. Farley came to her rescue.

"I don't believe that riding is in your best interests at this time, Mrs. Deveraux," he advised. "You are still recovering your strength."

"Thank you for your concern, Doctor. I shall abide by your wishes," replied Rorie, pretending disappointment.

"Well, then, if you have no further need for me, I shall be leaving on the morrow also," Farley announced. "Thank you for your hospitality, Your Grace. And Mrs. Deveraux, please consider very carefully *all* that we have discussed."

Cameron regarded the doctor and his wife with veiled curiosity. As bright pink spots appeared on Rorie's cheeks, his eyes narrowed to two dark blue slits, and his lips drew together in a harsh line. The doctor, though a few years older than himself, was not an unattractive man, and for the second time Cameron wondered if there was something between them. The muscles in his arm tightened as he bid a stiff good evening and pulled a surprised Rorie from the room.

"Captain Deveraux, either release my arm or slow your pace!" Rorie demanded angrily.

Cameron stopped in midstride at the foot of the stairs and searched her face closely. "What is between you and the doctor, Rorie?" he asked evenly.

The question caught her off-balance, and she lowered her eyes to hide the emotional turmoil that clawed at her insides. "There is nothing that concerns you," she responded tightly. And, jerking her arm free, she raced up the stairs to her room.

When Cameron burst into his chamber, slamming the door loudly behind him, Rawlings cast his eyes heavenward. Lord, but the captain has known nothing but foul moods since setting foot on this soil. He would be glad when this nasty business was done, and they could set sail for the colonies. "Have our plans gone awry, Cap'n?" he finally asked with some trepidation.

Cameron looked at Rawlings as though surprised to see the little man there. "No, everything stands for tonight," he growled, flopping onto the bed. " 'Tis Farley, damn his eyes. There is something between Rorie and him!"

At the risk of further angering his master, Rawlings snorted. "Yer marriage be only a bargain, sir. Why, 'twill be dissolved afore ye leave. Ye'd be in Lady Eleanora's bed yerself, but fer Lord Dandridge. Even so, I kenna see as how ye've managed ta ignore her ladyship this long. Pretty though she be, the Shelbourne lass ain't yer type anyway. So wha's the dif—" Rawlings broke off as he saw the murderous glint in Deveraux's eyes, and he quickly left the room shaking his shaggy head. What had gotten into the captain, he wondered dismally. What manner of spell had this lass cast on him, for never had the captain behaved so irrationally over a woman.

29

The minutes stretched into hours and the hours spread into the night as Rorie lay on her bed, straining to hear telltale sounds of stirring in the next room. Terence had said there was to be a drop tonight, and the captain and Rawlings would undoubtedly be in attendance, she surmised. That should give her time enough to search Cameron's room to know of his intentions. She just prayed that she would be in time to warn Terence, if necessary, before he left for the clearing.

She sat up abruptly, her nerves at the breaking point, as she heard a scraping noise, the shaking of a tree limb, and a faint thump as though someone had jumped from the window to the tree, which stood close to the side of the house, and dropped to the ground. Rorie hurried to the window in time to barely discern a figure blending into the black night.

Throwing a shawl about her light nightgown, she opened her door a crack and peered cautiously around before stepping out into the candlelit hallway. All was silent as she covered the few feet to Cameron's door and quietly let herself into his chambers. His scent of leather and sandalwood was so distinct that, for a moment, she fancied him standing there and nearly fled the room. Stop acting the silly, she berated herself with a shaky laugh. Hadn't she just seen him leave? Now to the task of searching the room for anything which would prove his allegiance, as the safety of her family stood in question.

She cursed the moonless night as she backed against a table and knocked over a glass. And against her better judgment, she decided to light a small candle from the dying fire. Holding the candlestick high, she surveyed the room before setting the light on top of the desk. After some minutes of rifling, the papers on the desk yielded nothing but typical business correspondence, and the armoire told her nothing except that the occupant had excellent taste in clothes.

Frustrated, nervous, and exhausted, Rorie stamped her foot in defeat and sat down heavily in a chair near the fireplace to think. Her head throbbed from the tension, and she massaged her temples as she propped a foot on the hearth. Suddenly she went very still. She had barely felt it, but she was certain that the brick beneath her heel had moved. Scrambling to her knees, surprise gave way to excitement as the corner brick pulled away easily in her hands to reveal a thrice folded parchment, yellowed with age.

Her eye caught the crest and signature of James Chardwellende, the previous duke of Lyndeforde. And she had read just enough to realize that it was a legitimacy of birth, when she

sensed a presence in the room. Her hand
smothered a gasp, and she nearly died on the
spot when she looked up to see Deveraux
standing across the room, his arms crossed over
his massive chest. He had the look of a father
who had caught his child in a naughty act.

"H-how long have you been here?" Rorie
stammered.

"Since after you knocked against the table. I
was coming down the hall when I heard your
attempts at stealth. 'Tis fortunate that thievery is
not your occupation, my dear, else your life
would be short, indeed."

"I—I saw you leave. You went out the
window."

Cameron raised his brow in surprise before
admitting, "You saw Rawlings leave. I was
restless and went down to the library for a
drink."

"And for Lady Dandridge," Rorie shot back,
catching a whiff of that lady's strong perfume.

"Tsk, tsk," he said with a hint of triumph in
his tone and a dangerous glint in his eye. "I
warned you before, Rorie, seeing is not always
believing. Now you shall pay the price."

He crossed the room in long, easy strides and,
yanking her roughly to her feet, he took the
paper from her nerveless fingers.

"I warned you not to make inquiry of me,"
he said, his voice low and husky. "You've
violated the agreement."

"I would violate any agreement where the
safety of my family is concerned," she retorted
with more bravado than she felt. "I know all
about your smuggling scheme, Cameron
Deveraux, and I won't let you set up my brother

and uncle for a hangman's noose to satisfy the desires of a scoundrel like Thornton."

Cameron looked at Rorie in surprise. "Where in the hell did you get that idea?"

"What difference does it make? Why didn't you tell me 'twas you at the rebellion, unless you were there to spy. Yes, Captain, to protect my family, I would violate a hundred of your arrogant agreements."

There was no reasoning with the wench in the mood she was in, Cameron decided. And as he, instead, swept her up into his arms, Rorie realized the recklessness of her statement. He had trapped her neatly, or rather, she had trapped herself.

"Let me go," she hissed, struggling to break free as he dropped her on the bed.

" 'Tis unfortunate for you, my sweet, that you had to be so inquisitive. Now I shall be forced to keep you close by my side at all times to ensure the success of my scheme, as you call it. No more separate rooms, Rorie," he warned. "From here on you're to be my wife in *all* meanings of the term."

Rorie gasped as he shed his robe and pulled the gown over her head with one swift movement. It was the afternoon in the cottage all over again, but this time she'd be damned if she would plead, cry or acquiesce under his hand. She had nothing more to lose, and fear no longer bound her. Anger was her strength now, and she would fight with every ounce she possessed.

Cameron was confident that once Rorie felt his velvet touch, she would readily surrender to him, for mankind was by nature sexual. Tonight there would be no interruptions, and he would at last have the chance to prove to her that the pleasures of love far exceeded the emptiness of abstinence. But the last thing he saw as he lay down beside her was a furious flash of green eyes, before being pelted with a hail of fists. Having been caught off-balance, it was a moment until Cameron could rally his stunned senses, for he was too busy countering her offensive. She was such a force of energy, twisting, turning, kicking and hitting, he couldn't get a hold of her. And when he tried to lay his leg across hers, he discovered that she had drawn herself up into a tight ball. As Rorie turned to roll off the bed, however, he was finally able to wrap his arm around her chest, tightly imprisoning her arms and hands. And as she unbent her legs to carry on the attack, his own muscular leg moved quickly to render her defenseless. For a moment both lay breathless from the exertion, but Cameron knew better than to relax his iron grip. He had already underestimated her determination once. He wouldn't do so again.

"It would seem, madam, that your convalescence is complete," he remarked dryly.

Laying on her side, her back drawn up securely against his broad chest, Rorie couldn't see Cameron's face, but she didn't mistake the hint of amusement in his husky voice. She started and shuddered then when he lifted up her heavy hair and began to lightly caress her neck and shoulder with his lips. She closed her eyes against the familiar weakening which was beginning to permeate her body with warmth.

Turning her on her back, Cameron stared deeply into her eyes, forcing her gaze to his. "It was meant to come to this, Rorie," he whispered.

"We've both known it since that night at the poacher's hut. The—ah—misunderstanding the afternoon of the picnic was a mistake I greatly regret, and I promise you I won't make it again."

Rorie's eyes grew wide in surprise. Was he going to release her? If this was an apology, she accepted. Her heart dropped as he lowered his dark head and pressed his mouth against hers with surprising tenderness, moving across her soft trembling lips with a coaxing sensuality until they yielded to him of their own accord. As his hand played across her stomach, down her leg, and inside her thighs, unlocking exquisite delights of shivering intensity, she was dismayed to feel her body once again overriding the refusal of her mind to respond to his masterful touch. In spite of her silent commands, her body soon ceased all efforts to struggle free.

"Relax, Rorie," he commanded softly in her ear. "I shall make you forget the pain of the past to remember only the pleasures of the present and the delights of the future."

The blood pounded in her brain. Rorie felt as though she had no will of her own, as his hands and mouth explored the pleasure points of her body, this time taking care to ready her for him. When she felt him separate her legs to move on top of her, she fought to bring herself under control one last time. Feeling the hardness of his manhood gently ease into that most private part of her body, fear clouded her eyes and panic threatened to overtake her.

"Easy, now. Don't fight me, Rorie," she heard him murmur soothingly through the haze of her mind.

As Cameron moved on her slowly, she began

to relax and respond to his commands as the initial shock receded. Her body moved rhythmically to his, imprisoned in a web of arousal. When she shyly put her arms around him, Cameron smiled, and, in the moment that their eyes met, both knew they had crossed a threshold from which there was no turning back. She moaned then as his pace quickened and tingles of teasing pleasure gave way to explosions of fiery sensation. Soon, she was greedily matching his pace thrust for thrust, movement for movement, until the mounting tensions of their bodies were at such a peak, she thought she could stand no more.

At last Rorie felt a heady and welcomed release, and she was drifting slowly, dreamily back to consciousness when Cameron exploded deep within her, seeking his own sweet release. Together they drifted as one, the tension easing from their bodies. And when Cameron moved off of her, Rorie felt a sense of loss this time rather than of relief that it was over.

This wasn't the act of shameful humiliation and cruelty she had once witnessed, once experienced, and had always imagined it to be. Cameron had been gentle and caring toward her, seeking to give as much pleasure as he had taken. A man who could give that much of himself couldn't possibly be the cold-hearted, ruthless blackguard she had thought him to be. Perhaps if they both hadn't been so angry, their first time together could have been much like this. In any case, she decided to follow her instincts now. She was no closer to understanding what was going on, but something told her that Cameron posed no threat to either her family or the village.

Indeed, the man might possibly be their salvation.

"Cameron, I—" she began tentatively.

He pulled her close and kissed her tenderly. "I know, darling," he said. "Let's get some sleep. We'll talk later."

Cameron was as shaken as Rorie at the shattering realization that he might possibly love this little wench, for love was such a foreign emotion to him. He had known many women over the years, but no had elicited from him the feelings of protectiveness and the desire to bring unselfish pleasure to them as had Rorie. The others had been there to merely satisfy his lust, and he saw now how empty and mechanical the act had been.

He had received his first inkling that he might feel something more for Rorie when she had lain so close to death at Marwynde. He wasn't sure why he had forced her to fight for her life, why he had impulsively married her to protect her. At the time, he had refused to admit he cared. She had been just a challenge to him. Now he could no longer deny his feelings for her.

Although not a religious man in the true sense of the word, he had felt a satisfying, spiritual union with Rorie, a oneness he had never experienced before. And as she lay peacefully asleep in his arms, he vowed to find a way to secure her love and trust. He could conquer her body, he realized, but he didn't yet have her heart and soul. And for the first time, he wanted all of a woman—he wanted all of *Rorie*—and he knew he would have to prove his worth to get her.

When Rawlings entered Cameron's room the

next morning with a tray of coffee and cakes, he stopped short at the unexpected sight of Rorie nestled in Cameron's possessive arms. Glancing from the relaxed, satisfied smile on his captain's face to the gown which lay carelessly discarded on the floor, Rawlings lifted one bushy, white eyebrow before a wide grin split his leathery face.

Cameron laid Rorie aside, careful not to awaken her, and quietly slid from the bed. Donning a garnet brocade robe, he took Rawlings by the arm and led him to the other side of the room.

"I thought she wasn't up ta yer style, Cap'n," said Rawlings slyly, setting the tray on the table.

"I discovered last night, Rawlings, that 'twas all the others who weren't up to my style."

At Rawlings' quizzical look, Cameron laughed. " 'Tis a long story, my friend. But know this," he said soberly, "when I leave, 'twill be with Rorie by my side."

"Could mean trouble, sir. What if the lass not be willin'?"

"She'll come," affirmed Deveraux, "willing or not. Now tell me of last eve's events."

"All went as planned, Cap'n. We got the goods all transferred to the tunnel just afore the pack train showed up. We kidnapped the guard, jest like ye said, an' left behind the scarf."

"Good. Be prepared tonight as well, same pattern. Have you found the connection?"

Rawlings shook his head. "The man ain't talked yet, but he will."

"Everyone safe? Terence?" asked Deveraux.

"Aye, Cap'n. The boy be a hard worker, an' a good lad."

"Excellent. Rorie's mind can be put at ease."

"She knows!" exclaimed Rawlings. "But Cap'n—"

"Easy, Rawlings," whispered Cameron, glancing at Rorie's still form. "Somehow, she found out about our plan. I suspect 'twas from Mrs. Fenton."

"But Molly would never talk," insisted Rawlings. "she be as tight-lipped as they come."

"You don't know my wife when she sets her mind to a task," remarked Cameron wryly. "She's very close to her family. She won't betray them. Besides, she was convinced that you and I were working for Thornton to set up her brother and uncle as smugglers for the hangman's noose. I came upon her searching my room last night for evidence to that effect. She found the paper."

Rawlings stared at Cameron in alarm. "This could be dangerous, the way she feels 'bout you, Cap'n."

Grinning boyishly, Cameron ran a hand through his wavy hair. "I think I succeeded in dispelling some of her opinions about me last night, but until we can gain her complete trust, Rorie shall stay by my side, night and day. When 'tis not possible to be by mine, she'll remain by your side. Do I make myself clear?"

"Yes, sir, though 'tain't ta my likin'," grumbled Rawlings. "The lass don't take kindly ta orders—like someone else I knows."

Cameron smiled. "You'll manage."

"Cameron?" came a low, throaty voice. "Cameron, darling, I've come to join you."

Deveraux turned to see Lady Eleanora standing in the doorway, clad only in a filmy lace gown which left nothing to the imagination. His frown of dismay instantly deepened to a scowl of disgust as she began to advance toward the bed, holding her arms out in invitation.

"There's not room enough in here for the three of us, Lady Dandridge," said Rorie. "I told you before that my husband is not available to you, but apparently memory dims with age." Her voice, cold and exacting, cut through the stilted silence like a well-honed blade.

Lady Dandridge's eyes narrowed to black slits as she stared back at Rorie. She didn't want to believe what she was seeing, but the facts spoke loudly for themselves. The thin sheet which Rorie clutched to her chest did little to disguise the fact that she was unclothed. And as Eleanora glanced from the nightgown on the floor to the bloom on Rorie's cheeks, she was filled with envious rage for the intimacy she irrationally felt should have been hers.

"I think you had best leave," said Cameron coldly. "My wife and I are otherwise engaged."

"No!" shrieked Eleanora. "You can't possibly prefer that conniving litle whore to me. Look. Look at what I can give you," she screamed hysterically, tearing at her gown. "I know how to please a man. Please, Cameron, please, get rid of the brat."

Rorie blinked incredulously, barely able to credit the scene before her. Her wide eyes pleaded with Cameron to do something. Just as he started to advance toward Lady Dandridge, an enraged voice suddenly boomed from the open doorway.

"Eleanora! I've always known you for the trollop you are, but this day, woman, you've overstepped yourself."

Lady Dandridge whirled about to face her husband. Stark, vivid fear contorted her features. "Robert!—I, the captain forced me—"

"I'll hear no more of your lies, Eleanora," Lord Dandridge interrupted scathingly, taking her roughly by the arm. "You have a half hour to get your things together. The coach will be ready to take you back to Marwynde. As I don't trust myself to ride in the same conveyance with you, I shall follow later—after I've been to London to petition Parliament for a dissolution of our marriage. Now get out!" He shoved her none too gently out the door. Struggling to compose himself, Lord Dandridge then turned to face Rorie and Cameron. His voice trembled with the rage he felt. "I heartily beg your pardons, Mrs. Deveraux, Captain, for my wife's outrageous behavior." And he quickly left the room to carry out his threat.

Appalled by Lady Eleanora's behavior and upset over the humiliation that Lord Dandridge had been forced to suffer, Rorie wrapped the sheet around her and jumped from Cameron's bed.

"I may have shared your bed, Captain, but I'll not share your favors," she shouted, her face livid with fury. "How could you do it to that poor man! After last night, I was hoping you had changed, but I can see that a rat never changes!"

Cameron was stunned by Rorie's outburst. After the intimacy that they had shared earlier, it angered him that she could have so little faith in him.

"You little fool!" he thundered. "You can't possibly think that I invited Lady Dandridge to my room!"

"The facts speak for themselves, Captain," she spat. "You didn't know that I would be here through the night, and you and that woman were together in the library earlier last evening—no doubt making plans. Don't deny it. You reeked of her perfume."

"No, I won't deny that she pursued me into the library last night, but I told her in no uncertain terms that I wasn't interested. I left her there and returned to my chambers—only to find you ransacking my room. 'Tis truth, Rorie, I swear. I've never encouraged that woman. Lord Dandridge knows that. 'Tis been only you I've wanted since first we met."

"I ken vouch fer tha', ma'am—" Rawlings started to say in defense of his captain. But when Rorie rounded on him in full temper, her green eyes spitting fire, the last of his thoughts died on his tongue.

"You! You're no better than the rake you serve!" she yelled at Rawlings' cringing form.

With that she swept from the room, leaving Rawlings and Cameron to feel as though they had been in the midst of a malestrom.

"Whew!" whispered Rawlings, wiping his brow. "Tha' be some temper the lass has there. Wha' are ye goin' ta do? She might tell someone 'bout the paper."

Deveraux frowned darkly and walked over to the window. Placing a hand on either side of the casement, he sighed wearily. "I'll deal with her later. In the meantime, lock her in the room and I'll—"

His voice dropped off as his attention was caught by a man on horseback charging into the courtyard. Quickly he motioned Rawlings to the window, and their mouths slowly curved into a satisfied smile as they watched the rider frantically gesturing to Roger Thornton. As the rider continued to gesticulate, waving his arms and holding out a scarlet-colored scarf, Deveraux and Rawlings grinned broadly. The duke stood with his back to them, but they didn't have to see his face to know the astonishment and rage he was most assuredly experiencing by now. Thus, they were not surprised when Thornton suddenly grabbed the rider by the throat and forced the hapless man to his knees. After delivering a savage kick to the messenger's groin, the duke strode quickly back into the house.

Unable to contain his mirth, and relieved that all had gone as planned, Rawlings broke into laughter. "It 'pears the duke hath a problem, sir."

"Aye," agreed Cameron more seriously. "But from this point on, my friend, we must watch our steps carefully. A cornered animal is very dangerous."

Minutes later, at the opposite end of the hall, Thornton broke into his startled cohort's chamber.

"Do you know what this is!" he shrieked, waving the scarlet cloth in front of Percy's face.

"Well, if I were a bull, I would charge, old boy," replied Percy with a smirk.

Thornton stared at Osborn, thoroughly exasperated. "Go ahead, Percy, laugh now, for you won't be laughing when I tell you the news."

"Calm down, Roger. You always overreact to a situation. Every problem has a solution. So what is it now? Hurry up, man, I've packing to finish before the coach to Portsmouth arrives at the inn."

"I don't think you'll be going," said Thornton, collapsing shakily into a chair.

Percy stopped packing and regarded his partner more seriously. "What's happened? What does this piece of cloth have to do with anything?"

"When Davey Billings' cut throats arrived with the pack train last night, the goods were gone."

"What! Didn't the smugglers drop anchor?" Percy cried, alarm piercing his complacency.

"Aye, the goods were dropped off all right, and a man was left behind to guard them. But when the Warwicke Gang arrived back to transport the booty, everything was gone—including the guard. This scarf was left in his place. Look at it, Percy! See the coat of arms? 'Tis that of the House of Chardwellende!" Roger finished shrilly.

"So what of it!" snapped Osborn. "Davey Billings and his gang must be pulling a prank."

Thornton shook his head emphatically. "Billings and half of his gang are accusing us of the same thing. The others believe 'tis my uncle returning to avenge his murder."

"And those fools actually believe that!" Percy laughed, but anxiety was becoming evident in his reedy voice. For the first time, control was being wrested from his manipulative fingers.

"Well, what would you make of it!" demanded the duke. "The guard and the goods vanished without a trace, in a three-hour period of time, and the scarf of a deadman suddenly appears. . . . My God, Percy, 'tis the end of the month, and it isn't Fenton at all," he cried, his voice rising hysterically.

"What are you talking about?"

"The gypsy, she said—"

"Shut up, Roger! And let me think."

With his hands behind his back, Osborn slowly paced the floor. " 'Tis someone who is taking us for fools, and I won't be taken for a fool. Now I've promised a bill of goods to Matthews, and I've taken part of the payment up front. If we don't deliver, Matthews can be as nasty as Billings. I suggest we find the answer and put an end to this nonsense soon, before our profit is ruined. That fool Eleanora and her bloody escapades haven't helped matters, either. If we are to know success, she'll have to reconcile with her husband. If she can't be convincing enough, we'll have to deal with the earl later."

A shiver went up Thornton's spine as he considered his alternatives: a life in debtor's prison, a hangman's noose on Tyburn Hill, or death at the hand's of Matthews or Billings. All were equally unsatisfactory. With shaking hands, he reached for a goblet and the decanter of brandy.

"Pull yourself together, Roger. That's not going to help anything," said Percy disgustedly. "I'll send word to Billings to post five of his best men when the second ship arrives tonight. Nothing had better happen to these goods or to the goods expected tomorrow night—or else, my dear Roger, you had best plan to take the first ship leaving for the colonies."

The goblet slipped through Thornton's nerveless fingers to shatter on the stone floor. God's blood! He had never even considered that course of action. Exile in that barbaric country, where noble titles carried little weight, was almost a fate worse than death.

30

Deveraux dressed quickly in a white cotton tunic with loose fitting long sleeves and brown cloth breeches. He was anxious to keep track of Thornton and Osborn to keep abreast of the events which were quickly unfolding. He was just pulling on his boots when a knock sounded at the door.

"Sir," said Rawlings, coming close and lowering his voice. " 'Tis a message from Molly Fenton. She hath a need ta see ye straightaway. She be waitin' in the clearin'."

Cameron frowned in consternation. "I thought you said everything went according to plan."

"It did, sir. I don't know wha' be troublin' Molly."

Within the half hour, Cameron had mounted a horse and rode off in the opposite direction. When he was sure that he hadn't been followed, he circled around to the clearing. Molly hurried to meet him.

"Thank ye fer comin', Cap'n," she said, wringing her hands and casting an anxious eye to his tall, imposing figure.

Dismounting, Cameron struggled to hide his alarm, for he knew Molly Fenton to be a sensible woman not easily given to flights of fancy.

"What is it, Mrs. Fenton? Has something happened to Will or Terence?"

"No, Cap'n. It concerns Rorie. I must know of yer feelin's fer the lass. Do ye love her, sir?" she asked bluntly.

Cameron was confounded and irritated. He had come expecting the worst and was instead being forced to face what he had been trying so hard to avoid. Running a hand across the back of his neck, he looked off into the distance, struggling to subdue the war within himself. The moment of truth had come.

Turning to the diminutive lady standing so distraughtly and expectantly before him, he at last answered, "Rorie and I have had a few—misunderstandings. But when this business is ended, I intend to straighten them out. For, heaven help me, I've come to love that little witch—handful that she be." His sincerity was evident when he added, "And I intend to take Rorie with me when I leave."

Molly let out a deep sigh of relief and gravely extended a folded piece of paper. "Then I think ye had best read this. 'Tis a letter my sister, Sirena, wrote afore she died. I had forgotten 'bout it, 'til a Mrs. Winton come round—she bein' the housekeeper fer Marwynde. I dinna believe wha' she had ta say 'til I read it fer meself in this letter."

With reluctant curiosity, Cameron took the

letter and began to read. When he had finished, he was speechless. He had never expected such a turn of events. It was rather like being shot between the eyes, and his mind grappled with the information in an effort to assimilate it. Things were getting so complicated. He had come to England with the singular purpose of exposing and ruining Roger Thornton and, in the process, had fallen in love with a troublesome, spirited female with an unsettling secret. Consternation puckered his brow.

"Who else knows of this, Mrs. Fenton?"

"Jest me, you and those mentioned in the letter. I didna know who else ta turn ta, Cap'n. I take ye ta be a good man. I figured ye could best protect Rorie of us all—an' would know how ta handle things later on. 'Twill change things much."

"That, Mrs. Fenton, is an understatement. Thank you for your confidence—and if you don't mind, I should like to keep the letter."

Molly nodded. "I know that I have done the right thing, Cap'n."

Rorie had watched from her window as Deveraux mounted a horse and rode off in a northwesterly direction. She wondered where he was going as she quickly dressed in a simple cotton dress, disdaining stays and hoops. What did it matter where he went, so long as she could be free of him. With the captain around she appeared to have no will of her own, and her thoughts always seemed to be a confused jumble as she found herself succumbing to his virile appeal. Indeed, the man radiated a force which drew her to him like a magnet. She needed to be free from Deveraux's influence, to think for herself.

What was that parchment she uncovered last night in his room? Though he hadn't actually admitted to anything, Rorie knew he lay at the head of the smuggling scheme to ruin the duke, but why? This was not his fight. Why should he care about a small English village?

Coming to a decision, she quickly twisted her hair into a knot, securing it with pins, and tied her bodice. She sensed there was a storm brewing, and she had to know what forces were causing it. Running to the door to follow after him, a small cry escaped her lips when the latch refused to lift beneath her hand. The door was locked! And as the dismaying revelation penetrated her numbed mind, Rorie fell upon the thick, wooden door in a rage, hurling every oath she could think of at Deveraux. She kicked, screamed, pounded, and cried until she was sore and hoarse, but her tantrum yielded no results. Like a caged creature, she then raced to the windows to assess her chance of escape by that route. But her heart fell when she saw the steep decline and knew that she was trapped. She was laying on her bed in abject defeat, when she heard a knock at the door.

"Mrs. Deveraux, 'tis Rawlings. I've a bit of food fer ye."

"Come in, Rawlings," she answered dejectedly. She grimaced as she heard the key in the lock. Minutes later, Rawlings shuffled into the room with a loaded tray. For a fleeting moment, Rorie had thought about falling upon the manservant and knocking him unconscious, but as the spry, little man regarded her with such grave concern, she didn't have the heart to hurt him.

" 'Tis sorry I am fer yer treatment, ma'am, but 'tis fer yer own good," he assured her apologetically.

"Mine—or Deveraux's?" Rorie muttered under her breath.

As Rawlings turned to set the tray on the table, Rorie noticed that he had left the key in the lock, and her spirits lifted. Quietly, she slid off of the bed, pulling the coverlet with her. And in a flash, she threw the counterpane over top of him. Pushing him to the floor, she ran for the door. She almost cried in frustration when she found it locked from the inside. Perspiration dotted her forehead, and her hands shook as she frantically worked the lock. Looking over her shoulder, she saw Rawlings struggling to throw off the cover. In another moment, he would be free. She forced herself to stay calm, refusing to give into hysterics. When she gave the key a final turn, the latch finally gave way. She had just slipped out the door and was locking it from the outside when she heard Rawlings pounding on the heavy portal.

Her heart was beating furiously as she blindly raced down the backstairs, through the servants' quarters and out the kitchen door. Concerned only with gaining her freedom, Rorie was oblivious to the curious, gawking stares of the servants as she flew past them. Angry and confused, she was no longer certain whom she could trust. It was too late to follow Deveraux now; she had no idea where he had gone. So Rorie skirted the village and the Fenton farm to make her way to the only other place where she had known any measure of solace.

When she entered her parents' cottage, her eyes were drawn inevitably to the coverlets on the hearth. Memories of that humiliating afternoon with Deveraux flooded her disturbed mind. Taking a knife from the shelf, she fell upon the covers in a burst of fury, shredding them into small pieces. She then filled the bucket with water from the nearby well, and, using pieces of the shredded coverlets, Rorie threw herself into a mindless flurry of action—scouring, cleaning, polishing and sanitizing the little thatched dwelling from floor to rafters.

She refreshed the bedding as best she could and was replacing the course linen on the bed of her parents' first floor bedroom, when she glanced up, startled and dismayed to find Wiley Pate watching her. His hands were raised above his head and rested casually on top of the doorframe.

"Hello, Rorie," he greeted, his hooded eyes roving lazily over her. "We meet again."

Rorie's face twisted into a mask of loathing. Physically and emotionally exhausted, she had no patience for amenities. "What are you doing here, Pate? I don't remember inviting you. Get out!"

His swaggering smile told her that he had no intention of leaving, and his next words only confirmed it.

"I'm afraid, dear Rorie, tha' we have a bit of unfinished business," he said, not bothering to hide his lustful hunger for her.

Noting the glazed look in his eyes, Rorie became truly alarmed. He slowly began to advance on her, his intentions obvious. She stood up to frantically survey the tiny room for any avenue of escape. Although Deveraux's manliness had always frightened her, she never felt the revulsion for him that she instinctively felt for Wiley. Retreating until her back was against the wall, she felt like a cornered animal and strived to keep the apprehension from showing in her face.

But Wiley saw the fear in her eyes, and it only served to excite him all the more. He laughed huskily. "I'm gonna change yer mind 'bout a few things, Rorie."

Planting his hands against the wall on either side of her head, he pressed his body close to hers. Feeling the rigidity of his manhood and the heat of his passion, Rorie fought desperately to push him away, but he easily imprisoned her arms. His mouth came down hard on hers bruising her soft lips as he hungrily devoured her. Suddenly he drew back with a yelp of pain, and his astonishment changed to rage, as he tasted blood where she had bitten his lip.

"You bitch!" he yelled, backhanding her across the side of her face.

Rorie staggered as bursts of light exploded in her head, and only the force of his hands on her arms kept her from sliding to the floor. Dazed, she tried to jerk her knee up against his groin as he tore at her dress, but he was too quick for her.

"Oh, no, sweet," he said, chuckling unpleasantly. "Not this time. No one makes a fool out of Wiley Pate twice."

Rorie screamed as he threw her to the bed then and fell on top of her, yanking up her skirts with one hand and pressing against her throat with the other. Gasping for air and fighting against the blackness which began to envelope her, Rorie raked her sharp nails across his face as she fought to throw him off. Viciously, Wiley slapped her again, this time drawing blood. Just as she was slipping into unconsciousness, a terrible commotion, punctuated by shrill screams, pierced her consciousness. She felt Wiley's weight being lifted off her, and she opened her eyes in time to see him being thrown through the air and slammed against the wall. By the time she had struggled off the bed and stumbled into the kitchen, Wiley was nowhere to be seen. Deveraux's large form blocked the sunlight from the open door. As he stood staring at her with grim, narrowed eyes, a tense silence enveloped the room. Rorie knew that he was fighting to control his rage.

She eyed him nervously, pulling her torn bodice together, as he slowly crossed the room to her. She didn't know what to expect, having tasted his fury before, and she flinched when his fingers reached out to cup her chin. Her whole frame began to tremble then, as he gently turned her head to examine her cheek. When he saw the bruise on her face and the cut on her lip, a deep scowl creased his features.

"Are you all right?" he asked hoarsely.

Rorie nodded, bursting into tears as Deveraux pulled her close and tenderly wrapped her in his arms. The wall of defense they had both sought to erect against each other crumbled between them.

"How did you know where to find me?" She sniffed, wiping away the tears and struggling to control her rioting emotions.

"I didn't. When I returned to Lyndeforde to

find Rawlings locked up where you should have been, I set out to look for you. Terence told me you might be here. When I was in view of the cottage, I saw Pate entering. Good Lord, Rorie, do you know what could have happened to you if I hadn't come when I did!"

He didn't mention how he had raced headlong to the cottage in a murderous rage, expecting to find her and Pate in a lovers' tryst—until he heard her screams.

"Why the hell didn't you stay put! Rawlings is quite abashed that he was outmaneuvered by a young woman. It makes him feel that he's getting old."

"I—I won't be locked up like a child, Cameron."

Deveraux laughed without humor. "Rawlings and I came to that conclusion." His eyes suddenly narrowed in suspicion as he noted the cleanliness of the cottage, the scrub bucket, the smudges on her face and the dirt on her dress. "What's this all about, Rorie?" he asked sharply, indicating the room. "What are you doing here?"

By now Rorie had regained a measure of her spirit and, still clutching the remnants of her bodice together, she reluctantly stepped away from the warmth of Deveraux's protective arms.

Taking a deep breath, she announced with a hint of defiance, "I've decided to make this my home after my part as your wife is done, and you have returned to the colonies."

Deveraux frowned. "We'll talk of this later. But for now, let's get you cleaned up. Have you another dress?"

Rorie nodded. "There's a trunk of my

mother's clothes in the bedroom."

"Good. I'll get you some water."

Rorie entered the little room off the kitchen, slipped off her torn gown, and smoothed her disheveled petticoat before rifling through the old trunk. When Deveraux appeared with the bucket of water, she instinctively reached for the discarded dress to shield herself.

"A bit late for modesty, isn't it madam?" he remarked with a grin, his eyes turning dark. Moving closer, he rinsed his handkerchief in the cool water and proceeded to wash the grime from her hands and face. His jaw tightened, and he lightened his touch when she winced as he bathed her cheek and cleaned the dried blood from her mouth.

Glancing up into his eyes, Rorie was surprised to see the concern mirrored in their depths. In the weeks that she had known him, she had seen lust, fury, mockery and arrogance reflected in his face, but never concern. The notion that he might truly care touched something inside of her.

Seeming to act of its own volition, her hand reached up to caress his strong, chiseled features. Shyly, she traced his dark brow, the length of his straight nose, and the curve of his full, sensuous lips. When she once again lifted her gaze, her eyes met his in silent accord. A smile playing at the corners of his mouth, Cameron reached behind to release her hair from the pins. As it tumbled down her back in a shiny, golden mass, he reveled in the luxury of it for a moment, before dropping his hands to encircle her waist and bring her tightly against his hard, muscular thighs. Putting her arms around his neck, Rorie raised herself up on her toes to meet his lips, and he kissed her with a slow, tender mastery which left her breathless—and wanting more.

At the question in his eyes, Rorie stepped from his embrace. And with a sure, steady movement, she untied the ribbons of her shift and petticoat to let them fall down around her slim ankles in a soft mound. She stood before him proud and tall in all of nature's glory, with no hint of shame. And as she moved toward him with outstretched arms, the gesture was not lost on Cameron. This time she was coming to him.

"You're not afraid?" he whispered huskily.

Her smile of calm assurance was all the answer he needed. Her skin was incredibly soft and satiny beneath his hands as he pulled her into his arms to kiss her again with an ill-concealed urgency. When at last he could bear to break away from her, he lifted her onto the bed and quickly shrugged out of his clothes.

Rorie couldn't resist him if she wanted to, for he had already awakened the dormant sexuality of her body. After the violence of Wiley's attack, she needed to experience love the way she now knew it was meant to be. Her desire for Cameron overrode everything else.

She felt as though she were floating above herself as she surrendered completely to him. His lips traced a fiery path down her body, and his tongue teasingly caressed her sensitive nipples, as his hand—searching and exploring—sent currents of desire through her. She heard him inhale sharply and felt the muscles cord in his chest as her hands hesitantly reached out to explore his long form. Soon their bodies were at such a feverish pitch that Cameron pulled her beneath him to send them both into spiralling heights of ecstasy.

They drifted back to earth, locked in a tight embrace, reluctant to part. Rorie thought she had never felt so complete and so much at peace as when she lay cradled in her husband's arms. Not wishing to jeopardize the fragile moment with unintentionally mischosen words, neither spoke for a time; they didn't have to. Their minds and bodies were perfectly in tune.

"Cameron, what is happening in Drumfielde?" Rorie asked at length, snuggling deeper into his embrace. She thought it to be the safer subject.

He kissed her brow and smoothed the hair from her face. "What do you mean?" he murmured lazily.

"Everyone seems to be involved in a scheme of sorts—the duke, Percy Osborn, Terence, Uncle Will, you. I want to know what is going on. Oh, I know all about the smuggling, but there is much more to it, isn't there?"

"I'll admit that I've haven't done much to gain your confidence, but you'll have to trust me on this, Rorie. The less you know for now, the better."

"That's the problem. I don't know you. What has that paper I found in your room to do with you?"

Cameron's muscles tensed and his voice was low and firm. "Know this, Rorie: if you mention that paper to anyone, you will more than likely have signed my death warrant. The only concern you need have is that of being my wife."

Rorie was at once alarmed by her husband's warning and irritated by the way he put her off.

"Now see here, Captain—"

"No more questions now," interrupted Cameron, slipping a large hand around Rorie's waist and drawing her to him.

Rorie shuddered and all further thoughts escaped her as he lightly ran his hand up the inside of her thigh and leaned over to capture her lips with unrestrained passion. Just then a voice shouted urgently from the kitchen.

"Captain Deveraux! Where are you? Rorie!"

" 'Tis Terence!" cried Rorie in a hushed whisper.

Cameron groaned and rolled away from her. God's teeth, was their love destined to be forever interrupted! He threw a cover over Rorie and was pulling on his breeches when Terence appeared in the doorway.

Upon eyeing Rorie huddling red faced beneath the coverlet and Cameron fastening his breeches, Terence's boyish face suffused with color. "I—I guess you found her, Captain," he stammered, grinning self-consciously. "Sorry, Rorie." Suddenly he noticed the bruise on her face, and his grin changed to a frown as he glanced at Deveraux suspiciously.

"Did you do that!" he demanded.

"I don't hit women," Cameron retorted, annoyed that the boy could think otherwise.

" 'Twas Wiley's doing, Terence," interceded Rorie. "He must have seen me come here. He was attacking me when Cameron arrived to put him off."

"I'll break his bloody neck!" growled Terence, relieved that the captain was not at fault, for he greatly admired and liked the man.

Cameron put a restraining arm on the boy.

"Easy now, lad. 'Tis my fight. I'll deal with him."

"I saw Wiley streaking across the field as though the hounds of hell were on his heels, but I had no idea. Are you all right, Rorie?"

"She is now," Cameron remarked with a grin as he noted the blush staining her cheeks. "Now what news have you that is so urgent?"

Terence's face fell as he remembered the reason for seeking them out. "Rorie, 'tis Lucy Finley. She was found in the river an hour ago."

Rorie sat up slowly, pulling the cover around her, and stared at Terence in disbelief. She felt as though her stomach had turned over, and for a moment, she feared that she would be sick. "What happened? Did she slip? No, no, Lucy was terrified of water. She would never have gone near the river."

"She looked as though she had been knocked about pretty good," admitted Terence. "But some children said they saw her walk over to the bank on her own this morning and just jump in. Others have said that she hasn't been herself for the past few weeks. I'm sorry, Rorie, I know you were friends."

Rorie stared vacantly off into space. " 'Twas Wiley," she declared, her tone hard and cold. " 'Twas he who killed her as surely as if he had pushed her into the river himself."

"Wiley? What has he to do with this?" asked Terence, glancing at Deveraux nervously. He knew Rorie would be upset, but he didn't think she would take the news this hard.

Rorie continued on in a vague harsh tone, as though her brother hadn't spoken. Indeed, she was hardly aware that Terence and Cameron were even in the room as she drew her knees to her chin and rocked back and forth.

"Lucy was so happy that May Day morn. She thought Wiley was going to marry her."

Rorie looked up at them, then, with pleading eyes. "I told her Wiley was no good. She must have discovered the truth for herself."

Deveraux motioned for Terence to leave. "I'll take care of her," he said. "You have a job to see to tonight."

Casting a worried glance at his sister, Terence gratefully deferred to his brother-in-law's wishes.

Rorie allowed her mind to shut down, neither knowing nor caring how she got back to Lyndeforde. All she knew when she awoke in Deveraux's arms the next morning was that the pain and guilt were still there. Poor Lucy. She hadn't deserved that fate. Maybe Rorie should have made Lucy understand before it was too late. Maybe, maybe, maybe. Too many maybe's pecked at Rorie's anguished mind.

"There was nothing you could have done, Rorie," said Cameron softly, reading her thoughts. "Tragedies such as this are a fact of life." He held her close and kissed her tenderly. "Here, now, Rawlings has just brought in a tray. Have something to eat, and you will feel better." He paused, then, reluctant to continue, for he wasn't sure what her answer would be. "Listen, Rorie, I have some business to see to now, and I won't be back until late. Can I depend upon you not disappearing from here while I'm away?"

She saw the relief in his face when she nodded unhesitatingly. But then, she would have agreed to anything to get Cameron out of the room, for this morning she felt miserably ill and wished to be alone.

Cameron had just left the chamber, when Rawlings entered to retrieve the breakfast tray. He frowned, for the young mistress had eaten very little and was looking pale and listless. "Ma'am, ye must keep up yer strength," he lectured, waving a buttered biscuit beneath her nose.

Rorie gagged and retched the contents of her stomach into the chamber pot. "Get that food out of here," she moaned, sinking weakly into a chair. She had hoped that the doctor's diagnosis would prove to be wrong, but she could no longer ignore the obvious. She was going to have Cameron's baby.

Rawlings stared at his mistress in alarm. "I'll fetch the cap'n."

"No!" ordered Rorie, the command in her voice stopping him in his tracks.

" 'Tis the wee one, ain't it, ma'am?"

Rorie looked at the little man in astonishment. "How did you come by this?"

"Doc Farley asked me ta keep an eye on ye."

"Dr. Farley! He promised me he wouldn't say anything."

"The doc ain't tha' way, ma'am. He promised not ta tell the cap'n, is all. An' much as it pains him, he has kept his promise."

"Why should he care?"

Rawlings shifted uneasily beneath her hard, questioning gaze. "The doc be the cap'n's ship doctor, ma'am. Like the rest of us, he be fiercely loyal ta the cap'n."

Rorie groaned. "I might have known. The captain seems to have a curious way of controlling every aspect of my life of late," she remarked sharply.

"Beggin' yer pardon, ma'am, but there's goin' ta be the divil ta pay, when the cap'n learns he ain't been told of the babe. He takes his obligations serious like."

Fire blazed anew in Rorie's eyes. "That's precisely why he's not to know, Rawlings. I won't be an obligation—or just another bedmate!"

Rawlings scratched his head in confusion. What else was there, he wondered? He knew dozens of women who would kill for the opportunity of changing places with this young woman—without the benefit of the captain's name. Suddenly he felt older than his years and yearned for the simpler days of his youth. Since these two headstrong people had come together, there was no figuring either one of them. Rawlings left the room, shaking his head and mumbling to himself.

Rorie spent the next hour pacing the floor, her restless anger mounting with the realization that she was developing deep feelings for Cameron. And it was getting more difficult to deny each time that he took her in his arms. It pained her to think that when his mission was completed, the marriage would be annulled, and he would leave her without a backward glance. That there were dozens of women to take her place in his bed, Rorie had no doubt. She was just one more in a long line. And she had no illusions about the fact that he had given her his name only to save her from Thornton. She knew that he wanted her—his passionate lovemaking was testimony to that fact—but he had never once said he loved her. No, she decided with fierce determination, she would not be another prize for his collection. Maybe someday, many years from now when the hurt was gone, she would tell Cameron that he had a child.

31

In spite of the danger yet ahead, Deveraux walked down the wide stairs of Lyndeforde with a spring in his step. After the arrival of the last shipment from Calais tonight, his business here would be ended, and he would be free—free from the past, free to make a new life with Rorie.

At the thought of Rorie, he smiled. At last she was his—heart, body and soul—and this was a lady he meant to keep for all eternity. Her long, slender legs; her waist, so small he could encircle it with his hands; her high, rounded breasts; her smooth satiny skin; and her finely molded features all conspired to drive any rational thought from his mind.

He actually needed her, he realized with a start. He, Cameron Deveraux, who swore allegiance to few men and to no woman, needed this obstinate, unpredictable sprite. There was a sense of wholeness and a deep inner peace, which flowed between them following their lovemaking, that he had never experienced in any of his other numerous liaisons. And if his and Rorie's willful minds were not always in agreement, their bodies were bound together by a perfect harmony and tempo. Yes, he could admit it now. Somehow she had pierced his carefully constructed defenses to claim his heart, and he loved her with a singular intensity. If it hadn't been for his clandestine meeting with Captain Hedrow, he would have turned on his heel to retrace his steps back to Rorie's bed.

"Hedrow, how you try a man's soul," Deveraux murmured with a sigh of resignation.

Nearing the drawing room, Cameron slowed his steps as voices raised in anger—or was it panic?—reached his ears. He recognized Thornton's shrill, nasal tone intermingled with Osborn's affected speech as they argued desperately with a low, menacing voice.

"God's teeth, man," shrieked Thornton, "you must be mad to turn up here. There are still guests about!"

"He's right, Billings. 'Tis dangerous for you to be here," agreed Osborn. "If the connection is made, 'till be all our necks."

Percy's ferretlike eyes bulged as the burly visitor grabbed him by the neckcloth and lifted him off his feet.

"Shut up, ye foppish jaybird! Oi dinna give a damn fer yer precious necks. All oi cares abou' is me goods. After last night, that makes two shipments missing. Davey Billings don't take kindly ta havin' his goods lifted," the smuggler sneered, releasing Osborn and sending him sprawling to the floor.

Thornton retreated a step and rubbed his neck as though he had been the one to feel the man's rough hand. "Mr. Billings, I—I assure you, the loss of your goods cannot be attributed to us," he stammered, white-faced with terror.

"Speak English, ye bugger! Iffen yer sayin' ye dinna take the booty, then who did? None else knowed of the plan but us. Davey Billings don't loik bein' made the fool."

Thornton backed away from the bearlike leader of the Warwicke Gang as Billings began to advance on him, kicking furniture out of his path as he went.

"No, wait, Billings," shouted Percy hoarsely, picking himself up from the floor and massaging his throat. "Are you sure the goods were delivered?"

Billings eyes narrowed beneath bushy black brows, and his cruel mouth twisted into a scowl. "Be ye callin' Davey Billings a liar?" he roared. "I see'd ta the unpackin' of the ship meself. Posted five guards loik ye says. When me men returns with the pack train afore dawn, the goods an' the guards all be gone, but fer this rag."

As the smuggler yanked a piece of red silk from his pocket, Thornton and Osborn stared mutely at the familiar gold crest emblazoned on the scarlet scarf.

"The Chardewellende crest," breathed Thornton. " 'Tis Uncle James' scarf again. Percy what if it's true? 'Tis the gypsy's curse, I tell you!"

"Shut up, Roger!" hissed Percy.

Billings looked from one to the other. "Me men be spoutin' some nonsense 'bout a ghost. Part of 'em is threatenin' not ta show up tonight. Iffen this be yer handiwork—"

"I assure you, Billings, 'tis not of our doing," responded Percy hastily. "We have much more to lose from this mishandled affair than goods. No, there is another force at work here, one which I intend to find the source of this night."

"See tha' ye do!" thundered the smuggler. "Cause 'tain't a pretty sight wha' me men 'll do ta ye iffen the goods be lost agin tonight," he warned. For emphasis, he ran a thick finger down the length of a purplish, puckered scar which ran from his temple to the corner of his mouth, grotesquely pulling one eye lower than the other.

Thornton cringed and even Percy was hard put to hide his fear as Billings stormed out of the room through the French doors. Thornton's hand shook convulsively as he reached for the brandy decanter, sloshing more of the liquor onto his hand and the floor than into his glass.

"Dear God, Percy, what do ye make of it?" he whispered desperately, downing the contents of the glass in one swig, his eyes wide with panic.

"Trouble, gentlemen?"

Both Percy and Roger jumped and turned to see Deveraux striding easily into the room.

"What makes you think there is trouble about, Captain?" asked Percy suspiciously, wondering how much Deveraux had overheard. "Roger and I were merely having a difference of opinion on a matter. Is there something you wish?"

Cameron smiled, seeing through the thinly disguised bravado. He could almost smell their fear. "I've come to tell you that my ship has been sighted and will be alerted to drop anchor in Portsmouth in two days. My wife and I shall be leaving on the morrow. I trust all arrangements have been made pertaining to certain goods. I don't wish to delay our partnership or my departure to the colonies any longer than necessary."

Ordinarily, Thornton and Osborn would have been cheered by this news, but at the moment they were distracted by a more pressing problem: the preservation of their lives. Percy waved off Deveraux impatiently.

"Yes, yes, Captain, all will be ready."

"One other thing," continued Cameron. "I have business matters to tie up with the squire and shall not be returning until late. My wife is not feeling well and will take her supper in her room."

"Fine, we shall discuss the final arrangements in the morning," answered Thornton dully, refilling his glass for the third time. "Mayhaps you'll have two extra passengers."

"Beg your pardon, Your Grace?"

"Nothing, Captain. Now if you'll excuse us, Percy and I have other matters to take up."

As Deveraux turned to leave, he missed Percy's appraising eye. For the hundredth time since first setting eyes upon Captain Deveraux, Percy wondered how to bend him to his will. But all men had a weakness, and somehow he would find the captain's, he vowed, as he walked to the window and watched Cameron lithely swing himself into the saddle.

"Percy!" growled Thornton angrily. "Set your mind to matters at hand. 'Twas your ideas what got us into this mess, now find us a path out!"

Percy regarded Thornton with ill-concealed disgust. "You're losing your backbone, Roger. You whimper like a frightened woman nowadays. Pull yourself together man, and we'll see to the end of this trickery. Send for that villager whom your bailiff recommends so highly, but tell him to come around after dark."

All through the afternoon and into the evening, something niggled at Percy's memory, refusing to be put to rest. His thoughts were full of Deveraux, but yet it wasn't Deveraux. He kept seeing fleeting images of two people: one, a tall, slim, bitter and withdrawn youth; the other, a strong, self-assured, coolly possessed man. And always he saw the thick, black hair; the firm, sensuous mouth; and the deep-set, cold, blue eyes, arresting in their intensity. Suddenly, Percy jumped to his feet, his small, beady eyes opening wide as he stared at Thornton in astonishment. "My God, Roger, 'tis him!" he exclaimed in wonderment.

Thornton swiveled wildly about, the look on Percy's face unnerving him completely. "Who!" he shrieked, expecting to encounter Billings' terrifying bulk once again in the doorway. Finding no one there, however, he shakily dabbed at his perspiring brow and sank deeper into the chair. "What's the matter with you, Percy!" Thornton snapped with exasperation.

But Osborn just laughed excitedly, his high-pitched cackle grating sorely on Roger's nerves. " 'Twould seem that the captain is more than he appears, dear boy," he finally answered with more control. " 'Tis small wonder that he walks these grounds with such easy familiarity. The man plays a good game."

"What gibberish are you spouting!" snapped Thornton, a chill playing up his spine as he noted the dazed, feverish glow in Percy's eyes.

"Don't you see, Roger? 'Tis Captain Deveraux who is stealing our goods. 'Tis he who is avenging Chardewellende's death," Percy explained impatiently.

The silence was deafening as Thornton stared at Osborn. "You must be mad," he uttered at last. "It can't be. For what reason?"

"Ah, yes, I'm mad, Roger. But mad like a fox." Percy laughed maniacally. "The reason will become obvious to you after I've proven my suspicions."

Roger's mind reeled from the unexpected disclosure as he considered the ramifications. "If 'tis true, we'll have to send out a man to warn Billings. Tell him to turn out all one-hundred men and to keep a lookout for Deveraux. The captain could ruin everything."

Osborn shrugged, his thin lips set in a dark, vicious smile. "I daresay we shall have to find a new partner, for after tonight, Deveraux shall no longer be available—to anyone."

Rorie hovered uncertainly outside the door. She had grown restless in her room and had decided to explore the library. Hearing Thornton's and Osborn's voices as she approached, however, she had started to retrace her steps when she overheard Cameron's name mentioned. As she listened, terror gripped her emotions, and she had only one thought. She had to warn Cameron. But how, when she wasn't even sure where he had gone? Rawlings! Rawlings would know. And she turned, intending to seek out Deveraux's trusted man-servant, when a rough hand clamped across her mouth and a heavy arm went around her waist to lift her off her feet.

"Rorie, my sweet," came a voice, low and silky and in her ear, " 'twould appear tha' we was meant ta be together after all, ay."

She was propelled into the room and sent sprawling to the floor beneath Thornton's and Osborn's startled gazes.

"Pate, what is the meaning of this!" demanded Thornton, nervously dotting his mouth and forehead with a lace-edged handkerchief. He didn't know how many more surprises his nerves could withstand.

"Found her outside the door, listenin' in, Your Grace," replied Wiley as he leaned down and pulled Rorie roughly to her feet.

The duke eyed her narrowly. "Mrs. Deveraux, what do you know of this business?"

Jerking her arm free of Wiley's grasp, Rorie shot her captor a look of pure contempt. "I do not know to which business you refer, Your Grace," she declared with as much indignation as she could rally. "Your man, here, is mistaken in his facts. I was approaching the library to search for a book to read, when I heard your voices. Not wishing to disturb you, I was going to return to my room when this ape pounced on me. And may I add, Your Grace, that if this is an example of your hospitality, I intend to leave immediately."

As before, Rorie's authoritative and forthright manner threw Thornton completely off-balance so that he momentarily forgot her actual origins. He looked uncertainly from Rorie to Wiley Pate, wondering what to do.

But Percy had no such reservations. He smiled, realizing that he had just found the captain's weakness, for he had noticed the change in the couple's relationship. "Still the uncooperative lady, ay, Mrs. Deveraux? Well, I believe we shall enjoy your presence a while longer. You had cause to ruin our plans once. You shall not do so again." He signaled to Wiley. "Lock her in her room, and return here for further instructions."

As Wiley escorted Rorie upstairs, he kept an arm so tight about her shoulders, his fingers dug into her tender flesh. "Not so fast, my pet. I happens ta like yer company."

"I should have known that you were a part of this," said Rorie contemptuously. "You told them that Will Fenton was my uncle, didn't you?"

Wiley laughed. "I warned you that you would come to regret that knee in my groin."

"You are a rapscallion, Wiley, but I had never thought you to betray your own kind."

"My own kind?" he scoffed. "They couldn't even put on a proper revolt without someone to spur them."

" 'Twas *you* who was inciting the crowd, then!" exclaimed Rorie, enlightenment dawning. "And the duke's emissary?"

Pate snorted derisively. "The villagers couldn't even do that right. Your pitiful excuse for a revolt had only bruised the man. The duke wanted him dead, so I had to kill him as he left Drumfielde," Wiley admitted matter-of-factly.

"You bastard! And you would let my uncle hang for it!"

"I didn't know the duke was planning to use it against your uncle. He jest tol' me he needed a reason to seize the shops. Now, iffen ye was to show some appreciation, mayhaps I could talk the duke into forgettin' 'bout yer uncle," he murmured, nuzzling her ear.

Rorie pulled away from him and spat in his face. For a moment, Wiley lost his swagger, and his features turned ugly before he checked his temper. There was no need to lose control, he reminded himself, as he wiped his face. He held all the cards now; he had Rorie right where he wanted her—at his mercy. The wench always was too headstrong for his taste, but now he perceived her defiance as a direct challenge to his manhood.

"Ah Rorie, ye shouldna done that. It coulda been real nice fer ye. Now I'll have to be rough," said Pate with a sigh of feigned regret.

"I'll fight you to the end, Wiley, most especially after what you've done. You've betrayed your people and you killed Lucy—"

"What are you talkin' abou'? Lucy was a silly-minded fool. The ninny jumped inta the river when I tol' her ta stay away from me. Had ta get a li'l rough with her, but she finally got the message tha' 'twas ye I wanted."

"You killed her as surely as if you had pushed her," continued Rorie relentlessly. "You killed her with your lies. I tried to warn her about you, but she loved you."

"Bah! Love is a silly woman's notion. A man don't need but one thing."

As he pulled her into the chamber and shoved her onto the bed, Rorie glared up at him with all the defiance she could muster.

"Ain't got time fer you now, sweet, but I'll be back," he promised with a low chuckle. "After I've taken care of yer husband."

"You're a sorry, twisted excuse for a man,

Wiley," sneered Rorie.

Pate grinned at the challenge. "You'll see wha' kinda man I am when I return."

When she heard the key in the lock, Rorie flew off the bed in a panic. How could she get word to Cameron? She knew from previous experience that there was no other way out of the room. But opening the window, she once again gauged her chances. Maybe, if she could negotiate the narrow ledge to Cameron's room, she could climb down the tree, the way Rawlings had done the other night.

The night was so dark, she couldn't see one hand in front of the other. One false step would send her plummeting to her death, and she shivered at the thought. But her mind was made up. Hastily, she shed her hoop and petticoat. Closing her eyes, Rorie prayed for courage. Then, wiping sweaty palms on her gown, she inhaled deeply before swinging a leg over the window-sill. She was about to lift the other leg over when she heard a scratching noise coming from the armoire. Suddenly, the door burst open and Rawlings came tumbling out amidst a string of oaths and an entanglement of gowns.

"Rawlings!" she cried.

When Rawlings looked up and saw Rorie hanging half out of the window, his heart skipped a beat. "Ma'am, what be ye doin' there!" he exclaimed in alarm, scrambling to his feet and running to pull her back in.

"Rawlings, how did you get in here?"

"The armoire has a connecting door to the one in the cap'n's room," he explained breathlessly. "Give me quite a turn, ye did, hangin' out the window like tha'—"

"Where is Cameron?" Rorie asked brusquely, cutting him off.

As Rawlings hesitated, Rorie's heart sank. "He's in the marsh, isn't he? Are my brother and uncle with him?" But she already knew the answer to that. "Rawlings, listen to me," she said urgently, grasping the little man by the shoulders. "They must be forewarned. The duke and Percy Osborn know of Cameron's plan to ruin their smuggling scheme. They're dispatching Wiley Pate to warn the smugglers."

"Don't ye worry none, ma'am, the cap'n gots his crew ta back him up."

"Rawlings, the Warwicke Gang is one-hundred men strong! Cameron must be warned!"

Apprehension flooded his face as Rawlings clearly realized the danger. If the captain and his crew were jumped before Captain Hedrow and his cutter of support troops arrived, the men wouldn't stand a chance. They would be outnumbered by four to one.

"I thought there was somethin' amiss when a chambermaid told me you was locked in yer room. Come, I'll get ye out of here."

"No," protested Rorie. "You can move faster by yourself. Go out the window and down the tree like you did the other night. I'll be all right here. Go! Hurry!"

After Rawlings climbed out the window, Rorie paced the room in a state of high anxiety, helpless to do anything, as icy fear gripped her heart. Her nerves were so tense, they threatened to snap like the string on a bow. God help her, she loved the man! The thought of Cameron lying dead upon the ground somewhere was more than she could bear. Fifteen minutes later, she nearly collapsed with relief as she heard a horse galloping out of the stables.

32

Cameron crouched low behind a rock on the bluff, looking down at the bustle of activity on the beach below. The Warwicke Gang was a dangerous lot to be sure. Their swaggering arrogance was all the more evident by the uniqueness of their dress. Disdaining the wide-brimmed, low-crowned felt hats which most smugglers used, they sported expensive, bell-shaped beaver hats with broad, satin bands specially ordered from London. Their coats were long and tight, their stocks and waistcoats elaborate, and their knee-length boots were usually compliments of ambushed dragoons.

Light signals from a shielded lantern had been exchanged. And Cameron guessed that the captain of the French sloop was now tacking around and steering a course just beyond the reach of any revenue cutter which might be patrolling the waters.

For the next few hours, he watched as the shore party ferried the goods from the French sloop to shore in small fishing boats. Soon the goods would all be transferred to the cave, and it would be time to signal for Captain Hedrow's cutter to move in. Cameron whistled softly as he estimated there to be nearly one hundred men, and he frowned at the odds his crew would have to face if Hedrow didn't arrive on time with adequate reinforcements. Just as he had surmised, the smugglers intended to stay with their booty until the pack train arrived. They were leaving nothing to chance after two losses. And it would be a simple matter now for the Navy to round them all up with one swoop of the area. It was time; Cameron reached out to light the lantern.

"I wouldn't if I was ye, Captain," came a low, threatening voice from out of the darkness.

Cameron turned quickly to find a pistol leveled at him, point-blank, with Wiley Pate on the other end. Raking a cool eye over the smugly confident boy, he evaluated his chances of overtaking Pate.

As though reading his mind, Wiley smiled easily. "Go ahead, Cap'n. Take a chance. I'd jest as soon shoot ye, though Billings no doubt wants that honor fer himself. Either way, Rorie will be mine with no one to interfere."

Cameron's heart lurched at the thought of Rorie at the mercy of this brute, and it was with great effort that he concealed his emotions. Only the tightening of his jaw muscles and the narrowing of his eyes betrayed the war which raged within him.

Wiley had hoped to make the captain squirm, but, to his eye, Deveraux showed no flicker of emotion, not even at the mention of Rorie's name. Disconcerted at the captain's self-possession, Pate angrily motioned Cameron to his feet. He nervously fingered the pistol and licked his lips when Deveraux rose to tower over him by some eight inches. He knew the captain's body was tensed and ready to spring, and it was with vast relief that he sighted two other members of the band making their way up the bluff toward them.

"Over here," Pate called.

Moments later, Cameron stood on the beach surrounded by a fearsome group of cutthroats, their hideous scars and mutilations reflecting grotesquely in the low light of a small lantern. Wiley Pate seemed nearly harmless compared to these desperate and twisted men with much more to lose than to gain. Cameron knew that they would fight to the death.

Davey Billings was a bear of a man. Although not as tall as Deveraux, he had the extra poundage and the meanness to make him feared by all. The smile he wore as he approached Cameron did nothing to conceal the malicious cruelty in his eyes.

"So ye be the one wha' steals me goods, ay? Shortie, suppose ye show the cap'n wha' happens ta thieves."

A small, gnomelike man stepped forward to display a hand with no fingers. Cameron didn't flinch, and Billings' eyes glittered furiously as Deveraux's face refused to register visible signs of fear. At a signal, two men then grabbed Cameron's arms and held him as Billings delivered three punishing blows to his midsection. When the smugglers' leader stepped back with a satisfied grin to the rousing cheers of his men, he was staggered by the scornful defiance in Cameron's piercing gaze. With a loud bellow of raging fury, Billings charged at Deveraux, determined to rip him apart with bare hands, for no man had ever stood up against him and lived to tell of it.

Bracing himself against the men who stood on either side of him holding his arms, Cameron lifted his feet and crashed both heavy boots into Billings' chest. As the leader lay prone on the sand, gasping for air, Cameron shrugged off his surprised captors and smashed his fists and feet into faces, stomachs, groins, shins—whatever he could come into contact with. He knew he couldn't fight off every man and would most probably die trying, but for the moment, his fury knew no bounds as he imagined Rorie helpless in the hands of Thornton, Osborn—and Wiley Pate. Five men finally subdued him. Insane with rage, Billings slowly approached once again, stopping to pick up a broken bottle along the way.

"I'm gonna carve up tha' purty face of yers so good, Cap'n, no woman 'll want ye," he hissed. "Then I'm gonna cut off yer fingers, one by one. Iffen ye still have yer wits abou' ye, yer gonna wish you didn't, cause I'm gonna slit yer throat slow and easy." The others broke into a whoop of bloodthirsty cheers.

Feeling the jagged edge of the bottle cut into his cheek just below his eye, Cameron winced. And he braced himself for the slow, downward sweep which would lay open the entire side of his face, probably severing nerve endings and muscles in the bargain. Damn! Where were Hedrow and his men? They should have been here by now. No, they were all awaiting the signal that he was not able to send, he remembered. As the bottle cut deeper, Cameron felt a wet, sticky substance trickle down the side of his face, and he bucked, fighting for time.

Off in the distance, a faint rumble sounded. Thinking it to be thunder, several of the smugglers looked skyward. An uneasy tension permeated the group, however, as the muffled rumble became more distinctly the sounds of shouting and the explosion of cannon balls. Billings ceased his mutilation and dropped the bottle as his men broke rank to stare warily down the shoreline.

The man who had been posted as a lookout approached at a fast run. "Davey! Davey! There be a mess of people comin' down the beach with torches, pitchforks, axes an' I dinna know wha' all. An' there be a revenue cutter followin' the shoreline."

As pandemonium broke loose and smugglers ran in every direction, Cameron took advantage of the chaos to break away from his captors.

"Stand an' fight, ye cowards!" screamed Billings as several smugglers began to scramble up over the bluff. Putting a knife to a few of his own men, he soon managed to gain control and organize them into a formidable unit.

For a moment the smugglers stood spellbound, staring in amazement as Cameron's crew, brandishing pistols, cutlasses and knives, spilled out through a tunnel they had never known existed. Billings' men quickly sprang to action, however, as bloodcurdling war cries broke upon their heads. The fighting was fierce, and the men of the *Homeward Bound* were in danger of being beaten back when a horde of people broke into the melee on the side of the crew. Looking up, Cameron grinned broadly when he caught a glimpse of Rawlings at the forefront, waving a sword and leading the villagers of Drumfielde into battle.

As the British cutter sailed into view, discharging several long boats of soldiers and a few well-aimed cannons over their heads, the smugglers gave up trying to fight their way out and began to scatter.

"Captain! Your back!"

At his first mate's warning, Cameron whirled around in time to see Billings at his back, a knife raised high in the air. "This be all yer doin', ye bastard," he screamed, swiftly plunging the blade down toward Cameron's chest.

Cameron raised his arm to deflect the blow just inches away from his heart, and the two men feel grappling to the ground. Although Cameron was younger and more physically superior, Billings' strength, fired by rage and desperation, was considerable. And as the smuggler fought to press the knife closer to his throat, Cameron knew he had to end the contest now, for his own strength was beginning to ebb with the beating he had taken. With an uppercut to the right, he smashed his fist into Billings' jaw. Blood spurted from the smuggler's mouth, throwing him off-balance just enough for Cameron to gain the advantage. Yanking Billings to his feet, Cameron then delivered four well-aimed blows to the man's fleshy midsection, and, with one last punch to the jaw, the smuggler crumbled to the ground at Captain Hedrow's feet.

"Nice of you to come, Hedrow," quipped

Cameron wryly, rubbing his bruised and skinned knuckles.

"I wouldn't have been here at all if we hadn't seen Rawlings and his band of villagers running down the beach with their torches. Knew something was in the wind then. What happened to your signal?"

"I'll explain later."

"Nasty gash ye have there. Best have someone see to it."

Cameron had forgotten the cut on his face and winced as he fingered the gash below his eye. The blood was drying; the wound could wait, he decided. "I have to find Rawlings. Give the townspeople a hand. They're not used to fighting."

"I think they're doing just fine," Hedrow replied with a hearty laugh as he watched one farmer gleefully jabbing a pitchfork into the behind of a shrieking smuggler.

Canvassing the area in the aftermath of the battle, it was several minutes before Cameron spotted his valet. "Rawlings, but you were a fine sight to a doomed man!" he exclaimed gratefully. "How did you know I was in trouble?"

Rawlings beamed with pleasure as he looked over the horde of subdued, moaning smugglers. It was a satisfactory battle, hard fought, with no fatal casualties among the crew or villagers. Most decidedly, the smugglers had gotten the worst of it.

"Well, Cap'n 'twas the missus. She was comin' ta warn ye tha' Osborn figured yer hand ta be in this, when Pate caught her listenin' in. Osborn ordered her locked in her room, an' sent Pate ta warn the smugglers. When the missus tol' me ye was up against a hundred men, I ran ta collect the villagers. I jest tol' 'em who we was an' wha' we was doin', an' they all followed me without another word."

Cameron clasped Rawlings affectionately by the shoulder. "Thanks, old friend. You saved my life. How did Will and Terence fare?"

"Will got a scratch on the arm. Few stitches is all he needs. And by the time Terence got out of the tunnel—him bein' shoved ta the end of the line—the fightin' was well in hand." Rawlings laughed. "But the lad got in a few good licks, jest the same."

"Any serious wounds or losses?" inquired Cameron tensely.

"Nothin' tha' Doc Farley kenna make good. Course, kenna say the same fer the smugglers." Rawlings frowned as he took a closer look at Deveraux. "Speakin' of the doc, ye best have him look at the cut on yer face. Wha' happened?"

"Billings' handiwork," Cameron replied tersely.

"Cap'n, there be some other news. The smugglers we took prisoner over the last two days finally talked. The way station to Portsmouth is Marwynde."

Cameron stared at Rawlings in disbelief. "Lord Dandridge?"

"Lady Dandridge."

Deveraux exhaled, vastly relieved. He hated to think that he had misplaced his trust, though, more for Rorie's sake than his own.

"Relay all this to Hedrow. Tell him to send half his men to Lyndeforde to arrest Thornton and Osborn. The rest should go to Marwynde when he's done with them here. And have Ian gather the crew to meet me at Marwynde with the ship. I'm going by horseback. I want to handle this matter myself, to spare the earl as much humiliation as possible. Rorie should be safe enough where she is until I can get to her."

Rawlings nodded and set off to carry out his errand.

When Cameron entered Marwynde, the house was strangely and ominously still. No sound greeted his ears as he moved from floor to floor, searching every room. No fires had been laid, no meal was cooking in the kitchen, and only a few candles had been lit throughout the house. A sense of foreboding gnawed at his insides as he cautiously made his way through the servants' quarters, only to find the pattern the same. No sign of life was to be found anywhere, and his pulse quickened when he came to the last door. It was locked. With a strength born of increasing desperation, Cameron gave it a mighty kick, but the solid mahogany panel held firm. After three more attempts, the lock finally gave way, and Deveraux broke through to find Edmonds, the butler, and Mrs. Winton, the housekeeper, bound and gagged, their pale faces full of fear.

"Where are the others?" Cameron asked brusquely as he took off their gags and hurriedly untied them.

"Oh, Captain, thank heavens you have come!" cried Mrs. Winton with an undeniable urgency in her tone. "Lady Dandridge gave all the servants the night off. When she found that Edmonds and I had overheard her plans, she had us bound. Ye must stop them. They are in the tunnel."

"They?" questioned Cameron, catching the plurality.

Edmonds nodded, rubbing the circulation back into his wrists. "The duke of Lyndeforde and Master Osborn are here. They've been smuggling ye know. They are on their way out to meet a boat which will take them to France."

"How do I get into the tunnel?"

"Through the dairy, off the kitchen," directed Mrs. Winton. "There is a trap door beneath the rushes."

Cameron turned on his heel and ran from the room.

"Captain, wait," called the housekeeper. "They have—" But her words were lost to Cameron as he raced along the narrow corridor.

Taking a lighted candle from the kitchen, Cameron surveyed the dairy room. He saw where the rushes had been disturbed in the far corner and, peering closely, he found the heavy trap door. When he opened it, the draft from the tunnel extinguished the candle, and he instantly felt the cold dampness as he blindly lowered himself down through the opening. The stone steps were steep and slippery, and Cameron had to move slowly as he felt his way along the slimey walls in the inky blackness. Presently he heard voices and saw the flickering of torches ahead of him. He had no plan, and he had no backup, but somehow he would have to delay their departure until his men arrived. Thankfully, he had thought to arm himself, and he pulled out a pistol as he quietly approached the group.

"Stop complaining, Eleanora!" Thornton was

shouting angrily. "The plan went awry, and we're lucky to be escaping with our lives. Either your trunks stay behind, or you do. Count your blessings that we even stopped at all for you."

Eleanora laughed harshly. "Who do you think you're fooling, Roger? You only came here because you needed money—my money. Well, the only way you'll get it is by my terms. The trunks go."

"Shut up, the both of you!" screamed Percy. "We must all survive to return and wreak vengeance upon all those who have brought us down."

"I doubt you shall have that chance, Percy," said Cameron, stepping into the light, his pistol raised.

All three whirled around in shocked amazement. Eleanora, with all her foolish vanity, was the first to recover. A pleased smile spread across her features as she assumed her customary seductive manner.

"Cameron, you've come for me. I knew you couldn't resist me."

"Stay where you are, Eleanora," Cameron ordered. " 'Tis true I've come for you, but to deliver you and your friends to the authorities."

As Eleanora shrieked and let loose a volley of oaths, Percy smiled so complacently that Cameron felt a twinge of uneasiness.

"I think not, Captain," he said with a certain swaggering confidence. "In fact, 'tis you who shall aid us in our escape."

"Oh, and why should I do that?" inquired Cameron with forced casualness.

"Just look behind me and to the side. Pate!"

At Osborn's command, Wiley emerged from

409

a small storage room, dragging Rorie in front of him. As Pate held her tightly with one arm around her waist and the other across her throat, Cameron's insides turned over at the fear and hopelessness in her eyes and at the knife in Wiley's hand.

"You see, Captain," Osborn explained, "when the fighting broke out on the beach, Wiley slipped away to warn us and to make arrangements for a boat to meet us here before daybreak. We brought your wife along for added protection, in case we happened to meet with trouble." Confident that he now had the upper-hand, Percy's thin lips curled into a malevolent smile. "Now, Captain, drop the pistol, or I shall instruct Pate to cut her throat," he ordered succinctly.

Wiley drew the blade lightly across Rorie's throat for emphasis until Cameron threw his firearm to Thornton. Rorie closed her eyes in defeat and tears of humiliation rolled down her cheeks as Wiley switched the knife to his other hand and gloatingly ran his fingers down her arm and inside the front of her gown. Goaded beyond reasoning by Rorie's distress, Cameron coiled to lunge.

"Easy, Captain," warned Wiley, thoroughly enjoying himself. "One slip of the knife, and she's dead."

Cameron struggled to regain his composure while mentally debating the alternatives. He had to throw them off-balance, to distract them long enough to gain the advantage. It would be dangerous, but he had no choice. He would have to play the only trump card that he had.

"Pate, I don't think you'll want to compound

your offenses by killing the earl's daughter," said Cameron, affecting a casualness he was far from feeling.

There was complete silence in the tunnel as all turned to stare from Cameron to Rorie. Uncertainty crossed Wiley's square face, and he slightly relaxed his hold on Rorie.

"What's he talking about!" demanded Thornton in alarm.

"Ask Lady Eleanora," Deveraux suggested coolly.

All eyes then swiveled to Eleanora. " 'Tisn't true," she whispered half to herself, her ashen face twisted in disbelief and her dark eyes darting madly about the tunnel. "The gamekeeper saw to the brat's death over sixteen years ago. He told me 'twas done. He demanded payment!"

Suddenly, Eleanora burst into bitter laughter which bounced eerily off the cavernous walls, grating on everyone's nerves like a fingernail scratching across a slate surface. "How I hated that child," she declared vehemently, "and I hated Robert when it became clear that the only reason he had married me was to provide a mother for the brat. His whole life revolved around her. When I found out that she was to be the major benefactor of his estate, I decided to be rid of her for good. I knew the gamekeeper had an eye for me, and I promised him a free hand if he would do this deed. And he did it. I know he did it!"

"He just made you think he had completed the task," explained Cameron, playing for time. "In truth he confided the scheme to Jemmy, and Jemmy, in turn, alerted Mrs. Winton and

Edmonds."

"That's preposterous," Thornton broke in impatiently. "How could the child have disappeared for sixteen years only to be living unnoticed in a village just twenty miles from here? Enough of your fanciful stories."

"Sirena Rutledge had been a maid as well as a close and loyal companion to the first Lady Dandridge, and had always held a special fondness for the child," Cameron continued. "After Lady Dandridge died, Sirena moved to the village where she married Richard Shelbourne and bore a son of her own. As the earl was in France at the time of your plan, Eleanora, Mrs. Winton turned to Sirena for help. When told of your plot, the Shelbournes agreed to take Aurora as their own and moved to Drumfielde where the child would not be readily recognized. The gamekeeper and Jemmy kidnapped Aurora as planned, but they met the Shelbournes at the edge of the woods to give them the child. No one ever suspected a young couple with two small children a year apart in age. It was to be a secret well kept until it was safe enough for Rorie to return and reclaim her true identity."

"You're lying!" screamed Eleanora. "What proof have you?"

Cameron looked anxiously over at Rorie's white, shocked face. Hold on Rorie. Hold on just a little longer, he silently cried out to her.

"Yes, Captain, pray tell us, what proof have you?" insisted Percy.

"A letter written by Sirena when she knew she was dying, and a broach that was given to her by Rorie's true mother. It was prearranged that if something happened to Sirena, the broach would pass to Rorie so that Edmonds and Mrs. Winton would know of her identity," concluded Deveraux. "But tell me, Eleanora, why did you kill the gamekeeper?"

Eleanora nervously licked her lips. "How do you know that?"

"Jemmy was waiting outside the hut. He heard you arguing and saw you run out. When he went into the hut, he found Finch with a knife in his belly."

She shrugged matter-of-factly. "The fool tried to collect his due." Then she turned blazing eyes upon Rorie, hatred and madness radiating from their dark depths. "Kill her!" she screamed. "Damn you, I said kill her!" And she ran to grab the knife from Wiley's hand. As Wiley tried to throw her off, Rorie broke free, and Cameron seized his chance. But he was too late—Thornton already had the pistol pointed at Rorie's head.

"If you don't stop screeching, Eleanora," he snapped, his control shaky at best, "I'm going to use this on you first. Now let's all of us move through the rest of the tunnel to the beach, so we're sure not to miss the boat, ay?" He grabbed Rorie and shoved her out ahead of him. "Any wrong move, Captain, and I'll blow her bloody head off," Thornton warned.

As they advanced to the beach, Cameron's heart sank when he could make out a boat putting into shore. There'd been no sign of his own men. "All right, Thornton, your boat is here, and I can't stop you. So let Rorie go now."

Thornton laughed nastily. "I'm afraid I can't do that, Captain. You see, Percy and I have limited funds, and some barbary cutthroats will undoubtedly pay handsomely for a woman of her beauty and noble blood."

"Jemmy, did ye hear tha'?" whispered Eloise in horror, from the seclusion of their hiding place. "We kenna let it happen!"

Having the luxury of an evening off, Jemmy and Eloise were staying in the hut which Jemmy had built for them on the side of the bluff. It was where they came when time allowed them to be alone with each other. Tonight they had heard voices on the deserted shore and had come to investigate, hiding themselves behind the rocks.

"Wha' ken we do, Eloise? We hath no weapons," answered Jemmy helplessly. "Eloise, Eloise come back!" he shouted as Eloise bolted into the night.

Eloise ran on blind instinct, hardly even aware of what she was doing. She only knew that the debt she owed Rorie would not allow her to surrender the girl to this horrible fate. She shot through the darkness, screaming like a banshee, to throw herself at Thornton. Eleanora screamed, and Roger, thinking that a mad animal had pounced on him, fired point-blank, his nerves at the breaking point. Sensing trouble, the men in the boat put out to sea again, while in the confusion Osborn and Wiley Pate scrambled toward the bluff. Seeing that Rorie was unharmed, Cameron raced up the rocky cliff in hot pursuit, his mind bent on a single goal.

At the top, Osborn stood fifteen yards away, as though he were awaiting his pursuer. Sensing a trap, Cameron approached stealthily. A chill raised the hair on the back of his neck, stopping him in his tracks, however, as Osborn began to laugh maniacally.

" 'Tis you, isn't it?" Percy called.

Dawn was just beginning to peak above the horizon, and in the rosy light, Cameron could see the crazed look in Percy's glazed eyes. "Yes, 'tis me, Percy," he answered.

"I knew it. Your eyes. The eyes that can penetrate a man's soul. How could I not remember?" Percy chortled, as though he were party to a well played joke. "Tell Roger. You must tell Roger. 'Twill more than likely push him over the edge, but Roger must know." With a long, wistful look at Deveraux and a sigh of regret for what might have been in his twisted mind, Percy then threw himself over the bluff onto the sharp rocks below, his high pitched screams lost in the thunderous crashing of the waves.

Staring down at Osborn's battered and broken body, draped grotesquely over the rocks, Deveraux was barely able to credit the scene. At the sound of stirring behind him, however, he pulled himself back to the danger at hand and turned his head just in time to see Pate charging at him from the side. Quickly, Cameron jumped back from the edge, narrowly sidestepping his assailant. Not willing to risk a confrontation, Pate saw that he had missed his chance and turned to flee. But guessing Wiley's intentions, Cameron reached out to collar the boy. Just as his hand made contact, Wiley turned and jabbed a sharp object into his chest. A searing pain ripped through Cameron's side. Looking down, Deveraux stared in wonderment at the blood seeping through his shirt where Wiley had knifed him.

As he staggered nearer to the edge in a state

of confusion and exhaustion, he felt the dirt breaking loose under his weight, and he struggled to regain surer footing before being catapulted over the side to share Osborn's fate. Breaking into a cold sweat, he moved back from the ledge slowly, gingerly, the earth continuing to crumble beneath his feet. When he at last reached safety, he leaned back against a wind-swept tree to recover his strength. Though his mind was now clear, his side throbbed un-ceasingly, and he could feel that the gash on his face had split open again.

Clutching his side wound to stem the flow of blood, Cameron slowly and painfully navigated his way down the bluff, continually fighting against the dizziness which strived to encase his mind in unconsciousness. Only sheer willpower and the thought of Rorie moved him down the steep embankment. As he neared the bottom, he felt a strong hand on his arm and gratefully accepted his first mate's support.

In the melee following the pistol shot, no one had heard Rorie cry out as Eloise slumped to the ground, a gaping hole in her chest. Letting out an anguished bellow which issued from the depths of his soul, Jemmy lunged at Thornton in a mad rage, pummeling the duke into a bloody pulp.

"Oh, Eloise," sobbed Rorie, cradling the maid in her lap, "why did you sacrifice yourself so?"

In spite of her agony, Eloise smiled up at Rorie. "Ye once saved my soul, little one, when ye gave me yer cloak," she whispered hoarsely. "Yer kindness give me back my pride an' let me ta live with my shame. I had a debt ta repay."

"What kindness?" cried Rorie. "We have only just met. Eloise! Eloise!"

But Eloise just continued to smile. "Give the

captain a chance," she said, her breath coming in ragged gasps. "I tol' ye he would balance the slate." And with a fluttering of her eyelashes and a convulsive shudder of her body, Eloise left her pain behind to at last find peace.

Rorie gently shook the girl, stricken beyond words and tears now, but the kindly maid didn't respond. What did Eloise mean about a cloak? With a thunderous jolt, realization broke upon Rorie's mind, and she suddenly understood. Eloise had been the young servant maiden so brutalized by Thornton and his friends on that fall day so long ago—the girl whose bruised body she had wrapped her cloak around. As a child, Rorie had been so profoundly affected by the anguish on the girl's face that her mind had blocked out all memory of the maiden's features, until now. At long last, the victim of her nightmare had an identity.

"Oh, Eloise, such a large price you have paid for so small a debt," she murmured sadly.

" 'Tweren't no small debt ta her, ma'am. Her always swore ta somehow repay ye," said Jemmy, unashamedly wiping tears from his eyes. He bent down and tenderly picked up Eloise's still form to carry her back to the hut where they had shared their happiest moments, and where he could freely grieve for her in his own way.

Rorie glanced up then as a hand touched her shoulder. She was neither surprised nor relieved to see Dr. Farley, as he helped her to her feet, for she was beyond all feeling. Her mind was numb, and she reeled from the series of shocks that had been dealt her. As she stared off into the distance in an effort to erase the whole ordeal of the night, she saw Cameron, supported by another man, stumbling towards her, his side and face covered with blood. A strangled cry escaped her lips. It was too much, and her body rebelled. Clutching her stomach, she doubled over as pains coursed through her lower midsection. Just before slipping into unconsciousness, she heard Cameron call out her name.

With Ian Hawkins supporting Cameron and Dr. Farley carrying Rorie, the little group slowly made its way back through the tunnel toward the house. When they came to the stairs, however, they found their way barred by a form which layed crumpled at the bottom. From the grotesque angling of the body, it was apparent that the neck had been broken. It was Eleanora. No one had even missed her in the chaos. At the top of the stairs stood Lord Dandridge, his ashen face frozen in disbelief.

"Instead of going on to London, I decided to turn back and see to Eleanora's leave-taking personally," he said dazedly. "When I arrived, Edmonds explained the situation. I was coming to help when I met Eleanora on the stairs. I must have startled her, for she lost her footing and fell to the bottom."

"Lord Dandridge," began Cameron grimacing with pain, "there is something else you should know."

"I know, Captain, Mrs. Winton has told me."

Coming out of his shock-induced stupor, Lord Dandridge noticed Rorie's inert form and Cameron's weakened state. Regaining a measure of his old self, he saw to their hasty exit from the damp, chilling underground, and, once inside the house, he busied himself with their welfare and comfort.

33

Cameron grimaced and bolted shots of brandy as Terence cleaned and stitched his gaping side wound with a needle and strands of horsehair.

"Nice work, son," said Dr. Farley, examining the neat latticework of stitches. "Where did you come by your knowledge?"

Terence beamed from the unexpected praise. "I was apprenticed to the apothecary for two years in Drumfielde. He taught me to stitch wounds as well, since there was no doctor nearby. I lost interest in the profession when my folks contracted the fever, and I couldn't help them."

Dr. Farley nodded with understanding. " 'Tis the unfortunate lot of a doctor that he must lose almost as many people as he saves. But you should go to London and study under Drs. William and John Hunter. You would make a fine surgeon."

"Ow!" yelled Deveraux. " 'Tis flesh and blood you sew here, not an animal's thick hide!"

"In your case, 'tis one and the same," quipped

Farley, leaning over to take a closer look at Cameron's face. "Luck was with you, Captain," he declared. "A half inch closer and a little deeper, and you would have lost that eye. Just missed the nerves. Afraid you'll have a bit of a scar, though. Too bad I can't say the same for Thornton. The poor bastard will be crippled for life after the beating Jemmy gave him."

" 'Twas a fate well deserved," Cameron stated grimly. "How is Rorie? When can I see her?"

"Naturally she is still in shock. I think we all are, after that untimely revelation of her true identity. Aurora Dandridge! But she's strong; she'll survive this. She just needs time. Lord Dandridge, Mrs. Winton and Mrs. Fenton are with her now, trying to sort it all out."

"She had to be told sooner or later, and, at the time, I didn't feel that there was a choice," Cameron explained in his own defense.

"Maybe, but it was almost too much for the—"

The doctor cut himself off when he realized what he was about to say, but he knew that Cameron had caught the slip. And even as he looked away, Farley could feel the captain's sharp eyes boring right through him, demanding to know the truth.

"Damn it, Charles, you know what it is I want to know!" Cameron exploded with impatience as Terence took another painful stitch. "Is she in danger of losing the baby?"

"Baby!" Terence halted his stitching in midair. "Rorie is going to have a baby, and she didn't tell me? That's a fine thing to hear in an aside like this!"

"You're not the only one the doctor and your sister have been trying to keep in the dark," grumbled Deveraux irritably.

Terence blinked in surprise. "She didn't even tell you?" Hurt that Rorie had not seen fit to confide in him, he was somewhat mollified that he, alone, hadn't been the dupe.

Dr. Farley stopped trying to pretend ignorance of the matter, and the relief was evident in his voice. "Sorry Cameron, but Rorie insisted. How did you come to know? Rawlings?"

"Rawlings! God's blood, do you mean to tell me that he knew, too?"

Farley nodded. "I wanted him to keep an eye on her."

Cameron didn't know whether to be angry that the information had been kept from him or relieved that it was all out in the open now. He had felt rather than seen the subtle changes in Rorie's body of late. Her breasts had become fuller and the sharper angles of her form were beginning to take on a softer, more rounded appearance. Sensing that something was in the wind, he had begun to observe her closely, remembering the shared confidence he had perceived between her and the doctor. Still, he hadn't been sure, not having had any previous experience in this field, and he had spent the last few days trying to find a way to confront her with his suspicions. He had been about to take his chances while they were together in the cottage, but then Terence had interrupted them with the news of Lucy Finley, and the opportunity had never presented itself again.

"How did you know?" repeated Dr. Farley.

"Suffice it to say, Doctor, I have a *feel* for

these things. I know my wife—well," Cameron said, grinning through clenched teeth as Terence took the last stitch.

Farley laughed knowingly, satisfied that he hadn't breached Rorie's confidence.

"So far the baby seems fine. The pains she felt were a warning signal. The baby cannot survive another shock like tonight, Cameron," Dr. Farley warned firmly. "Since you've come into Rorie's life, I gather that she's known nothing but turmoil. She needs to get her life in balance again and to know a little serenity now."

Cameron moved to stand. "I want to see her," he said. But as he stood up, the pain shot through his side, and he staggered and swayed dizzily. Terence and Dr. Farley each grabbed an arm and forced him back into the chair.

"Easy, Captain," admonished Farley. "You're in no condition to see anyone. You've lost a lot of blood. The only place you are going is to bed—in here," he added, noting the look in Cameron's eye.

"He's right, old man. You look as though as you've been keelhauled," broke in Captain Hedrow, striding into the chamber.

"You don't exactly look as though you're ready for a levee yourself," Deveraux shot back, noting the exhaustion in the British captain's face and glancing pointedly at his torn and powder-stained uniform.

Hedrow grinned and poured himself a healthy glass of brandy. "Heard you took a knife in the side. How is it?"

"Hurts like the very devil, but I'll live. Any word on Pate?"

"No, not yet," responded Hedrow, rubbing a

hand across his weary features. "The bastard took off into the marshes. It'll take some time until I can get all my men together again. We rousted the Warwicke Gang, though. Thanks to your help, Davey Billings and two of his top men are on their way to London to stand trial. A dragoon regiment has been sent into Rye to round up what is left of the others. Sorry about Lady Dandridge."

"Don't be. 'Twas a destiny she had long courted," Deveraux replied tersely.

Hedrow's eyes narrowed in bemusement then, as he swirled the amber liquor in his glass. Scrutinizing Cameron with a steely gaze, he said, "You've a good and loyal crew—Delacroix."

Cameron glanced up sharply at the name, his eyes staring deeply into Hedrow's and a slow smile curving the corners of his mouth.

"Reed Delacroix! By God, I knew 'twas you!" declared Hedrow triumphantly. "I didn't believe for a moment those stories that you were dead. You are always too stubborn to die. Had my suspicions that day you walked into my office, though I must say I was confused at first. You've changed much from that skinny, hot-headed youth," he noted with approval.

Cameron winced as he shifted his weight in the chair. "What made you suspect, Alan?"

"I'm the one who taught you to fight all those years ago at school, remember? I'd recognize that style anywhere. Aside from that, those eyes of yours always could freeze a man at ten yards. Too bad Percy never knew."

"He knew—in the end," said Cameron tightly.

Terence and Dr. Farley stared at each other in

confused astonishment.

"Reed Delacroix! 'Twas you who was the son of the murdered duke of Lyndeforde!" proclaimed Terence in awe. "I can remember my parents and aunt and uncle wondering what had happened to you. You just disappeared."

" 'Tis a long story, Terence, and I shall enlighten you all later."

Farley groaned and wagged his finger in stern admonition. "Cameron—Reed—whoever you be, I warned you. No more surprises! Good heavens, man, I've sailed with you for seven years. You could have told me! God only knows what this will do to Rorie!"

"No one knew, Charles—except Rawlings and my grandfather. Thornton had his spies everywhere, looking for me until he thought me dead. 'Twasn't safe for anyone else to know until I had achieved what I had set out to do. And don't worry about Rorie. I think she suspects."

Terence's shoulders slumped dejectedly. "Rorie is the daughter of Lord Dandridge and not my sister after all. You are Reed Delacroix and not really my brother-in-law. Who else isn't all he pretends to be?" he asked sullenly.

Cameron smiled at the disheartened boy. " 'Tis not the name two people carry, but the relationship they have between them, Terence. Rorie has cherished you as her brother for all of her remembered years. In her heart, you always will remain her brother. I shall be equally proud to claim you as my brother-in-law. And Terence—the name is Cameron now."

Terence cast his eyes to the floor in an effort to hide the emotion he felt, for the captain's acceptance meant a great deal to him. "Thank you, Cap—Cameron."

Similarly, the others in the room were moved, and Dr. Farley stepped forward to gruffly defuse the emotionally charged moment. "All right, now. Let's get this man to bed, or we may all be burying him on the morrow."

For the next five days, Rorie kept to her room, refusing to see anyone but Lord Dandridge, Dr. Farley and Molly Fenton as she tried to piece together the puzzle of her life. Her mind still reeled from the shock of who she was, the reality of the past, the violence and terror of her near escape from an unthinkable fate, the death of dear Eloise who gave her life—and Reed Delacroix, the catalyst of all these events. For good or for bad, everyone whose life he had touched in his short stay had been altered for all time.

In his chamber down the hall, Cameron was a very reluctant and disagreeable patient as he was continually denied access to his wife's room. Rawlings had just come scurrying out of Cameron's chamber amidst a chorus of oaths, when Dr. Farley approached.

"How is our patient doing today, Rawlings?"

Rawlings shook his head. "He ain't gonna stay in there much longer, Doc. 'Bout ready to tear the room apart now tha' the fever's gone. Nearly broke his stitches open pacin' the floor. I wouldna go in there jest now. He be in a fine temper worryin' 'bout the missus."

Dr. Farley laughed. "So the always cool and self-possessed captain is at his wit's end, ay? Do him good to stew in his own juices. But I've some news that'll make him fit to live with again."

When Farley entered the chamber, Cameron stopped pacing to look at the doctor expectantly. His sore state of mind was clearly evident by the untidy condition of the room and by the scowl on his face.

Farley smiled and nodded. "She'll see you now."

Relief flooded Cameron's face, and he flew past the doctor and out the door.

"Mind your tongue!" Farley called after him sternly.

Standing outside Rorie's door, Cameron took a minute to compose his raw emotions before entering her chamber. Once inside, he was at a loss for words. She was standing at the window, her back to him, the sun dancing upon her golden head. Her hair hung in loose, shimmery waves, and she was dressed in a satin day robe of dusky rose and silver gray. She looked like a goddess standing there, bathed in the early morning light, and Cameron was reminded of the time when he had mistaken her for an angel in Lord Dandridge's London home so many weeks ago. He was hard put to restrain himself from taking her in his arms, but the rigidity of her back and the proud tilt of her head warned him that this was not the time.

Rorie finally broke the unbearable silence which lay between them like a heavy mist. "I saw you had been hurt, and I wanted to come to you, but Dr. Farley had confined me to bed. Later on, I couldn't bring myself to face you until I had worked through a few things in my mind," she said softly, not turning around.

Cameron could hear the tremor of uncertainty in her voice and struggled against the familiar feeling of helplessness she had always had the power to evoke in him.

"I know," he answered simply. "I'm sorry about Eloise. Jemmy told me of the past you two shared. It explains much."

"Eloise repaid her debt to me. How am I to repay mine to her?" choked Rorie.

"Some debts are better left unpaid. Rorie, Eloise was in the beginning stages of consumption. She traded the few years that she had left for your life."

Rorie turned to stare at Cameron, shaking her head in disbelief.

" 'Tis true," he said gently. "Jemmy told me a few days ago."

"Oh, poor Eloise," cried Rorie. "That her life should have been so filled with misery."

"No," corrected Cameron. "She knew more happiness these last years with Jemmy than many people know in a lifetime. Grieve for your loss of her if you will, but not for the life she has lived."

Seeing the wisdom in his words, Rorie smiled gratefully as she struggled to maintain her composure.

"What do I call you now—Cameron or Reed?" she asked at length.

" 'Reed Delacroix' died the night I was put on board that ship bound for the colonies, Rorie. I couldn't take the chance of Thornton tracing me before I was ready to deal with him, so I adopted my middle name of Cameron and my mother's surname of Deveraux."

"But your mother was a Delacroix."

"When my mother began her liaison with my father, my grandfather opposed it bitterly and broke off all communication with her. Being of the French nobility, she adopted her mother's surname of Delacroix to save the family further embarrassment.

"How is it your grandfather is a colonial then?"

"As the second son of a Marquis, with no immediate hope of inheriting the estate, he immigrated to the colonies to seek his fortune," Cameron explained. "By the time he could forgive my mother enough to reestablish communications with her, I had already been sent off to school in the northland."

"You never knew you had a grandfather?" asked Rorie in surprise.

"The opportunity never presented itself," replied Cameron with regret. "Later, Mother felt the secret would be better kept in case a safe harbor would be needed for me."

"Why should she think that?" pressed Rorie, determined to know everything there was to know about her husband.

"The duchess and Roger Thornton had tried to have my mother and me kidnapped once before. Mother never trusted them after that. And according to Rawlings, three weeks before my parents were killed, a gypsy woman—to whom the duchess had tried to sell me as a child—warned my mother of some further danger. Mother gave her a ring in payment. Rorie, the gypsy who visited my mother and the old crone who spoke to you at May Day were one and the same. She stopped me as well and pressed that very ring—the wedding ring you now wear—into my hand as proof. Among other things, the woman said that I had come full circle."

Despite the warmth of the fire which dispelled the early morning chill in the room, Rorie felt a shiver go up her spine as she remembered the old woman. And her brow knit in puzzlement. "I don't understand, Cameron."

"You see, Rorie, my father's wife had died the previous year, and my parents were planning to be married. With Reverend Wickersham as a witness, Father signed two documents naming me his legitimate son and heir. He and my mother were on their way to be married in your father's London home and to post the one copy with the solicitor, when Thornton had them ambushed and killed. Unbeknownst to anyone, my mother had sent the other copy to my grandfather earlier, along with instructions that should anything untoward befall her or the duke, Rawlings would be entrusted with seeing me safely delivered into my grandfather's hands."

"That was the paper I found in your room?"

Cameron nodded. "I only learned of its existence myself when my grandfather gave it to me before I left Charleston. Prior to that, I had assumed that the second copy had fallen into Thornton's hands as well."

"Why couldn't you have been honest with me?" Rorie asked, her eyes glistening like faceted emeralds.

Cameron ran a hand through his hair in a slow, thoughtful movement as memories of a lonely, bitter young boy, refusing to forgive his parents' betrayal of love, washed painfully over him.

"I haven't been honest with myself for

years," he at last admitted, more to himself than to Rorie. "How could I be honest with you? Besides, you were so determined to see me as a blackguard, it didn't seem a prudent measure at the time to confide in you. 'Twas a dangerous game I played, and I didn't know who was to be trusted."

Rorie nodded and plucked tensely at the folds of her gown. "When did you know that I was Aurora Dandridge, Cameron?"

"Not until your aunt showed me the letter which Sirena had written—after we were already married," he emphasized, following her train of thought. "When I married you, Rorie, I thought I was marrying a schoolmaster's daughter, not the daughter of the earl. Titles and social status make little difference to me. I didn't disclose your identity at that point, because it wasn't a safe time for you to know then."

"I see," she said, her voice seeming to come from a long way off. "In the tunnel when you disclosed my true identity, I thought it was a trick to distract Eleanora and the others. Then I remembered a portrait of Lady Caroline Dandridge that I had viewed in the gallery here. In the painting, she is wearing a gown which I've seen in my mother's—Sirena's—trunk of old clothes. Mrs. Winton said that Lady Caroline often gave clothes she no longer wore to Sirena. I used to wonder how my mother—Sirena—came to possess such finery, and why my parents would never discuss the past." Rorie's voice broke with confusion and misery, and her eyes pleaded for answers. "Cameron, how can I stop thinking of the Shelbournes as my family? They raised me, loved me. I can't foresake their memory."

Cameron's heart constricted, and he ached to take her in his arms as he read the anguish in her face and heard the pain in her voice.

"No one expects you to forget the Shelbournes, Rorie, least of all Lord Dandridge," he replied gently. "In time, you'll work it all out so that you're comfortable with both the past and the present."

Rorie turned back to look out the window again, her mind struggling to force her confused emotions into order. "Is the marriage legal?" she asked suddenly, though she wondered why it should matter.

"Have no doubt on that score, Rorie. The vows are binding," Cameron assured her, his voice deep and sensual, sending a shiver of awareness through her.

Rorie started, then, when Cameron came up behind her and put his hands on her shoulders, his fingers lightly massaging the smooth skin before slowly moving up the column of her neck. As he pressed his lips against her fragrant hair, curling one arm across the top of her breasts and slipping the other protectively around her waist, Rorie gave up trying to control the trembling in her body. She had forgotten how his slightest touch could stir her senses. When he turned her around to face him, she closed her eyes, willing herself to resist the tremors of excitement that he sent coursing through her.

"When Wiley came back to Lyndeforde for me, I thought he had made good on his promise to kill you," she whispered, a sob catching in her throat as she reached up to caress the thin, jagged scar on his cheek. "When you came staggering down from the bluff covered in blood, I was sure of it."

" 'Twill take more than the likes of Wiley Pate to kill me," he responded huskily, cupping her face with large hands and bringing his lips down to meet hers.

His kiss, slow and gentle at first, became more urgent as Rorie's resolve melted and their primal need for each other emerged. His masculine scent of sandalwood filled her senses, and the nearness of him paralyzed her mind, refusing to allow her to think. He continued to kiss her intimately and deeply, while he loosened her gown and deftly slipped his hands inside to caress her softness. As he guided her toward the bed, she somehow found the strength to break away.

"Cameron, please don't. We have to talk," she pleaded, straightening her gown.

Cameron frowned, unable to understand her sudden reticence. He knew he hadn't mistaken her desire for him, but he made no further move toward her as Dr. Farley's warning rang in his ears. Instead he searched his mind for casual conversation to dispel the high tension of the moment.

Hoping to bridge the gap, he said off-handedly, "In a few days the *Homeward Bound* will return from taking on supplies in London, and I'll be ready to sail for Charleston—"

"But you are now the duke of Lyndeforde. What of your estates? What of Drumfielde?" she interrupted with a curious mixture of panic and relief in her voice—panic that he was leaving her, yet relief that her secret would be kept.

"Charleston is my home, Rorie. And that's

where I belong. I'm arranging with trusted bailiffs to see to my estates—what is left of them. Will Fenton, now that Terence has been able to make him see the merits of modern farming methods, will manage Lyndeforde. The land is very poor. If it is to be restored, much must be changed. The village will still hold its open fields, but 'twill be with a few rules. The rest of the land shall be enclosed—for the benefit of the village—as well as for Lyndeforde," Cameron hastened to add when her head shot up at the mention of that dreaded word. "Enclosure is needed, Rorie, if the yield of the land is to be increased," he warned. "All profits shall be shared by the villagers and the estate. If handled properly, enclosure doesn't have to spell the disintegration of a village."

"What of Terence?" Rorie asked.

"Dr. Farley is seeing about having him admitted to the Hunters' school of surgery in London, and Lord Dandridge has offered Terence residence in his London home." Cameron grinned. "If I don't miss my guess, Terence won't be alone in London for long."

"Why? What do you mean?"

"Mary arrived last night, and they seemed to have found quite a bit to talk about."

"They would be good for each other," Rorie agreed when she had recovered from her astonishment. Though she smiled, her eyes still reflected her own pain as she struggled to hide her inner turmoil. "May I assume that you will take care to sign the document for the dissolution of our marriage before you leave for the colonies?"

Cameron felt as though the wind had been

knocked out of him. A scowl darkened his features, and his fingers gripped her forearms. "What are you saying, Rorie? You're sailing to Charleston with me. Do you think I would leave my wife and child behind!"

Her eyes widened in surprise as she wondered how he had found out about the baby. "Cameron, the agreement was that—"

"To hell with the bargain we struck, Rorie. I agreed to that before I knew I was going to fall in love with you, before I knew you were carrying my child. No child of mine will be born a bastard! Besides the marriage has been consummated—more than once, if I need remind you," he added wryly. "It cannot be annuled without a special act of Parliament now."

It was just as she had feared. "This has all been a misunderstanding," cried Rorie, giving vent to all the hurt and pent up emotions she had been harboring for so long. "I won't be thought of as just an obligation for you to take care of."

"Obligation? You little fool! Don't you know by now that I love you!"

Once, Rorie would have given anything to hear him say that, but so much had happened, so many secrets had been kept that now it was too late. "Do you know how to love, Cameron?" she asked, searching his face.

Cameron massaged the knot of muscles at the back of his neck, clearly disconcerted by the question. "I haven't had much experience at it," he finally admitted ruefully. "So much of my life has been mired in cynicism, bitterness, and a thirst for revenge, but that's all in the past now. I want to spend the rest of my life with you— loving you, protecting you, providing for you and the baby."

But Rorie wasn't convinced. "How many Eleanoras are there back in Charleston, Cameron? I won't share your favors, and I'm too tired to fight any more battles," she responded with a note of finality in her voice that made Deveraux distinctly uneasy.

"I won't deny that I've known many women, Rorie, but there has been no one of consequence since first we met, and certainly none since our marriage. I swear it."

"Since you have come into my life, I've not known a moment's peace," she lashed out. "I don't know what to believe any longer. I think 'twould have been better had you never returned."

Cameron was stunned. "I can't agree with you," he said slowly but firmly, forcing his temper under control. "The reality is that Drumfielde was barely self-sufficient when I arrived. The people were on the brink of starvation. If Thornton had had his way, Drumfielde would have been forced to the mines—Terence included. Lord Dandridge might never have known you as his daughter. Mary would have been married to a man who would have abused her, ultimately running through her fortune and bringing shame upon her head. You would never have been freed from your nightmare of Eloise's attack—free to know love as it is meant to be known. And in all likelihood you would have been either forced into Squire Balfour's bed or forced to submit to Wiley Pate's heavy hand. Lucy Finley's fate could well have been your own!" he added with brutal candor. "The only other truth of importance here is to be found in the times we have lain together and the baby we have created."

Rorie winced, recognizing the truth in his words, and it didn't make the decision she had reached any easier to accept or to announce. "I'm not going with you, Cameron," she said with sad resolution. "I'm sorry about the child. I had hoped that Dr. Farley wouldn't break my confidence."

"Dr. Farley didn't have to tell me, Rorie. I had guessed as much. When were *you* going to tell me?"

Rorie's evasive eyes and the blush suffusing her face spoke volumes. And as realization flooded Cameron's mind, he stared at her incredulously.

"You weren't going to tell me at all, were you? Were you!" he shouted, barely able to suppress his fury. His hand jerked her face up to meet his eyes, so full of accusation and pain. "I threw away the years I should have had with my father and mother because of foolish pride. I won't be denied a chance with my own child, Rorie. Can you honestly deny that you love me?"

Rorie could see the relief in his face as she shook her head, her eyes shimmering with unshed tears. "I do love you Cameron, perhaps more than is good for either one of us."

"Then come with me."

"I can't. I love you, and I owe you my life, but I don't trust you. I can't trust a man I don't understand, and I can't give of myself to a man I don't trust. You of all people should comprehend that, for we are much alike in that respect. Besides that, I can't leave a father I've only just found. We have a lifetime to make up for."

"All right, Rorie. There is some truth in what you say. And I have yet to gain your trust," he conceded wearily. "But it doesn't have to be this way. Give me a chance. There is much more between us than you know. I could force you to come with me."

"Yes, you could; but then ours would be an empty marriage like Lord Dan—like my father's and Eleanora's. We would only hurt each other, and soon that hurt would turn to hate. As we have seen, many evil things are done in hatred, Cameron. I couldn't bear that between us. At least this way, we part . . . friends."

As Cameron gave Rorie a long, considering look, hope, pain, love, and regret flashed across his handsome face. He felt as though he had had his guts wrenched out of him, and he could see that she was faring no better. For the sake of the precarious state of the baby, Cameron gave in.

"All right, Rorie. We'll leave it at this—for now. But I'll be back," he promised with a determined glint in his eye and a firm resolve in his tone. "Just grant me one favor. Don't move to dissolve the marriage for one year. Give me time to change your mind."

After a tension-filled moment, Rorie slowly nodded her head. "Although I don't know what good will come of it, you have your year, Cameron. I owe you that much."

34

The *Homeward Bound*, her supply-laden hull riding low in the water, bobbed proudly upon the vast expanse of the sea. The wind blew life into the sails as the crew unfurled her masts in readiness for the journey home.

Cameron stood on the rocky shore below Marwynde and watched as the dinghy approached to transfer him to the ship. In the brightness of the day it was hard to believe that this beach had been the sight of so much earlier violence. But the tide had washed away the blood, and the wind had blown away the ugliness to restore the sandy bluffs to their former desolate beauty.

It was time. As Cameron turned, reluctant to say his good-bye's, Lord Dandridge stepped forward, his once saddened features wreathed in happiness.

"Captain, you have restored my life and my honor to me. Anything I have is yours."

Cameron's smile was bittersweet. "All that I desire of yours, milord, is not for the taking. I'm sorry for the charade Rawlings and I had to play out, but 'twas vital to our safety."

Lord Dandridge nodded with understanding. "Though taller by an inch or two, you possess the same manner and presence of your father and the shrewdness of your mother. They would be proud to call you son. And 'tis my honor to be your father-in-law."

" 'Tis long I hope you shall have that honor, sir."

As Cameron moved on to Captain Hedrow, their eyes met and the years fell away. Nothing more needed to be said as they grasped each other by the shoulders, their camaraderie re-established.

"By the way, Cameron, don't worry about Pate. There is evidence to the fact that he met certain death in a sinkhole in the marsh. You needn't concern yourself over Thornton, either. The deformity of the injuries, the appalling conditions of the prison, and the loss of position have reduced the duke to less than those he sought to subjugate. He spends his days whimpering and snarling like a mad dog, beating off rats and inmates."

Cameron's jaw clenched and his features hardened. " 'Tis a relief to know that Rorie shall be safe."

Rorie, Rorie, Cameron screamed out in silent anguish. *Where are you?* He scanned the small group, hurt by her conspicuous absence. Though he had hoped, he had not expected her to be here. They had said their farewell in her room that one morning. God, but it seemed an eternity ago instead of just four days. He had seen her only once since then—at Eloise's funeral.

Cameron looked down as he felt a timid hand on his arm.

"She loves you, Captain. Just give her a little time," Mary said with a smile of encouragement.

Cameron took her hand respectfully. "You've been a good friend, Mary. I know how hard you have tried. How is the squire faring?" he inquired with a chuckle, seeking to mask his seething emotions behind a light moment.

"I'm afraid he hadn't yet recovered from the news of Rorie's marriage before it was known that the duke had played us for fools." At the thought of Thornton, Mary's eyes clouded momentarily before a twinkle of amusement replaced the unpleasant memory. "Poor Father hasn't been able to venture farther than the bed and the wine closet since. Suffice it to say, Captain, I shall be determining the direction of my own future from here on."

Cameron didn't miss the gleam in her eye nor the blush on Terence's youthful features as the young couple exchanged shy glances. Watching the love blossoming between them and sensing their expectations for the future—expectations that he once had—his loss was all the more keenly felt. "Don't be the fool I've been, Terence," he counseled.

"I won't, sir." A red stain immediately spread across the boy's freckled face when he realized what he had said.

For the first time in days, Cameron burst into laughter. It felt good, and the others joined in to dispel the glum, emotion-charged atmosphere which pervaded the Captain's leave-taking.

" 'Tis proud I am ta know ye, Yer Grace," said Will Fenton with gruff admiration.

Deveraux smiled. "And 'tis proud I am to count you a friend, Will. Take good care of Lyndeforde. And you, Mrs. Fenton, watch after Rorie for me."

Molly nodded and returned his smile tremulously, tears glistening in her gray eyes. "We all owe ye much, Cap'n."

"Your faith and that of the villagers when most I needed them has repaid me tenfold."

As Cameron turned to leave then, he heard his name being frantically called.

"Captain! Captain, wait!"

They all looked to see Reverend Wickersham's rotund figure clumsily navigating the hill down to the beach. Chafing at the delay, Cameron went to meet him.

"Captain," the clergyman puffed out of breath, "I only just learned of your true identity yesterday, as I have been away. I thought you should see this."

And he handed Deveraux a page from the church's registry which read: "United in matrimony according to the tenements of the Church this 20th day of April, 1740, His Grace James Chardwellende, Fourth Duke of Lyndeforde, and Lady Claire Delacroix."

Cameron was stunned as Reverend Wickersham confirmed the question in his eyes.

"I married them five days before they departed for London, Captain. Their plan was to await your arrival and be married at Lord Dandridge's residence there, but your mother seemed to feel a greater urgency to proceed beforehand. When you disappeared, I thought it more judicious to keep the ceremony a secret. Drumfielde was suffering enough at the hands of that scoundrel Thornton, and then, of course, there was always the hope that you might return."

Cameron turned away to look far out to sea. When he at last spoke, his voice was low and full of sorrow. "Ten years ago, Reverend, this knowledge would have meant much to me."

"And now?" asked the reverend, curiously.

"Now, it proves my father to have been ennobled with more honor than I had ever credited him with. His death will forever be my loss. Guard the document well, Reverend."

"Don't you want it? Ye shall have need of it to claim yer title and yer place in the House of Lords."

"What need have I for a title in the colonies? No, Reverend, you keep it, but see that Rorie gets a copy to safeguard the future of our child."

With that, Cameron walked to where two members of his crew waited with the boat to ferry him out to the ship. As the dinghy cut through the rolling waves, Cameron glanced up at the bright blue of the sky and watched as gulls circled overhead. All seemed so right with the world, why not with him? he wondered desolutely as his eyes scanned the shore and the surrounding areas. Then he saw her—a lone figure standing silhouetted against the sun at the top of the hill, her golden hair whipping in the wind, her cloak billowing about her gown. His jaw tensed, and he felt a tightening in his chest as she slowly lifted her arm in silent farewell. His wounds were healing, but he doubted that his heart ever would until all was right between them. Though miles now separated them, Cameron could see every feature in her lovely oval face, smell the fragrance of her long, wavy hair and feel every curve of her exquisite body. He didn't raise his hand, for this was not good-bye. He would be back.

Soon after the Captain boarded the *Homeward Bound*, the sleek, graceful vessel was turned into the wind and headed out to sea. Long after the shoreline was no longer discernible, Cameron stood at the railing.

"I'm sorry about the lady, Captain. Rawlings told me. He's worried about you," said Ian Hawkins coming to stand by Cameron and looking out over the watery landscape.

"Then know this too, Ian. The present soon becomes the past, and the past forever has the capacity to haunt and shape the future," responded Cameron with quiet introspection. "Someday you'll better understand what that means, but pray that it won't be too late when you do." Sighing deeply, Cameron reluctantly pushed himself away from the rail. "I'll be in my quarters."

Rorie watched the *Homeward Bound* sail further and further away from her, and with it, taking her soul. Grief and despair tore at her heart as she looked down at the water breaking against the shoreline. She doubted that she could feel as much pain as she was feeling now, were her body being dashed against the rocks. With startling insight, she suddenly understood Lucy Finley's state of mind when the unhappy girl chose death over life those many days ago. Lulled and entranced by the rolling of the waves, Rorie edged closer to the precipice. Suddenly, she cried out as an old woman abruptly materialized before her. It was the gypsy from the May Day.

Small and frail, her black eyes boring into Rorie's, she once again repeated her earlier words: "Two forces: love and pride. One ye must avoid, the other ye must not fight. . . . Flow with the tide an' ye shall know rewards. Flow agin it an' ye shall reap sorrow."

As quickly as the old woman had appeared, she vanished again, and it was a few minutes before a shakened Rorie decided that the gypsy must have been a vision in her mind's eye, the recollection of a memory. "Oh, Cameron, what have I done?" she cried out in anguished sobs, as sudden comprehension of the old woman's words broke upon her consciousness.

"Mrs. Deveraux."

Rorie jumped, startled to find Captain Hedrow standing beside her.

"Mrs. Deveraux, I have a story to tell you," he said softly, his voice and expression telling her that he understood her torment. " 'Tis of a young boy who was brutally stripped of his faith, self-respect and pride."

"Captain."

Cameron looked up from the maps and navigational tools which littered his desk.

"Well, what is it, Hawkins?" he snapped moodily.

" 'Tis a ship, sir, off the starboard bow and bearing down. Baskins makes it out to be a frigate of the Royal Navy."

Cameron frowned. He wanted no more delays. What the hell could a naval ship want with them? "The crew didn't take more than our share of the booty, did they?" he growled suspiciously.

"No, sir. We took only what was specified. Could be impressment, sir?"

The same thought had occurred to Cameron, for the British were notorious for preying upon merchant ships and impressing the crew into the ranks of the Royal Navy. Almost immediately though he dismissed the notion, for England was not at war. Pirates? It wasn't uncommon for a cunning pirate to capture a British ship and continue to fly her flag until close enough to register a crippling blow. Whatever the reason they were being pursued, Cameron didn't like the prospects.

"Tell Richards to ready the cannons and arm the men," he ordered.

"Hold your britches, Cap'n," yelled Rawlings, poking his head in the door. "I know ye be spoilin' fer a fight, but 'tis Cap'n Hedrow signalin' to come aboard."

"Alan! What the devil could he want?" Cameron turned on Hawkins once again. "You are sure there is no excess bounty in the hold, Ian?" he demanded sternly.

"None, sir," Ian insisted.

"Rawlings, how soon until Captain Hedrow boards?"

" 'Bout twenty minutes, Cap'n."

"All right. I have a few calculations yet to finish here. Send me word when he's on the deck."

"Aye, sir."

Some twenty minutes later, Cameron heard the scuffle of feet, and the scraping noise of a ship pulling alongside.

"Him is here, Cap'n," yelled Rawlings from the open doorway.

Cameron nodded, distracted by the maps. "I'll be there in a minute."

"Beggin' yer pardon, sir," responded Rawlings, gravely. "Methinks ye best come now. 'Tis a serious matter we have before us."

Cameron looked up, the alarm plain on his face. "Has something happened to Rorie?" And he bolted up the steps two at a time without waiting for an answer.

"Alan, did you have second thoughts and come to rescind the goods?" Cameron joked half-heartedly in an attempt to cover his fear while the knot in his stomach drew tighter.

Captain Hedrow's manner was solemn as he shook his head. "Actually old friend, I've come to do the opposite. I've come to deliver."

At the perplexed look on Deveraux's face, Hedrow grinned as a group of Cameron's crew parted to reveal a tall, slim figure with the same green eyes, pert upturned nose and dimpled smile that Cameron had come to love so much. As in a dream, he moved slowly toward her, his mind afraid to register what his eyes were seeing.

"Rorie," he whispered, fearful of shattering the illusion, " 'tis really you?" And he held out a hand to touch her cheek for proof that he wasn't dreaming.

As he looked questioningly into her eyes, Rorie smiled and nodded, with no hint of uncertainty. "Yes, Cameron. I'm here to stay— I'm homeward bound."

A slow smile spread across Cameron's rugged features. And a rousing cheer went up from the crew as he crushed Rorie to him and kissed her with all the abandon of a man long denied, oblivious to his surroundings.

"What made you change your mind?" he asked curiously when he could at last tear himself away from her. "I thought you didn't trust me? What of Lord Dandridge?"

"I'm tired of flowing against the tide," she answered cryptically. Noting his confusion, she laughed. "I'll explain later. And while 'tis true, you have yet to gain my trust, Cameron Deveraux, you have my love. Thanks to a story which Captain Hedrow relayed to me, the other will surely follow, for with understanding comes faith. As for Father, as soon as arrangements can be made for his affairs, he will join us in the colonies until after the baby is born."

Cameron turned to Hedrow. "Alan, I—"

Hedrow smiled broadly. "There's nothing to say," he answered gruffly, struggling with his own emotions. "I'm merely returning a favor, though I had the devil's own time catching you. Mrs. Deveraux, take care of this thick-headed rogue."

Rorie extended her hand in friendship and gratitude. " 'Tis farewell, Captain Hedrow, but I hope not good-bye. Thank you."

Scanning the crew, Deveraux chuckled when he caught sight of Rawlings sitting in a far corner blowing his nose and dabbing at his eyes. "Rawlings!" he roared. "Break out the cask of rum. Double rations all around."

Rawlings jumped, smiling sheepishly when he realized he had been caught in a weak moment, and rushed off to do the captain's bidding as Cameron turned to address his men.

"I trust you men can sail a ship for a few days on your own, ay?" he said with a rakish grin, his clear, blue eyes twinkling meaningfully.

And among renewed shouts of cheer and laughter, Cameron swept up a flushed Rorie in his arms and strode purposefully toward his cabin. He intended to make up for a lot of lost time.